31472400501148

DATE DUE

			PRINTED IN U.S.A.

NOV 2 1 2022

1637

THE TRANSYLVANIAN
DECISION

**To purchase any of these titles in e-book form,
please go to www.baen.com.**

1637

THE TRANSYLVANIAN DECISION

ERIC FLINT
ROBERT E. WATERS

A Baen Books Original

Baen Publishing Enterprises
P.O. Box 1403
Riverdale, NY 10471
www.baen.com

ISBN: 978-1-9821-9223-5

Cover art by Tom Kidd

Maps by Michael Knopp

First printing, November 2022

Distributed by Simon & Schuster
1230 Avenue of the Americas
New York, NY 10020

Library of Congress Cataloging-in-Publication Data

Names: Flint, Eric, author. | Waters, Robert E., 1968– author.
Title: 1637 : the Transylvanian decision / Eric Flint, Robert E. Waters.
Other titles: Sixteen hundred thirty-seven
Description: Riverdale, NY : Baen, 2022. | Series: Ring of fire
Identifiers: LCCN 2022035879 | ISBN 9781982192235 (hardcover) | ISBN
    9781625798817 (ebook)
Subjects: LCGFT: Alternative histories (Fiction) | Science fiction. |
    Novels.
Classification: LCC PS3556.L548 A618694 2022 | DDC
    813/.54—dc23/eng/20220729
LC record available at https://lccn.loc.gov/2022035879

Pages by Joy Freeman (www.pagesbyjoy.com)
Printed in the United States of America
10 9 8 7 6 5 4 3 2 1

For Eric Flint

1947–2022

You will be missed.

Contents

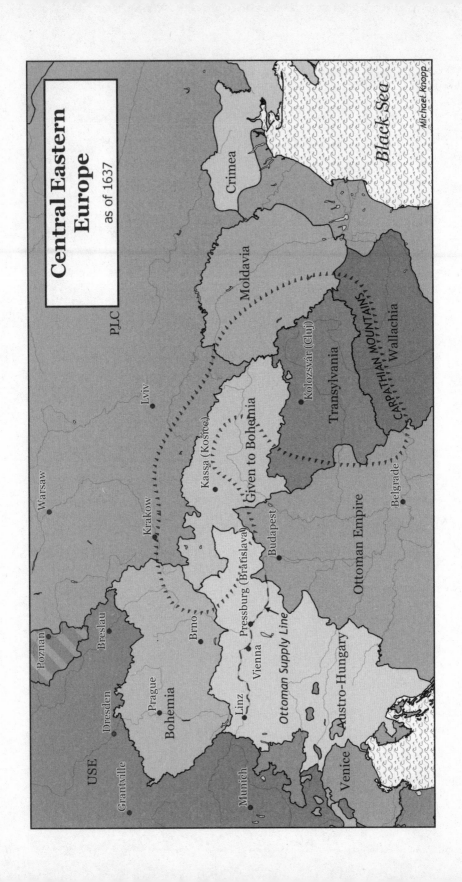

Central Eastern
Europe
as of 1637

Michael Knopp

Black Sea

Crimea

Moldavia

PLC

Warsaw

Lviv

Krakow

Kassa (Košice)

Kolozsvár (Cluj)

Transylvania

Given to Bohemia

CARPATHIAN MOUNTAINS

Wallachia

Poznan

Breslau

Dresden

USE

Grantville

Prague

Bohemia

Brno

Pressburg (Bratislava)

Budapest

Belgrade

Ottoman Empire

Linz

Vienna

Munich

Ottoman Supply Line

Austro-Hungary

Venice

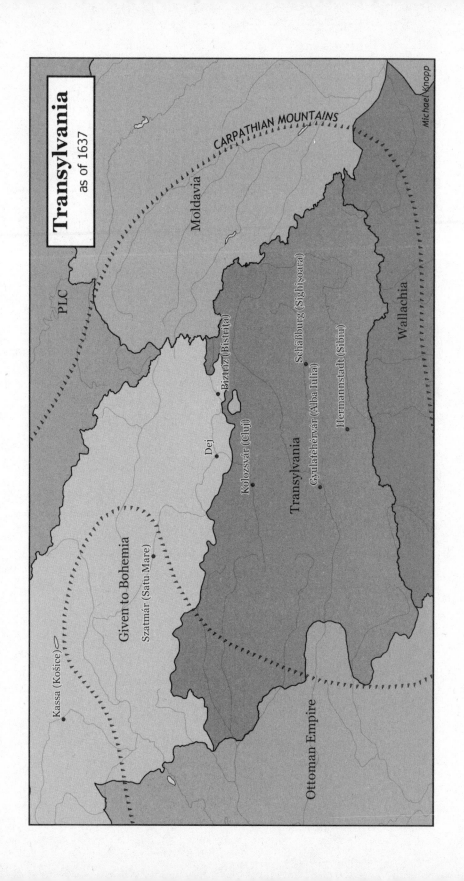

Part One

April–May 1637

Our prince of the old and kingly line
—Sophocles, *Ajax*

Chapter 1

Field hospital
Grand Army of the Sunrise
Near Krakow

An arch of arterial blood sprayed across Isaac Kohen's blue scrubs, followed by the angry voice of Doctor Oberheuser.

"Keep that hemostat locked, boy!" the army's chief medical officer shouted, "or I'll kick your worthless ass back to medical school!"

"I'm sorry, Doctor," Isaac said, reaching with his forceps into the mangled thigh of the badly wounded soldier. The font of blood, fortunately, helped guide his hand. "These forceps are useless. They keep slipping, tearing the artery, and—"

"Don't give excuses, boy! Find that artery and clamp it down... now!"

Isaac leaned in despite the blood pouring from the soldier's leg. He was trying to clamp the femoral artery so that they could amputate the right leg above the knee. A tourniquet had been put in place in the field. It had stopped the bleeding long enough to get the lad back to the hospital, but it wouldn't do for a removal. Proper anesthesia had been administered. The nurses were standing by with the bone saw. Everything was ready to go, save for Isaac's task: clamping down the artery before the man bled out.

The sound of artillery echoed in the distance, shaking Isaac's

3

hands, his nerve, juicing his anxiety. The battle was close. A mile or so at most. General Morris Roth's Grand Army of the Sunrise locking horns with Polish-Lithuanian forces. This field hospital was closest to General von Mercy's cavalry, so most of the soldiers being brought in were cavalrymen. The soldier splayed out on the table before them, however, was an artillerist whose leg had taken a nasty bounce from an enemy cannonball. The ball had ripped most of the calf muscle away, leaving nothing but scraps of meaty red flesh, broken bone, and tattered uniform below the knee. The femoral artery itself had been damaged such that a proper ligation was necessary before amputation. He could be saved, if Isaac could just find...that...artery...

"Got it!" he shouted, almost making another mistake of holding up the hand that held the clamp tightly against the artery, just to prove to the old, grumpy, son of a bitch surgeon that he had it. But he kept his hand in place and further supported the clamp with the index finger and thumb of the other hand. "Cut!"

No cutting. He said it again, but the nurse holding the saw just stood there with a sad expression, her eyes cast down toward the bloodstained ground.

"He's dead, boy," Oberheuser said, stepping away from the table. "He's dead."

The lifeless eyes and pale, sallow face of the soldier confirmed it. Oberheuser ran his hand over the man's face to close the eyes. He then sighed deeply and wiped his sweat-stained sleeve across his forehead. "Very well. Take him away. Place his body in line outside with the others. Quickly, now. We have other wounded to attend to."

Isaac stepped away from the table to let the orderlies come up and carry the man away. He stood there holding the forceps, letting blood drip from his hand onto the ground. His heart raced. He was sweating. He felt like weeping.

"My apologies, Doctor. I did the best I could."

Oberheuser took off his gloves and tossed them into the bucket where all soiled prophylactics were tossed for later sanitation. He pulled his mask down to his chin, shook his head, said, "Don't worry about it, boy. It's not your fault. You're too young and inexperienced to be doing this. Herr Roth put you in the field too soon. You're not ready."

Oberheuser was never one to mince words or belay his criticism, especially during times of great stress. *Criticize me all you want,* Isaac thought as he placed the forceps in a bowl nearby, *but you aren't suited for fieldwork at all, old man. You may be a good surgeon, but* you *don't have the proper temperament for this.*

The old doctor was, in fact, a *very* good surgeon. He was in his fifties, Isaac knew, though he wasn't sure of the man's exact age.

Karl Oberheuser had been an army physician for the Catholics and Habsburgs before the Ring of Fire, but had quickly aligned himself with the up-timers and their Swedish allies when he had, apparently, seen the writing on the wall. He had received some modern medical training in Jena and had served on Torstensson's medical staff near Ahrensbök. When General Roth had asked the USE for additional medical support for his own army, Oberheuser had quickly volunteered, which in truth, had come as a complete surprise to Isaac. The old doctor wasn't an anti-Semite in the strict sense; Isaac had grown up in the ghetto of Prague and knew what true anti-Semitism was. If Oberheuser were, he'd have never volunteered to serve an army comprised primarily of Jewish infantry.

He treated Isaac as if he were a child, something to tolerate, but not to take seriously.

"Doctor Oberheuser," Isaac said, his voice trembling. "You persist in calling me 'boy,' but I will remind you that I am twenty-one years of age. I am trained in up-time medical techniques. I am more than qualified to be here, and I would ask that you refer to me as 'Doctor' or 'Herr Kohen' or I'll even accept, 'Hey, you.'" Isaac swallowed against the strong pulse in his throat, the nervous shake of his hand. "I will no longer answer to 'boy.'"

The vein on Oberheuser's forehead grew into a deep purple line that ran to the bridge of his nose. He looked like he was about to explode. Then another report of musket fire echoed through the tent, reminding them both about the matter at hand.

"Then get on outside . . . *Doctor,*" Oberheuser said, thumbing toward the open flap of the hospital tent, "and check on the wagonload of wounded that just arrived." He pointed to a soldier waiting in pain on a stretcher. "I'll tend to this man's shoulder."

Isaac nodded politely. "Yes, Doctor."

He removed his bloody gloves and mask and affixed a clean apron around his waist. He washed his hands and arms to the elbows; he scrubbed them thoroughly as he had been taught at school. Then he toweled himself off, took a deep breath, and stepped outside the tent.

Inside the tent, all he could ever smell was feces, urine, blood, and body sweat, despite the fact that Doctor Oberheuser understood the value of good ventilation. It was just that, inside the tent, no amount of airflow could staunch the odors that floated up to the canvas ceiling and hung there like a pall over the desperate, but necessary, work being conducted below. Outside, the air was cool and fresh, if not a little sickly-sweet with the smell of sulfur and niter from drifting musket and cannon smoke.

Wounded were lying everywhere, though most were noncritical and could be tended to by nurses. The wounded that Doctor Oberheuser was referring to were Sunrise men who had just arrived from the front.

Nurse Bayer was already tending to them. She addressed Isaac without turning. "All walking wounded here, Isaac. Some more serious than others, but no one a priority, thankfully."

Devorah Bayer was from the Prague ghetto as well. Her son had been killed at the Battle of the Bridge, and her husband had died a month later from a heart attack. Shortly thereafter, she volunteered her services to Morris Roth's cause. She did not have as much up-time training as Isaac would like to see in all their nurses, but she was driven and seemingly immune to the sight of blood and suffering. That was always a good skill for a nurse to have.

Her name came from the great prophetess who, in the Book of Judges, led a revolt against the Canaanite king. It meant *bee* and some even suggested that it meant *to speak with kindness*. Isaac was all for that right now. The calming voice of a nurse was sometimes the best medicine for a wounded soldier.

"Go ahead and take a respite, Devorah," Isaac said. "I'll take care of these men."

Men! Isaac huffed. *Hardly.* Oberheuser would be correct in calling these soldiers "boys." By the innocent look of their faces, they were barely out of their teenage years.

He inspected a sword wound on a young cavalryman's arm. The slash had cut through the man's buff coat with one clean swipe. Someone had cleaned the wound and had pulled the lacerated skin together with three strips of surgical tape cut to butterfly. Isaac was pleased to see it. There were a couple field medics near the front, Isaac knew. One of them had probably done this. He inspected the work. He nodded. Nice. *I'm having an impact.*

"The killing never stops at the front," Devorah said, helping one of the wounded climb out of the wagon. His left hand was wrapped in a length of his own bloody sleeve. He was in a lot of pain, but he was conscious and could breathe and walk. He was practically ready to return to the field. "You need all the help I can give."

"Nevertheless...take a break. You've been at it nonstop for six hours."

"So have you," she threw back.

"Yes"—Isaac winked and shared a sly smile—"but I'm younger than you. Just a *boy*, remember?"

Devorah got the joke but waved it off. "Fine, fine, Herr Doctor. I'll give this one some water and a fresh dressing, and then I'll *take a break*."

Isaac nodded his thanks. "*Danke, meine Dame.*"

It was true that in war, there was always killing at the focal point of the battle. Where exactly that was right now—a mile, two miles, three miles away—Isaac did not know. More casualties would surely come in. They needed every doctor, nurse, orderly, and medic on duty. But fatigue was a devil in a battle situation; just a thirty-minute rest could be the difference between saving a life or losing one.

Isaac turned his ear to the wind. Cannon and musket fire echoed again in the distance. The focal point had either shifted, or the battle itself was winding down. Isaac hoped the latter. The *entire* staff needed a break, needed to pause for one of those cool drinks of water Devorah's wounded soldier was about to have. That would be most welcome, indeed.

But not yet.

Isaac climbed into the wagon and inspected the head of a Silesian mercenary leaning exhausted against the railing. Nasty wound. Blunt trauma with deep purple bruising, overlaid by a ragged cut from a serrated edge. Isaac winced. "Serious wound there, my friend."

The soldier nodded and replied in Polish, "*Tak.*" He lacked the energy to say anything else.

"Can you walk?" Isaac made his fingers move like they were walking across the ground.

"*Tak.*"

"Go in there." He motioned to the tent. "You need stitches for that wound. The head bleeds a lot, you understand, and so if we don't stitch you up properly, you'll keep losing blood and then once it does heal, you'll have terrible scar tissue where no hair will ever grow again. Go in there and tell them 'stitches.' You understand . . . 'stitches.'"

The man seemed to understand. He mouthed the word back a couple times and then crawled to the end of the wagon.

As Isaac was helping the man get out, an argument erupted inside the tent.

Doctor Oberheuser was shouting angrily again.

Isaac held the man back. "Stay here," he said, taking the man's hand and placing it over the clean bandage on his head. Isaac pressed down hard and smiled. "Hold it tight over the wound like this. I'll return shortly."

Inside, a hussar from the Polish-Lithuanian side of the engagement was laid out on a table. He was fighting two nurses and a field medic trying to hold him down.

"What is going on here?" Isaac asked.

Doctor Oberheuser stopped his vile stream of cursing long enough to answer. "I'm supposed to save *der feind* here, as per the standing orders of our General Roth. What nonsense! We have neither the time nor the supplies to give aid and comfort to *der feind*. I won't do it!"

"Sir," Isaac said, coming over to assist the nurses with their struggle. The man was out of his mind, mumbling in Polish and casting terrified glances left and right. Isaac could tell right away that he had been given morphine. Too much, in fact. "General Roth's orders are clear: we are to give aid to enemy soldiers, wherever possible, so long as it does not impede in the care of our own soldiers. We don't have any serious, pressing cases at the moment, so—"

"He's lost too much blood!" Oberheuser barked, his frustration and exhaustion on full display. "It's a ZB-2 Santee wound. The round shattered the right humerus. We'd have to amputate too close to the shoulder. I can't do it without serious risk and likely failure."

Isaac looked at the damage despite the man's writhing. His stomach clenched. It was, indeed, a very nasty wound. The up-time-inspired round had torn through the man's clothing, pulling fabric deep into the arm and twisting it around the brachial artery. Isaac could see bone fragments peeking out of the muscle tissue, like tiny fangs ready to bite. Luckily, the artery itself was mostly intact. The hussar had lost a lot of blood, but the tourniquet had staunched a full bleed out.

"I can do it," Isaac said, marking a place on the soldier's arm with index and middle finger. "You do the ligation and clamping here. You're more qualified to do those than I am. I'll do the cutting here." He moved his fingers to where the bone had been shattered. "There's no bone left here, so it'll be an easy amputation. I'll cut, you clamp. I'll stitch the flap afterward."

Oberheuser started to object, but Isaac knew that giving the compliment about the ligation and clamping was just the right amount of butter to spread across the old doctor's bread. All Isaac wanted was for the foul-mouthed physician to try; that was all. They both needed a little medical redemption for earlier mistakes in the day, and despite such a terrible wound, this hussar was not dead, nor did he have to be.

"Very well," Oberheuser said, wagging his finger, "but we've no time for proper reapplication of PPE or for scrubbing. We've got to do it now, or in five minutes, it won't matter."

Isaac agreed. "Let's move him into better light."

With the nurses' and medic's aid, they lifted the table and moved it into the center of the tent where there was light from two oil lamps swinging from the scaffolding. The center of the tent did not offer the best ventilation, but it offered the most space for such a serious surgery.

"Wait..." the cavalry soldier said, his eyes glossed over in fear and confusion. "What are you going to do?"

"Ah, you speak German." Oberheuser seemed pleased. "That is good. We don't have to waste time now trying to figure out what you are saying. Simply put, *Mein Herr*, we are going to save your life. We're going to remove your arm to keep you from bleeding to death."

"No!" the Polish soldier barked. He tried lifting himself up, sliding his legs off the table, but the nurses held them in place. He winced and lay back down. "Don't take my arm. Please. I'd rather die than lose my arm."

"You're going to be fine, young man," Isaac said. "Trust me. We're going to take care of you. Get that rolling table over there," he said to a nurse and pointed to his left, "and get the combat shears and cut off his coat."

"No, no..." The hussar struggled. "I won't let you take my arm."

"We should give him a shot of morphine," Oberheuser said, thumbing through a set of scalpels to pick the proper one for ligation of the artery.

Isaac nodded. "You're probably right, but he's already loopy with his first dose. I'm loath to give him another."

"Nevertheless, give him one. Otherwise, we'll be fighting him the whole time."

They didn't have many doses left, but Isaac directed a nurse to fetch him one. For that matter, they had few clean syringes as well. Smaller soiled equipment like syringes and scalpels and clamps were currently being sanitized in one of the pressure cookers that Isaac had snagged in Grantville before answering General Roth's call. But they still had a few doses ready to go, and at least one of them could be used on *der feind.*

Isaac pushed out a small stream of morphine to ensure all air bubbles were gone. "Hold down his left arm."

Isaac moved to the patient's left side. The hussar was cursing them in Polish—Isaac knew enough of the language to know that—and trying to wrest his arm free from their grasp. He grabbed the man's wrist and forced the arm down. "Keep him still..."

He managed to find a vein just below the bicep. He pushed the clear liquid in slowly while Oberheuser waited for the nurse to put the rolling table beside the hussar and carefully lay his wounded arm across it. As she did so, the Polish soldier howled in pain, but Isaac noticed that he was no longer flailing about. That was good. The extra morphine seemed to be doing the trick.

"I'm ready," Oberheuser said, standing there holding his scalpel.

Isaac accepted two cutting knives from the medic. The bone saw was unnecessary, for there was no bone to saw, just shards that could easily be pushed aside during the procedure. He walked over to the other side of the table and got into position. He nodded to Oberheuser. "Ready."

"Don't...don't take my arm...don't..."

The man was fading fast. "Have no fear, young man," Oberheuser said, leaning over to begin the ligation. "In fifteen minutes, you're going to be just fine. You'll fall asleep, and you won't even remember—"

The hussar moved so fast, Isaac didn't see him reaching with his good arm into his boot and drawing out a small blade. As soon as Isaac saw it, he howled, dropped his own knife, and reached for it, but failed to knock the soldier's arm away.

The blade struck Oberheuser's neck. It was a solid strike, and one that sent the doctor reeling backward and clutching his neck as blood poured from the wound.

"Guards! Guards!" Isaac screamed as he tried grabbing the hussar's arm. The makeshift blade pierced the shoulder of a nearby nurse before they managed to pile on and knock the weapon from his hand. Isaac was screaming, the soldier was screaming, the nurses were screaming. The guards rushed in. One of them hiked up the butt of his musket and smacked the hussar in the head.

They dragged his limp body away. Isaac recovered and went to Oberheuser immediately.

"I'm so sorry, Herr Oberheuser. I tried to—"

"Herr doctor!"

The new voice was commanding. Isaac turned and saw four men burst into the tent. Two were holding a third between them. The other, carrying no one, was a cavalry officer.

"We have an officer here who needs immediate attention!"

Isaac was about to protest and turn back to Oberheuser, when he felt a hand on his shoulder. He turned. Devorah smiled at him. "Go, and tend to them, Isaac. I'm done with my break. I'll take care of Herr Oberheuser."

"Are you sure?"

"Do what she says, boy," Oberheuser said, using that derogatory term again, but in a weakened, muted voice. Isaac let it go. The wound had not, unfortunately, damaged the old man's vocal cords. "He didn't hit the jugular. I'll be all right. Go do your duty."

Isaac nodded, mouthed *thank you* to Devorah, and stood.

"What is the problem?" he asked, helping the two cavalry soldiers carry the officer to a chair. Isaac knelt in front of the man and began checking his wounds. They were serious.

"He took a sword slash across his face and shoulder, and his eye is badly damaged."

Isaac nodded and looked up. "And who are you, sir?"

"I am Colonel Gerhardt Renz."

Isaac looked back at his patient. The man was groggy but awake. "And who are you?"

"Christian von Jori."

"Captain von Jori, to be clear," Colonel Renz said, "and you have to save him, sir. Please...I beg you."

Isaac examined the eye. A hastily applied dressing had been

wrapped around the man's head. Isaac lifted the eye patch slowly. *Oooh! Ugly!*

"It hurts when I blink," von Jori said.

Isaac put the patch back in place and stood. "Then I'd advise you to stop blinking."

It was meant as a joke, but no one was laughing. Neither was Isaac, for that matter. It was a bad joke. He just needed to blow off some steam, some tension. Nothing was going right today.

"You're going to save his eye, aren't you?"

Isaac had never seen a colonel show so much concern for a lower-ranked officer. The patient did have "von" in his name, so perhaps Christian *von* Jori was an important person.

Isaac looked across the tent to Doctor Oberheuser. Devorah was still tending to his wound. Isaac then looked at the line of smeared blood and dirt where the Polish hussar had been dragged out of the tent. He shook his head.

What a miserable day.

He turned back to Colonel Renz. "Yes, sir, I will try." Then he said the quiet part out loud. "But I haven't been very successful at saving anyone today."

Captain von Jori's wound was a long saber slash across his forehead, over his eye, down his chin and neck, and into his shoulder. The shoulder cut was the deepest, but the least worrisome to Isaac. The buff coat had prevented the slash from cutting the artery in the arm. They cut away the damaged coat, cleaned the wound, and bandaged it right up.

The neck wound was of more concern. It too hadn't struck an artery, thank God, but it was deep enough that, with continued movement by the patient, the artery could tear and there'd be nothing Isaac could do about it, being now the only qualified field surgeon still in action.

The most critical wound at present, however, was the right eye. The slash had split the eyelid, although it looked like the eye itself had been spared the cut. A lot of blood had poured into Captain von Jori's eye and down his face. For some odd reason, small bits of shrapnel and large grain powder had been spread all along the slash line, and one of the most egregious pieces was lodged *in* the captain's eye, just under the lid. Isaac had tried extracting it with tweezers. No luck.

"Fetch me that satchel over there," he said, motioning toward a small leather bag on the ground. "I need my magnet."

"Magnet?"

Isaac nodded as the nurse fetched his satchel and handed it over. He reached into the bag and drew out a small U-shaped piece of metal, smaller than his palm. He smiled and waved it like a horseshoe. "Courtesy of Imperial Tech in Magdeburg. With this magnet, I'm going to try to extract that little piece of metal you have lodged up under your eyelid. All that painful blinking you've been doing has drawn it in too far; can't get it out by normal means, so we improvise. Now, Captain von—can I call you Christian? Please be still. And *don't* blink."

"Wouldn't it be best to knock me out first, or give me a sedative, or whatever it is you physicians do to keep your patients calm?"

The question both surprised and impressed Isaac. Most soldiers who came through the white flap were either in too much pain, too weak, or so ignorant of medical procedure that they never asked questions—never said a word, in fact—except scream or grunt or howl in pain. "We're preparing anesthesia now, but it isn't ready yet. We can't wait for it. If I don't get that bit of metal out of your eye now . . . well, you just be still. And *don't* blink, no matter how painful it is."

The nurse who had handed Isaac the satchel now leaned over Christian and placed her gloved hands near his eye. With tender thumbs and index fingers, she carefully spread Christian's eye open. The captain tensed at the pain; she cooed soft words of encouragement to soothe and keep him calm. Blood flowed freely down his face, into his ear, and onto the table. Isaac moved closer, identified the errant piece of metal with a magnifying glass, then slowly moved the magnet toward the eye.

"Still," Isaac whispered, "still now."

The metal fragment responded immediately, standing up in its lodged state like a soldier itself. Isaac inched the magnet closer while he mouthed a small thank-you to the duo of Wilhelm Fabry and his wife Marie Colinet who had perfected the practice of using a magnet on pieces of metal in the eye. They were still alive today, somewhere in Germany, and Isaac made a point to one day meet and thank them in person.

Christian lay still and calm, and Isaac drew strength from the man's courage. *If he can show strength and courage in a time like this*, Isaac thought, *so can I.*

He moved the magnet closer until it touched the piece of metal. He let it linger there a few seconds, took a deep breath. Then slowly, slowly, he drew the magnet away to ensure the metal fragment did not slip back into the eye. *One . . . two . . . three . . .*

The fragment was out. Isaac placed the magnet on a nearby tray. "Very good," he said with a big, happy sigh. "That's a relief. Good job holding still, Captain. Your calm demeanor is impressive."

"Thank you. Please, call me Christian."

Isaac smiled. "Indeed. There's still work to be done on your eye, but now we move on to your neck."

"Anesthesia is ready, Doctor."

Devorah had taken a moment from treating Doctor Oberheuser to get a morphine shot ready. It was the last full dose they had. Isaac wasn't sure that Christian even needed it. The man had proven his ability to withstand searing pain, but better safe than sorry, as they said in Grantville. One errant move of his neck while Isaac was stitching the wound might drive the needle right into the artery.

Isaac accepted the syringe. He felt Christian's hand on his arm.

"Doctor," the young captain said. Isaac could see tears forming in Christian's undamaged eye. "If I die, will you ask Colonel Renz to send word to my mother and father in Zurich? Tell them that I was thinking about them in the end, and that I am sorry for leaving without saying goodbye. Will you tell him that?"

Isaac nodded. "I will, Captain, I will. But I won't have to because you're not going to die. I promise."

Christian nodded and then turned his head to the left to expose his mangled neck. Isaac pushed the syringe into Christian's arm, and then slowly squeezed the plunger until the barrel was empty.

He set aside the empty syringe and grabbed a stitching needle and suture material. He chose to use the good silk thread for this wound. Good quality silk stitching thread was in short supply, but for a wound this delicate and unstable, the best was required. Non-peppermint-flavored dental floss and tennis racket strings from Grantville, sheep gut sutures, and even iodine-treated horsehair were available, but no. Silk all the way.

"*Will* he live, Doctor?" Devorah's question was sincere.

"I think so," Isaac said, making the first puncture on the neck wound and pulling the silk through. "But I don't know for sure."

Chapter 2

Roth town house
Prague, capital of Bohemia

"Checkmate!"

Morris Roth purposely avoided Len Tanner's smug satisfaction as he studied the board for any possible escape his king might make. A brand-new chess set, carved in nice, polished birch; the pieces smooth and on well-balanced bases. A "welcome home" present from his wife, Judith, who had commissioned it from one of the most skilled Jewish woodcarvers in what used to be Prague's Jewish ghetto. The "Josefov," they called it, after an up-time historical reference that wasn't really appropriate in this universe. The Josefov was still a very self-enclosed community, but was no longer legally a ghetto.

Morris studied his options. Nothing. Not a damn thing he could do about it. He'd made the wrong choice three moves ago. His king was trapped in a corner with no way out and no one coming to the rescue. Not even the queen, who sat quietly off-board, despondent in capture.

He sighed, shook his head, and flicked his king over. "You win."

Len smiled and rubbed his hands together with great satisfaction.

"Don't gloat too much, Len," Morris said, taking his remaining pieces off the board and placing them aside, "you only won two out of three games. You're no Bobby Fischer."

"I don't need to be," Len said, taking his victorious pieces off the board and placing them alongside Morris' vanquished. "As long as I'm better than you more often than not." He winked.

Morris chuckled. "That's not hard to do."

He and Judith had invited Len Tanner and Ellie Anderson over for dinner, good wine, good conversation. They now sat huddled in the second-floor room that Judith had designated as the home's official "living room."

Home! More like a mansion, Morris thought. A beautiful home, in its way, but big and vacuous. In truth, too much for a humble up-time jeweler—and these days, military contractor—but the status he'd acquired in Bohemia in the years since they'd moved here pretty much required that he and Judith live in such a domicile. He insisted on calling it a "town house" even though most Jews in the Josefov and a fair number of Gentiles elsewhere in the city called it the Roth Palace.

Morris hated having to break up the pleasant conversation Judith was having with Ellie Anderson, but time was money, as was often said. The day was drawing to a close, and there were still other matters he needed to attend to before nightfall, other people he needed to see.

"Thank you both for coming by," Morris said, snapping the chess pieces into their case. "I'm so glad to see you two again. I wasn't even sure I'd be able to return so soon, but now that I have, I wanted to talk to you both about an important matter."

"Oh, shit," Ellie said, rolling her eyes in wide circles. "Here it comes."

Morris held up his hands like Job. "What?"

"Whenever you get serious like that," she said, "you're about to make my day fucking miserable."

"Ellie," Judith said, allowing a playful smirk to cross her face. "At least give my husband a chance to say something *fucking* bad before you accuse him of it."

Ellie Anderson was, in up-time parlance, a potty mouth. This was nothing new, and four years in Prague, and six years down-time, hadn't divested her of the trait. In truth, both he and Judith had never minded Ellie's foul language. But in this case, Morris agreed with his wife: *At least let me say something bad first before you accuse me of it.*

"You both have done a marvelous job here in Prague," he

said, closing his chess set and leaning back comfortably with a fresh glass of wine. He took a sip. "I don't think there's a city in the world as interconnected as this one. I'd say, AT&L Bohemia has done well for itself."

Which was very true. Len Tanner and Ellie Anderson were communication specialists, and in the four years that they had lived and worked in Prague, they had set up one of the most modern communication grids in all of Europe. Nothing so modern as to rival a moderately sized up-time city, but in the here and now, Prague was becoming the envy of the world in up-time-inspired communication systems. A radio and telephone system that stretched from one end of the city to the next. And a telegraph system as well, which oftentimes was more reliable than the other two. Bottom line: every block in Prague had some form of communication station, including the old Josefov whose once restrictive walls now had as many gaps in it as the South Mountain ridgeline in up-time western Maryland. Morris thought of that stretch of mountain range that had, in his old world, proven to be a critical juncture during the American Civil War. The skirmishes fought in those gaps had preceded the Battle of Antietam. He thought about all those up-time battles as he gathered his courage for the skirmish he was about to fight.

He cleared his throat. "When we first arrived here, you agreed to a five-year deal. You'd stay in town and establish AT&L Bohemia and make Prague an epicenter of modern communication. You've done that, and I thank you. I suppose that if you wish to leave Prague and go elsewhere, you'd have your pick of a dozen cities or more begging for the same treatment. If you wish to do so, then I will, in the end, not stand in your way. But—"

"Here we go..."

"—I'd like you to help me continue, and complete, the Anaconda Project."

"I understand that the Sunrise is still HQ'd near Krakow," Len said, rising from an opulent, stiff-backed wooden chair and taking a more comfortable recliner near his wife. He accepted a fresh glass of wine from Judith. "Thank you, Judith."

"Yes," Morris said. "No reason to move the army until I know *my* next move."

Len sipped and nodded. "I hear that Pappenheim has pretty much given you the boot. Is this true?"

Morris resisted a laugh. Stands to reason, he thought. In a city as connected as this one, word gets around. "More or less true, yes. He's allowing me to pull the army back as far as Brno. He doesn't want two armies in Bohemia at the same time, and I can scarcely blame him. If I were in his shoes, I'd not want a competing force in my country either, especially one comprising as many mercenaries as I have.

"We've achieved a great success in Poland against the magnates, but it's not enough. Not yet. There's more to do."

"Where the hell are you going with this?" Ellie asked, waving off another glass of wine from Judith. "Thank you, no. And why do you need us? You've got good radio people, don't you?"

"I do," Morris agreed, "but we need more. Success breeds success, Ellie. Our success against the magnates has literally opened the floodgates. New volunteers are pouring into camp daily—most of them young Jewish men in and around Krakow. But also from Prague." He motioned to the window. "Right now, there's a caravan forming in the Josefov ready to head out at first light. New Brethren have come also, as well as more mercenaries offering their services—for a price, of course. Bottom line is, by end of May, the *Grand* Army of the Sunrise will have doubled, if not tripled, in size. Which means I don't have enough communication equipment, specialists, you name it. I need you both to help me coordinate the effort."

There was a pause as Len shot a glance at his wife. Ellie did not respond, which was more troubling to Morris than her frequent outbursts of colorful language. Her silence meant that she was either so angry that she couldn't speak, or that she was actually contemplating the offer. Well, it wasn't much of an offer yet.

"Why don't you just refuse the new volunteers?" Len asked, finishing his wine, and handing the glass back to Judith with a smile and a nod. "Do you really need any more men, especially with the Galicians and Mike and his USE forces—"

"Yeah, well, see, therein lies the rub," Morris said, relieving an itch on the back of his head. "I've already told the Galicians that we'll not be fighting alongside them any further. It isn't necessary, anyway. It'll be a while before the Polish-Lithuanian powers-that-be can mount any sizable counterattack, if at all; they got badly whooped. And Mike has a nasty little fellow by the name of Murad IV to contend with. I cannot rely on him or the USE moving forward; perhaps they might assist in some small way, but I can't rely on it. No. We're going forward alone, guys, and that means I need communication techs like you."

Len rubbed his chin, said, "What's your need? Any prelim thoughts on that?"

Morris shook his head. "Not certain. At a minimum, I want to mimic the USE model of seven to twelve radios per one thousand men. I'd like more, of course, but I doubt there's enough reserve radios in Prague to get by."

Ellie grunted. "And I dare you to try to take them, Morris. Even at a good price, these Bohemians are going to push back hard. People are pretty comfortable now with the ease at which they can communicate with their neighbors. It's like toilet paper: take it away, and you get shit everywhere."

They all laughed at that one, though Morris did not disagree with her foul warning. "Not only that," he said, "but getting them out of town without the mayor—or Pappenheim, for that matter—knowing of it . . . will be a challenge. But we'll work it out. We have to. We don't have a lot of time."

Len crossed his arms. "Where do you intend on going, Morris? Where's the Sunrise headed?"

"Don't know yet." He resisted checking the clock on the wall. He didn't want to seem rude, nor was it right to suggest with any body language that their visit and this conversation wasn't the most important thing on his mind right now. But he had a lot of things on his mind, and all of them queuing up and demanding equal attention.

Ellie lowered her brow. "Shouldn't you know where you're going before you make plans for us? I mean, a lot of what you're going to need in terms of communication equipment will depend greatly on where you're going."

Again, a very true statement. "I know, and I apologize. I'm meeting with someone soon who may help provide counsel on that decision. But in truth, it doesn't matter. No matter where I take the Sunrise, I'd want you with me. I *need* you."

The pause this time was longer. Morris looked at his wife. She smiled, leaned over, and squeezed his hand. Judith had chosen not to engage in the conversation, and instead provide simple moral support. Under the circumstances, Morris preferred it that way. He didn't want the offer to seem like they were both piling on the pressure. He needed Ellie and Len badly, but in the end, if they chose to decline and stay in Prague, he was not about to force them. He had no authority to do that, and even if he did, he would not exercise it.

Len whispered into Ellie's ear. Ellie did the same with Len. They discussed the offer in whispers for a good five minutes. Finally, Ellie said, "Thank you, Morris, for the offer. But...Len and I have a good life here in Prague. The people rely on us for their radio and telephone services. Yes, there are more than enough good radio and telephone techs in the city that we wouldn't be missed. But we're in charge, and we have a responsibility to—"

She paused while she and Len watched Judith hand Morris a pad of paper and a pencil. Morris tore a sheet off the pad and scribbled something with the pencil. "Here's my final offer."

He handed the note to Judith who passed it over to Len.

Len and Ellie stared for two long minutes at the sizable number Morris had scribbled. Finally, Len took a breath and said, "You're joking."

Morris shook his head. "No, sir. As Staff Sergeant Barnes said in *Platoon*...'I shit you not.'"

"Well, Ellie," Judith said, letting her famous smile spread across her face, "did my husband just ruin your *fucking* day... or did he make it?"

Len folded up the paper and put it in his shirt pocket. "Okay, Morris. You win. When do we leave?"

"I know why you've asked me here," Jason Gotkin said, again refusing a sifter of wine from Morris Roth. He pointed his thumb toward the living room door. "I just saw Len and Ellie leave."

Morris shrugged, pointed to his chess set. "Len and I just played a game of chess, that's all. And Judith hadn't seen Ellie in—"

"Morris, please. Enough with the small talk, the obfuscation. I have a bris to attend."

"Mazel tov, by the way." Morris finished his wine and set the glass down. "Being a rabbi suits you."

"Morris—"

"Fine, fine." Morris sat on a chair opposite Jason. He sighed, folded his hands together, sighed again. "Okay, here it is: I need you, Jason."

"No!"

"The Sunrise *needs* spiritual guidance if we are to see the Anaconda Project to completion. I've got a lot of new recruits—*raw* recruits—joining by the day. They need someone like you, an up-timer, who can—far better than me—put their sacrifice into the proper context."

Jason took a handkerchief from his pocket and wiped his brow. He couldn't decide if he was sweating because he was hot, or because of their conversation. Maybe both. "And what is that proper context?"

Morris seemed shocked at the question. "That their lives *matter*, Jason. That we, you and me, the people who came through that ring of fire, can give them a better life."

Jason rubbed his face. "I provide that service here, in Prague, every day."

Morris nodded. "Yes, I know you do. But Prague is not the focal point of our problems right now, Rabbi. Our cause is East. We've got to see this through, my friend, and I need you at my side."

So true, and yet, it couldn't come at a worst time. His *semikah*, his ordination, had occurred not three months ago. He was just getting his feet beneath him, winning the respect and trust of those he guided. It wasn't easy for down-time Jews to trust an up-time rabbi. He was just earning that trust, and now he was being asked to leave?

"My wife will not allow it."

"Like her father, Sarah understands this cause even better than you," Morris said. "She's a down-timer. She's lived the oppression of the Josefov. And, I've spoken with Judith about it. She wants Sarah and the kids to come and live with her here until you return. It would be an honor."

Jason grunted, eyed the half-full wine bottle, and tucked away his handkerchief. "And when will that be? When would I return?"

Morris shook his head. "I don't know, my friend. When the project is finished."

Months, years, perhaps. His kids would grow up in the dim light of a mansion. He wouldn't even know his own children when he returned.

"Please, Jason." He could see the desperation in Morris' eyes. "I need you."

Jason stood and walked to the window. He put his hands on the sill, ran his fingers over the smooth carpentry. Outside now, not far away, a caravan of Jewish recruits was assembling to march to Krakow and join the Sunrise. In fact, Jason had spoken just this morning to a few of the young boys packed up and ready to go. Boys who had no idea what they were marching to, and yet, they wanted to join that rising sun, no matter the cost. The cost could be their deaths, and yet, there they went. "You are sons of Abraham," he had told them loudly as they readied to depart. "Be proud of who you are."

"Okay, Morris," Jason said, turning away from the window and the cool breeze. It felt good on his face. "I'll go. But only on one condition."

"Name it, my friend."

Jason pointed to the wine bottle. "Pour me one of those. In fact, make it two."

Chapter 3

Roth town house
Prague, capital of Bohemia

The man introduced himself as Pál Rákóczi, brother of George I Rákóczi, prince of Transylvania.

He was not dressed in an ostentatious manner, though that could easily be excused by the distance he had traveled and the manner in which he had arrived: all cloak-and-dagger, in the back of a covered wagon that had pulled up to the gates of their home, with the driver begging admittance to discuss a most important matter. After a complete security check of the occupant of the wagon, the man claiming to be Pál Rákóczi was let in.

He was a short man. He wore a burnished red doublet with gold buttons. Hanging from his neck was a modest silver chain from which dangled a crude wooden cross. His headdress was more fur than felt, and in it, a single dark feather, dry, worn, crooked, and ready to fall apart. His beard and mustache were well-kept but filled with strands of gray. His breeches, a shopworn tan; his boots, a hard tarnished black leather.

He smiled, nodded quickly, and said, "It is an honor to meet you, Herr Roth. Your legend grows as we speak."

"My legend?"

"Oh, yes," Pál said, following Morris down the hall. "Your military successes against the Polish and Lithuanians, specifically, in addition to your great success here in Prague at the Battle of the Stone Bridge. How many years ago was that engagement? Three? Four?"

Morris shook his head, opened the door to his study, and stepped aside to allow Pál Rákóczi entry. "I've lost count, to be honest. Please, have a seat."

"Thank you."

They sat on opposite ends of the large rectangular table that filled the middle of the room. The space served both as a study and a library. Judith had commissioned three large bookshelves to be constructed and bolted into the far wall. Now all they needed were enough books to fill them.

The room itself was ample, like most rooms in the house, but the tall windows behind Morris' chair captured the light of the sun and cast it across the space. Unfortunately, the sun had already set for the evening, and so, the young lady who had followed them in, carrying a tray of wine and tea, set the refreshments down on the table and lit two lamps. The hot glow from the light made visibility tolerable.

"*Hakaras HaTov,*" Morris said, nodding to the young woman. She nodded in kind and curtsied to both him and their guest, and then left quietly through a small side door.

"Would you care for a drink?" Morris asked, motioning to the tray.

Pál Rákóczi nodded. "Yes, thank you. Some wine, please."

Morris rose and went to the tray. As he poured, he was intrigued by the man's expression. "Do you find it odd, Herr Rákóczi, that I am serving you, instead of the young lady?"

Rákóczi shook his head. "No, Herr Morris. Although I must wonder why any man who would bother having a servant girl, would not expect her to complete her duties."

Morris shrugged and passed the drink over. He prepared a cup of tea for himself. He'd had enough wine with Len, Ellie, and Jason; his head was throbbing under a mild buzz. "I do it for two reasons. First, security. The absence of servants at a discussion that might require confidentiality makes it less likely that gossip will spread. Secondly, she brought in the tray and lit the lamps. What more could I have asked for? I like to think that I am still humble enough to serve a guest in my own home. The Talmud teaches us that humility is a great virtue."

"It is true, then. You are a Jew."

The statement took Morris by surprise. "You didn't know that already?"

"Oh yes, yes. But it is always best to get the confirmation from the source. Rumor, conjecture, hearsay... have all converged in Transylvania to make you a Moses, an Attila, the second coming of Saint Stephen I, though he was a Christian. But now, I know for sure."

"And does *that* bother you?" Morris asked, returning to his seat with a simmering cup of tea.

"Not at all, Herr Morris. It is one of the reasons for my visit."

"Indeed, sir. Why has the prince of Transylvania sent his brother to me?"

Assuming that the man was the brother of the prince—and Morris was not entirely convinced yet that he was—the question was valid.

Rákóczi took a sip of his wine. He nodded. "Very good. I would request a bottle upon my return home. But...let us put that matter aside for now and get to it." He set his glass down, leaned forward with hands and elbows on the table. "Herr Roth. The prince of Transylvania, my brother, feels that it is time to reconsider his current political relationship with the Ottoman Empire. He would like to explore the possibility that an alliance with Bohemia might enable him to restore his principality's independence."

Morris almost did the classic spit-take from up-time comedy shows. He stopped and collected himself right before a dribble of tea escaped his mouth.

This was indeed a surprise. When he had been told that an envoy from the Transylvanian court had arrived in Prague requesting a meeting, he figured it would be some minor dignitary at best, afraid of where the Grand Army of the Sunrise might venture next. He imagined the little oaf pleading with him not to "invade" his country, and then throwing wild, and probably unenforceable, threats at him to try to scare him into another direction. Or, at worst, making serious threats on behalf of Sultan Murad himself. Transylvania was, after all, a vassal state of the Ottomans. But this?

He tried to remember what he knew about Transylvania's history. Had Transylvania *ever* been an independent realm? He wasn't sure, but his impression was that the area had always been some other power's vassal, or at least subordinate, going all the way back to the Roman Empire.

He might be wrong about that, however. He was hardly an expert on the subject. Happily, his spymaster, Uriel Abrabanel, probably did know—and as luck would have it, was in Prague right now.

Morris cleared his throat. "That's quite a proposition, sir."

Rákóczi nodded. "And a sincere one, I can assure you. I speak for the prince."

Did he? Nothing in the man's countenance suggested otherwise, but Morris knew enough about Transylvania's history to know that the term "turbulent" was appropriate. Competing political, social, and religious interests were as common there as the fog that skirted the vast Carpathian mountain range hugging the central basin. So many invading forces had marched through its fields and foothills, its forests, its towns, that it was, even today, a hodgepodge of ethnicities, a soup of religious denominations and cultures. Could this man be who he claimed to be, or was he playing a role? Was he a spy?

"I have been further instructed to offer you this, Herr Morris: Prince Rákóczi will agree to an alliance with Bohemia, and do so publicly, in exchange for military support from you and your army. He is also willing to cede portions of our northern territory so that you may continue to move into Ruthenian lands." Rákóczi smiled. "And thus, continue your Anaconda operation."

Morris raised a brow. "Anaconda?"

"Come now, Herr Roth." Rákóczi smiled and waved as if he were swatting a fly. "I mean no disrespect to you in your own home, but Transylvanians are no fools, nor do we tread into situations that we are unprepared for. My brother is well aware of your political and religious goals. And he has no quarrel with them, especially if you agree to our proposals and conditions."

Morris sat up in his chair, near giddy with equal amounts of excitement and dread. "And what might those be?"

The sun had risen too soon, Morris hadn't gotten enough sleep the night before, and now his head throbbed with a nasty headache. Uriel Abrabanel seemed to find it quite amusing. But then, Uriel found most things amusing.

"I would think that, being back in Prague," the Sephardic agent said, "you'd find time to rest, my old friend. What ails you that you lose so much complexion...and sleep?"

Morris rubbed his face vigorously to help himself come alert. "Well, since you claim to have known the man, how's this little quip from Shakespeare: 'One may smile and smile, and be a villain'? I need to know if the man I have in my home, sleeping in one of my guest rooms, is a villain or what he claims to be. And I need to know *now*."

Morris dropped his hand and made a face. "Very soon, at least."

Uriel nodded. "I can confirm this with certainty: the man you have in your home is indeed Pál Rákóczi, brother of Prince George I Rákóczi. He has another brother too, by the way: Zsigmond. I don't know where he is or what he is up to at the moment. I can find out if you like, but it will take some time. Gyulafehérvár, the capital of Transylvania, is at least five hundred miles from here—and farther than that, when you include the detours that have to be made to avoid Ottoman territory."

"It's *that* far?"

Uriel's little smile broadened. "Even after all the years since the Ring of Fire, you Americans keep thinking that Europe isn't nearly as big as your homeland. Yes, it's that far."

Morris shook his head, not as a gesture of negation but in an effort to clear it. "Is there any reason I need to know about Zsigmond?"

Uriel shrugged. "Two brothers, two competing interests? The prince sends one brother as his envoy. Why not the other? Why not both? Things to keep in mind if you decide to pursue this offer."

That was the trouble with spies: always seeing crosses and double-crosses in everything.

"Very well. What do you know of the Rákóczi family?"

Uriel stroked his beard. "George himself came to power not long ago: 1630, thereabouts. He succeeded Stephen Bethlen, who was prince for only one year. Catherine of Brandenburg came before Stephen, and her reign wasn't long either. She was the second wife of Gabriel Bethlen, who ruled Transylvania for sixteen years. George was a great supporter and admirer of Gabriel, and I don't doubt that he considers himself the rightful successor to the man."

"Seems like quite a tangle."

Uriel nodded. "As dynastic successions so often are. The Rákóczis, the Bethlens, the Báthorys, the Bocskais. And on and on and on. All of them, and more, have held power in Transylvania for as long as history has been recorded."

"Was Gabriel Bethlen a good leader?"

"Many consider him one of the finest princes to have ruled Transylvania—but he ruled as a vassal, and there is a fine line between 'good ruler' and 'obedient puppet' under those circumstances. He was king of Hungary for a short time as well; the duke of Opole and Ratibor. The history of Hungary, Transylvania, and the Ottoman Empire are inextricably woven together, Morris. You must understand that going in...if you do go in."

He did understand that. Since the Ring of Fire and his acceptance of the Anaconda Project, Morris had become a student of history. There was still much he hadn't learned, but he had made a point to become knowledgeable about the history of Bohemia, Poland, and Lithuania. He knew much less about Transylvania since it hadn't seemed especially relevant to his interests. He knew a fair amount about Transylvania's current relationships with larger and more powerful kingdoms and empires around its borders. But the day-to-day machinations of the Transylvania court he did not know.

"And the Rákóczi family, specifically?"

"They are neither angels nor devils, Don Morris. They are one family in a line of pragmatic rulers of Transylvania that goes back centuries. They rule in their own self-interest, and if it aligns with Transylvania's interests, then all the better. There are good people and bad people in all families, including royal ones."

"And George himself? What is he like?"

"He is new to power, but he has a lot of military experience. And, as I said, he was a confidant to Gabriel Bethlen, which puts him in good stead with many in his country. I do not know the man personally, but I have heard good things about him. Then again, I've also heard that he is an ass in the world."

More Shakespeare? Uriel preferred up-time Westerns to iambic pentameter. He should be quoting Louis L'Amour, not The Bard.

"What would you do, Uriel, if the decision was yours?"

Uriel laughed softly. "I'm sorry, my friend. I don't wish to make light of the matter, but that is a question you will have to answer on your own. It is your army, your men, your cause. I fully support what you are trying to do, and if you believe that moving the Grand Army of the Sunrise into Transylvania is the right course of action, then may God guide you. God—and I strongly recommend you get my niece's advice as well."

"Well, that's a given," said Morris. Rebecca Abrabanel was the Secretary of State of the United States of Europe. There was no way Morris was going to make any decision over a matter like this without consulting her. He'd already sent a radio message to Magdeburg. He'd sent copies of the message to Krakow and Linz as well, since he didn't know where Rebecca was at the moment. The down-timer had taken to up-time-style "jet-lag diplomacy" as if she'd been born to it.

Over the next few days, Morris had several meetings with Pál Rákóczi—although calling them "meetings" was more of a courtesy than anything else. Nothing substantive was discussed. The meetings were more in the way of social encounters; basically, a way to be polite and attentive to the Transylvanian nobleman without making any commitments.

Rákóczi did not object. He understood perfectly well that the commander of the Grand Army of the Sunrise was not going to make any decisions without collecting as much intelligence as he could and discussing the situation with the powers-that-were in Bohemia. That meant General Pappenheim, first and foremost— and Pappenheim was in Linz, confronting the Ottomans. It would take him a while to get back to Prague.

And while Rákóczi had no way of knowing that Morris had asked Rebecca Abrabanel to come to Prague as well, he would certainly not have been surprised. The likelihood that Bohemia, or even an officially "detached" Grand Army of the Sunrise, would make common cause with Transylvania against the Ottomans without consulting first with the United States of Europe was effectively nil.

Morris did spend quite a bit of time studying the two up-time atlases he had that showed modern Romania and its many counties. He also questioned any of his officers he could find—there were more than he would have thought—who'd spent time in Transylvania.

The result was to heighten his interest in the Rákóczi proposal.

The northern area that the prince was offering basically comprised the up-time Romanian counties of Satu Mare, Maramureş and Bistriţa-Năsăud. Together, they would provide an excellent avenue through which to move the Grand Army of the Sunrise eastward to advance the Anaconda Project.

Morris continued to use that term for it, for lack of a better alternative, even though it was no longer very appropriate. Wallenstein, who had launched the enterprise, had had the simple and fundamentally crude goal of expanding his kingdom and turning it into what amounted to an empire. Morris' aim, on the other hand, had overlapped but had been quite different. He didn't care whether Bohemia expanded its territory, except insofar as that might advance his own goal, which was to torpedo or at least forestall the Chmielnicki Pogrom depicted in the up-time histories. Unless that history was changed, a dozen years in the future a great Cossack rebellion would erupt that carried in its train one of the worst slaughters in Jewish history. Not comparable to the Holocaust, certainly; but probably as bad as the 1919 pogroms carried out in the Ukraine by Petliura and Denikin's White armies during the Russian Civil War.

Truth be told, Morris still had no clear idea how to achieve his aims. But since it seemed self-evident that the more power he accumulated, the more leverage he would have, he had continued to proceed along the lines laid out by Wallenstein. But was that the right course of action now?

Airstrip southeast of the Horse Market
Prague, capital of Bohemia

Morris waited to approach until after Rebecca's plane taxied to a halt and the pilot cut the engines. That wasn't so much due to any apprehension on his part that the propellers might accidentally fire up again, as it was to the necessity to watch where he was treading. The ground bordering the small airstrip was rough enough that you couldn't take your eyes off it, lest you stumble and plant your face square in the dirt.

The pilot, Captain Laura Goss, was the first to emerge from the cockpit. She was holding a pair of aircraft wheel chocks and looking rather disgruntled. Normally, chocking the wheels would be done by one of the attendants at the airfield, which, in this case, was...

Well, nobody. The airstrip had only one person on duty, and since he was officially a "controller" and it was a cold day for late April, he'd decided to exercise his authority to stay inside what passed for a control tower.

"Why the hell did you have us land here, Morris?" Goss asked, a bit grumpily, as she placed the chocks. She waved her hand in the direction of Prague's regular airport, which was in Malá Strana on the other side of the river. "What's wrong with Wallenstein Field?"

"There's nothing wrong with the field," said Morris. "Except that it's too close to Wallenstein's palace. We have a guest staying there *now* who is the reason for your coming, but someone we don't want to know that you're here. Yet, anyway."

By the time he finished those sentences, both Rebecca Abrabanel and General Pappenheim had emerged from the cockpit, in time to hear.

Pappenheim chuckled, looking in the direction of the city. The rather far distant city. "I'd forgotten this airstrip even existed," he said. "We must be a mile beyond the Horse Market."

"Not quite, but pretty close." The Bohemian general had used the traditional name for what was now officially Wallenstein Square—and in the universe Morris came from, had been called Wenceslas Square. A lot of people had started doing that since Wallenstein's death. The man had named so many things after himself that it got hard to keep them straight.

Laura Goss was looking somewhat alarmed. "Uh...boss. I don't think—doesn't look like it, anyway—that there's anywhere suitable here for me to camp out."

Knowing Laura, Morris was pretty sure her major complaint was more along the lines of *and for sure nowhere to get a drink and join a party.* But he kept a straight face. "Relax, Captain. You'll all be staying with Judith and me in the Josefov."

He pointed to the northwest. "See? Here come our rides."

Turning, they saw a young man on a horse leading a string of them in their direction. The mounts were already saddled.

Laura's expression now got a bit on the sour side. Like many Americans since the Ring of Fire, she'd learned how to ride a horse. But she didn't have to like it.

"So, what is this all about, Morris?" asked Rebecca. She wasn't fazed by the oncoming equestrian mode of transport. Raised a Sephardic girl in London and Amsterdam, Rebecca had never ridden a horse before the Ring of Fire either, but she'd become quite a good horsewoman in the years since.

"I'll explain along the way," he said.

Roth town house
Josefov district, Prague

There was silence in the room for at least a minute after Morris finished the presentation that he'd begun while they were riding from the airstrip. That presentation had taken quite some time, since by then Morris had gathered a lot of information. Most, though by no means all of it, had come from Uriel.

Rebecca was the first to speak. But all she said was: "Well."

Pappenheim's contribution was no more effusive. "What does the Queen's Council say? As you know, I've been preoccupied with dealing with the Ottomans lately." He pointed to the south. "Down there."

Morris smiled. "It will no doubt astonish you, Gottfried Heinrich, to learn that the entire council, including the queen herself, has deferred the matter to your judgment. The grounds, of course, being that the main parameters involved would seem to be military in nature."

Pappenheim made a little snorting sound. "Astonished? No. Irritated, yes. For the love of all that is holy, this is *not* primarily a military affair, it's a political and diplomatic one. If we form an alliance with the prince of Transylvania, the impact on... on... will be..." He ground to a halt.

Roth's smile became very close to a grin. "You see the quandary. In point of fact, the diplomatic repercussions of us forming an alliance with Transylvania are practically nil. The Ottomans will become our enemy? They already are."

He shrugged. "In fact, Gottfried, the council is right. The issue is almost entirely military. On the positive side, we would be opening another front against the Turks—and one which, if we suffer a loss in it, doesn't make our situation any worse. On the negative side..."

"It would require a certain commitment of forces that we might prefer to use elsewhere." The general gave Morris a look that wasn't exactly unfriendly but had no warmth in it either.

"As to that, *General* Roth," said Pappenheim, "the situation is as simple as could be. We will suffer no diminishment in our ability to fight the Ottoman Empire because the only Bohemian forces that would be involved in this enterprise would be yours."

That came as no surprise. Morris nodded and looked to Rebecca.

"So now, I plop the matter into your lap, Secretary of State Abrabanel. What if any military or other support might we expect—hope for, at least—from the United States of Europe?"

Rebecca was chewing on her lip. A small, what you might call ladylike portion of it, anyway. She was not someone given to excessive public displays of concern, or uncertainty.

"To be honest, I have no idea," she said. "I will need to discuss it with..."

She left off the lip-gnawing, took a deep breath, and slowly sighed it out.

"Several people. Gustav Adolf and Ed Piazza, of course. My husband. Probably some others." After a moment, she added: "Certainly some others, rather."

She looked at the big standing clock in a corner of the room. What Americans called "a grandfather clock," for no good reason she'd ever been able to determine. The thing looked very modern to her.

"How accurate is that clock?" she asked.

Morris glanced at it. "We adjust it every day. It's accurate within five minutes."

"Good. I still have plenty of time."

"Time for what?"

"Time to fly back to Linz before nightfall. Prime Minister Piazza might be able to make the flight from Magdeburg by then as well. He can certainly get there by tomorrow midmorning." Rebecca rose to her feet. "Please have one of your servants summon Captain Goss, Morris."

Chapter 4

Encampment at Kazimierz
Grand Army of the Sunrise
South of Krakow

The campground for the Joshua Corps was busy. So busy, in fact, that Isaac Kohen nearly missed seeing Jason Gotkin among the hundreds of new Jewish volunteers who had arrived within the past several days.

He waved and raised his voice in salutation. "Shalom aleichem, Rabbi Gotkin!"

The up-timer looked up and around to find the greeter. When he saw Isaac, he smiled. "Aleichem shalom, Brother Kohen!" He waved him forward.

They met in the middle of the mass of men, greeting each other warmly. "I heard that you had arrived in camp, Rabbi. I'm so glad."

"Call me Jason, my friend. I may be a rabbi now, but we've known each other long enough to dispense with such proper greetings."

"Very well...Jason."

Isaac's father, Chaim ha-Kohen, was a rabbi himself. He was also Eva Bacharach's brother, so Isaac's family, through its intimate connection with Morris and Judith Roth, had known Jason Gotkin since his arrival in Prague. In fact, Isaac remembered when he and Jason first met: at the Battle of the Stone Bridge, when Isaac was still just a lad, aiding the wounded during the battle.

"When did you arrive?"

"Three days ago," Jason said as they walked toward the field hospital. "Morris Roth has made me army chaplain for the Joshua Corps."

General Roth had implemented a new faith services program where each religion represented within the ranks had a chaplain on which to rely for spiritual needs. A new Catholic chaplain had been appointed just yesterday, and tomorrow, the new Calvinist chaplain would receive his appointment.

"Mazel tov!"

"Thank you."

But Isaac could see that the new responsibility and title weighed heavily on Jason's spirit. "Why are you troubled, my friend? It is a great honor."

"It is, Isaac, it is. I'm both humbled and grateful for the appointment. But, I'm concerned."

Isaac stopped, turned to Jason and put his hand on his shoulder. "Why so?"

Jason sighed and scratched his beard. He looked around again, looked through all the young men coming and going, wandering about the camp trying to find their companies, their sergeants. So many fresh faces, so many anxious, hopeful expressions. "I don't believe one rabbi is enough, Isaac. With so many new men arriving daily, one just isn't enough to maintain their spiritual needs. I've sent word to Morris in Prague requesting at least one more, maybe two."

Isaac nodded. "I'm sure he'll approve."

"Let us hope, but the thing is, I don't want to create a problem within the army where members of the other faiths feel that their spiritual needs are being overshadowed. If so, then they'll request more priests and pastors, and then we'll have an arms race on our hands."

"A what?" Isaac asked, confused by the term.

Jason shook his head. "Never mind. In short, I don't want the Jews and Gentiles of our chaplain corps at war with one another about their own recruitment numbers when a lethal enemy force is breathing down our necks.

"Also," he continued, "all these new, untrained, unskilled

boys." He leaned in and whispered. "They don't know a damned thing, Isaac. And you know as well as I do: the greener they go in, the redder they come out."

Isaac agreed wholeheartedly with that. In time, these young boys would get the training they needed to face an enemy army. They'd learn how to march, load and fire their muskets and pistols, use a sword, a knife, and all the other myriad things a soldier learns in preparation for war. But such training would take time, and did they have that kind of time? There was no word yet on when and if the Grand Army of the Sunrise would march again. No word either on where.

There were rumblings, of course, rumor and speculation. Some said they weren't going anywhere, that they were going to stay here in Poland and hold the line for possible counter attacks. Others said that they would strike the tents soon and keep heading east. Still others suggested such radical moves as heading south, through Hungary, or the Principality of Transylvania and Wallachia, to strike the Ottomans in the Levant. Isaac did not know the truth of any of it, but he agreed with Jason completely: these new men needed to start their training soon, or they'd be paying him and his medical staff bloody visit after visit.

"Oh, that reminds me," Isaac said, "I have been put in temporary charge of new recruitment and supply for the medical corps."

"Mazel tov!" Jason said, returning the congratulations.

Isaac chuckled. "Trust me, there's no glory in it. But it's very important. With our chief medical officer down for a good while, I'm responsible for obtaining medical supplies and recruiting new nurses, medics, orderlies. I'd like to recruit from the Ashkenazim, if possible. As you conduct your daily faith services and prayers for them, if anyone expresses interest in assisting me and mine, I'd be most grateful if you would send them my way. And not just women for nursing positions. Men are just as qualified to perform those duties, whether they wish to admit it openly or not."

Jason nodded. "Yes, I will do so. But that's another thing I'm not happy about: wives and children in the baggage train. Sarah and our children will be staying in Prague, thankfully, but many, many women and children are in camp right now, and they intend on following us like it's some goddamned parade." The up-timer scrunched his shoulders and neck, realizing that he had made the mistake of blaspheming out loud. "Sorry, my friend. I must be careful not to allow my emotions, and latent up-time sensibilities, get the best of me."

Isaac suppressed a laugh. "That's quite all right. We've all had those outbursts of late. My father always said that, in times of war, men resort to their baser instincts. He was not saying that as a compliment, but I think he understood that, under great stress, a man often shows his weaknesses. And in those moments, it is God that we must look to, to regain our strength."

Jason nodded. "Your father is a wise man, and his son is wise beyond his years. Perhaps you should have been a rabbi."

Isaac shook his head. "No. I knew my calling the minute I stepped onto that stone bridge. Speaking of which..." Isaac stopped and looked toward the large hospital tent where many soldiers still convalesced with wounds. "I must say goodbye. I have my rounds to conduct."

They said their goodbyes. As Jason walked away, he turned and pointed at Isaac's head. "I'm happy to see you wearing your kippah."

Isaac touched the soft, dark fabric of his cap. "They call it a yarmulke around here."

"Kippah, yarmulke, yamaka, whatever you call it. Wear it every day, Isaac. Now is our time, my friend. Be a proud Jew."

"Always," Isaac said, waving Jason away. He reached for his cap again and resisted the urge to remove it before entering the tent. In this one, there were currently more Gentiles than Jews, and even now, amidst all these young Ashkenazim recruits, regardless of what Morris Roth had accomplished in Prague, regardless of what liberation the Sunrise had brought to the Jews in Poland, he still fell back upon old habits of trying to hide his identity.

Be a proud Jew... Isaac heard Rabbi Gotkin's words loudly in his mind. He nodded to himself, removed his hand from his yarmulke, and stepped into the tent.

I will try to be, Jason... every day. I will try.

"How's our patient, Devorah?" Isaac asked as he stood near the flap and accepted a clipboard from, in his learned opinion, the best nurse on staff.

"The one in the corner," she said, pointing there, "or the one in bed three?" She pointed there.

The one in the corner was Doctor Oberheuser who, thankfully, for once, wasn't filling the air with a stream of expletives. He had fussed and groused so much about being confined with common soldiers that they had agreed to, at least, give him the best space in the tent: a nice, spacious corner that gave ample light and ventilation. The one that needed the light and ventilation, however, and the one whom he wanted to visit the most, was in bed three.

"How's Captain von Jori today?"

"Quiet," she said. "Stoic. But polite, which is a great virtue in the tent." She folded newly cleaned and sanitized sheets while she gave Isaac the basics. "His wounds are healing. We'll need to redress his eye soon. No infection that I can see or smell, though you're a better judge of that than I. Otherwise, he's fine. His neck is swollen, his cheek, the flesh around his eye. We've done our best to keep the swelling down. He refuses pain medication. I can't decide whether that's excessive courage or stupidity."

Isaac huffed. "Perhaps a little of both."

"Greta is quite taken with him," Devorah continued with a wry smile, motioning toward a small group of nurses tending to Doctor Oberheuser. "She keeps casually stopping by his bed, even when she's not assigned to him, and chatting. She laughs at everything he says. She's even loaned him an up-time book that's been translated into German."

Isaac wagged a finger at her with his own wry smile. "You keep that she-wolf away from my patient, Devorah. He needs to devote his full energies to recovery...nothing else."

He tucked the clipboard of Christian's chart under his arm and made his way through the maze of beds. He greeted all nurses and orderlies moving from patient to patient, and stopped to give solace to a young Jewish footman crying for his mother. They prayed together, and Isaac held his hand. He then took off his yarmulke and placed it on the boy's head. That calmed him immediately. The boy then laid his head back, smiled, closed his eyes, and died.

Isaac didn't bother retrieving his cap. He just left it on the poor boy's head as two orderlies came up and carried him away.

Isaac took a moment to gather himself. Then he greeted the cavalry officer, two beds away.

"Good morning, Christian. How are you feeling?"

Christian propped himself up on his elbows. He winced in pain. "Did that man just die?"

Isaac nodded. "Yes. A gut wound. Very severe. There was never much chance that he would survive it."

"You gave him your cap."

"It's called a yarmulke, and yes, I did. We wear the cap as a sign of respect and fear of God. It reminds us that there is a great separation between us and God, and that He is above us all. The boy *needed* that connection in his last moments, to remind the world, perhaps to remind himself, that he was Jewish." Isaac sighed and looked down at his shoes. "So many of us have to hide that fact just to survive. I'm glad he was able to be himself at the end."

He grabbed a stool nearby and placed it alongside Christian's bed. He took a seat. "But what is done is done. Let us talk about you. I'll ask again: how are *you* feeling?"

Christian laid back carefully with a long exhalation of breath. "I'm doing fine, I suppose."

Isaac picked up the book that young Greta had loaned the captain. "*The Adventures of Huckleberry Finn.* Do you like it?"

"For the most part, yes. I don't understand a lot of the context, though. The way they talk bothers me. I don't know if it is a very good translation. But Fräulein Greta said it was—"

"You let me know if Greta is causing you trouble, and I'll take care of her."

"No, no. She is very sweet. She reminds me of my sister."

Isaac smiled. "Just so it stays that way. Your energies must be confined to recovery right now, nothing else."

"Oh, don't fret about that. I'm in no shape for such things."

"Speaking of which"—Isaac leaned in—"may I check your wounds?"

Christian nodded and lay still while Isaac did his examination.

Christian was naked from the waist up, a pair of loose tan breeches from the waist down. A thin sheet covered his legs. His right arm, neck, face, and eye were wrapped with up-time gauze and bandages. Isaac carefully reviewed each afflicted area and reported his findings aloud, as he was trained to do at Imperial Tech in Magdeburg. "Your arm and shoulder are fine. The stitches are holding, your cuts are healing well, though I will caution you that you must keep moving them both or they may grow stiff and never fully recover. Human muscle, Christian, takes great offense at trauma. Scar tissue will develop and harden, severely undermining your mobility. Unless you fight against it."

He examined the neck and peeled away the dressing just

enough to have a look. He nodded. "Neck is doing fine. Swollen, but again, stitches are holding and cuts are healing." He put his nose near the wound and sniffed. "No infection that I can see or smell, though you do need a bath."

Christian snickered. "Every soldier here needs one, I suppose."

Isaac moved to the eye. He ever so gently peeled away the dressing. He winced, though made sure Christian did not notice. "Your stitches are holding, praise God. No sign of infection, but your eyelid is swollen shut. And that will be so, I imagine, for quite a while. I'll have Nurse Devorah come over soon and clean and redress—"

"Am I going to lose my eye, Isaac?"

"I don't know yet, to be honest. The eye is one of the most delicate organs in the human body. I successfully removed all the debris and there's no evidence of any serious structural damage. But it suffered a great trauma. It will take time."

"Will I be able to see again?"

That was an even more difficult question to answer. "That, I do not know. My instinct suggests that yes, you will. But you may have some impairment. We will have to wait until the swelling goes away and you can open your eye again to know for sure."

Christian sighed deeply and shook his head. "A half-blind cavalry soldier. Might as well have died up there."

It looked as if Christian was about to cry. Isaac wondered if he might be suffering from what the up-time medical texts called PTSD: Post-Traumatic Stress Disorder.

"The way Colonel Renz tells it," Isaac said, shifting to the positive, "you saved a lot of lives in the fight. You prevented a near full slaughter of an infantry company. Can you tell me what happened?"

Christian huffed. "Colonel Renz is too kind. I did very little."

"Tell me anyway."

Christian paused to rub away a tear before it ran down his cheek. He cleared his throat and winced at the pain of doing so.

"It was right before General Mercy ordered a withdrawal of his cavalry to allow Colonel Higgins and the Hangman Regiment to come up and engage. My unit, Captain Tideman's company, Colonel Renz's regiment, were at the spearhead of a charge that had initially gone well. We'd smashed into the flank of dismounted dragoons. We had them flailing and on the run.

"Not too far away from us, a company of Brethren was heavily engaged with Lithuanian infantry. They seemed to be doing rather well, but they had been pulled into an almost untenable salient that was concerning to my captain. When we got word that a column of hussars was trying to move around the Brethren and strike them from the rear, Captain Tideman ordered a redress of the lines and a redeployment to try to catch those winged bastards unawares before they could commit to their own charge.

"We moved quickly and took the interior line. We were ready. When they came up over the ridgeline, Captain Tideman ordered the charge, and just as he raised up in his saddle to make it, he took a round right in the face from, I assume, the infantry brawl going on nearby. You've never been in battle, Isaac, so perhaps you don't understand just how rare it is for a single shot from a musket to strike the face. Point-blank from a pistol, sure, especially if it's from one of our Santees. But a down-time musket from distance? A one-in-a-million shot that tore right through his face, through his mouth and out the other side. His face was gone, Isaac. Just... gone.

"I tried catching him as he fell from the saddle, but I was too slow. I jumped down to him and I held him, praying to God that he was all right. I'm a Calvinist, Isaac—my family is—but I've hardly ever prayed in my life. I did that day, but God wasn't listening, or perhaps he was busy elsewhere. It did not work. My captain was gone, and my company was in disarray.

"Men up and down the line were reining their horses back, shouting retreat and all manner of blasphemy. I was angry. I wasn't brave or noble or anything else. I was just mad! I saw those winged devils coming on, and I remember standing up, pulling my sword, and screaming, *Attacke! Attacke!* I got back onto my horse, and I charged the sons of bitches.

"Suddenly, company men were all around me, charging too, and we slammed into them. Next thing I remember, I was crossing swords with an officer, I think, though there was so many colorful men and horses moving in and out of my view and range, all that horrifying whistling from their wings, I couldn't be sure. One of my stirrups broke, and I slipped in the saddle. I raised up my arm to try to maintain balance. That's when he struck and slashed me right across my face, neck, and shoulder. I remember shouting my uncle's name, hearing and feeling the explosion of a cannon shell nearby, and then falling from my horse.

"Next thing I remember was being dragged from the field by none other than Colonel Renz. He and one of the other fellows you saw when they brought me to the tent. On the way here, Colonel Renz gave me the field commission of captain." He paused, then, "That's all I remember."

Impressive. "I suspect you got that shard of metal in your eye from the exploding cannon shell."

Christian shrugged. "Maybe, though it could have come from the man's sword. A cavalryman's sword can get pretty beaten up during a fight, Isaac. Hacking and slashing thick buff coats, armor, flesh, bone. It's not uncommon. When he made that final slash, it could have chipped right off."

"Well," Isaac said, his heart racing from the story, "however it happened, you survived. And you may think you failed, and yes, I suspect conducting that charge in lieu of your captain's death, did cause some of your fellow cavalrymen to die as well. But I've no doubt that you saved many lives." He put his hand on Christian's hand. "That matters. Colonel Renz seems to think that your quick action prevented the Brethren from being slaughtered."

Christian nodded. "Colonel Renz is a good man, a good commander. I just hope that I can live up to his expectations. Now, I need to get out of this damned bed."

He moved as if he were rising. Isaac stopped him. "Hold on, Christian. You need to start exercising, yes, but not today. You've still got a few days here before I'll release you."

Christian pulled away and glared at Isaac. "You don't have the authority to keep me here. If I want to leave, I will."

Isaac held his tongue and temper. He breathed deeply, rubbed his brow, paused to collect his thoughts. "Christian, you see that son of a bitch in the corner? That's Doctor Oberheuser, chief medical officer of the Grand Army of the Sunrise. If I tell him you are in no condition to leave, he will place guards around your bed, and they won't let you even get up to piss. Now, please, be still, and trust me. Trust your doctor."

Christian fell back into his bed, clearly despondent, restless, and more than a little angry. Isaac let him stew for a few moments, then continued. "Christian, the most important thing I've learned as a care provider is that a person's health is comprised of three basic things: physical, mental, and spiritual well-being. Body, mind, and spirit. I promise you, your body is healing, and on my honor, I vow to make sure that you recover fully. You are feeding your mind by reading; I fully approve. Your spirit? Well, we'll take care of that later."

"If you think I'm going to become a Jew," Christian blurted, "you have a—"

Isaac waved him off. "Not on your life. I'm no rabbi. I wouldn't dream of proselytizing or witnessing as you Protestants may call it. Besides, you reek of Gentile."

There was an awkward pause, and then they both laughed. It felt good. It was clear to Isaac that they both needed that, Christian perhaps more so. There were so few moments in his profession where laughter was afforded. It felt, and sounded, good.

"I'm worried, Isaac," Christian said, sitting up again, "that if I don't get back to my company soon, they may pick another captain. Colonel Renz may require it. A company cannot go long without a leader, especially those men. If they don't have one, they'll just disband the company, drift away or sign up with another captain and company."

"I'll speak to Colonel Renz and make sure he doesn't move on that." Now was the time to set the hook. "On one condition."

Christian wrinkled his brow. "Yes?"

"That when it is time for you to be discharged, you come and work for me."

"What are you talking about?"

"Due to Doctor Oberheuser's continued convalesce, I've been put in charge of medical supply and refit. And this is an order straight from General Morris Roth. I need a good second to help me coordinate the effort with the quartermaster. Since I must share responsibilities between that and my normal medical duties, I need someone who can step in for me when I am otherwise occupied, a person who can both handle the mental and physical rigors of the position. It'll be a great way for you to recover your physical strength and mental acuity." *And, it'll help allay your depression and general malaise.* "Do you accept?"

Christian took a long time to decide. So long, in fact, that Isaac stepped aside a moment to address an issue with a patient in bed seven. When he returned, Christian said, "Very well. I will agree, if you agree to speak to Colonel Renz immediately, and allow me to return to my men as soon as I am able."

Isaac nodded. "On my professional honor."

"Isaac!"

Doctor Oberheuser's voice was loud and obnoxious. As always. "Come over here. I've a bowel movement ready for your examination!"

Isaac put his face in his hands and groaned. "You Gentiles will be the death of me."

He stood slowly. "I'll be by again later to check on you." He bid farewell and turned to leave.

"Isaac," Christian said. Isaac stopped and turned. "Thank you for saving my life. I—I just wanted to tell you that."

Isaac smiled. Hearing that was as welcome as the man's laughter. "You are quite welcome, my friend."

Chapter 5

Emperor Gustav II Adolf's headquarters
Linz, Austria
Temporary capital of the Austrian-Hungarian Empire

After Rebecca finished her summary of the situation, the three men in the room looked at one other. More precisely, Mike Stearns and Ed Piazza looked at Gustav Adolf for a few seconds, then at each other for even less time, and then back at the emperor. For his part, Gustav Adolf studied one of the paintings on the wall of the rather small room he used for meetings like this one. It was a portrait of his grandfather, Gustav Vasa, who had led Sweden's war of independence against Denmark and founded the Vasa dynasty of which Gustav Adolf was a member.

There was a portrait of Gustav Adolf's grandfather anywhere he went, except for brief visits. Occasionally, he would add another and invariably smaller portrait of his own father, Charles IX. There were never portraits of the other rulers of Sweden who had followed Gustav Vasa until Gustav Adolf came to the throne in 1611.

And for good reason. Mike Stearns liked to joke—although not in the emperor's presence—that Sweden had been ruled during that era by the Brothers Grimm. The founder of the dynasty had been succeeded by his oldest son, Eric XIV, who had gone mad and been overthrown by his younger half brother, John III.

45

(Who, for good measure, had seen to it that Mad King Eric was then poisoned.)

Brother John was not mad, but he was no prize as a ruler. He was hot-tempered and violent, and prone to paranoia. A worse legacy, though, was that he married a princess of the ruling family of Poland and Lithuania, Catherine Jagiellon, and had a son by her named Sigismund. This not-so-jolly fellow would become Sigismund III, the king of Poland and Grand Lithuania in 1587, to which he added the titles of King of Poland and Grand Duke of Finland upon his father's death in 1592—only to lose those titles three years later when the Swedish Riksdag forced him to abdicate to his uncle Charles—the third and last of the Brothers Grimm—because Sigismund insisted on remaining Catholic instead of accepting the Lutheran church which now dominated Sweden. This was the origin of the bitter feud between the two branches of the Vasa dynasty that had now been raging for decades.

After contemplating his grandfather for a while, Gustav Adolf turned his attention back to the other occupants of the room.

He looked to Mike first, which was a breach of protocol given that Piazza was now the prime minister of the USE and Stearns was a mere major general. But Ed didn't take offense. Reality was what it was, and all of them knew that while Mike was scrupulous about not formally intruding onto Piazza's turf—or his wife Rebecca's, for that matter—he didn't mind informally wandering through it rather freely.

Besides, this was primarily a military issue. For now, at any rate.

"What do you think?" the emperor asked.

"We should go for it," Mike replied immediately. "Leave aside Morris Roth's concerns. It is to our benefit to open as many fronts against the Ottomans as we can."

Gustav Adolf stroked his mustache and then gave his goatee a little tug. He favored a Vandyke, as did many men of the time.

"I doubt if Murad will devote many of his own troops to the task of suppressing Transylvania," he said. "He'll order his vassal states of Wallachia and Moldavia to do it. And since neither Wallachian nor Moldavian troops are among those we're facing, it wouldn't really take much pressure off us."

His tone was that of a man simply making an observation, not being argumentative.

"I don't disagree with any of that," said Mike. "You're right, Your Majesty—for the moment. But if our intervention alongside Bohemia's succeeds in establishing an independent Transylvania, that situation could change."

The emperor issued a soft snort. "The Balkans being what they are." After a moment, he added: "You're right, of course."

The complexities of Balkan politics went back centuries. The relations between masters and vassals were a lot more fluid than the terms themselves suggested. A strong and independent Transylvania would put pressure on all the neighboring vassal states of the Ottoman Empire. Even if they remained formally "vassals," they would have greater room for maneuver—which would, in turn, force the Turks to devote more attention and quite possibly more military forces to the region.

For the first time, Piazza spoke up. "What concerns me is our own resources. *Can* we do it? What I mean is—"

"Do we have the military forces we could free up?" the emperor finished for him. He hadn't taken his eyes off Mike, though. "What would you propose?"

Again, Mike's answer came immediately. "Send in the Hangman." His lips quirked. "Sorry, old habit. I mean the Silesian Guard."

"All of it?"

Mike nodded. "That will immediately add about three thousand troops to the ones the Bohemians already have. Not a lot, perhaps, but they've got a solid core of veterans and very high morale. And we should be able to feed in more forces as time goes by."

Rebecca was frowning. "Can we rely on just one newly trained brigade of Thorsten Engler's to defend Silesia?"

Gustav Adolf planted his hands on his thighs and leaned forward. That was a sign that he was getting enthusiastic. They were all familiar with his mannerisms, by now.

"Not a problem," he said. "First, there is little chance anyone will be threatening Lower Silesia in the near future. The Bohemians have ceded it to us and the Poles and Lithuanians have more than enough on their plates, between our forces besieging Poznań and the thrashing the Galicians just gave the Lithuanian magnates outside Krakow. So..."

He stroked his mustache again. "Just as I explained to Brigadier

Engler not so long ago. Silesia is a superb location in which to complete the training of the new divisions he has been building up. That will provide the province with more than enough military forces for their needs. By all accounts, the situation there has settled down nicely. I will readily state that whatever disputes I have with the young woman's reckless political views, she is a superb organizer."

His eyes widened. So did Mike's.

So did Rebecca's. "But, you can't—"

"Of course!" said the emperor. "We'll send in Richter as well."

Mike was nodding. "Not alone, of course. She'll need a staff; other organizers. A printing press, that goes without saying."

"You can't be serious!" protested Rebecca.

Piazza shook his head. "Sure they can, Rebecca. These two?"

Roth town house
Prague, capital of Bohemia

Once the small talk was over and the servants had all been dismissed, Francisco Nasi gave Morris Roth a quizzical look. At least, his gaze was quizzical. The twisted little smile below it... not so much.

"So why is a younger brother of the prince of Transylvania— what's that American expression?—'camping out' with you for so long? He's been here in Prague quite a while."

"He's not 'camping out' with us now." Judith had a startled expression on her face. "He's been moved to Wallenstein's castle."

Morris' expression was just exasperated. "I *knew* he was being careless. Hopefully, you're the only one who noticed."

"That's doubtful," said Francisco, blowing on his teacup to cool the liquid down. "If Rákóczi were Jewish and had restricted his outings to the Josefov... maybe. Even then, the odds would have been no better than even. Don't think for a moment that the Ottomans don't have Jewish spies."

He blew on the cup again. "But gallivanting the way he did all over Prague? I don't think there's much chance he wasn't spotted by an enemy agent. It's always a problem, conducting diplomatic relations when you don't have radio access to the other party—the one who can decide, I mean, which in this instance is Prince George Rákóczi. The envoy has to dawdle about for weeks—sometimes months—while a decision gets made. Naturally, they get bored, and unless they're very disciplined, they will get careless."

Now he took his first sip. "Still too hot," he pronounced, and set the cup down on the side table next to his chair. "On a more positive note, at least he kept his mouth shut—seems to have, anyway—on the subject of *why* he was here."

The cocked, quizzical look was back. "So. Are you going to tell me or not?"

It didn't take Morris more than five minutes to fill Nasi in on the situation. The Sephardic spymaster, once a courtier in the Sublime Porte, was so familiar with the politics of Europe and the Middle East that he could fill in most of the blanks himself.

Once Morris was finished, Francisco took a drink from his tea, which had cooled enough. As he set the cup back down, he said: "And you want me to do what for you, Morris? Please be specific. Precise would help, too."

Morris wasn't surprised by the bluntness. Nasi had moved to Prague more than a year earlier and he'd come to know him fairly well.

"Two things, mainly. I need the best intelligence I can get, and that generally means you."

"You already have Uriel," Nasi pointed out. "He's very good."

"Yes, he is—and he will continue to work for me. But he's gotten pretty old for fieldwork."

Nasi didn't argue the point. Morris thought he'd mostly raised it just to buy himself a little time to think.

"What else?"

"The use of your pilot and plane whenever possible."

Nasi took another sip of tea. He'd obviously expected that request as well. "And what else?"

Morris shrugged. "Hell, Francisco, you'd know the answer to that question better than I would. Whatever else might help the commander of an army about to blunder its way into a region of the continent he knows almost nothing about except that it's reputed to be full of vampires."

"That's incorrect, you know. Wallachia is where Vlad Tepes started those silly fables. The Transylvanians had little to do with it."

Morris spread his hands in a triumphant gesture. "You see how great my need is for good intelligence?"

Nasi smiled, drained the rest of his cup, and set it down. There was something decisive about the movement.

"All right, Morris. I'm a bit ashamed of myself, since to a degree I'm toying with you."

Both stared at him. Judith said, "Huh?"

"I wasn't sure exactly why Pál Rákóczi was here, but I could make an educated guess—and my guesses on subjects like this are *very* educated. Assuming I was right, I realized I'd finally have to make a decision regarding your so-called Anaconda Project."

It was Morris' turn to say "Huh?"

Francisco spread his hands. "I've been skeptical since the beginning that your scheme would do much good. The size of the populations involved—Jewish and Gentile both—and the intractability of the conflict seemed like insurmountable problems, at least in the time you had available. Which was no more than fifteen years when you started and is now down to a dozen."

He shrugged. "I thought the best you'd be able to do would be to provide a refuge for a portion of the Jews caught up in the coming pogrom—and a small portion at that."

"But you've changed your mind?" asked Judith.

"Not...exactly. I still think it's a daunting challenge. But I no longer think it's insurmountable. Especially—and this brings us back to the matter at hand—if you can find an anchor in Transylvania."

He leaned back in his chair. "It's an unusual place, in so many ways. Between the ethnic and religious mix, you have everything in Transylvania. Mostly Hungarians and Germans—whom they call 'Saxons' there. And the offshoot of Hungarians known as Székelys. When it comes to religion, you have Christians of every stripe, Jews, even a Christian sect that's becoming Jewish."

Morris frowned. "Who is that?"

"You never heard of the Sabbatarians? They began as a radical Unitarian group of Hungarian extraction, but as time went on they came to believe that the logic of Unitarianism was that the Jews had been right all along." He chuckled. "Mind you, there aren't too many rabbis outside of their own ranks who agree with them—or welcome their evolution, for that matter."

Judith shook her head. "I—we"—she glanced at her husband—"never heard of them."

"That's hardly surprising. Why would anyone in a small mining town in what used to be your West Virginia have heard of a small—there aren't more than twenty thousand of them—and rather peculiar sect of Jews in Transylvania who were wiped out centuries earlier?"

"What do you mean, 'wiped out'?" demanded Morris.

"The Transylvanian Diet gave the Sabbatarians an ultimatum. As of the end of 1635, they had to join one of the four accepted Christian denominations—those are Catholicism, Calvinism, Lutheranism, and Unitarianism—or be persecuted. Most of them refused, naturally, and the persecution has already begun in this timeline. So far, it has not been too severe, though."

Morris' face grew hard. "And as soon as the Grand Army of the Sunrise shows up, it'll stop altogether."

Nasi nodded. "Yes, I imagine so. I imagine Prince Rákóczi understands that himself—and is quite willing to forego the persecution. The point I'm making is that if you can link Bohemia with Transylvania, you will have taken some great strides toward creating a political situation—call it a political reality, rather—that will make pogroms such as Chmielnicki's impossible. Or at least squelchable, if they do get started."

His own expression grew hard. "Having thousands—eventually tens of thousands, I think—of well-armed Jews with military experience living in the region will make even Cossacks think twice. And you are the one creating that new reality."

He planted his hands on the armrests. "So here is what I will do. Yes, I will provide you with as much intelligence as I can—which will be quite a bit, because I can get Denise and probably Minnie to travel with your forces."

Judith didn't look entirely thrilled with that news. "Uh... Francisco... Denise Beasley... well, what I mean is..."

Nasi laughed outright. "The rambunctious girl you remember has changed a lot, Judith. Grown a lot, anyway. She's still pretty rambunctious. For her part, Minnie is as shrewd as anyone comes and an extraordinarily good student. Which, I'll admit, is not Denise's strongest suit."

Judith muttered something that sounded like *to put it mildly,* but Morris shook his head. "Honey, leave off. I was at Krakow; you weren't. I don't have any problem with Denise—especially if Minnie's with her."

He cocked his head. "But will she be? The last I heard she was pregnant with Archduke Leopold's kid and was planning to settle down with him. At least by seventeenth-century royal mistress values of 'settle down.'"

Nasi laughed again. "She's not that far into her pregnancy. More to the point, she's getting bored. Life as the paramour of an Austrian archduke isn't as glamorous as it sounds. Yes, I'm sure she'll agree. Provisions will have to be made, of course. But—"

He shrugged. "Whatever its faults in other ways, the seventeenth century is quite good at making provisions for the delivery and care of royal bastards."

Judith muttered something else. It might have been *talk about damning with faint praise.*

But Morris didn't really hear. He was thinking ahead. "If Denise and Minnie come..."

Nasi nodded. "Yes. That means you just also got what amounts to your own little air force. Not so little anymore—we'll have a Jupiter, a Dauntless, and two Dvoraks, with no doubt more to come later." He smiled. "I'm even thinking of calling them Nasi's Tigers."

Morris chuckled. "After Chenault in World War II, eh?"

Francisco shrugged. "Eddie would quit if I didn't let him join them with his plane. *My* plane, technically. But he'll be spending most of his time learning to fly the new Jupiter. The USE air force agreed to train a couple of other pilots for us, who can fly the Dauntless and flesh out the Jupiter's crew."

"Don't you need it yourself?"

"Eddie or Tuva can handle my occasional needs. Which are very occasional these days, on account of the demands"—he gave Judith a glance that could be translated as *what is it with women and weddings, anyway?*—"of my marital negotiations."

Judith smiled. "How is that coming, by the way?"

"Slowly and sometimes painfully. Marrying into the inner circles of the largest Jewish community in the world is easier said than done, even if you come with my resources and connections."

Her smile was now bordering on a grin. "Especially a Jewish community that is so orthodox they haven't even invented the term 'Orthodox' yet. And they're Ashkenazim, to boot, where you're not only Sephardic but Ottoman. In your origins, anyway."

"Very recent origins—so recent that most of my family still

lives in Istanbul. It would be a lot easier if I was trying to marry a girl raised in the Reform tradition, but so far the only Jews in the world who fit that description are the two of you."

"And Jason Gotkin," Morris said, sounding defensive.

Judith looked dubious. "I think the best you can say about Jason's convictions these days is that they might fit within Conservative Judaism. Except that doesn't exist today either."

Francisco shook his head again. "We're drifting from the subject I want to raise next."

"Which is?"

"My need for the occasional use of a plane is about to get easier to fill anyway." He sat up straight and smiled. "As you must have heard by now, Bohemia has developed its own aircraft industry."

"Is it really that far along?" asked Morris. "I got the impression they were still at the prototype stage."

"A foul calumny. They have just completed the first functional aircraft. Three of them, in fact." His smile widened. "And we've already sold them!"

"To who?"

"Well, one of them to me, of course. At a cut-rate price, I might add."

Morris gave him a suspicious look. "Aren't you a part owner of that company?"

"I own a few shares of stock, yes. But the company could well afford to give me a discount since we just sold the other two planes to the richest Jew in Prague."

Morris' eyes widened. Judith laughed. "And now you've got your own air force, husband!"

Chapter 6

Roth town house
Prague, capital of Bohemia

Morris led Pál Rákóczi into his study. This time, the large table
in the center of the room would prove quite useful.

"Have you made a decision?" Pál asked, crossing the room
and taking his usual chair.

Morris did not bother sitting. He could see stress and impatience on Pál's face. It had been nearly three weeks since the man
had arrived. *He's wondering if I've decided, or if this is going to
be another one of our pleasant "chats."*

Morris did not waste any further time. "Yes, I have," he said,
setting a manila folder, with two copies of the agreement inside,
on the table. "After much consultation and consideration, I and
Gottfried Heinrich Pappenheim agree to a Bohemian alliance with
Transylvania." He opened the folder, took out the documents, and
pushed them across the table for Pál to review. "All agreed-upon
conditions are defined in this document. General Pappenheim
has already signed it. It now only requires our signatures to be
official, and we consider your signature to be a procuration for
your brother, George I Rákóczi, the Prince of Transylvania. If
you sign it, it is as if the prince himself is signing it, and you
will complete your signature with two small p's to denote *per
procurationem*. Do you understand?"

Pál nodded. He stood slowly, leaned over the table, and reached for the agreement. He pulled it closer and read it thoroughly, and twice. Morris found it amusing that the man's lips moved when he read.

Pál held out his hand. "If I may have a quill, please, sir."

Morris reached into his breast pocket and pulled out two ballpoint pens. He handed one to Pál. The man accepted it, but looked at it as if it were a poisonous snake. Morris chuckled and shrugged. "It's an up-time quill. Sign with the pointy end. It'll work."

Pál did so, showing surprise at how smooth and effortless it was to use. "It does not require an inkwell. What a relief."

Morris nodded. "It carries one on its back."

Pál signed both copies with the required "pp" at the end of his signature. Morris did the same. "We are official, Pál Rákóczi. Please present your copy to your brother upon your return to Transylvania." Morris tucked his copy back into the manila folder. "Now, let's get down to business."

Morris cleared the table and then produced a large map that had been given to him by Francisco Nasi. He rolled it out onto the table and weighed down the curled ends with the lanterns.

"Impressive map," Pál said. "Very precise."

Morris said nothing. He was not about to reveal any of his intelligence contacts to this man. Yes, they had just signed an alliance between Bohemia and Transylvania, but there was no need to show his entire hand. Not yet, anyway.

"The Grand Army of the Sunrise is here," Morris said, pointing to a sketched image of a sun, "at Kazimierz, south of Krakow." He moved his hand down the map to Transylvania. "These are your cities of Kolozsvár and Gyulafehérvár, the up-time Romanian cities of Cluj and Alba Iulia, respectively. It's a distance of over five hundred miles, assuming we take the route I consider the most viable in order to keep from running afoul of Ottomans.

"But, we're not going to do that. We're not going to take such a long, arduous trek and have our supply lines strung out over, potentially, hundreds of miles. As I reminded someone recently, sir, success breeds success. The Sunrise is in the middle of an expansion, a refit, and a restructuring."

"How many men can we expect?" Pál asked.

Morris shook his head. "I cannot give you those numbers today. I'll be leaving for Krakow soon. I'll have a better sense of it once I'm there. But I suspect we'll be able to field eight, maybe ten thousand, by the end of June."

Maybe more, maybe less. "But I'm sure you know all too well that a green army is not an army for long. Before we enter Transylvania per our agreement, they require time and training."

Pál stood and looked Morris straight in the eye. "Then what do you propose, Herr Roth?"

Morris took a step to the left, took a pen out of his pocket, and circled a city which lay near the border of Austria-Hungary.

"Kassa?"

Up-time, it was known as the Slovakian city of Košice, but like most cities and provinces in this part of seventeenth-century Europe, Kassa had been controlled by many political factions in the decades leading up to the Ring of Fire.

One of its most recent owners—and the one that interested Morris the most—was the Principality of Transylvania itself. Prince Gabriel Bethlen, with the military assistance of Pál's brother George, had seized the city in an anti-Habsburg insurrection in 1619. Bethlen held the city until his death in 1629, when it was then returned to Habsburg control.

Then the Ring of Fire occurred, and who owned the city now? That was even unclear to Francisco Nasi. Certainly, there was some municipal authority that held the city together and maintained the peace, but otherwise, it was ripe for the picking, and a perfect stepping-off point for the Sunrise, and for future Bohemian and USE military operations.

"Yes, Kassa," Morris said. "Your family is well aware of its strategic significance. Located roughly halfway between Krakow and Kolozsvár. Moving there first will allow the Sunrise to continue its refit and training before heading into Transylvania. And, it will be a useful place for the USE and its continued campaign against the Ottomans...if such a need ever arises."

Pál piqued his interest immediately. "So, the United States of Europe *will* be involved in this endeavor?"

Morris smiled, stepped back from the map, and said, "Yes... with just a bit of a fig leaf. The units they will be sending are from the Silesian Guard, not the USE army proper."

Pál shook his head and flashed confusion. "I wasn't aware that the Silesians were capable of fielding a force of their own. How many men? Who will be in command?"

"Colonel—now Brigadier—Jeff Higgins, the former commander of the Hangman Regiment of the USE's Third Division. You have perhaps heard of him?"

Mutely, Rákóczi nodded.

"The core of the Silesian Guard is the former Hangman Regiment. So, it's quite a formidable force, built around veterans."

Pál rubbed his beard and nodded again. "That would certainly be true. That regiment has a ferocious reputation." He leaned over the map, placed his finger on Kassa, and drew an imaginary line into Transylvania all the way to their capital of Gyulafehérvár. "This would be the route that I would suggest, Herr Roth. It will keep you free from Ottoman entanglements."

Morris nodded. "Your thinking is consistent with mine own, but I will not commit yet to an entry point. I must confer with my lieutenants first before a final decision is made on the route." He smiled. "I'm a supply guy, Herr Rákóczi, not a field commander."

"You have taken on quite a responsibility, then, putting yourself in charge of an entire army."

How true that was, Morris admitted to himself. This foray into Transylvania could go south quickly in so many different ways. On paper, it made perfect sense: provide military support for Transylvania's alliance with Bohemia and its declaration of independence, in exchange for northern territory such that Bohemia could continue its expansion into Ruthenian lands. The military support that the Grand Army of the Sunrise would provide should be relatively easy as these things went. Fighting against the vassal armies of Moldavia and Wallachia using up-time-inspired weaponry should not present much of a challenge; assuming, of course, that Sultan Murad did not turn his attention toward his vassals and engage in force himself. That, unfortunately, was entirely possible. But Francisco Nasi, Rebecca and Uriel Abrabanel, and others would begin their misinformation campaign soon. With any luck, the Sunrise's move into Kassa would be seen as a move to bolster USE forces against Murad's main column, or not seen at all.

With any luck . . .

Morris tapped a finger on Transylvania. "It is my understanding that over the years, as a vassal for the Turks, the military readiness of your country has been weakened. Murad has drawn men from your cities and towns as replacements for his own losses. How many soldiers can you put into the field, Herr Rákóczi?"

Pál considered, by again running his fingers through his beard and sighing like a bear. "As many as you can field, I suspect."

Morris was surprised. "That many, eh?"

Pál smiled politely. "Herr Roth, when my countrymen learn of this agreement, they will understand the risk, and they will *volunteer* to defend their homes. The Székely, the Hajdu, even our Saxon populations, will fight like mad dogs to protect their families, their farms. We cannot hope to raise enough to stand against a combined force from Moldavia and Wallachia, however. That is why we are asking for your support.

"But we will be there, in the field, in numbers to help defend our country. That, I can promise."

The meeting was over. There was nothing more to speak about right now. Everything else about this operation was still unclear, unsettled.

"My only concern, Herr Roth, with this entire endeavor," Pál said as they walked out of the room and toward the foyer, "is how Sultan Murad will respond."

Morris nodded but kept moving. His heart leapt into his throat. "Yes, Herr Rákóczi. That is everyone's concern."

Part Two

May 1637

Our great grim man of power
—Sophocles, *Ajax*

Chapter 7

Temporary headquarters
Lady Protector of Silesia
Krakow, Poland

"For Chrissake," grumbled Jeff Higgins. "Can't these people make up their minds about *anything*?"

He glared at the door of their small apartment—a converted workshop, actually—in the Cloth Hall that served simultaneously as the temporary headquarters of the Silesian Guard as well as the Lady Protector of Silesia. Aside from a desk overloaded with papers and documents, most of the workspace of the headquarters consisted of the bed they shared. During Rebecca Abrabanel's visit, she'd sat in the one chair in the room while Jeff and Gretchen had perched on the side of the bed.

As Jeff had put it when they moved in, theirs was a jury-rigged arrangement—with a hung jury. Once he explained the American idiom, Gretchen had been amused.

Mildly amused, anyway. Gretchen had a view of the world that was more philosophical than her husband's. Stoicism squared, you might call it.

She studied her husband, for a moment. He didn't notice, because he was still glaring at the door through which Rebecca had left just a short while ago. For all the love she had for Jeff, she'd understood for years that in some ways they were very different.

She was a revolutionary, and Jeff wasn't. He shared most of her beliefs and political goals, certainly, and he was always supportive of her. But when all was said and done, he simply didn't have the fire in his belly that she did.

Gretchen didn't fault him for it. They came from two worlds quite foreign to each other. His had been a world which, for all its many faults, had been fundamentally a decent one. Hers had been savage; both brutal and profoundly unjust.

She hated that world. She would hate it until the day she died—and while she was alive, would do everything in her power to destroy it. Burn it to bedrock and pour salt over what was left. *Early modern era delenda est.*

So, when Rebecca proposed to them that they participate in overturning yet another portion of that despised world, Gretchen had been all for it. Immediately and unreservedly. Whereas Jeff had seen the proposal largely as a nuisance. *Dammit, he already had a job to do!*

He left off glaring at the door and looked at her. It didn't take him more than a moment to understand what she was thinking. Whatever separated them, they were extremely close.

"Fine," he grumbled. "We'll do it. Tata will be in charge of Lower Silesia while we're gone, and Thorsten Engler will take charge of its defense. And I'll organize the troop movements we need. But as Napoleon said—or maybe Frederick the Great—an army marches on its stomach. Stomachs need to be filled, which means food either gets bought or stolen. And given that the Hangman tradition is at the heart of the Silesian Guard, we're not going to be stealing. So, who's going to finance all this? The last I looked—well, you and Tata looked—the coffers of the government of Lower Silesia would be ridiculed by homeless beggars."

Gretchen grinned. "You don't need to worry your little head about that." She reached out and patted her husband on the head. Jeff scowled.

Now, she shrugged. "I'll see to it, one way or the other. I'll start by flying back to Breslau and giving Tata the news. While I'm at it, I'll count the coins in the province's treasure. That won't take any time at all. Then..."

She pursed her lips, thinking. "I'll start with Ed Piazza in Magdeburg, I think. He'll be easier to squeeze money out of than

Gustav Adolf—unless the emperor takes it up as one of his hobby horses. Which...he might."

"What about the kids?"

She shrugged. "We'll figure something out. There's always a way to have children taken care of."

Different worlds. In the one Jeff had come from, Dr. Spock had been a big deal. In this one, he was more alien than a Vulcan.

Encampment at Kazimierz
Grand Army of the Sunrise
South of Krakow

Isaac had established Christian's physical therapy through tedious work, a daily routine of supply management and exhaustive labor. "Bend at the hips, lift with your legs," Isaac would say over and over as crates of newly acquired medical supplies needed to be off-loaded from wagons and piled near the hospital tent for inspection and ultimate use. And then, the unused portions would be repacked and placed on wagons in preparation for the inevitable march to...where? That, unfortunately, was still unknown.

Fortunate and unfortunate, as it turned out. Unfortunate because the army, the men, were getting restless, even the new recruits being put through daily drills. Fortunate, because Colonel Renz had accepted Isaac's plea on Christian's behalf and had simply assigned Christian to his company as captain with no threat of dismissal. Unfortunate, because Christian had yet to meet his men—many of whom were new—to get to know them. Doctor Isaac Kohen had not released Christian from his service, and as the days wore on, it seemed as if he never would.

"Must you constantly put me through these stretching exercises, Isaac?" Christian asked as they and other patients worked near a copse of trees that had been designated as the physical therapy center for the army. "It was my eye, face, and shoulder that were wounded. Not my legs."

Isaac lifted Christian's right leg into a bend and pressed it against the soldier's abdomen. "Your entire body experienced a trauma, Christian. Your muscles are stiff everywhere."

"People are beginning to talk," Christian said, looking left and right and lowering his voice. "All this so-called therapy that you and the nurses are conducting. I've heard rumblings among the men. They think it's...odd."

Isaac chuckled and lowered Christian's leg. He took the left leg and performed the same stretch. "There's a lot of up-time medical practices that we down-timers find odd, even offensive. I care not. Let them talk. In the end, when those that have gone through my therapy sessions are back in the field facing the enemy, they will thank me and my cadre of *odd* nurses for our dedication to their physical well-being. Including you."

"And when *will* I be put back in the field?"

Isaac paused, looked at Christian, and smiled. "When you're ready."

Christian didn't bother pursuing the matter. He'd asked the question before and had gotten pretty much the same response each time.

"Now," Isaac said, standing and stepping back a pace, "rise, remove your eye patch, and let's check your reflexes and visual acuity."

Christian rose, removed his eye patch, and took his normal position ten feet from Isaac. The doctor pulled a palm-sized rubber ball from his white coat, squeezed it, and tossed it underhand to Christian, who caught it perfectly.

Isaac stepped back five feet and tried again. Another five and again, until he was thirty feet away. He then began to toss overhand to the left, then right, left then right, forcing Christian to move quickly to seize the ball before it flew by. Over and over until Christian was panting. He caught nearly every throw to his left, but only about two-thirds to his right.

Isaac placed the ball back in his coat pocket and nodded. "Better than last time. Your energy is up. Your flexibility is good. Your visual acuity is excellent on your left side. Your right? Well, you still have some depth perception problems. You caught about seventy percent of my tosses."

"If you tossed the ball better," Christian said, gulping air to catch his breath, "I'd catch more."

Isaac smiled. "I'm a doctor, not a baseball pitcher."

"Baseball?"

"Yes, an up-time sport. You've never heard of it?"

Christian shook his head.

"I attended a few games during my residency in Magdeburg.

It's fun and sometimes quite exciting. Someday, perhaps I'll recommend to General Roth that he implement an inter-army league. It would certainly give the men something to do in their free time." He stepped up to Isaac. "Now, I want to check each eye to see how far you can see without blur. Just like before. And I want you to be honest, Christian. I can't help you if you bend the truth."

Bend the truth? The nerve of this guy! Christian was about to argue the point. Instead, he sighed and nodded. "Let's get on with it."

"Let me check your left eye first," Isaac said. "Cover your right."

Christian placed his hand over his right eye, making sure he did not press down too strongly. The swelling had gone down considerably. Isaac's delicate stitching of the eyelid had proved successful, and the eye was in fine shape overall. But the right side of his face was still tender and all purple and black as if a big, beefy Lithuanian had worked over his face with a club.

Isaac stepped back five feet. He raised his arm. "How many fingers am I holding up?"

"Three."

"Good. Now, I will continue to back up. When I reach a place where my fingers become blurry, you tell me, all right?"

Christian nodded again.

Isaac slowly backed away. Ten feet. Twenty. Thirty. He was out one hundred feet before he stopped. It was a good distance, and obviously, Christian could not see the fingers as easily as he had done ten feet away, but no blur.

There was no need for Isaac to back up any farther. The left eye was fine.

"Now the right!"

Isaac began one hundred feet away and slowly walked closer. Blur, blur, blur...*My God, when will it stop being this way?* Christian could see Isaac's body shape and even see the shape of his arm, his fingers. But there was no definition, no clarity. Just a fuzzy blob, that... "Yes! Now, I see you clearly."

Isaac lowered his arm, smiled. "Good. That's five feet farther than two days ago. Ten feet more than last week. You're improving." Isaac motioned to the wounded eye. "Let's have a look."

Christian moved his eyeball left, right, up, and down while Isaac leaned in with his small magnifying glass. "I sincerely wish that we had a fully qualified ophthalmologist on staff, but we don't. I've done my best over the past few years to understand the human eye and all its many facets, but a certified professional, dedicated exclusively to the eye, would be ideal.

"The good news is, the eye can also heal faster than almost any other organ in the body. You're on the mend, Christian von Jori. You're on the mend."

"Will I ever see as well out of the right as I do the left?" Christian asked. "Or is this permanent?"

Isaac sighed, shook his head. "I don't have an answer for you on that. We'll just have to wait and see."

He was tired of waiting. Waiting for his body, his eye, to heal. Waiting for the opportunity to return to his regiment and take command of his company. Waiting for the generals of the army to decide when and if they would march again. And where? He was, in truth, a mercenary cavalryman, having served under General von Mercy for going on almost two years now, even before the creation of this Grand Army of the Sunrise. A mercenary lives and dies by his pay, Christian knew, and there were always armies elsewhere willing to pay more. A small stipend was being given out to all soldiers in General Roth's army to keep them loyal and in place, but how long would that last? Colonel Renz had awarded him the position of captain, but if his men began drifting away due to "waiting" and short pay, there would be no company to return to.

Christian put his eye patch back on, put his boots back on, and collected his coat. "What's for dinner tonight?"

Isaac snapped his fingers. "I forgot to tell you. I'm having dinner with Rabbi Gotkin, along with a half dozen or so prospective nurses and orderlies. You're welcome to join us."

Christian shook his head. "No, thank you, Isaac. If I have to endure another one of Gotkin's kosher meals, I'll—"

A persistent high-pitch whirl of propellers caught their attention. Christian shielded his left eye from the sun and looked up.

The plane was a dot on the horizon growing larger and larger until the sound of its engine was nearly deafening. Christian ducked as it flew past overhead, then felt foolish because it was not that close to the ground. He'd seen up-time aircraft before, on more than one occasion, but the sight of them always made the hair on his arms prickle.

"Marvelous," he said, his eyes wide as lamplight.

Isaac nodded and smiled. "Yes, in more ways than one. General Morris Roth has returned."

Chapter 8

Grand Army of the Sunrise Encampment
Kazimierz
South of Krakow

Morris could barely hear Denise Beasley over the roar of wind in his ears as they descended. "You need a better landing strip, Morris!" she said from the seat in front of him, speaking loudly over her shoulder. "This one sucks! Get your men to build a better one!"

He nodded, though she couldn't see the gesture from her vantage point. "Don't worry," he tried to say, white-knuckle-clutching the side of the cockpit. His voice sounded like it was blowing through a fan—which, with the pusher propeller behind him, it effectively was. "Wee...won't...be here...fooor long."

Unfortunately. He was finding this flight just short of terrifying and wasn't eager to do a return flight any time soon.

Part of the problem was his pilot. Morris had known that Francisco Nasi's regular pilot, Eddie Junker, had been training his girlfriend Denise to fly. But he hadn't realized until this morning that the training had proceeded far enough that *she* would be flying him to Krakow.

Morris had great confidence in Denise's coordination, athleticism, eyesight—if it was physical, the girl was in great condition. Mentally... Well, she was very smart. And very bold. And he couldn't help but think of the well-known quip: *There are old pilots, and there are bold pilots, but there are no old bold pilots.*

Mostly, though, his anxiety wasn't caused by the pilot but by the aircraft he was in. This was the very first of the new Dvorak planes, created by the almost-as-new Zizka Aeronautics Company. It was described as a "light aircraft" and was promoted as a plane that was "superb for reconnaissance."

Put the two descriptions together...

Light plane superb for reconnaissance was a salesman's way of saying *cockleshell way up in the air.* And just in case he hadn't figured that out on his own, Denise had enthusiastically filled him in on all the specific details.

The dry weight—some might have called it curb weight—of the aircraft was only five hundred pounds. It was a high-wing, tandem two-seater with a pusher propeller driven by a fifty-five horsepower, two-stroke two-cylinder engine.

Cruising speed, fifty to seventy-five miles per hour; maximum speed, ninety-five mph; stall speed, twenty-eight mph. The stall speed was twice as fast as he wished she were flying. He figured he could probably survive a crash going fifteen miles per hour or less.

And two five-gallon gas tanks, one on each side.

Ten measly, pitiful gallons. God help them if Denise got lost at any point. Fog of doom, coming up.

Last but not least, the girl had named her plane *Dixie Chick*, after the very popular country music band the Dixie Chicks. Morris was okay with that, except that Denise was currently singing their song "Wide Open Spaces."

Loudly. He could hear every word.

"She needs wide open spaces—"

The crappy little landing strip—she was right about that; it did suck—was approaching at what seemed NASCAR race speed.

"To make her big mistakes—"

The plane touched down and taxied to a bumpy halt. *Thank you, God!* Morris was never so happy in his life. They had survived, he was finally back in Poland, and the sun was shining.

General Franz von Mercy and his security retinue were waiting for him.

Morris stepped down from the plane. He thought about kneeling and kissing the ground like he had seen Vietnam veterans do on their return home. It was tempting, but he refrained and instead accepted a hug from Denise.

"You going to be okay, General?" Denise asked.

Morris nodded and pulled away. "Yes, I will, now that I'm on solid ground. And call me Morris, please."

Denise nodded and put her fancy leather flight helmet back on. "Anything you say...General." She winked and then added, "And don't worry about your air force. It'll be waiting when you need it again."

O frabjous day!

But he didn't say it out loud. That would have just been mean. Denise was at that age when her cocky self-confidence was only matched by easily bruised feelings.

General Mercy saluted. "Welcome back, General Roth."

Morris returned the salute. "Glad to be back, General von Mercy." He accepted the reins of a horse, and with some assistance, climbed into the saddle. He was no expert horseman, for sure, but anything was better than a screaming death trap with wings. "I trust things are in proper order here?"

"Yes, sir," von Mercy said, pulling on his reins and leading them off the crude airstrip and back toward Kazimierz. "There is much to discuss."

Morris nodded. "Yes, there is."

They crossed the Vistula into Kazimierz. The narrow streets were lined with young Ashkenazi men shouting, clapping, and giving their full-throated thanks. *Don't praise me*, Morris thought as he acknowledged their appreciation with salutes, smiles, and short, efficient tips of the hat. *Praise your field general.* But von Mercy was not a Jew, and these men were not so much cheering for Morris, he knew, as for what he represented: one of their own, at the head of a real, honest-to-God, ass-kicking army, leading them to a better life, a better future.

I sure hope so...

Von Mercy had selected a modest home for the Sunrise's HQ. The home lay just inside the wall surrounding the Jewish quarter, a separate section of Kazimierz known as the Oppidum Judaeorum. Morris was pleased with the selection. Modest, yes, but with a large enough dining room to serve as a comfortable place to conduct their war councils. Morris figured at least a dozen, and possibly as many as fifteen, officers could be in attendance at once.

"You travel light, General," von Mercy said, setting his hat, sword, and belt on the table.

"My personal provisions and military accoutrements will be arriving with Ellie Anderson and Len Tanner," Morris said, laying his own hat aside and taking the big chair at the head of the table. "They managed to acquire a couple of wagonloads of radios and much needed communication equipment. They're moving with a wagon train of men and materiel that left Prague several days ago. Should be arriving any day now."

"Then you've made a decision on where we are headed."

Morris nodded and patted the sweat away from his brow. He was still suffering a bit of light-headedness and air sickness from the turbulent flight. "Yes, and we will speak about that in good time. But now, I need a full briefing." He cleared his throat. "What is the state of the Sunrise?"

Von Mercy collected papers from a pile at the end of the table and took a moment to get them organized. He handed batches, one by one, to Morris. "These are preliminary muster rolls for each regiment, sir. Each regiment down to each man by company."

Morris nodded and sifted through the pages, one after another of names, dates, unit assignments, etc. *Impressive.* "We've gone through quite an expansion, haven't we?"

Von Mercy nodded. "We've nearly doubled our numbers since reaching Krakow. Many Jews, of course, from the Oppidum and towns and villages in the region. We've also gathered additional mercenaries, both foot and horse. Mostly horse. Even more Brethren. By end of June, we may be near ten thousand men... give or take a thousand."

"That would be a good number to achieve."

"Yes, sir. But with your permission, I'd like to cap that number. Make it official so that the stream of new recruits slows down."

Morris finished accepting the last batch of musters, thumbed through them quickly, and set them aside. He leaned back and motioned to a chair behind von Mercy. "Please, General. Have a seat."

Von Mercy sat. Morris continued. "What's troubling you about the numbers, General? Is it their pay? Supply?"

"I'm troubled by a number of things," von Mercy said, letting his breath out slowly, as if to collect his thoughts and his tongue before speaking out of turn. Morris could see the man figuring out what to say first. "Pay, indeed. Mercenaries shed blood for a commander only if their pay is equal to their sacrifice. I'm very pleased with our cavalry corps, sir. We have some of the finest cavalry soldiers and officers available. Their pay will have to increase, sir, and soon, if we wish to keep them under our command. There are many other armies in the field today—the USE, Pappenheim's, the Ottomans, to name a few—and men who fight by the coin will drift away if they aren't paid adequately—and perhaps just as importantly, in a timely manner. Some will turn their swords and pistols against you if they find another employer."

"I understand that well, General," Morris said. "Pay will increase soon, now that I have returned, and a decision has been made as to our next move."

"Where are we going, sir?"

Morris shook his head. "Let us delay that discussion. Proceed with your concerns."

Von Mercy moved as if he were going to protest such a delay. The muscles in his jaw worked rapidly. "I—my next concern is, indeed, supply. So far, we have been fortunate. As you ordered prior to your return to Prague, new weapons and ammunition have been arriving. Many of the men, especially the cavalry and Brethren, have their own firearms. Not as efficient as our up-time ZB-1636 rifles or ZB-2 Santee pistols, but assuming we will be marshaling against forces that do not possess similar weaponry, we should be in fine shape when, and if, we do engage.

"Our stores of medical supplies are increasing at pace. The citizenry of the Oppidum have been most generous in offering whatever they can along those lines, and young Doctor Kohen, who is in charge of that endeavor, per your orders, has been mustering as much supply as he can by soliciting the aid of some officers during their convalescence." Von Mercy huffed. "He's denuded the tails and manes of many of our horses to make suture material."

Morris smiled, nodded. "Remind me later to speak with him. To both of you, in fact. I have some adjustments I'd like to make to our medical team. Continue, please."

"My biggest concern about supply, sir, is food. We have been collecting as much nonperishable foodstuffs as we can, but as you have told me a number of times, 'Battles are fought once in a while, but an army must eat every day.' I know you do not like the idea of excessive foraging on the march. You do not wish to deprive the citizenry of its ability to simply survive, to feed itself, its families. Doing so leaves a disgruntled countryside in our wake, which may be a serious detriment to us further down the road. I understand that.

"The Brethren have volunteered drovers to handle a small herd of cattle, but that will not be enough. We *must* forage as we march, or that concern I have about mercenaries leaving in droves—excuse the pun—will consume the entire army."

Morris sighed, loudly. "I understand that, General. I don't like it, but I understand it. We need to be as respectful as possible as we move. I can't claim to be the head of an army whose chief purpose is liberation and then have that army abuse the citizenry. We need to make sure that we take great care in treating the people along our march with respect and kindness. We pay for what we can, and we take what we need as kindly as possible."

What does that mean, actually? Morris heard himself saying those last few words, and didn't really understand them himself. How *does* one *take* something kindly from someone? He didn't know the answer to that, but perhaps they'd discover ways to do so on their march to Kassa.

"Finally, my biggest concern..." Von Mercy took a deep breath, clasped his hands together before him, paused, then said, "...is the state of the army itself. Our new recruits are the most unprepared men I've ever seen. The mercenaries and the men who fought with us against the magnates, they are skilled and ready to go. The rest, all the Ashkenazim, who have volunteered in the past month...well, I've never seen any group of people so ill-prepared for war. I mean no disrespect, sir, but they are not ready to fight."

Morris put up his hands as if to protest, and snapped, "What do you expect, General? These are people who have never had the opportunity to own firearms themselves, at least in no great numbers. Have never had the chance to defend themselves against men *with* said firearms. They've spent their whole lives looking down barrels, not pointing them at anyone. Most of them have probably never even touched a musket. What do you expect?"

An awkward pause filled the room. Morris was immediately sorry for his outburst. He chalked it up to fatigue, exhaustion, and a headache that was slowly building behind his forehead. He closed his eyes, took a moment, and then put up his hands in surrender. "Peace, General. Peace. I understand your concern. We'll discuss readiness later. Let's move forward. Tell me your TOO/OOB."

"My what, General?"

Morris almost laughed, remembering where he was. *Go light on the up-time lingo, Morris.* "The organizational structure of the Sunrise. I can infer it through your muster sheets, but from top to bottom, what's our new chain of command?"

A light went off in von Mercy's brain. He stood and gathered up additional pages. He motioned Morris forward. "If you please, General."

Morris went to his side. Von Mercy then proceeded to lay out the pages on the table like a puzzle, with a page dedicated at the top of the pattern with the names of all the generals and regimental commanders. He then placed additional pages below them like cue cards that one might use to fit together the pieces of a crime scene or errant branches of a family tree. It was all very efficient, very orderly.

Morris leaned over the display and focused on the names of his top commanders. He pointed to von Mercy's name. "I see question marks alongside officer positions unfilled. But why is there a question mark next to your name, General?"

Von Mercy cleared his throat. "Well, General Morris, I thought that perhaps you'd like to discuss the possibility of, and perhaps the necessity of—"

Morris put up his hand. "I know where this is leading, sir. You are wondering if it'd be prudent to assign field command to an Ashkenazi, given the fact that nearly half, if not over half, of the army, when it's all said and done, will be Jewish. My answer to that question is no, sir, a resounding, unequivocal *fucking* no. If you're looking for the top Jew in this army, that's me. But I'm a jeweler, a contractor, a supply guy. I am no tactician, no skilled field commander. You're the field general of the Grand Army of the Sunrise. Put any concerns about that out of your mind. That's an order."

Von Mercy nodded. "Very well, sir."

Morris leaned over the display again. He worked carefully through each page, taking mental notes of various details. "Interesting," he said. "I see that the Ashkenazi have decided to collectively call themselves the Joshua Corps."

"Yes, sir."

"Good choice. I like it. And they have no problems with my directive that their companies be differentiated by letter designation?"

"No, sir. Unlike our mercenaries, they have no particular affiliation with one officer or another. They really don't seem to care what company they belong to, so long as they are a part of the experience."

Morris nodded. "And I assume our mercenaries refused the same directive."

Von Mercy gave a regretful sigh. "I'm afraid so, sir. Most mercenary units are mustered, and function, on the company level, and their unit name is most often the name of their captain, although it can vary from time to time. I think we're just going to have to deal with a designation split to keep the peace among our mercenaries. We can't afford to lose the cavalry."

Morris pointed again to the top page. "I see that you have assigned a major general as provost marshal of the army. Very good. Is security a big concern right now?"

"It's becoming one. Restless men, low pay. Fights have broken out. A Brethren was shot and killed the other day in a dispute over a goat. Each regiment will have its own provost marshal and a small cadre of—what did you call them—military police? They will all answer to Major General Luther Lange. He's a good officer. Stern, but fair. He'll take care of it."

Morris was about to ask if there had been any expressions of anti-Semitism among the rank and file, but decided against it. Not now, at least. Tomorrow, he'd meet with this General Lange and discuss all of that in full. For now, it was time to move on to the question that von Mercy desperately wanted answered.

Morris returned to his chair. "I'm impressed with your care and attention to detail. You've done great work to expand this army in my absence. I'm truly grateful that you're on our side."

Von Mercy nodded. "Thank you, sir."

Without question, Franz von Mercy was one of the best field commanders in service today. His best qualities revolved around his skill as a cavalry officer, but there was no army in the world who would pass up making him their own. Even Mike Stearns would snatch him away in a heartbeat.

"Now," Morris said, feeling the pangs of hunger. "Given everything that you have told me, taking into consideration all of your concerns, give me a frank assessment as to how long it will take to put this army into the field as a viable fighting force. In your honest opinion, General von Mercy, how long will it take to whip this ragtag army of Jews and Gentiles into a reasonably effective army?"

Von Mercy considered. He leaned forward in his chair, placed his elbows on the table, chewed on the bottom of his lip. His jaw muscles worked overtime. Finally, he said, "End of July, sir. Maybe early August. By then, everything should be in place."

Morris smiled and nodded. "Good. That's what I wanted to hear."

Von Mercy ruffled his brow. "Forgive me, sir, but I'm confused. Are we going to stay here for that long? I thought your return meant—"

Morris chuckled. "Our friends Rebecca and Uriel Abrabanel, along with Francisco Nasi, have begun a misinformation campaign saying the very same thing you just confessed to me. It's good to know that that is, indeed, the truth of it. Sometimes, the truth is the best misinformation. If everyone knows it and believes it, and sees that it is true, then perhaps the Ottomans will as well.

"But you're absolutely right, General. I did not come back to waste our time standing still. We'll be leaving, and soon, in spite of what you just said. Within days, Krakow will be in the rearview mirror."

Morris could see that his up-time expression confused the general, but von Mercy shook it off and said, "Then, sir, at the risk of repeating myself, I ask again: where are we going?"

"Clear the table, General," Morris said, standing and finding his energy. "Collect your maps, and have your aide-de-camp call in some food and wine. We've a long night ahead of us."

Chapter 9

Ennsegg Castle
Enns, Austria, eight miles east of Linz

Murad IV, Sultan of the Ottoman Empire, Commander of the Faithful, and Custodian of the Two Holy Mosques, was angry. A foul mood was not out of sorts for him, though this flare of rage was due to the missive he held in his hand, one that he had not anticipated.

He tore the letter to tatters and tossed the pieces into the fireplace. The flames consumed them immediately. "How dare he do this to me? How *dare* he?" He picked up his mace and swung it as if he were trading blows with a sworn enemy. "If I were facing him now, I'd take this mace and dash his head from his neck, and let his corpse bleed dry as it was paraded through the streets of his capital."

"It is only an alliance with Bohemia, My Sultan," Halil Pasha said, showing extreme deference and respect. "Not the alliance that we had feared."

Murad tossed the mace to the floor. Its mass and weight chipped the stone, sparked, and clattered to a halt. The sound echoed through the room. "I am aware of the contents of the letter, Halil. Very much aware."

In truth, he had always expected the USE to open a new front against him. Their supreme commander, Gustavus Adolphus, had proven himself an excellent strategist as well as tactician, willing to take calculated risks, and more often than not, benefitting from those risks at critical moments in battle. Such risks would, in time, fail him—indeed, it already had on a few occasions. Murad knew this despite his youth, for in war, one's fortune always ran out.

Allah be Praised.

Yes, Murad had always expected a new front to open against him. He just never expected it to involve the Bohemians. Though, perhaps he should have.

He breathed deeply to calm himself. It would not do to show such anger and surprise in front of Halil or any other assistant, any other councilor. He was Murad IV, emperor of the Ottoman Empire. He had to act like it.

"What have you learned of Bohemian military assets and readiness?" he asked, turning from the fireplace and addressing Halil Pasha directly. "Have they mobilized?"

Halil dared to move forward and shook his head. "No, My Sultan. There appears to be some dispute between Pappenheim and that up-time commander, Morris Roth."

Murad raised his brow. "Ah, yes. What a silly man to be at the head of an army. A jeweler! What kind of dispute?"

"Apparently, Pappenheim has refused to allow the Jew's so-called Grand Army of the Sunrise to return to Bohemia."

"It is currently engaged with Polish-Lithuanian forces, no?" Murad asked.

"Yes, My Sultan. It is going through an expansion. Jews are pouring in by the hundreds, the thousands, placing an enormous burden on its resources." Halil smiled. "And, as it is near Krakow, as you say, currently engaged in battle with the—"

"And thus, because of these maladies, you believe that his army is incapable of moving, and that we have nothing to fear from this alliance between Transylvania and Bohemia?"

Halil shook his head strenuously and bowed low. "No, My Sultan. I did not say that. Any alliance between two countries in opposition to Allah's, and your, cause is always of concern. I am merely saying that the dispute that seems to have erupted between Generals Pappenheim and Roth is causing delays in their military preparedness. They have declared an alliance with Transylvania, yes, but it seems to be an alliance in name only. Nothing that our spies in Bohemia and Poland have seen suggests an immediate threat."

"How soon, then?"

Halil paused, rubbed his beard. Murad could see his advisor worrying over the best answer to give. Murad did not like bad news, which is what he had just received, but he expected accurate—or as nearly accurate as possible—intelligence from his advisors. Anything else deserved punishment.

Finally, Halil said with great care, "If this Grand Army of the Sunrise is the one that Bohemia moves against you, My Sultan, I do not think it will happen until late summer, perhaps early fall."

"And they will then most likely move straight into Transylvania?"

Halil nodded. "That is our assessment, My Sultan."

Murad turned back to the fireplace. He put his hands out to warm them. Despite the rising heat of early summer, Ennsegg Castle was always cool. Today, that was a blessing, for it kept his own temperature and temper in check.

If his spies were correct, then Murad did not have to concern himself with any Bohemian army moving into Transylvania until late summer...if it ever moved there at all. He could continue to focus all his attention on the USE and its occupation of Linz. That, indeed, was his most pressing concern, and it needed to remain so.

"What does the Koran say about patience, Halil?" Murad asked, not waiting for an answer. "'Allah stands with the patient.' Therefore, we shall be patient."

Murad turned. "But, not too patient. It is prudent to send word to Moldavia and Wallachia to order them to immediately muster and move against Transylvania. Their collective armies should bring George Rákóczi and his treason to heel. And tell them that they may divide the spoils up however they wish thereafter. Transylvania is theirs, Halil, if they succeed. And they must."

Halil nodded. "Yes, My Sultan. Will we also be sending them military support? Advisors?"

Murad shook his head. He knelt and retrieved his mace. "Vasile Lupu and Matei Basarab are loyal subjects. They are enough to deliver our message to George Rákóczi in force. But, let us at least prepare."

He pointed the mace at Halil and waved it subtly. "Gather my commanders—Suleyman, Ahmed, all of them—and bring them to me. We will discuss what forces we may send into Transylvania, when and if the need arises."

Halil bowed low. "Yes, My Sultan."

The room was quiet again, save for the crackle of fire. Murad looked at the glow of the flames on the head of his mace. There, he saw the faces of his enemies.

"With Allah's strength," he whispered, turning the mace over and over in his hand, "I will bring this mace down upon all of your heads. All of you. One by one."

Chapter 10

Inside the great narthex of the Dealu Monastery
Principality of Wallachia, five miles north of Târgoviște

Matei Basarab, voivode of the Principality of Wallachia, had had fitful dreams the night before. He had dreamt of being chased by wolves through the thick forest of the Codrii Vlăsiei. He ran and ran and ran, and each time he thought he had outrun their vicious and snarling maws, they would take him down by the ankle and tear him to shreds. He'd awaken from this in sweats, breathing heavily, not clear of where he was. Eventually, he'd fall back asleep, but it would start all over again.

He could not decide if being torn to shreds by wolves was any worse than the impertinent order he was being given at this very moment.

"Sultan Murad, Commander of the Faithful, demands that you attack at once," Stroe Leurdeanu said, letting the lengthy and overly verbose letter slip though his hands like a scroll. "You are to attack Transylvania, capture and/or kill their prince, and seize their capital of Gyulafehérvár. And in exchange, you and Voivode Vasile Lupu will be allowed to divide Transylvania as you see fit. In the name of Allah, peace be upon Him, and on and on and on." He dropped his arms to his sides, letting the corners of the long letter scrape the floor. "This is an official communiqué, My Prince. It holds Sultan Murad's official seal, and it was given to me by a courier in whom I have absolute trust."

Matei turned toward Stroe Leurdeanu and smiled weakly. The man was a rising presence in the Wallachian court, one with military experience, and one in which Matei himself had absolute trust. Stroe was like the son he never had. Matei wished the letter were false, a foolish trick played upon him by some ambitious boyar wanting to embarrass the Craiovești family. Or, perhaps even better: Matei was still dreaming, and this was nothing more than wolves sinking their fangs into his tender flesh.

"Is there anything in the Sultan's missive that indicates his financial and, more importantly, military support for this directive?"

Stroe shook his head. "No, My Prince. It is believed that any Bohemian force that would move into Transylvania in support of Prince Rákóczi's misguided declaration of independence will not occur until late summer, early fall. Thus, Sultan Murad does not feel the need to preemptively send military support."

"Then we must, indeed, move quickly."

Vasile Lupu had been uncharacteristically quiet through Stroe's recitation of the letter. The voivode of Moldavia now stepped away from one of the many burial vaults in the narthex and came forward with a wild glare in his eyes that matched the wolves of Matei's dream. "If Sultan Murad is correct, then we have two, maybe three, months of time to act."

Matei shook his head. "Do not think that this . . . invasion of Transylvania will be easy, Vasile. We are in the midst of the Carpathian Mountains. The Transylvanians understand this country as much as we do. They will be prepared."

Vasile's expression was one of impatience. He was a man who, Matei knew very well, owed his success and rise to power to the Ottomans, and Murad specifically. Vasile Lupu was one of the richest men in all of Eastern Christendom, and even though he had become prince of Moldavia but three short years ago, his ambition knew no bounds. Rumor suggested that Vasile considered himself a Byzantine emperor. Matei had to stop himself often from laughing in the man's face at that notion.

"Our combined armies can sweep arrogant and rash George Rákóczi from the field. And with the time that we have—"

"We are not military men, Vasile," Matei said, interrupting what he figured would be a long diatribe about seizing the wondrous Transylvanian plateau. "We are statesmen, administrators. We did not come to power to kill our subjects. We rule to make their lives better, or so we try."

Vasile Lupu's eyes flared agitation. "Do not lecture me, Matei, on what my duty is to my own people. I understand the situation completely. But the simple truth is this: Sultan Murad IV has given us an order to move upon Transylvania. The only question to be answered now is: will you comply, or will you be hanged?"

"Of course I will *comply*," Matei snapped, growing weary of Vasile's assumption that *he* had been the courier who had brought the message to him and not Stroe. As if the voivode of Moldavia would deliver their answer back to Murad in person. *The arrogance!*

"I will comply," Matei reiterated, calming himself. "I just do not like the fact that Murad refuses to send us assistance. If and when a Bohemian force enters Transylvania, they will have those devilish up-time weapons with them. My contacts in Lithuania have been giving me reports about the utter devastation that those weapons bring to the battlefield. I doubt that anything that we can muster would match them."

"My Prince," Stroe said, "Sultan Murad did not say that no aid was forthcoming. He simply stated that they would not be sending aid immediately, that he needed to devote his military assets to more pressing matters: namely, the United States of Europe. If circumstances change, My Prince, surely Murad will send forces to assist."

Matei said nothing to that, but knew enough about military operations to know that any delay—a month, a week, a day—might as well be a year. If the Bohemians entered Transylvania with a force armed with modern weaponry, those wolves he had been dreaming about would not be so easy to subdue. So, maybe Vasile was right after all. It was imperative that they move and move now, seize George's capital and be there, entrenched, when the wolves came howling. At least then, they might have a chance.

"Thank you, Stroe," Matei said, smiling and placing his hand on the young man's shoulder, "for delivering, in haste, this message to us. You may go now. I will find you later to discuss our preparations."

Stroe bowed, turned, and left the narthex.

"He's an interesting young man," Vasile said, as he walked beside Matei down a row of burial vaults holding the remains of some of the most important, wondrous, and dangerous voivodes of both Wallachian and Moldavian history. "I wish I had one like him at my side."

"He is," Matei agreed, "and I am blessed to have him in my court. But let us speak now about what truly matters."

"Which is?"

"How can we hope to raise an army large enough, and in time, to take Transylvania? I will say again... we are not soldiers."

Vasile sighed, shook his head. "The world has changed, Matei. This so-called Ring of Fire has interrupted our lives in ways that we are only beginning to understand. Here, in our little corner of the world, its effects have been minimal at best. But no longer. The fire is now upon us, and so we must rise to meet that threat."

Matei shrugged. "Perhaps we should join Transylvania in its declaration. What difference does it make if we live under Ottoman or Bohemian rule?"

What a dangerous thing to suggest, especially to one like Vasile, who could so easily send word to Murad and have Matei executed and his headless body pulled through the streets of Istanbul while Janissaries pissed in his empty eye sockets. But Matei didn't care. If the world was changing, then by the grace of God, he was going to speak his mind, and damn to hell where the pieces fell.

Vasile paused, stared at Matei, and forced a smile. A dangerous, nay, angry smile that told Matei that he needed to tread cautiously. Vasile said, "What is that up-time idiom? 'Better to ride with the devil you know than the devil you don't.' Murad has been good to us. We must support his order." He wagged a finger in Matei's direction. "And do not forget, my friend, that you stand to lose the most in defiance of this missive. Wallachia's border is long and directly adjacent to the empire."

Matei deflated, sighed himself. "You are right, of course. I am just frustrated that the prince of Transylvania, *our* confidant and friend, has put us in such a delicate position. I have half a mind to go to Gyulafehérvár myself and string the son-of-a-whore up by his manhood."

Vasile laughed. "And I beside you."

That emotion was sincere. To Matei, this declaration of an alliance with Bohemia and of Transylvania's independence, was a sincere betrayal of their friendship. Not once had George even mentioned his interest in forming a new alliance, and they had kept each other's company several times within the past year.

"I can field perhaps four, maybe five thousand men by early July," Matei said, refocusing his attention to military details. "I will speak with my Serbian and Levantine contacts and see what mercenary cavalry they may send. My Hungarian contacts as well."

Vasile nodded. "And perhaps your Lithuanian friends. They may be more than happy to assist us in this endeavor. At least give us some cavalry. I suspect they are quite sore with Bohemia right now."

"Yes, it is possible."

"And I will muster the same," Vasile continued. "I will speak with my boyars and direct them to levy their peasants. I will also reach out to acquire Tatar cavalry. They will be more than happy to join us, I'm sure. By early July, we will have a sizable host with which to attack our *impetuous* friend George Rákóczi. And I will see to the terror campaign as well."

Matei wished he possessed Vasile's enthusiasm, but he knew George Rákóczi. The prince of Transylvania was no novice when it came to battle. Much of his youth had been spent assisting Gabriel Bethlen against Habsburg aggression. There would be no easy march into—"Wait! What do you mean by 'terror campaign'?"

"I mean exactly that." Vasile halted, turned to face Matei. They stood now in the center of the narthex, one of the largest in the world. His voice echoed through the vaults. He held up his hands. "Like many of our predecessors have done, and against the Ottomans no less. You know of which Wallachian prince I speak. Like him, we will strike fear into the hearts of any Bohemian army that dares to march into Transylvania."

Matei shook his head. "No, I do not like this idea. Innocent civilians are always harmed in such endeavors, even if you confine your strikes to just enemy forces. Villages are burned, crops destroyed, innocents killed."

"It must be done!" Vasile said, the echo of his stomped boot moving through the narthex. "You know this. This is how war is fought in the Balkans, my friend. If we allow our enemy to move unfettered through the plateau, they will become fat and contented with the hospitality of their host. They will love the citizenry, and they will be loved back. No. We must make it difficult for them, perhaps impossible . . . or we have little hope of victory."

He was right. Matei hated that fact, but it was true. It had to be done. He nodded. "Please promise me, at least, as a man promises to his priest, that you will not purposefully harm any civilians in this endeavor. I understand the nature and necessity of guerrilla warfare, Vasile. I understand the need to scorch the earth so that the enemy cannot feed in comfort. But please, show compassion for the people. If you do not, then they will rise against us in time, and no amount of combined forces will take that beauteous garden."

He moved forward and placed his hand on Vasile's shoulder. "And I cannot stress this enough, my friend. Do not make any attempt on the life of the prince, his wife, his children, or anyone else in his family. I must have your word on that before I agree to support this terror campaign."

Vasile paused before answering. He rubbed his broad beard vigorously, as if he were rubbing away stubborn bread crumbs. He grimaced. "Very well. I shall take these actions against Bohemian troops only, for the sole purpose of harming them, and no others. There will be no violent actions taken against the citizenry of Transylvania, nor against any in Prince George's family or his court. You have my word, as a Christian."

Matei nodded and stepped back. "Very well. What else shall we discuss?"

They spent the next thirty minutes walking among the vaults, working idle banter into serious discussion about timetables, tactics, and other matters of state. Matei shot down immediate discussion about how they might divide the Transylvanian plateau between them. "Let us win the war first, Vasile," he said, as they finished their discussion and bid each other farewell, "before we enjoy the spoils."

The voivode of Moldavia exited the narthex, and Matei leaned heavily against the tomb of the great Radu IV. It was blasphemous, perhaps, to be so informal and loose on such sacred ground. But God had already punished Matei enough for one day. He had given him Vasile Lupu as a partner in this terrible operation.

Stroe Leurdeanu returned. "Did you and Voivode Lupu work out all the details, My Prince?"

Matei nodded. "Enough for now." He breathed deeply and gathered his strength. "But I want you to keep your eyes and ears in the Moldavian court watching and listening, Stroe. We may have no choice but to follow this edict from our suzerain, but I want to ensure that we do it in such a way as to not bring shame to our people, to our country, and to God."

Stroe bowed. "Yes, My Prince."

"We have a long, bloody summer ahead of us, my friend."

Stroe nodded. "And many sleepless nights as well."

To that, Matei Basarab not only agreed, but welcomed.

Chapter 11

Krakow
Capital of the FPLC
(Free Polish-Lithuanian Commonwealth)

Denise Beasley walked slowly around Jeff Higgins, examining him up and down.

"I don't see where this is going to work," she said. "You're not as fat as you were back up-time, but you're hardly what anyone is going to call 'svelte.'"

"Denise, has anyone ever told you that tact is not your strong suit?" That was what anyone would have called a rhetorical question, though, because Jeff wasn't really irritated. He and Denise had known each other since they were children. There was about a seven-year gap in age between them, so they'd never been schoolmates. But Grantville had been a small town. Up-time, anyway. In the year 1637, six years after the Ring of Fire, it was more in the way of a big town—even a small city, by some reckoning.

Denise grinned. "There's a rumor that some dimwit said that back in 1992, when I was five years old. I don't believe it, though. Nobody is that dimwitted."

The grin was replaced by a scowl. "Look, Jeff, I'm not trying to be rude. But facts are facts. Stubborn things, like somebody once said. Yogi Berra, maybe."

Jeff managed not to smile. "Actually, it was President John Adams."

Denise waved that away. So far as she was concerned, picayune historical details weren't exactly facts themselves. "Whoever. The point is—" Once again, she looked him up and down. "What do you weigh? And don't fudge, dammit. Our life and death could depend on it, and I am *not* exaggerating."

She pointed at the small—very small—airplane parked on the runway a short distance off. "In case you hadn't noticed, a Dvorak is not a Boeing 747."

"I weigh a little over two hundred and sixty."

"We'll make that two hundred and seventy. Since I weigh right around one hundred and thirty, that gives us an even four hundred pounds' worth of people that that poor little critter has to get up in the air."

Jeff frowned. "What's the problem? I thought you could lift five hundred pounds over and above the weight of the plane itself."

"I can. But that includes the fuel, too. The weight of the fuel tanks is figured into the *Dixie Chick*'s curb weight, but not the fuel since we can vary that. Gasoline weighs about—"

"Six pounds to the gallon," said Jeff, who'd now been doing military logistics for years. He did the calculations quickly. "Which means we can only carry about sixteen gallons."

"Instead of the forty gallons I can carry if the tanks are full. The problem is now obvious."

Jeff was still frowning. "Well, how many miles can you go on a gallon of gas?"

Denise shook her head. "This is a plane, not a car. You have to figure how many hours you can fly on a gallon of gas, not how many miles you can go. There are too many variables that affect mileage to make 'miles per gallon' mean anything. Wind speed and wind direction are the biggest ones, but even something like humidity can make a difference. When humidity goes up, air pressure goes down, figuring for the same volume of air. So, the wings have less air—technically, molecules of air—to move around, which means they have less lift."

Denise was so good-looking and had such a flamboyant personality that it was easy to underestimate how smart the girl was. Jeff reminded himself not to forget that.

"Okay," he said. "So how many hours can you fly on a gallon of gas?"

"Roughly, you've got to figure you need seven gallons of fuel to fly for an hour. That's at a cruising speed of fifty-five to sixty miles per hour, but I always shrink that down to fifty miles to be on the safe side."

By the time she'd finished, Jeff had already done the calculations again. "Figure two hours of flight time on sixteen gallons, in other words, allowing for a safety margin. Which would get us about one hundred miles."

"Whereas the distance between here and Breslau is about one hundred and fifty miles." With her hand, Denise made a gesture mimicking something plunging downward. "*Boom.* Our body parts are scattered all over the landscape somewhere in the vicinity of Opole."

She planted that hand as well as the other on her hips. "Now, if you guys had done the smart thing and built airfields every fifty miles or so—*with* a stock of fuel kept on hand—we'd be looking at a different situation. But the way it is, big fella, if you want to get from here to Breslau, you're going to need a horse."

By the time she'd finished talking, a droning sound could be heard. She turned her head and squinted into the distance. "Or you're going to need my boyfriend. What the hell is Eddie doing here?"

"What I'm doing here is what I was ordered to do by our mutual boss, Francisco Nasi—provide any and all assistance needed for the success of what he's currently calling 'the Carpathian Caper.' At the moment, that requires me to deliver a package to Morris and then do whatever he tells me to do. It's all very mysterious. Need to know and I don't, apparently." An aggrieved look came to his face. "And what sort of cantankerous question is that coming from my own girlfriend, whom I haven't seen in—"

"Less than forty-eight hours. We spent the night before last together in Prague and you got laid, remember?"

Jeff had to keep from smiling again. Denise had always been quite selective in her boyfriends and was not at all promiscuous, but she had the breezy attitude toward sex that you might expect from the child of bikers.

Eddie's expression now had a smug tinge to it, on the other hand. "How could I forget?"

✧　　✧　　✧

Rebecca Abrabanel's State Department plane arrived less than two hours later. The Dragonfly was a six-seater, and Thorsten Engler and Tata were passengers along with two of Rebecca's aides.

Jeff wasn't surprised by the presence of the aides, since Rebecca had turned her official aircraft into what amounted to a mobile office. But he hadn't expected the other two people. Tata was the new governor of Lower Silesia and Thorsten was in command of the province's military forces.

"Why are they here?" he asked.

Eddie shrugged. "Got no idea. Rebecca must have stopped in Breslau to pick them up. But look on the bright side. This saves us a trip to Breslau, at least."

"What I'm doing here," Thorsten explained to Jeff once they were all seated at a conference table in a big meeting chamber on the second floor of the Cloth Hall, "is negotiating with you over a division of our military forces, since I have a new assignment which"—he held his hand up in a gesture of rigid warning—"I can't talk about because it's top secret. If you have a problem with that"—he lowered the hand and pointed an accusing finger at Rebecca—"take it up with the Secretary of State."

Rebecca gave him a glance which, coming from a less serene person, would probably have been an exasperated roll of the eyes. "He's going to another continent, never mind which one. We've finally decided to intervene in the slave trade. That's hardly a secret since we're in the process of assembling a very large fleet in Hamburg—and some other places—that we could hardly keep under cover. We just don't want our enemies—that would be Spain and Portugal—to know exactly where we're going."

"I'm taking my whole brigade with me—the one I just got done training and was *supposed* to be bringing to defend Lower Silesia," added Thorsten.

Tata had a very sour look on her face. "I just found that out myself—and I'm the governor. What I want to know is who's going to replace Thorsten and his brigade in that assignment."

"We haven't settled that yet," said Rebecca. "But we don't think there's any immediate threat to the province that the militia can't handle."

Jeff agreed with that assessment, but he wasn't surprised to see that Tata's expression didn't lighten up any. If he was the governor of a now undefended province right on the border of Poland, instead of a somewhat detached observer, he wouldn't be any happier than she was.

But he had his own problems to deal with, so he got immediately to the issue at hand. "Can you give me some of your volley gun companies?" he asked, trying not to sound too eager. Engler was the universally recognized master of volley gun tactics—and he'd been the one training the new companies.

"You can have all of them, including the veteran units. They won't be any use where I'm going. But I'll want something in exchange."

Try as he might, Jeff couldn't help but wince a little. He lusted after those volley gun batteries, which were murderous against the kind of cavalry forces he'd be encountering in Transylvania. But what Thorsten would want in exchange were mortar units that Jeff also doted on.

Perhaps...

"Light artillery?"

"Give me a break, Jeff. The reason I won't be able to use volley guns is because I won't have any horses. So, what good would ordnance do me that's even heavier? A four-pounder cannon weighs about a ton. No, I want mortars and mortar crews. Infantry weapons."

"Well..."

"I suggest that the two of you take this subject up later," said Rebecca. "Right now, with the people present at the table, we should discuss the use of the various aircraft we have available for the Transylvania campaign. You're what we have in the way of experts on the subject of the Dvorak and its proper use, which"—here she gave Thorsten another glance—"will interest Brigadier Engler since he's going to be taking two of the planes to—"

She waved her hand. "Where he's going."

Denise spoke up. "I figure I'm the expert we have on Dvoraks, since I've been flying them for a while now. While Eddie's been flying for a lot longer than I have, he's only flown a Dvorak a few times."

She paused and looked at Eddie. There was perhaps a challenging glint in her eye. Wisely, Eddie just nodded and thrust his hand forward, inviting her to continue.

"So, here's the thing," Denise continued. "The Dvorak has some great pluses and some not as bad but still pretty lousy downsides. The pluses are that it flies great, it's very maneuverable, and you can land and take off anywhere as long as it's flat and there aren't any rocks and big sticks in the way. A meadow will work just fine, you don't need an actual airstrip—although that's always handy, of course. Best of all, you don't need much room to take off and land. You can be airborne in seconds. Landings, the same."

"And the downsides?" asked Jeff.

"The biggest one is range. It's a really small plane and can't lift much more than five hundred pounds over and above its own weight. That doesn't leave you with much in the way of fuel capacity unless you're flying solo—and for reconnaissance it's a lot better to be carrying an observer as well as a pilot. Plus, it's a small engine so it's got a low cruising speed; it takes you a while to get anywhere—and while the top speed is somewhere around eighty miles an hour, you're just going to burn more fuel so you don't get any benefit in terms of range."

She took a deep breath, while thinking. "And . . . oh, yeah. When I said it flew great, that's only true if the weather's good. The Dvorak really doesn't handle poor weather well. As in, you may as well not even bother to get off the ground because you'll be coming right back. If you haven't crashed in the meantime."

Jeff nodded. "Which limits the reconnaissance capability. A lot, in this part of the world."

Stoutly, Eddie rose to the defense. "Jeff, bad weather makes for lousy reconnaissance even if you have a plane like my Dauntless. It'll handle the weather a lot better, but you still can't see much of anything."

"Yeah, I understand. I wasn't criticizing, just making an observation. The main lesson I take from this, though, is that we need to figure out ways to create a lot of small landing strips spaced not more than fifty miles apart."

"You really don't need much, Jeff," said Denise. "I meant it when I said a meadow works fine. Just make sure any sizable rocks or other obstructions have been removed, and any holes have been filled in."

He shook his head. "That's not the problem, Denise. It doesn't do you any good to have a small airstrip where you can refuel if there isn't any fuel there. Which means the strips have to be maintained, resupplied—and most of all, guarded. And unless you have enough troops to station an actual garrison—which we won't, outside of major towns and maybe a few big villages—then you're vulnerable to cavalry raids."

He gnawed on his lip for a few seconds. "Let me think about it. We should be able to figure something out."

He now looked at Eddie. "And what about the Dauntless? Will we have it available whenever we need it?"

"Pretty much. It's not impossible that Nasi might call me back, but it's not likely and even if he does, he should be able to give us a fair amount of warning. But it really *isn't* likely he would. He supports what we're doing and there are enough commercial planes now that if he needs one, he should be able to just rent or lease it, with a pilot."

"Speaking of renting or leasing," said Jeff, "does anyone know what the chances are we could get the services of a Jupiter or Saturn from the Netherlands for a few weeks? Better still, for the duration of the campaign. I have a feeling we'll find having an airlift supply capability will be worth its weight in gold. The Dvoraks are useless for that and even the Dauntless won't be much use."

"I could carry a few hundred pounds of cargo," said Eddie, "but that's about it, even if I'm flying solo." He leaned forward to look down the table at Rebecca, who was seated on his side of it. "Jeff's right about this. If nothing else, unless we can start hauling hundreds of pounds of fuel for the planes into forward locations, we'll be caught in something of a logistics loop."

"I don't have an answer to that question, but I'll see what I can find out."

Jeff had to bite his tongue, figuratively speaking, to keep from snarling that he and other military commanders had continually carped and complained to the civilian authorities that they spent too much of their time worrying about weapons and not enough worrying about the humdrum needs of military supply. *Amateurs study tactics; professionals study logistics.* It was simply inexcusable that the USE still hadn't produced its own version of the big Dutch cargo planes. Yeah, they were pretty slow and they weren't in the least bit sexy. So what? They could carry a lot of cargo way faster than any horse or mule—and with their air cushion landing gear they could even handle rough terrain.

Being fair about it, the problem with getting a big cargo plane for the Grand Army of the Sunrise wasn't due to pigheadedness on the part of Morris Roth or General von Mercy. Both of them understood how valuable such an aircraft would be to their efforts. The problem, insofar as Jeff had been able to determine—Morris was being very close-mouthed about it—was that obtaining one of the planes built by Markgraf & Smith Aeronautics could sometimes be politically tricky. Theoretically, Markgraf & Smith was just a private company, but in the real world, King Fernando had a great deal of influence over who could and who couldn't get one of the big planes. Jeff couldn't see where selling a Jupiter or Saturn to a Bohemian army that was marching to war almost halfway across the continent of Europe, against an enemy that was no friend of the Netherlands, would pose a problem for King Fernando. But... who knew?

He reminded himself of what was probably the human race's oldest military saw, going back to the Paleolithic: *You fight a war with the army you got, not the one you wished you had.*

"What the hell," he murmured under his breath, "we're still probably in better shape than the guys on the other side."

I hope.

Chapter 12

Grand Army of the Sunrise headquarters
Oppidum Judaeorum, Kazimierz

Isaac heard the soft, breathy sounds of fornication before he reached the covered wagon.

"Oy, Fakakta!" he whispered with an exhalation of agitated breath. He winced, shook his head, and gave a light wrap of knuckles on the wagon bed. "Christian. Christian, I know you're in there. Come on out, please."

Silence. Then giggles, a shuffle of bodies as the wagon rocked slightly. Whispered voices, more giggling, and then a smiling young lady stuck her head out the back. "*Guten abend, Herr Doktor*," she said, blowing a wisp of hair out of her face.

"*Guten abend*, Greta," he said with a roll of his eyes. He thumbed her out. "*Loslegen.*"

She giggled, climbed out, then ran off, holding her modest dress closed tightly at the chest.

Christian climbed out shortly thereafter, even more disheveled than Greta. He dropped down into a small puddle of water and paused to tuck in his shirt. He buckled his belt and flashed a contented smile. "I must say, Isaac, Greta is a far better physical therapist than you are."

Isaac ignored the crass comment. "I thought you said she reminded you of your sister."

Christian straightened his collar. He winked. "Well...perhaps a distant cousin."

Isaac wagged a finger in Christian's face. "Listen here, if you get that girl in trouble, we'll lose a good nurse, and I'll put you in her place permanently."

Christian chuckled and slapped Isaac on the shoulder. "Don't worry, my friend. I was nothing if not careful, and a gentleman."

There were many things Isaac wanted to say to that, but he tucked away his agitation and tugged at Christian's shirt. "Come, now. I'm taking you to see the boss."

"I've already met Oberheuser."

Isaac shook his head while guiding Christian toward the stone bridge that crossed the Vistula. "No, not that boss. *The* boss."

Isaac had expected something smaller, more intimate, perhaps even a one-on-one with the commanding officer, to go over medical supply and further needs. Such was not the case.

Sunrise HQ was packed.

It seemed as if the entire command staff was in attendance. General von Mercy was there, of course, standing beside Morris Roth. Next to him and going down one entire side of the large table in the center of the room, were the newly appointed provost marshal, Major General Luther Lange; Colonel Samson Shalit, First Regiment of the Joshua Corps; Colonel Reznik Makovec of the Brethren; Colonels Friedrick Burkenfeld and Gerhardt Renz, First and Second Cavalry Regiments. There were others, too, but Isaac did not know their names, or their faces, very well. Like the provost marshal, many of them had just been appointed to their positions. It was intimidating to be in the presence of so much "brass," as an up-timer might say. He was thankful, though, to see Jason Gotkin huddled with the rest of the chaplain corps at the end of the table. And Doctor Oberheuser too, who had managed to weasel his way up to stand close to General von Mercy and was talking to him as if they were old friends.

There was one woman in attendance as well, Ellie Anderson, who stood near Morris Roth and didn't seem to mind her minority status. Isaac recognized her from Prague. He could hear her laughing and speaking casual obscenities as she and Morris engaged in a private conversation. There was a lot of elevated banter going around the room. Their voices created a cacophony of noise that made it difficult to hear anything clearly.

Isaac stepped up to the table, pulling Christian with him. Morris caught his eye and brought the attending to silence.

"Thank you, Isaac, for coming," Morris said with a pleasant smile and a wave as the conversation in the room dwindled, then stopped.

"Honored to have been invited, sir," Isaac said.

"Who is your companion?"

"This is Captain Christian von Jori. He has been serving as my medical supply assistant during his convalescence and therapy."

"How are you, young man?" Colonel Renz asked from across the table.

Christian nodded. "Very well, sir, thank you. I'm anxious to get back in the saddle."

"Von Jori," von Mercy said, casting his eyes to the ceiling. "Why does that name sound familiar?"

"He is the young man I told you about, General," Colonel Renz said. "The one who saved a Brethren company from rout."

"Then I should thank you," Colonel Makovec said, his deep, rough Bohemian accent catching the attention of everyone at the table. "Perhaps I should take you back to my regiment, make you my aide-de-camp."

Light laughter spread across the table. Christian smiled, nodded, said, "Thank you, sir, but I'm a cavalry officer. I've no desire to be anything else."

"And you're not going to steal him from us, Colonel Makovec," Colonel Renz said with a sly smile and a twitch of an eye. "The cavalry needs good company commanders."

"The need is great throughout the army, gentlemen, both for foot and horse," Morris said, bringing the conversation back to him before it broke into an inter-regimental squabble. "Let's focus now on why we are all here. Why I've called you together."

Morris placed his hands on the large map spread across the table. "I've already discussed this matter with General von Mercy and our regimental commanders. This conversation is more for the benefit of you serving civilians." He looked at Doctor Oberheuser, Isaac, Jason Gotkin, and the rest of the chaplain corps. "Simply put: in seventy-two hours, the Grand Army of the Sunrise will strike its tents and march to Kassa."

The announcement was no surprise to Isaac. The fact that Morris Roth had returned from Prague was a clear sign that a decision had been, or would be made soon, as to the Sunrise's next move. He was a little surprised, however, at the destination. The talk about camp pertained to Bohemia's and Transylvania's newly declared alliance. Why, then, were they marching in a more southerly direction and not simply moving straight away into Transylvania? For that matter, why not keep moving east into Ruthenian lands to further what the Grand Army of the Sunrise was supposed to do, what Morris Roth had told Isaac in person what it was supposed to do: destroy any possibility that the Chmielnicki Pogrom could ever take root. How could that be accomplished by moving to Kassa and therefore, moving closer to Ottoman battle lines?

But all of it became clearer as Morris laid out the plan, and once he did in full, it made perfect sense. At least most of it. Isaac was no soldier, no officer. When he heard grand strategies about military movements and operations, all he could see in his mind were the number of casualties, the number of wounded, the number of corpses that such plans could produce.

Isaac was young, yes, but no fool. He understood the cost of war; he had become a military surgeon to help mitigate that cost. This move to Kassa did not appear to be overly dangerous. Naturally, whenever armies marched, there was always death. Men would die simply by accident: one of the axles on a wagon in the baggage train would snap, and in the process of fixing it, a soldier's leg or arm would get crushed. Foolish horseplay during bivouac would end in a knife fight and someone's throat cut. One of the Brethren's APCs would topple into a deep ditch, injuring everyone inside and probably killing some of them. Death always happened with armies on the march. The question in Isaac's mind as General Morris Roth laid out the plan was, where would they go next? It was the second move, after Kassa, that worried him the most.

Christian, on the other hand, stood at the table in rapt attention, listening intently as the plan was articulated. He even dared raise his hand and ask questions about which regiment might take point and lead the army into Kassa. That created a small debate about whether it should be the Joshua Corps or a cavalry regiment. There were good rationales for both options, but Morris shelved the final decision. He finished his presentation and stood back from the table.

"All right, gentlemen," he said, "that's the plan. Now, before I go around the table and ask each of you to give me a status report, I want to introduce you to Ellie Anderson. She and her husband, Len Tanner, will be taking command of our radio and communication network."

Ellie stepped up to the table and waved. "Howdy!"

Everyone was cordial and either gave her a small wave, a nod, or a curt "hello," but it was clear to Isaac that many of them were uncomfortable being in a war council with a woman. For her part, Ellie kept her cool, which was more than he ever remembered her doing in Prague.

"What's the status of our communication network, Ellie?" Morris asked.

"A work in progress, Morris," she said, ignoring proper military protocol. "Len and I just got here yesterday late, and unfortunately, didn't escape Prague with as many radios as we had hoped. Your dream of seven to twelve radios per thousand men is just that. More likely, four or five per thou for now. And we'll be starting a training program using the radio techs you have. Len and I would prefer we not move until at least the radios are distributed. But you know what they say about military movements and pissing: if you gotta go, you gotta go."

Her frank, vulgar comment brought a few chuckles, but clearly shocked everyone else. Especially in the chaplain corps. How *dare* a woman speak harshly and in front of so many important men? Isaac noticed Rabbi Gotkin lower his head and force himself not to burst into laughter.

Morris moved on. "Very well. Colonel Shalit?"

Colonel Sampson Shalit was much revered among the Joshua Corps. He had been in command of the Jewish infantry that had fought against the Polish-Lithuanian Magnates, so all the men in his regiment were veterans. His opinion carried weight among the Ashkenazim. Isaac was glad to see him wearing his yarmulke.

Wish I had worn mine.

Colonel Shalit nodded. "We are ready to move, sir, though we do so without a full refit. Some of the promised ZB-1636 rifles have arrived, but not all. Many of our companies will have to make do with regular down-time muskets and equipment for now."

"I noticed in your most recent TOO that you are sticking with roughly two hundred men per company?" Morris asked.

"Yes, sir. We don't have enough qualified company commanders to reduce that number per your request. For now, at least. We will, in time, have a more qualified pool of officers, but we must assign the men to someone before we move. We'll reassess the Joshua Corps' command structure once we reach Kassa."

Colonel Shalit turned to Ellie. "Frau Anderson, I have discussed the issue of radio coverage with Colonel Burkenfeld, and I agree with his assessment. For now, the cavalry requires more radio coverage, as it is likely that their companies will be used for reconnaissance, scouting, flanking. I will speak with you and Herr Tanner afterward about all this...with your permission, of course."

"Of course," Ellie said. "Let's get this matter taken care of as soon as possible."

"General Lange?" Morris said, moving down the table. "What's the security situation?"

"Horrible," he said flatly, "but improving. I'll have provost marshals assigned to each regiment before we leave Krakow. Increasing the men's pay, sir, has improved spirits and mood considerably." He narrowed his eyes and glared around the room. "But it has been made clear to me that there has been some discrimination and harassment between the Ashkenazim and, specifically, the cavalry. This will not be tolerated. Is that understood?"

General von Mercy had promoted Luther Lange to major general, so he was, in effect, the third-highest ranking officer in the Sunrise.

Looking around the room, waiting for the other officers to acknowledge General Lange's warning, Isaac could see real tension in the promotion. Lange was a favorite of von Mercy's. They apparently went way back, even before the Ring of Fire. Lange was reported to be fair, but very harsh, and he was not above hanging a miscreant on sight.

Everyone nodded their agreement to General Lange's warning, and Morris pressed on. "Colonel Burkenfeld? Colonel Renz? What's the status of our cavalry?"

"The cavalry is ready to move, sir," Colonel Burkenfeld said. "Like the infantry, our supplies are low. We are limited in our ZB-2 Santees, along with ammunition. If we were to distribute them all evenly among the companies, we'd have only two per man. We've decided to give those precious howdahs only to our elite companies, sir. The rest of the men will have to make do with the weapons they have. Until, of course, our resupply arrives." He turned to Colonel Renz. "Do you concur, Colonel?"

Colonel Renz nodded. "Yes, and I would like to reinforce what Colonel Shalit has said. We suffered command losses during our tussle with the Lithuanians. Some of our companies are short-staffed. I'm having to combine companies for the time being, until I can find—"

"I'm ready to go!"

Christian's interruption startled Isaac. It startled nearly everyone at the table.

"I'm ready to go," Christian repeated, this time at a more respectful volume. "Colonel Renz, I'm ready to take command of my company."

Isaac tugged at Christian's sleeve and whispered, "Christian... hold a moment. We should discuss this."

Christian pulled away. "No, Isaac, I'm sorry, but I'm ready to go." He turned to Colonel Renz. "Sir, with your permission, I will take my position as captain in your regiment."

All eyes fell upon Isaac, as if he were the one to make the final decision. But was he? Did he really have the authority to refuse Christian's declaration? If Colonel Renz said yes, then there was nothing he could really do about it, especially in the presence of all these high-ranking officers. This was a military matter. No, in fact, it wasn't. It was a medical decision, and it came down to a simple question: Was Captain Christian von Jori ready to assume his duties as a cavalry officer? Isaac sighed, rubbed his forehead, said, "Very well. If you wish to return to duty, then you may do so. I release you from my service."

Colonel Renz nodded. "Very well. Captain von Jori, attend to me after this meeting, and we will discuss your reinstatement."

There was a pause, then Morris moved on. "Colonel Makovec?"

"I'll simply reiterate what has already been mentioned," the Bohemian commander of the Zizka Brigade said. "We do not have sufficient weapons or ammunition. I am less concerned about additional training, General Roth, as most of my men are well-rehearsed in the art of war. But... we have commissioned two additional APCs, and they have not arrived yet."

What that really meant was six more vehicles, two locomotives and four armored wagons. After some terminological fumbling around, the Brethren had settled on the definition of "an APC" being a locomotive and two wagons. That definition could get ragged around the edges in the field, because a locomotive could wind up pulling anywhere from one to four armored wagons.

Morris nodded. "I have spoken with the quartermaster, and he has assured me that they are en route and can be easily diverted to Kassa in order to accommodate our departure."

Colonel Makovec shook his head. "That is not acceptable, General. I am concerned that the additional travel time to Kassa will stress the carriages to such an extent that, by the time they reach Kassa, they will be less than useful. So, we either wait for them to arrive here so that my men can take control of them to ensure their survivability of the march, or we await them in Kassa and hope for their safe arrival. It's a risk I'm not willing to take on such delicate, and expensive, machinery. We *must* wait another full week before we strike out."

Morris shook his head. "No, we can't afford a delay. General von Mercy," he said, turning to his second-in-command. "Any tactical concerns with leaving the Brethren here in Krakow while we move forward?"

Von Mercy considered. "Negligible, assuming we receive little resistance in Kassa. We can manage it for a few extra days."

"Very well." Morris turned back to Colonel Makovec. "Leave just enough crew behind to await your new APCs, but you and the rest of the Brethren will come with us. Understood?"

Colonel Makovec paused before nodding agreement. Isaac couldn't help but smirk. Makovec was a good officer, but he bristled at being bossed around. He preferred to do the bossing, and while he was never openly insubordinate to superior officers, he did not like being put into situations where his manhood was challenged.

Isaac had heard about this from some of the nurses tending to wounded Brethren. *It is amazing what men will tell women when they need mothering.*

"Rabbi Gotkin," Morris said. "How goes the chaplain corps?"

Jason Gotkin bowed humbly. "Very well, General Morris. I have tried to attend to the spiritual needs of the Joshua Corps as best as I can, but we need additional rabbis, sir, if applicable.

I'm afraid that my meager support is not sufficient for the thousands in camp."

"Understood," Morris said. "I was unable to convince any in Prague to come with me. You've had no success in Kazimierz?"

Jason nodded. "Three have volunteered, but two of them are elderly, and I fear that they may not survive a long move. The third is very young, younger than me. His family, unfortunately, refuses to let him go. I'll be speaking with his mother tomorrow. Maybe I can convince her."

"Don't take the boy away from his mama," Ellie said to a fair amount of laughter. "It would break her heart."

When the laughter died away, Jason said, "I promise I'll be kind, Ellie. I understand their concern, but I need help. I just need to convince her that her son will be doing righteous work."

"I'm sure they know that already, Jason," Morris said. "Ellie's right. Don't force the issue. If they refuse to give him up, let it go. We'll find you additional support in Kassa, someone not so old, or so young."

That did not seem to put Rabbi Gotkin's mind at ease, and Isaac wondered why Morris was being so impatient and so unwilling to offer sympathy. He stared at Morris as he had a brief, private conversation with General von Mercy. The up-timer was tired, exhausted actually. Isaac could see it on the man's face. *The weight of the world is on his shoulders.*

Isaac made a mental note to recommend to Morris that he and Isaac and Jason spend some private time together in prayer. There was need for all three of them to give pause and ask God for strength.

The rest of the chaplain corps told roughly the same story as Rabbi Gotkin. They too would like more pastors and priests to cover the army. Morris made the same promises to them.

"General von Mercy," Colonel Shalit said, raising his hand, "if I may ask you a question, sir, before we proceed?"

Von Mercy nodded. "Yes, Colonel. What is it?"

"What decision has been made about artillery distribution? How many cannon are we likely to receive?"

"The artillery will model the USE method of six guns per company," von Mercy said, "with two companies combined to form a twelve-gun battery. For now, each regiment within the Joshua Corps will receive one battery each." He motioned to Colonels

Burkenfeld and Renz. "The cavalry will provide teams to deploy the guns as needed. When our supply of barrels and ammunition increase, the number assigned to each regiment will increase."

Colonel Shalit nodded. "Thank you, General. That will be fine."

Morris paused to ensure no further discussion on the matter. Then he continued. "Okay, Isaac. Your turn. How are we set for medical supplies?"

Isaac looked to Doctor Oberheuser in deferment, got a nod, then spoke. "Yes. Like everyone else, sir, some supplies are low. We need more pain medication, more sanitation equipment and PPE, but we have eight wagonloads of supplies—one of which will have to be *thoroughly* scrubbed before we leave"—he shot a hard glance as Christian—"and I hope to have two more wagonloads before we depart. That is no guarantee, unfortunately, but we'll try."

Doctor Oberheuser then gave a final assessment of medical staffing, which to Isaac's relief, was coming along well. On the nursing and orderly side of the equation, they had plenty of women—and some men—volunteer for those positions. But his hope of having a field medic assigned to each company was not possible before Kassa, and probably not afterward either. Each regiment would have two, and they would be deployed as its commander saw fit.

In order for that system to even work, he and Doctor Oberheuser had implemented a strict triage program wherein the field medics had absolute authority to decide who was expectant (who would die) and who would be removed from the field for "priority" medical care. The walking wounded would have to deal with their own wounds and would not be admitted into the tent unless their condition worsened. And this system would be in place until the surgical staff was increased to sufficient numbers.

To that end, they had acquired two volunteer surgeons from Kazimierz. Isaac was grateful for that, but neither had any up-time medical training. They were old school, down-time physicians who could provide basic medical services only: conduct simple sutures, reset broken bones, remove a limb with assistance. Simple stuff. The rest fell on him and grumpy old Oberheuser.

A few more questions, a few follow-up answers, a few random conversations, and the council was concluded.

"Thank you, lady and gentlemen," Morris said. "I appreciate

your frank, honest assessments. But we are, as Len Tanner might say, and Ellie can attest to, one piece in a larger game of chess. An important piece, and dare I say, the *most* important. But there will be no delay in our departure, despite your concerns. We will deal with these supply and training deficiencies as we go along. We move to Kassa in seventy-two hours. Make your preparations. We will meet again in forty-eight for a final review. Thank you all. God bless you all."

Isaac found Christian outside. "Couldn't we have spoken about this, my *friend*, beforehand? Shouldn't you have confided in me first before making such a snap decision?"

Christian put up his arms. "I didn't know the chance would come up."

"I realize that. But there was no reason to blurt it out there, in front of everyone. You could have waited for us to discuss it afterward."

"And what would you have said?" Christian's expression grew tense. His face reddened. "You would have said no, insisted that I stay in your service, and for how long? Days? Weeks? Months? No. I've got to get back in the saddle, Isaac. I'm bored. I'm restless. My place is with my men. My company."

Isaac paused, saw the sincerity, the desperate need to return to service, in his friend's eyes. He did not like it, but he understood it. Christian was experiencing the same call to duty that Isaac had felt on that stone bridge in Prague four years ago.

"Fine, fine," he said, relenting. "Just promise me that you will keep the eye patch in place. Your eye is much better, but it still needs time. It's still very sensitive to bright light. You work it too hard, you strain it, and it may get worse. Please, keep the patch on, and come to see me from time to time, so that I can check on it. I'll tell you when you can remove it for good. Agreed?"

Christian smiled and nodded. "Agreed."

That night, after Morris examined the contents of the package Eddie had brought to him from Prague, last-minute changes in plans were made. The army would still make its departure to Kassa in seventy-two hours, but Morris himself wouldn't be playing a direct role in the preparations. He had to fly back to Prague immediately to do something he was not at liberty to discuss. Eddie would fly him.

Since they had to make a refueling stop in Breslau anyway and the Dauntless could carry three passengers, they could drop Jeff off so that he could coordinate the effort of getting the Silesian Guard to Kassa with Eric Krenz. Jeff had considerably less than half of the guard with him in Krakow. More than a third, but probably not over forty percent. But since that portion consisted mostly of what used to be the Hangman Regiment and was comprised of the guard's veterans, Jeff had to get them into Transylvania as soon as possible. Krenz—Colonel Krenz, now—would bring the rest from Breslau...whenever he could manage it. That was likely to be a ragged affair.

You fought a war with the army you had, not the one you wished you had.

Chapter 13

Breslau (Wrocław)
Capital of Lower Silesia

Gretchen Richter hated to fly. But her reaction to having Denise Beasley as her pilot was quite different from Morris Roth's. Denise had made Morris nervous. The effect she had on Gretchen was not to lower her anxiety—that was a given, and would have been if the pilot was Saint Peter—but to increase her political resolve.

Gretchen was not what up-timers meant by the term "feminist." She thought a lot of the premises of that viewpoint were questionable and some were downright absurd. But she also believed very strongly that the world would be improved in direct proportion to the extent women wielded power and influence, since it was blindingly obvious that hers was the more sensible of the genders.

And thus, the more female pilots, the better. That would certainly reduce the chances of planes colliding in midair, for one thing. Granted, that chance was not very great to begin with, given the small number of planes in the skies of the current day. But however few there were, the more male pilots you had the greater the chance they'd do something stupid. Whereas the more women you had behind the controls, the greater would be the rationality.

"I'm about to start our descent!" Denise shouted over her shoulder.

Splendid. Gretchen approved of descents. Landings, even more.

✧   ✧   ✧

"That's better than I expected," Gretchen said, after she returned the financial ledgers to Tata.

Tata shrugged and used the motion to help place the heavy ledger into the big lower cabinet of her desk. "The economy of the province has been improving rapidly. A lot of the poverty of Lower Silesia was because of the political chaos. When people get nervous they hoard things—food, clothing, what little money they might have, anything—and that just makes things worse all around. Once they feel that conditions are more secure, all that hoarded wealth—such as it is—starts coming back out."

Now sitting fully upright again, she gave Gretchen a squinty-eyed look. "You do understand that 'more than I expected' doesn't begin to cover marching the whole Silesian Guard even as far as Krakow, much less however much farther Transylvania is from there."

"At least four hundred miles," said Gretchen. "Probably farther."

She shook her head. "Don't worry. I don't plan to use any of what little cash or income or loans Silesia might be able to come up with. No, I'll squeeze the wealth out of the USE."

"We're now part of the USE, remember?"

Gretchen waved her hand dismissively. "Call it the USE proper, then. Where all the fat German burghers are."

Tata laughed. "'Fat German burghers,' is it? I think your husband would scold you for being politically incorrect."

"No, he wouldn't. He's an American, true, but I've been educating him for years."

"Is *that* what call you it?" Tata was smirking now. "I've heard some of your so-called education sessions when the walls were thin."

Gretchen grinned. "Education is a very expansive term."

Magdeburg Airport
Just outside Magdeburg
Capital of the United States of Europe

"I'm impressed!" Gretchen said, looking down at the airfield. Denise was circling the *Dixie Chick* back around on the orders of the control tower. It turned out there was a new runway set aside for small planes.

"Impressed by what?" Denise shouted back.

"The airport! They have enough traffic now to worry about the difference between small planes and big ones!"

"Guess so! I haven't been here in a while myself!"

By then, Denise had the *Dixie Chick* on a new course. Gretchen had seen the little runway they were headed toward as they came around, but it was now hidden from her view by the nose of the aircraft.

As Denise began her descent and the nose came down, the runway came back into view. It seemed shorter now.

A lot shorter.

She told herself that that was just an optical illusion caused by their height, angle of descent. Whatever. But her knuckles got white again, as she gripped the armrests.

It didn't help that Denise had started singing what she called her "flying tune." About the last phrase Gretchen was in the mood to hear, given the circumstances, was *her big mistakes.*

The actual landing, though, came as both a relief and a surprise. This runway was in excellent condition and whatever reservations she might have about Denise's high spirits, the teenager's reflexes and hand-eye coordination were superb. Gretchen barely felt the impact at all. One moment they were in the air; the next they were rolling comfortably down the airstrip. It seemed to take no time at all before Denise took them off the runway and was taxiing toward the three hangars positioned just off to the side.

Gretchen was surprised again when she saw there was a delegation waiting to greet her. She'd assumed without really thinking about it that she'd have to make her own arrangements to get into the city.

Denise brought the plane to a stop, hopped out, and began setting the wheel chocks. Gretchen climbed out a few seconds later, after unbuckling herself and drawing her valise out of the small cargo compartment behind her seat.

The *Dixie Chick* really was a little plane. Gretchen had now flown in it twice and was starting to notice details. All she had to do to get out was unlatch her door, which was on the opposite side of the fuselage from Denise's to give both of them enough room, swing her legs out and step down—straight onto the ground. When she stood erect, she was about a foot taller than the top of the wing that sat atop the fuselage—what Denise call a "high-wing" design.

She tried to decide if the size of the aircraft should worry her or comfort her. On the worry side was the fact that it was almost downright flimsy. On the comfort side, that same flimsy quality made it seem rather leaflike. She'd seen leaves fall to the ground. Very gently. Hopefully the plane might do the same in the event something went wrong.

Leaf, she told herself firmly. *Think of a leaf.*

The delegation came up to her at that moment. It was a trio, with a young woman in the lead.

"Welcome, Lady Protector," she said, extending her hand. Gretchen shook it, managing not to grind her teeth in the process. As much as she detested the title, she *had* agreed to it, after all.

"I am Johanna Fetzerin, and I'm on the staff of the prime minister. I am here to take you to the lodgings we've arranged for you and then, at your convenience, to meet with Herr Piazza." She looked toward Denise, who had finished with the plane and was approaching with her own valise in hand. "Will your pilot need lodgings as well?"

"Yes, she will," said Gretchen. "Where will we be staying?"

"At the Hans Richter Hotel."

This time, it was her eyes that Gretchen had to control, lest they roll upward in exasperation. Was there *anything* in Magdeburg that the scheming politician Mike Stearns hadn't named after her slain war-hero brother?

Fetzerin must have sensed her feelings, because she smiled slightly and said, "The hotel was built recently. It was named after the square it fronts on."

Which Mike Stearns made sure was named for Hans. So, he was still responsible, as far as she was concerned. But there was no point getting irritated over it, this long afterward.

She felt a little pang of grief. It had been...how long, now, since Hans died in the Battle of Wismar? Three and a half years, already.

By then, a carriage had come up. It was more like a small bus, actually, although it was horse-drawn. Only two horses, though, which boded well for the condition of the roads. Magdeburg was one of the few cities in the USE that had good thoroughfares. Nothing up to the standards of Grantville, of course, but at least you didn't need to worry about having your teeth chipped because of a jolting carriage.

Office of the Prime Minister
Government House
Magdeburg

"I haven't got room in the budget to cover all the expenses of moving what amounts to a brigade of soldiers from Krakow to wherever you might wind up in Transylvania." Ed Piazza cocked his head slightly and raised a quizzical eyebrow. "Which is where, by the way? Do you even know yet?"

"I don't," said Gretchen, shaking her head. Then, as firmly as she could manage: "But I'm sure my husband and General Roth will have determined their final destination by now."

Ed smiled at her. "No doubt. Do you know how long they plan to take to complete the troop movement?"

"No. I don't. But Jeff did tell me it would take several weeks and quite possibly two to three months. It depends on the conditions of the roads in Transylvania, which..."

"Are probably glorified cow paths," Ed finished for her. "But at least he won't be hauling heavy artillery."

Again, he cocked a quizzical eyebrow. "Will he?"

That question, Gretchen could answer with some confidence. "No. Jeff told me he was planning to rely mostly on mortars and volley guns. The most he'd bring in the way of artillery would be what he called 'light field guns.' Four-pounders, I think I remember him saying—and not more than eight of them."

Piazza looked at one of his aides, sitting in a chair to the side. Gretchen had been introduced to him but couldn't precisely remember his name. Anton something. Gottlieb or Gottschalk. He was a man who looked to be in his forties and had the bearing of someone with a military background.

Without needing any prompting, the aide said: "That sounds about right, Prime Minister. A four-pounder field gun will weigh less than a ton. Even with the added weight of the shot and powder, that's well within the capabilities of a brigade. Even on bad roads, as long as they're not trying to cross mountains."

"And will they be?"

The aide shook his head. "Nothing I'd call 'mountains,' no. They'll skirt the High Tatras, of course, moving from Krakow to

Kassa. Once they reach Kassa, they'll be on the northern boundary of the Great Hungarian Plain. Crossing the plain and most of Transylvania, coming from the north as they will, should pose no problems at all." Here he made a face. "If they try to enter the Carpathians at the southern edge of Transylvania, though... That would be a different story altogether. But Brigadier Higgins is an experienced officer. He wouldn't be foolish enough to do that."

By the end of the meeting, Gretchen had gotten a commitment from Piazza that the USE would finance the movement of the Silesian Guard as far as Kassa, and would provide enough support for the guard to remain in Kassa, if need be, through the winter. If the guard did continue moving into Transylvania, the USE would maintain the support until the funds ran out. However soon or later that might be.

That was the best she was going to get. She hadn't really expected any more than that and wouldn't have been surprised if she'd gotten less.

"Next, I have to see what I can squeeze out of Gustav Adolf. So, tomorrow morning—early—we fly to Linz," she told Denise.

"Define 'early.'"

"Up-timers." Gretchen wasn't quite scowling. "When the roosters are making enough racket that you can't sleep anyway."

Denise wasn't quite scowling, either. "Down-timers. Who think it's reasonable to keep chickens in cities."

That night, at the dinner table, Ed's wife, Annabelle, said to him: "You seem distracted. What's up?"

Ed leaned back in his chair and sighed. "I'm just... What did Proust call those books he wrote?"

"*Remembrance of Things Past.* Sometimes translated as *In Search of Lost Time.*"

"Yeah, those. I was just remembering things past. The days when I was a high school principal and Morris Roth was a small-town jeweler and Jeff Higgins was just a teenage kid. Now... Prime Minister. General. Brigadier. Something is just plain screwy with the universe."

Part Three

June 1637

Yesterday's load of wretchedness
—Sophocles, *Ajax*

Chapter 14

On the road to Kassa (Košice)
Near the High Tatras

Groomsmen tied fetters around the front legs of the troubled horse. They ran ropes through the neck and girth straps to give themselves control and pull power if the horse decided to buck or try to bolt. Christian von Jori watched the procedure in dismount, waiting to give the word while the rest of the company continued to follow the Sunrise toward Kassa. He had hoped to make the entire trip without losing a horse, or horses, in this case. No such luck.

"Very well," he said, giving the nod as the groomsmen were ready. "Bring it down."

Together, three groomsmen pulled the ropes while the other two controlled where the horse would fall. It was proving to be difficult. The horse, even in its debilitated state, struggled to break free of the fetters. Two cavalrymen passing by stopped, dismounted, and gave assistance. The horse was then brought under control. Finally, it fell.

The fetters and rope were kept in place and held tightly as Christian came forward to inspect the right hind leg. He pressed his fingers into the swelled tendons. The horse whinnied and kicked, but the fetters held firm. He placed the leg down.

Damn!

"Stand back, please," he ordered. He pulled his pistol from his holster and aimed it toward the horse's chest. The modern Santee would do its work quickly, he knew, though he hated using it in this capacity.

He pulled the trigger, the gun fired, and the horse stopped fighting.

The groomsmen removed the fetters and used them to bring the second horse down in the same manner. Christian inspected its front left hoof. A small bone fracture that, if allowed to persist, would continue to grow until the horse simply could not walk, much less trot or gallop. Infection would set in and, ultimately, death.

He pulled another loaded pistol from his saddle holster and did the deed quickly.

"Have the regimental cooks field dress them both and have the meat packed in salt," he said to the horse's riders, climbing back onto his own horse and tucking away his pistols. "You can skin them as well and keep the hides if you like. Collect their tail hair and give it to the medical corps. They're always in need of suture material."

Christian turned away from the two bloody carcasses and regained his place in the line of cavalrymen making their way to Kassa.

Kassa (Košice)
Northern boundary of the Great Hungarian Plain

Christian rounded the corner and raised his gloved hand quickly to keep from being blinded by a hot, bright light rising behind the rolling hills beyond the city walls. He was disappointed, not only because he couldn't see the path forward and thus guide his horse effectively, but because his company, along with the rest of Colonel Renz's cavalry regiment, were entering the city as rear guard for the Grand Army of the Sunrise. Rear guard and protector of the supply train. An honorable duty, indeed, but not one that always garnered the most glory.

It had been decided that the Joshua Corps, supported by flankers from Colonel Burkenfeld's First Cavalry Regiment, would have the honor of leading the army into Kassa, to some fanfare and spectacle, for rumor had it that Jews were not permitted to live in the city itself. Those living outside the city walls could enter it by day, but were then ushered out every evening. When General Roth heard of this injustice, giving the Joshua Corps the lead was an easy decision to make.

"You should wear your hat, sir," Lieutenant Karl Enkefort said, bringing his horse up alongside Christian's. "The one I gave you?"

Christian paused, then said in a near whisper, "It doesn't fit me, Lieutenant. And the damnable brim keeps falling down over my eyes. Might as well wear a blindfold."

The lieutenant struggled to hide a chuckle. "Yes, sir. My apologies. Perhaps we can find you one that's more befitting the shape of your head...sir."

Karl Enkefort was one of the veterans of the company. He had been a sergeant under Captain Tideman, but Christian had promoted him to lieutenant. He had a terribly dry wit, one that could easily run him afoul of his superiors, but his organizational skills were excellent. Right now, Christian needed all the help he could get on that score. Being a company commander was an honor, save for all the administrative work, day after day, hour after hour. Keeping up with the roll to ensure men were being paid properly and on time for their service; ensuring that each man received his daily ration of food; making sure that men did not recklessly waste ammunition firing haphazardly into the wood line along the march, for sport or game; keeping them from drinking excessively on the march and thus, getting into fights which, more often than not, saw them injured or dead; ensuring that they had adequate clothing and bedding... An endless stream of tedious details that gave Christian a headache. Thankfully, Lieutenant Enkefort was good at keeping it all under control.

"My head is perfectly shaped, Lieutenant, and far better looking now with my new eye patch. It's the hat that's the problem."

At Isaac's request, Nurse Devorah Bayer had fashioned Christian a new eye patch out of black silk. The strap lay a little tight across his forehead, but it stayed in place even during a rigorous march as they had just finished. His eye patch was too tight, his hat too loose.

What a way to start a campaign!

The road sloped down, and the sun dipped behind the distant hills. Christian dropped his hand with a deep sigh and a head shake and guided his horse back to the center of the road. "How are the men?"

Enkefort nodded. "Very good, sir." He shifted in his saddle and pointed to the rear. "We're strung out from here back to Neuneck's men at the head of supply."

Christian nodded and looked back to where the lieutenant was pointing, though the column was too long and the road too winding to see the supply train. "Any concern with the horses?"

"No, sir, not since those two you had to put down. Fatigue, of course, both with the men and their steeds. We pushed pretty hard, as you well know. Otherwise, we're in good condition. Be nice to bivouac soon, though, to give everyone a good rest."

Colonel Renz had organized the Second Cavalry Regiment into ten companies of roughly one hundred men each, plus supporting staff. Right now, Christian's company was a little understrength, with only about eighty viable soldiers, a mixture of both medium and light cavalry. Now that they had arrived in Kassa, Christian hoped that their personnel issues would be addressed and solved. There was always that hope.

The road curved sharply along a wooded hillside. Colonel Renz came into view, waiting with his staff on the edge of a steep escarpment, spyglass in hand and trained toward Kassa.

Christian's horse clopped through a fresh pile of dung. The smell annoyed him, which was surprising because, as Isaac might say, Christian's sense of smell should be "blind" to such offal at this point in his military career. He rubbed his nose vigorously. "Keep the men in line and moving forward, Lieutenant Enkefort," he said. "I need to speak with our regimental commander."

"Yes, sir." Enkefort saluted quickly, turned his horse away, and disappeared down the column.

Christian waited while Colonel Renz finished his survey of Kassa. The colonel then handed his spyglass to his aide-de-camp. He sighed and stretched, then said, "It's a beautiful city, no?"

To Christian, Kassa was no better or worse than any other city he had seen in Bohemia, Poland, or anywhere else.

In the distance, nestled against the hills that protected the rising sun, was a walled city atop its own bluff. Two walls, in fact, protected the citizens and the buildings therein. From his vantage point, Christian could see the steeple of a great cathedral, a castle, and other towers rising through a dying fog. Below the bluff and outside the walls were common homes, farms, and cropland in support of the city. A typical eastern European city in Christian's mind.

"Yes, sir," he said, "it's quite lovely."

"Thank our God we're here," Renz said. "Another few days, and we might have been in a bit of trouble."

"My company only lost two horses, sir."

"Did you salvage the meat?"

Christian nodded. "Yes, sir."

"Very good. Then I want you to keep your men moving, Captain. Per General von Mercy's orders, we're not to enter the city." He pointed to the Hernád River, which snaked its way along the edge of Kassa. "Bivouac your men on the east side of the river. Find a good spot, set camp, and sit tight."

"Yes, sir. Have we encountered any resistance up the column?" Christian asked.

Colonel Renz shook his head and chuckled. "None. General Roth said they folded like a cheap suit."

Christian furrowed his brow. "What does that mean?"

"Damned if I know. One of those up-time expressions." The colonel huffed. "They're going to kill the German language with all of their silly talk."

Christian wasn't so sure of that, but said nothing. During his time as a mercenary for the Sunrise, he had found many up-time sayings delightful and oftentimes much more expressive of the situation than the more brusque German expressions. Perhaps it was a matter of personal taste. Colonel Renz had an air of the aristocracy about him, though Christian had never been able to learn the colonel's background. The colonel could like or dislike up-time expressions all he wanted, so long as he was a good commander. So far, Colonel Renz was proving to be one.

"Sir, will I have an opportunity to acquire more horses for my company?" Christian asked, leaning forward in the saddle to catch the colonel's eye. "I'm understrength. I need twenty, twenty-five more men. I know that there are companies over strength. I'd like your permission to—"

"You know as well as I do, Captain," Colonel Renz said, "that mercenaries are very particular about whom they serve. Especially the cavalry. They pick a captain and stick with him. But, you have leave to try." He turned to his aide-de-camp. "Which of our companies are over budget?"

The aide-de-camp, a man not much older than Christian, pulled some papers from his leather satchel and reviewed them quickly. "Truckmuller, Mitzlaff, and Horst."

"Very well. Speak with them and see if they can accommodate your needs."

Behind them on the road, the army moved right along. Christian's company had just finished passing. Neuneck's cavalry were now moving into view, clopping through piles of dung and muddy sloshes of evening rain.

"Catch up with your company, Captain," Colonel Renz said. "Keep moving forward. And remember. Smile and greet with kindness the citizenry that come out of their homes to observe our march. As the commanding general orders, we're to be seen as liberators, not conquerors."

Christian nodded. "Yes, Colonel."

Chapter 15

Ennsegg Castle
Enns, Austria
Eight miles east of Linz

"It would appear, Halil, that your intelligence on the jeweler's immobility was incorrect," Murad IV said as he gathered with many of his lieutenants in war council.

Halil Pasha, who had come late to the meeting, bowed in sincere supplication. "I am sorry, My Sultan. I did not anticipate such a foolish and misguided move by—"

Murad put up his hand and closed his eyes to seek patience. But patience was what had put them in this dangerous situation. No more patience. "Do not speak to me unless I call upon you, my *learned* adviser. Stand there, for once, in silence, and listen."

The room was so quiet, Murad could hear birds chirping through the open window in the adjoining chamber. A light breeze flowed through the space, shuffling the edges of the battle map that Suleyman had laid out on the table before them. Quiet, peaceful, unlike the siege raging nearby.

"The Grand Army of the Sunrise is now in Kassa," Murad continued, pointing at a stone on the map, "near halfway to Transylvania. If the Jew turns his column east and moves quicker than *anticipated*"—he turned to glare at Halil Pasha—"he'll be in Gyulafehérvár within the month."

Semsi Ahmed, commander of the Gureba-i hava, the Ottoman air force, cleared his throat and begged to speak. "If I may, Sultan." His words were calm, careful. "We must entertain the possibility that the up-time general has abandoned his plan to prevent the Chmielnicki Pogrom and intends on joining his army with the United States of Europe. If so, then his goal may be Pressburg."

Murad nodded. "And your opinion, Suleyman?" he asked.

The commander of the Akinji nodded. "It is a possibility, My Sultan." He pointed at Pressburg on the map. "It is a little shorter in distance than the Transylvania capital. In the opposite direction, of course, but the ground near Pressburg is more palatable for an army like his, My Sultan, a mixture of mercenary cavalry, Bohemian Brethren, and untrained Jews."

"An army of Jews and mercenaries that handily defeated their most recent opponent," Murad interjected.

Suleyman nodded. "Yes, My Sultan, with the help of the USE and their Galician allies. This move to Kassa may well constitute another gathering of forces, this time with the USE specifically, with the intent of moving upon Pressburg. It makes sense militarily."

Murad paused and considered. It certainly did make sense. Too much sense, in fact, for Murad to just discount the notion, no matter how badly he wanted to. Still, it seemed very unlikely to him that Bohemia and Transylvania would go through such a public announcement of their alliance, and then leave Transylvania to die at the hands of Matei Basarab and Vasile Lupu. Why would the prince of Transylvania announce the alliance to the world, unless he had had assurances that the Grand Army of the Sunrise would move to assist? Could that up-time jeweler be so deceitful as to turn his back now on a promise that he most assuredly had made to George Rákóczi?

Of course he could. He was a merchant, a jeweler, an up-timer, and a Jew. How could he not be so?

And yet... *what to do, what to do...*

Through his confused thoughts, Murad heard his father Ahmed's voice clear and precise... *Follow your own counsel, Murad. Follow your instincts.*

"No," Murad said, "I do not believe that the jeweler intends on moving his army to Pressburg. His success has called thousands of Jews to his ranks—we know this for certain—with assurances to seek and find a promised land. That is not toward Pressburg;

that way lies death and desolation to all who have answered his call. No. He will turn his column toward Transylvania. There is no doubt in my mind of that. The question before us now is... when."

Murad turned to face Halil Pasha. The cowed advisor responded immediately by snapping to attention, his face showing great eagerness to again be in the good graces of his suzerain. "Yes, My Sultan."

"Have my vassals moved against Transylvania?"

Halil nodded. "I have received confirmation from Voivode Lupu, My Sultan. His army will be ready, within days, to move. The Moldavians may already be in the field."

"And Matei?"

Halil shook his head. "I have received no word from Voivode Basarab, My Sultan. But I would assume that he—"

"That is your weakness, Halil," Murad snapped. "You sometimes offer too much of your own opinion. Do not assume. Say you have heard nothing and leave it there."

Halil nodded. "Yes, My Sultan."

Murad returned to the map. He gently guided his fingers over Austria, Bohemia, and Transylvania. "The forces I ordered to ready: are they ready, and where are they coming from? Bec? If so, there will be little or no chance of us jumping their march, even if the Jew waits a week to move. We're out of position."

"Your forces are mustered and ready to move on your order," Suleyman said.

"From where?"

"Timişoara, My Sultan," Semsi Ahmed said.

Murad ran his hand down to a small dot in the Eyalet of Temesvár. He then ran his hand up to Transylvania. He smiled. "Whose idea was it to position them there?"

"Halil Pasha's, My Sultan," Semsi Ahmed said, seemingly eager to help their beleaguered advisor crawl out from under Murad's rock. "He thought it best to find a place closer to Wallachia, in case you—"

"Congratulations, Halil," Murad said, his mood improving, "you have finally made a decision worthy of praise."

A smattering of light laughter filled the room. Halil grinned ear to ear. His face reddened with relief. He bowed. "Thank you, My Sultan. I live to serve you."

Be still, Halil, I had no intention of punishing you for your misinformation. We're all at fault here for allowing the heretic to confuse us, to guide us onto paths we know better than to tread. Not anymore...

"What troops have you mustered?"

"Two regiments of sipahi," Suleyman said, placing a stone atop Timişoara. "One regiment of Akinji. One regiment of Janissaries. One sapper crew. Four katyusha rocket launchers. Three tanks, plus eight wagonloads of provisions, weapons, ammunition."

"These tanks," Murad said, "they are the new model, yes? What some are calling *Ifrits*?"

Suleyman bowed. "Yes, My Sultan. Gone is the main cannon, and in its place, a flamethrower capable of shooting fire up to sixty yards. A battering ram for siege work has also been installed to its front. It is a most capable machine."

"Will these *Ifrits* keep pace with our forces?" Murad asked.

"No, My Sultan," Suleyman said. "They will have to arrive later. Two weeks behind, at least."

Murad wondered whether it was wise to even bother sending them. They were slow, big, bulky. Perhaps it'd be wiser to add more Janissaries, more sipahi cavalry. But the Grand Army of the Sunrise was a "modern" army, with USE weaponry, and they would most certainly wield those weapons to great effect. Armored fire tanks, though slow, could make a difference.

Does the jeweler have airships? Planes? Perhaps his spies could give them reliable intelligence on that.

"No airships?" Murad asked, leaning back from the map to stretch his back.

Suleyman cast his eyes down. "No, My Sultan. We do not have any to spare. That is why we have instead mustered three tanks. We can, at least, try to overwhelm them on the ground. Although I will say, Voivode Lupu is begging for an airship, and is, in fact, offering to buy one outright. He is convinced that it is necessary, given the rumors that the Jew's army will have an air force of some kind."

Murad sighed, paused, rubbed his well-kept beard. "Give him the ship with the two kafirs."

"The *Chaldiran*, My Sultan?" Semsi Ahmed asked.

Murad nodded. "It can leave immediately."

"Yes, My Sultan."

Murad walked to the fireplace. He picked up the mace leaning against the rough stone hearth. He hefted it in his hand, and then stuck the tip of it into the flames and watched as the fire singed the metal, scorched the wood. He pulled it out and fixed his gaze upon the blackened spikes. He puckered his lips and blew embers away, feeling the heat of them on his mouth. He smiled. The day had begun badly. It was ending much, much better.

"Gentlemen," he said, turning to his commanders. "Move our forces immediately from Timișoara. Move them day and night if you must but get them into the fields of Transylvania quickly. And tell the world we are doing it. Double, triple the numbers you announce. Let us give the jeweler and his not-so-grand army a reason to keep his commitment to Prince Rákóczi.

"Tell the world that Murad marches to Transylvania."

Chapter 16

Breslau, capital of Lower Silesia province

"It'll take you forever to get there," Tata predicted.

"No, it won't," countered Gretchen. She continued her slow walk around the wagon train, inspecting both the mules and the wagons themselves. "It's less than three hundred and fifty miles from here to Kassa, and from here to Krakow—that's about half the distance—the roads are quite good. I figure we'll get there in two and a half weeks. Three, at the most."

Tata's expression was dubious. "That's assuming you don't encounter bad weather."

"It's June, remember? The temperature is pleasant this time of year in southern Poland."

"Yes, it is. But June is also the rainiest month of the year. Rain on dirt roads—you're not in Grantville or Magdeburg out here—means mud and mess."

Gretchen stopped and frowned down at her shorter friend. "Why are you so grumpy?"

"I want to go with you."

"Mud and mess, remember?"

"So what? There'll be plenty of mud and mess here in Breslau, too. But if I'm with you, I'm doing exciting stuff. Here, I'm just the governor. Have to deal with the messes made by people as well as rain."

Gretchen shook her head. "You have your ambitions standing on their head."

"So do you! Every chance you get, you shed your proper responsibilities to go charging off on another crusade. *You* were the chancellor of Saxony, remember? *You* were the Lady Protector of Silesia."

Gretchen took a deep, slow breath. There was...perhaps a grain of truth in that charge. A very tiny little grain, to be sure.

"For what it's worth, Tata, I wish you were going with me too," she said quietly. "You're wonderful to work with. But..."

She shrugged. "Such are the demands of the struggle. We *do* need to consolidate our position in Silesia—and on a sound republican basis. I can trust you to keep the nobility properly squelched."

"Ha! I'm the one who was a duke's concubine, remember? I'm sure my soul is still tainted and soiled by that sordid episode."

Gretchen chuckled. "Won't work, Tata. Eberhard was one of the famous Three Good Dukes—and almost everybody thinks you're the one who persuaded him on his deathbed to bequeath his duchy to the entire population. The modern Esther, they call you."

"That's pure nonsense and you know it. Eberhard came up with the idea all on his own once he knew he was dying."

"Legends take on a life of their own. Way it is. Get used to it. I've had to. And to get back to where we started, it will *not* take forever to get to Kassa, even going by wagons pulled by mules. It'll be faster and easier to go by horseback, but—"

Again, she shrugged. "The demands of the struggle, once again. I have *got* to have a good printing press, where I'm going and what I'll be doing. No way to carry that size machine on horseback."

Tata really was in a sour mood this morning. She immediately spotted another anxiety to gnaw at and widen. "You know how valuable that thing is? Word gets out—which it will, don't think it won't!—and every gang of robbers between here and Kassa will be waiting for you."

"Let's be more precise. You're saying they will be waiting for me and my escort of fifteen stouthearted CoC organizers and militants, armed with the finest rifles, not to mention..."

She drew a pistol out of a shoulder holster. "My trusty 9mm, with which I have gunned down more than a handful of miscreants. And some of the other women in the expedition are armed and know how to use guns, too."

She returned the weapon to its holster, swiveled a bit, and pointed to the third wagon in line. "And did I mention how much ammunition I'm taking with me? For all the guns, not just mine. That whole wagon and most of the one behind it is carrying nothing else—well, except for more rifles."

The gaze she now bestowed on Tata was serene. Almost—not quite—angelic, you might say.

The wagon master rode up at that moment. "Let's get moving, everyone! We just got word over the radio that the weather is good in Krakow—but you never know. Weather is treacherous. We could find ourselves in a downpour if we dawdle."

"See?" demanded Tata.

Kassa (Košice)
Joshua Corps encampment

The blisters on the young soldier's foot were fat with fluid. They covered his heel and toes. He had high arches—a small blessing— so he was suited for the infantry. He just wasn't ready for the long march between Krakow and Kassa.

"How many are like this?" Isaac asked the medic standing nearby.

"At least a quarter of the regiment, Herr Doctor, has reported blisters and foot discomfort of some degree," Tobias said, reaching into his satchel as directed for a needle and supplies. "Most are not as bad as this, but still, bad enough."

Isaac accepted the needle, a small container of rubbing alcohol, mustard poultice, and a cotton swab.

"Is it what the up-timers call 'trench foot'?" Tobias asked, kneeling beside Isaac to get a better look.

Isaac shook his head. "We're not dealing with that here... yet, anyway. That occurs when the feet are kept wet for long periods of time. This is simply the result of young men walking ten to twelve miles per day with minimal training, in less than adequate footwear. They aren't used to the rigors of the march."

The quality of a soldier was directly proportionate to the

quality of his feet, Isaac knew. Take away a soldier's ability to walk, and you take away his ability to fight. And it was clear that these men were not following the foot hygiene rules that he had written and distributed among the infantry. He'd have to speak with each company commander and remind them—once again, and perhaps more forcefully this time—to make their men follow the rules. Or, well, this is what happens: a third of the company potentially down due to bullae, sore ankles, and tendonitis.

I hope we stay in Kassa for a long, long while.

Isaac took the cotton swab, doused it with alcohol, then rubbed the tip of the needle with the swab to clean and disinfect. "You do this first," he said, holding the needle tightly between thumb and index. "Then you rub the blister with some alcohol—gently, like this—and then you make a small puncture in the blister."

He drove the needle tip into the blister until the swollen skin burst, and the cloudy fluid began to seep out. "Now, normally," he continued, "you would allow the fluid to leak out on its own. But we're not in a clinical setting. We're an army on active operations, currently under a light canopy of trees"—he looked up—"bivouacked next to a river, and it's threatening rain. So, you can use your fingers to gently push the fluid out to save some time. Be careful not to push too hard, lest you tear the skin around the puncture hole further and cause pain such that you get kicked in the teeth by your screaming patient."

"I would never kick a man," the young Ashkenazi soldier said, grinding his teeth and wiggling his sore foot under Isaac's applied pressure. "Never."

Wait to say that after your first taste of battle.

Isaac continued. He punctured two more blisters on the soldier's foot, repeating the same steps so that Tobias could remember the procedure clearly.

"Once all the blisters are drained," he said, "you're supposed to apply antibacterial ointment. But, we don't have any of that. So, just wipe off the excess drainage with a clean rag—and I mean clean, Tobias, *clean.* Then, apply a little of this mustard poultice to the loose skin of the drained bullae, and then wrap the foot with gauze, or a clean strip of cloth if that's the only thing available."

Isaac finished the procedure, tied off the gauze, and slapped the boy on the leg. "All set now, young man, but I want you off your feet for the rest of the day."

"We're supposed to drill in a few hours, Herr Doctor," the boy said.

Isaac shook his head. "No. You tell your company commander that Doctor Isaac Kohen says that you are in convalescence for twenty-four hours, starting now. If he has a problem with that, you tell him to talk to me. Understand?"

The young boy nodded and, despite his obvious concern about the trouble that he might get from his commanding officer, grinned happily. The boy knew as well as Isaac what twenty-four hours meant. Within twenty-four hours Shabbos, the Sabbath, would begin. Thus, twenty-four would become forty-eight, and that was more than enough time for his punctured blisters to begin to heal.

Isaac handed the needle and rubbing alcohol to Tobias. "You understand the procedure now? Good. Repeat it for all of these men." There were about twenty Ashkenazim sitting about, waiting for care. Isaac leaned in and whispered, "Be judicious in your applications, Tobias. You have a limited supply of alcohol, swabs, and poultice. Treat only the bullae, the big blisters. And maintain good hygiene. I can't stress that enough. And order them all to convalesce for a full day. Understand?"

Tobias nodded. "Yes, Herr Doctor."

"Very well, then," Isaac said, patting Tobias on the shoulder. "I'll be off."

"Where are you going?"

Tobias' question was answered by Len Tanner's booming voice echoing down the embankment and through the light wood. "Come on, Isaac. Time to go!"

Isaac looked up the rise toward the narrow road. Len's wagon, loaded with communications equipment, waited. Ellie Anderson sat beside her husband, waving Isaac forward. He waved back to acknowledge their request. "We're headed over to the cavalry."

Near the Hernád River
Second Cavalry Regiment encampment

Christian didn't realize how hungry he was until he walked through the regimental field kitchen and smelled all that delightful meat turning on the spits: squirrel and rabbit and chicken and fish, crisping and browning as grease dripped and sizzled in the embers. The horse meat from the two that he had had to put down on the march was being removed from barrels where it had been packed in salt. He had a good mind just to stop, sit himself down near one of those barrels, and eat the meat raw. He was that hungry. But first, his own horse needed love and attention.

He passed through the fog of succulent smells, refocused his mind, and stepped into the area of camp where several horses were currently being shoed. New shoes had been attached to his company's steeds all day long, and a farrier had offered to take care of Christian's horse. He'd refused. "Thank you, no. He's my horse. I'll shoe him myself."

Besides, Christian's father liked to say that his youngest son had come into the world grasping a hoof nipper. For his mother's sake, Christian hoped that wasn't true. But the von Jori's were the best blacksmiths and livery stable owners in Zurich. They owned quite a bit of property as well. Before he was five, Christian knew pretty much everything one needed to know about animal husbandry. The skills of a farrier had come easily to him, and he felt it was necessary for a soldier to shoe his own horse. In such a large regiment, it was logical to employ blacksmiths and farriers to do that work for the companies. He understood that. But *Captain* von Jori didn't have to follow the rules. Not all the time, anyway.

He weaved his way through the chaos of horses and farriers and found his horse tied to a post, waiting.

He was a strong, beautiful dark brown Hanoverian and Christian's fourth horse since he had left home. The first had died of infected sword wounds. The second had broken two of its legs tumbling down a muddy embankment on a foolish misstep. The third fell just recently in the battle against the Magnates. This fourth one was the best of the lot and given to him by the men in his company. Thus, it was the captain's duty to take care of it himself.

"*Hallo*, Alphonse," Christian said, running his hand across the horse's broad neck. He cooed gently and laid his head against its smooth shoulder, let his hands run along its side. He took a moment to listen to Alphonse's breathing and recalibrated his own breaths to match. "*Ich bin deiner nicht würdig, aber ich werde versuchen es zu sein.*"

"He's ready to shoe, Captain."

Christian nodded to the farrier holding the reins and got to work.

He started with a front hoof. He used a nail clincher to remove the nails from the old shoe. He then pried the shoe off the hoof. Then he used a nipper and knife to remove caked-on dirt, dung, and excess hoof wall and sole. He then used a rasp to smooth out the rough spots. The farrier in assistance then handed him a heated shoe so that Christian could set it against the hoof, let the hot iron leave its scorch marks to indicate placement, and then, if necessary, determine what additional cleaning, cutting, and shaping of the hoof was needed to form a better fit. This took three tries. He dipped the shoe in water to cool it, and then tacked it on carefully with gentle taps from a hammer. He finished by running the rasp across the shoe a half dozen times. Finished!

He repeated the steps three more times until Alphonse was standing tall and proud with four brand-new shoes.

"Excellent work, Captain," the farrier said. "He's ready for war."

Christian nodded and patted Alphonse's smooth shoulder. "So am I."

"I'm not."

The voice startled him, but he recognized it immediately.

Christian turned. "Ah, Doctor Kohen. What brings you to the cavalry? Your boss has already made his rounds. Checking us all for saddle sores."

Isaac nodded. "Yes, Herr Oberheuser had the easy job today. Saddle sores are nothing compared to the miles of ruined feet I've had to treat within the past few hours."

Christian wagged a finger. "That's because you've never ridden a horse. You say an infantryman's feet are essential? Well, a cavalryman's ass is the same. Try bouncing on blisters for hours and see how it feels."

Isaac chuckled. "I suppose you're right."

Christian turned to the farrier and said, "Will you please take this fine fellow to the regimental blacksmith and ask him to double-check my work? Also, if my saddle is ready, please pick it up. They were supposed to fix it with a new girth strap."

"Yes, sir."

Christian and Isaac stood together and watched the farrier guide Alphonse away.

"He's a fine horse."

"Thank you," Christian said. "Best I've had so far." He tugged at Isaac's sleeve. "Come, let's have a meal. My treat."

Isaac followed Christian toward the field kitchen, but begged off the food. "No, thank you, Christian. Given the day I've had, I'm in no mood to eat."

"Very well. You can watch me eat. And again, why are you here?"

"I caught a ride with Len and Ellie. They are distributing new radios to each regiment. At some point, they'll call all the company commanders together and give instructions on their proper use." He chuckled. "Try not to be too taken aback by Ellie's brusque, up-time language."

They entered the field kitchen, and Christian accepted a plate from a server. "Slap the meat high, Rolf," he said. "I could eat a whole goddamn horse."

He and the server shared a laugh. Isaac didn't seem to understand the joke. "You find it strange that we laugh about eating horses?" Christian asked.

Isaac shrugged as they found barrels to sit on near an open pit fire. "I just find it odd that you would eat the very animals you depend upon for your service to the army. For your life."

Christian took a bite of the rabbit carcass that the server had slapped on his plate. He chewed, swallowed, and said, "Normally, I admit, I would not eat horse meat." He lifted his plate to show it to Isaac. "I'm not eating it now, as you can see. But if there is no alternative—and on campaign, there often isn't—a cavalryman must make do. And I like to think of it as the horse's final service to its rider, its company. The meat that it provides in death may save the life of its rider and all the other riders that it has served with. I look at it as a blessing."

They sat there for a long moment in silence, as the kitchen and campgrounds bustled with activity. Men playing card and dice games; men talking, laughing, cursing; men trimming their beards and being fitted with new uniforms; men napping beneath trees; men in prayer. Somewhere beyond the tree line, at least a dozen of Christian's soldiers bathed in the Hernád. Others were checking their wheellocks, flintlocks, and ZB-2 Santees. Others were grooming their horses. Others sat reading.

The entirety of it warmed Christian's heart and filled him

with excitement. He loved the energy of the camp. It gave him strength.

Isaac didn't seem to agree.

"What troubles you today, my friend?" Christian asked, finishing off the rabbit and flinging the bones into the fire. "You said you had a bad day, but it feels like something more. What's wrong?"

Isaac sighed and scratched his head cap. He was wearing his yarmulke today. "It's not just about sore feet, Christian. I have this sinking feeling that we're going to strike tents soon. Listening to Len and Ellie talk on the way over just made it worse. The way they talk, it's like they think the same thing. But we aren't ready.

"Over a third of the Joshua Corps are suffering from poor feet and spine hygiene. When the body breaks down, my friend, infection comes to call. If we leave Kassa now, we'll lose men on the march. Men who, if they had just a few more weeks to recover, to train and to prepare, they'd be ready. I fear General Roth is going to order the army to move to Transylvania any day now. It's too soon."

"Some are saying that we aren't going there at all," Christian said, wiping his mouth on his sleeve. "Some are saying that we'll turn toward Pressburg."

Isaac huffed and shook his head. "I'd prefer it, to be honest, but I don't believe it for a moment. We're heading to the plateau, and what medical horrors await us there?"

Christian waited to see if Isaac was going to say anything else. When he didn't, Christian said with a smile, "Don't despair, my friend. It'll all work out. Remember what the Bible says: 'Many are the afflictions of the righteous, but the Lord delivers him out of them all.'"

Isaac perked up quickly, opened his eyes wide. "You know Psalms?"

Christian waved him off. "No, no. I'm no biblical scholar, Isaac. But my mother would read verses at night, sometimes over and over, in times of trouble. She thought I was sleeping beyond the thin wall of her and father's room. But I heard her read passages. Some of them I remember well."

Isaac's mood improved. "That's good to hear. Remember what I always say: For good health, you must nurture..."

"Body, mind, *and* spirit."

"Exactly." Isaac pointed to Christian's eye patch. "Mind if I have a look?"

Christian nodded and leaned over. "Certainly."

Isaac, slowly and carefully, pulled away the patch. "Looks good. The bruising is nearly all gone. No more swelling. How's the light sensitivity?"

"Tolerable. I can even move the eye around with no pain or discomfort at all."

"Excellent," Isaac said, fixing the patch back into place. "Then you have leave to decide whether to wear the patch or not. I officially release you, Christian von Jori, from my care. You may go forward with God."

Christian nodded. He felt a sudden rush of joy. He never expected Isaac to utter the discharge. Hearing it now was the best thing he had heard all day. "Thank you, Isaac. You have given me excellent care these past couple months. I am in your debt."

Isaac waved him off. "Never mind that, Captain. Let us pray to God that you never have to be in my care again."

"That is definitely worthy of prayer. Now, Herr Doctor, what can I do for you?"

Isaac straightened on his barrel, cleared his throat, smacked his lips as if he were thirsty, and said, "I think, Captain von Jori, that you can get me something to eat. What's on the menu?"

Christian smiled and winked. "Want to try a little horse?"

Isaac chuckled. "Sorry, but I'll have to try something else. Horse meat isn't kosher."

Beč, formerly known as Vienna
Capital of the new Ottoman province (eyalet) of Austria

Usan Hussein knew that his life was about to change dramatically when Hasan bin Evhad handed him a musket and a yataghan and ordered him to follow. They did not stop walking until they were outside the city and standing beneath the *Chaldiran*, tethered to the ground and ready to launch.

"What is this all about?" Hussein asked, his blood pressure rising, his ruined right eye pulsing beneath the patch with each beat of his heart. "Are we going somewhere?"

"I go nowhere," Evhad said. "But you are going south."

"Where? And why?"

"That is not for me to say. I serve and follow the Sultan as directed, and he has directed me to deliver you to the *Chaldiran*. That is all I'm permitted to do." Evhad motioned to the airship. "The captain of the *Chaldiran* will explain everything. Peace be upon you."

Hasan bin Evhad was gone, and Hussein stood there staring at the *Chaldiran* like a toy soldier with tiny weapons in hand.

Hussein felt both joy and trepidation. The fact that he was standing there, holding Janissary weapons, could only mean one thing: he was being permitted back into the corps. Yet, he was standing before an airship, and he knew very well that Sultan Murad liked using his airships as execution platforms. *Hasan bin Evhad says that I'm going south, but I could be pushed over the side on the way.*

He took a step back and considered turning and running. A rope ladder tossed over the side of the ship stopped him from making such a rash decision.

A man swung over the side of the ship and worked his way down the ladder. He dropped the last few feet, settled himself, and then turned in greeting.

He took Hussein in a hug and kissed both cheeks. "As-salamu alaykum, Usan Hussein."

"Waʻalaykumu s-salam," he said back, though it felt odd doing so because the man who had just greeted him warmly was not Muslim.

"It has been a long time, Moshe Mizrahi," Hussein said, trying to remain calm, courteous amid so much confusion, uncertainty. "It is my understanding that I am to be taken south to..."

"Timişoara," Moshe said, "and immediately. Mordechai and I have been ordered to deliver you there, where you will take command of a new Janissary regiment."

"Me?" Hussein could not believe what he was hearing. "Why me?"

Moshe chuckled, though he did not bother to explain what was so funny about the question. "The Sultan's army has expanded recently. The Janissary corps has been a part of that expansion. They need good officers. Even with your impairment and humiliation in defiance and defeat, your experience and skills are necessary at this time."

Hussein rubbed the patch over his right eye. He shrugged.

"Why am I not being given a command at the front line, near Linz?" He asked the question though he had a good idea what the answer might be. *I am an embarrassment. A one-eyed freak that the Sultan does not want—*

"I cannot answer that question, Hussein." Moshe motioned for them to take the ladder up to the waiting gondola. "But the Sultan is giving you a second chance, my friend. I would not look so earnestly toward divining his reasons. Take the second chance, and be content."

Hussein sighed, nodded, and walked to the ladder. He bow-slung his musket over his back, buckled his yataghan to his waist, and grabbed the rungs. Moshe helped him climb.

"What are we going to do in Timişoara?" Hussein asked as he centered himself on the ladder and began to climb. "Guard duty?" *Again?*

"No. We will not be staying there for long."

"Where are we going?" Hussein asked as he reached the top of the ladder and was helped into the gondola by Mordechai Pesach.

"Transylvania."

Hussein shook his head. "Why, in Allah's great name, are we going there?"

Chapter 17

Kassa (Košice)
Grand Army of the Sunrise headquarters

"It's utter hyperbole, General Roth," von Mercy said as he found his seat at the table in the burgomaster's home. "Murad will *not* be marching on Transylvania himself."

"That goes without saying," Morris said, shutting the door of the room behind him and finding his own chair. "But his hyperbole does reveal a truth: the Ottomans have finally committed forces to Wallachia's and Moldavia's assault against Prince Rákóczi. We weren't expecting anything less in the end, but I think Nasi, Rebecca, and Mike—and hell, even I—were hoping for a slightly different reaction."

"That they would interpret our move to Kassa as an impending attack on Pressburg."

Morris nodded. "Indeed. And thus give us time to sit here, strengthen, and then we could jump the march into Transylvania in force on our own timetable, while he balks at moving men off the front line for fear of an end around into Pressburg. That would have put us in the plateau long before he got there, and with weapons and numbers that they couldn't handle.

"But Murad's no fool," Morris said, sighing deeply and running his hand through his thinning, and quickly graying, hair. "The only reason he's been bested by the USE more often than not is that he hasn't yet fully adjusted his equipment and tactics to meet nearly four hundred years of up-time military history. But he's learning...he's learning."

Morris leaned back in his chair and stared at the burgomaster's ceiling. An artist had started crafting a depiction of Jesus rising through storm clouds, but it was only half finished, and quite honestly, looked creepy against the stark discoloration of the exposed wooden frame of the roof. Jesus was a fine figure for the burgomaster to choose for his own home, but at this moment, Morris wished he were staring into the face of Abraham instead. He needed the guidance of someone who had suffered a long journey into foreign lands.

The citizenry of Kassa had been most generous so far with the Sunrise's stay in their modest city. The burgomaster in particular, a small, portly fellow with an uneven beard, was all too willing to allow Morris and his staff to use his home for their war council. Morris figured that, from the mayor's perspective, it was either bend to Bohemia, the USE, or the Ottomans. The choice was apparently easy for him to make. So easy, in fact, that he had even suspended the law preventing Jews from entering the city at night.

The question before them now was: how long would they remain in Kassa? They had to fulfill their agreement with the prince of Transylvania. Morris was not about to be a Benedict Arnold. But Kassa was almost the perfect location for a more permanent HQ. There was even a nice, long strip of ground abutting the Hernád that would make for a world-class landing strip. The USE could enter the city in time and, indeed, make its move against Pressburg when and if it so desired.

"Has Francisco Nasi seen any movement of Ottoman forces from Vienna, Pressburg?" von Mercy asked. "Any troops being pulled from the line and potentially diverted to Transylvania?"

Morris shook his head. "No, none, save for one lone airship that our contacts said landed near Vienna and picked up one passenger."

"In which direction did it fly?"

"South, I think he said."

Von Mercy stroked his beard. The tip of his tongue darted between his thin lips as his jaw muscles worked overtime. "That passenger could be the one who will lead the Ottoman forces into Transylvania. He could be en route to meet his army."

"But where, General?" Morris asked, slapping his hand on the table. "Where? That's the fucking problem with these Turks. They have an unlimited supply of troops that they can run up from Egypt, from Serbia, from the Levant, a constant stream of fresh bodies. It'll never end, unless someone does an end around and hits Murad in his own rear. If he's pulling troops from the interior of his empire, they could be coming from anywhere."

"True," von Mercy said, "but there are only a few cities along the Serbian-Wallachian line that are practical jumping points for an invasion of Transylvania. I am no expert on the lay of the land, as it were, in that part of the world, General, but I have at least a working knowledge of it. And if Murad is pulling troops from that area, the good news is, they won't be elite. The bad news is, they may already be on the move."

"Which means *we* have to go *now*."

Von Mercy nodded. "Yes, General."

But of course, they couldn't. It was one thing to move them quickly from Krakow. The ball needed to start rolling on that. Now that they were in Kassa, it was highly impractical for them to strike the tents again so quickly and move into a fighting posture. Supply was still pending. Colonel Makovec's APCs were on the way, but still out another week or two. Reports from the medical team told of at least a third of the Joshua Corps suffering dehydration and poor foot care. Provost marshals had not been assigned to each regiment yet. There were still companies without adequate officers. There were just too many plates spinning right now, and no immediate indication as to when they would settle.

Von Mercy raised his finger. "May I make a suggestion, General?"

Morris nodded.

"Let me take an advance force into Transylvania. Let me go in first, while the rest of the army stays behind to convalesce and regroup. I can jump Murad's march and be in the plateau before he gets there. You can then follow me in within a few weeks once you're ready."

Morris straightened in his chair, folded his arms across his chest. He curled his brow. "Who would you take with you?"

Von Mercy shrugged. "Those forces ready to move now. Those that are not suffering as much trauma, both physically and supply-wise, as the rest of the army. First Regiment of the Joshua Corps, the men who fought against the Magnates. They're veterans. Colonel Renz's Second Cavalry; he's got a good mixture of both heavy and light horse; shock and reconnaissance. Two additional infantry companies gleaned from the rest of our foot mercenaries: a company or two of Brethren for sure. At least one battery, maybe two. And of course, any and all supply and medical staff as needed."

Morris rose from his chair and walked over to a closed window, which he could not, unfortunately, open. The glass was thin enough, however, for him to lean his ear toward it and listen to all the myriad camp sounds wafting up from the Hernád.

Hundreds, thousands of tiny fires lit the scattered wood around the river. He could hear horses whinny, men shouting, muskets sounding. Even in the dark of night, some of the men were training by lamplight. All bivouacs active, save for the Joshua Corps, for it was Shabbos. From their place along the river came muffled songs of prayer and tiny candlelight. Morris smiled and wished he were with them right now, amidst the flickering mass of humanity that seemed content in their camps. He could use a good prayer session.

Divide the army? A crazy notion. Such a tiny force against, in essence, three armies. Make the wrong move, and the entire endeavor would collapse. Then again, such bold action had worked well throughout military history. That, and the fact that the Sunrise had an abundance of up-time-inspired weaponry, which made his army fight at least a third, if not a whole half, more effectively than any down-time army in the world. Then again, adding Turks with similar up-time weaponry changed the calculus altogether.

"When can you leave, General?" Morris asked, returning to the table.

"Just give the order, sir, and I can have us on the march in four days."

Morris nodded. "Very well. Then I so order. Begin your preparations as soon as we are finished here. Now, let us discuss the details of your plan.

"Let's begin with supply and medical staff." Morris reached over the table and grabbed a pen and pad of paper. "I know exactly the man I want to assign as your personal surgeon."

Isaac ran straight into Rabbi Gotkin as he hurried to his meeting with General Roth.

"Careful, Isaac," Jason said, catching him before they collided. "Where are you going in such a rush?"

"Apologies, Jason. I'm in a hurry. General Roth has called me to a meeting."

"Indeed. What for, if I may ask?"

Isaac shook his head. "I do not know, but I am late."

Jason let him go. "Very well, then. I'll speak to you later. *Zikher travalz.*"

Isaac nodded, straightened his yarmulke, and continued.

He was rushing from the Joshua Corps campsite, wherein he had delivered a baby from one of the wives who had followed her husband from Krakow to Kassa in the supply train. It had been a successful, but difficult, birth. The mother was sleeping soundly now with a spoonful of sedative while being cared for by Nurse Devorah.

Isaac entered the burgomaster's home and knocked gently on the door to the war room.

"Come in!"

Isaac opened the door. Inside the room, Morris and Doctor Oberheuser seemed to be wrapping up a heated conversation. "Hello, General Roth, Doctor Oberheuser. Am I intruding?"

"No," Morris said, waving him forward. "Come in, please. The good doctor and I are just finishing." Morris picked up some papers from the table, tapped them to straighten them out, then said, "That'll be all for now, Doctor. I'll send for you later, and we'll discuss further details."

Doctor Oberheuser nodded and turned toward the door. Before leaving, he placed his big, calloused hand on Isaac's shoulder and flashed a quick smile—or, as close to one as the grumpy old coot was capable of flashing. "*Viel Glük*, Herr Doctor. You will need it."

They were now alone, the first time since Morris had returned from Prague. Anxiety rose in Isaac's chest. Being alone with the commanding general meant only—well, it could mean a lot of things. He might just want to talk, catch up on old times. He might want to know the medical status of the army, an update on the status of supply. Or it might mean—

"How goes the Joshua Corps?" Morris asked, shuffling documents and placing them in a manila folder. He sat and motioned for Isaac to do the same. "What's its medical status?"

"Tenuous, General," Isaac said, seeing no reason to lie or shade the truth. Morris didn't seem to like that sort of thing from his staff anyway. "Men—boys really—who have never walked, much less marched, so much in their lives, suddenly asked to hoof it over a hundred miles, and on the quick step. It stands to reason that their bodies would break down somewhat, even as young as they are. It's a manageable situation, though. They just need time."

Morris nodded. "An up-time poet once said: 'Time is the fire in which we burn.' A little gloomy, even cynical, I grant you, but nonetheless, accurate. There never seems to be enough time for anything."

Morris motioned to Isaac's soiled hands. He had tried to clean up as quickly as possible, but there were still residual traces of blood on his palms. "A surgery?"

"No, General. A birth."

Morris smiled. "Successful?"

"Yes."

"A boy?"

"Yes."

"Mazel Tov!"

"Indeed. The father asked me to ask you if you might honor them by attending the bris."

Morris considered. "Yes, I might be able to, although it'll depend upon how the next few days go."

He said that last part almost under his breath, as if he were afraid that someone might hear it, but before the general had a chance to speak further or explain his comment, Isaac blurted, "I wanted to thank you, General, for a long time. For sending me to medical school in Grantville, Magdeburg—"

"It's your Aunt Eva who sent you, young man," Morris said. "She saw in you that spark. I just paid your way. And call me Morris."

"Very well. Nevertheless, Morris, I wanted to thank you. It changed my life."

The general seemed to blush, embarrassed, perhaps, at being the object of so much focused appreciation. Isaac could see that Morris was happy with the praise, but so overwhelmed with the tedium of command.

"Thank you, Isaac. You have paid me and the Sunrise back many times over these past few, and critical, months. Your debt has been paid in spades. Now," he said, again focusing his attention, "let us come to the reason you are here.

"I have spoken with Doctor Oberheuser, and I've decided to make some adjustments with the medical staff." Morris sighed deeply, ran his fingers through his hair, and again, seemed hesitant to continue. "Simply put: I'm sending General von Mercy and an advance force from the Sunrise into Transylvania, ahead of the full army. It's going to happen soon. I want you to be his personal surgeon and serve as chief medical officer of said advance force."

Isaac felt honor first, then anger. "Sir, Oberheuser hates me. He has it in for me. He wants me to go to get me out of—"

"Actually," Morris said, raising his hand, "just the opposite is true. He disagrees with my decision. He thinks you aren't ready to be a chief medical officer. He insisted that I send him."

"And he's right." Isaac felt his heart pounding. "I'm not ready. Sure, I can poke blisters, wrap wounds, treat infections, do stitchings, remove limbs, but he's far better at the more detailed work and—"

"On the contrary," Morris said, again interrupting. "I've been told that you have an excellent eye for the details. And you are far cooler under pressure than he is. Now *that*, you cannot deny."

Isaac chuckled, nodded. "I can agree with you there, Morris. But honestly, I don't believe that I'm qualified at this time to be General von Mercy's surgeon. A man with that responsibility needs to be more senior, have more field experience, than me."

"I need you to do this."

"Why?"

"Because we're sending the First Regiment of the Joshua Corps in with him. The first are the Ashkenazi elite. They're tested and ready, having fought against the magnates. They're the best we've got. But they are going to be far, far from home, in a foreign country with wolves everywhere. I want them to know that they have a person on the medical staff who represents them. I want to give them at least that much comfort. And that, you will agree with me also, is *not* Karl Oberheuser."

Isaac pondered the situation. This certainly was not what he had expected when summoned. He wasn't sure what to expect, but this? "What other regiments, companies, will be part of this advance force, sir?"

"A few companies from the Zizka Brigade," Morris said, "a cannon battery or two, the Second Cavalry Regiment, support staff, men and materiel as needed."

Christian's regiment.

Isaac nodded. "My medical staff will not have to be as large as it is to accommodate the entire Sunrise, of course, but still substantial. Do I have permission to choose my nurses and medics?"

Morris nodded. "Yes. I've asked Oberheuser to work with you to determine those choices." He smiled. "But don't take away all of his good people, Isaac. He has the rest of the Sunrise to treat with."

Devorah Bayer would be his capital demand. If Oberheuser rejected every one of his other choices, she alone, at least, must go with them. And he wouldn't mind plucking Tobias away from Second Regiment of the Joshua Corps. Young Greta? Well, perhaps she'd stay behind.

Isaac cleared his throat. His heart began to beat normally, the initial shock of the assignment beginning to dissipate. "I assume that you will also be assigning a rabbi? If you haven't made a decision on that yet, Morris, may I recommend Jason? Spiritual health is just as important as physical health."

"That is a good idea," Morris said. "I will speak with him."

Isaac paused again and gave his mind time to absorb what had just happened.

Being the chief surgeon of a field general was a big deal, especially for one as elite as Franz von Mercy. Despite his apprehension, it was a great honor, and it was what he wanted, right? To be recognized as a "chief" medical officer, not just an assistant with a few meager authorities given to him by the forced generosity of a grumpy old German surgeon who might well be a borderline anti-Semite. To be in command of a medical staff, to be respected, to practice medicine in God's name, as Isaac knew he needed to do on that deadly bridge years ago in Prague. What more could he have asked for?

And yet . . .

"Thank you, Morris," Isaac said, pushing his anxiety deep. "You honor me. I accept the position. When will we depart?"

"In seventy-two hours. But I want you to have your medical staff and supply needs assessed within a day and resolved. I know, I know. It's a ridiculous request, but I wasn't kidding when I said time is the fire in which we burn. We are up against the clock here. We must stay ahead of the flames."

Isaac's anxiety increased tenfold. He felt it in his chest, his head, on his face. He stood quickly. "Very well. Then if you will permit me, Morris, I must speak with Doctor Oberheuser, then General von Mercy, then—"

"Yes, yes, you must do all of that." Morris stood and moved around the table to stand beside Isaac. "But there is one important thing we must do first." He turned to the door. "Jason! Come on in!"

Jason Gotkin entered quietly, carrying three candles and two *tallis* prayer shawls draped over one arm.

"What's... going on?" Isaac asked.

"We, my good friend," Jason said, laying the candles on the table and handing a shawl to each of them, "are going to participate in Shabbos."

"You see, Isaac," Morris said, accepting the shawl and placing it over his head and shoulders. "As the commanding general, I rarely get an opportunity to do something like this. But we are about to go our separate ways, and it may be a while before I get an opportunity to see you both again. I want to take a moment—just a moment—to pray with you both before we say our goodbyes."

Isaac gave Jason a stern expression. "I just ran into you a moment ago and told you I was going to see Morris, and you said nothing about this?"

Jason shrugged. "It is not my place to reveal the decisions of the commanding general. We needed to make sure you were going to be okay with the decision. Now that you are, we should pray."

"So, you're coming with us?" Isaac asked.

"Of course I am."

Isaac placed the shawl over his head. Tears welled in his eyes as he remembered what Rabbi Gotkin had told him when they had met in the Ashkenazi camp at Kazimierz: *Be a proud Jew.*

He had never felt such pride in being Jewish as he did right now.

As they lit their candles together and stood side by side, basking in the warm glow of the flame, *Rabbi* Gotkin began to pray:

> *"Barukh ata Adonai Eloheinu, Melekh ha'olam,*
> *asher kid'shanu b'mitzvotav v'tzivanu l'hadlik ner*
> *shel Shabbat..."*

Chapter 18

Kassa (Košice)
Grand Army of the Sunrise headquarters

"How soon do you figure you'll get there, Morris?" Jeff straightened up from the map spread over a table in Morris Roth's headquarters. He resisted the temptation to take off his hat and wipe his brow with a sleeve of his tunic. That just didn't suit the necessary dignity of a general officer.

He wished he could, though. It was a hot day in June, and the concept of "air-conditioning" in seventeenth-century central Europe—anywhere in the world, outside of Grantville—came down to "open a window." Except they couldn't, because Morris had set up his headquarters in a room that had only three small windows, none of which could be opened because the architect had apparently designed the structure several centuries earlier.

"Hard to say," was the reply. Morris, showing a lack of respect for the dignity of office that was shocking in a man of his exalted rank, took off his own hat and wiped his brow with a handkerchief he drew out of a back pocket.

Jeff bowed to reality. "Where'd you get the handkerchief?"

Morris smiled. "Judith gave me a bundle of them when I left Prague. Remind me after the meeting's over and I'll give you a few. 'AC' in this day and age is pronounced 'are you kidding me?' To get back to the point, it's really hard to say. The straight-line distance from Kassa to Szatmár is about one hundred miles, as near as I can figure. But the route we'll have to take to get there will be quite a bit longer than that. Von Mercy's advance party should be able to get there within ten days or so, but the rest of the Sunrise..."

He paused, his lips pursed. "Being honest, I don't see where we'll get there before the middle of July."

Jeff grunted. "Which is about the same time as I can get there with the Hangman Regiment."

Morris frowned. "I thought you'd disbanded that altogether, when you formed the Silesian Guard."

"Officially, we did. But there are three regiments in the guard, which is roughly the size of a brigade. Hangman veterans are scattered across all three of them, but two-thirds or so wound up in the First Regiment. So, guess what they call it, and who cares what the official name is?"

Morris chuckled. "And I take it they're your premier regiment."

"By at least half a country mile. Mind you, the other two regiments are coming along nicely, but they just don't have the same depth of experience. That's why I'm bringing the First Regiment here by way of an advance unit. For them, 'forced march' means something."

"How long will it take you to get the rest of the guard here? And who's in command of that? Krenz?"

"Yes. As far as how long... Figure they'll reach Kassa by the end of July at the earliest. But it's more likely they won't get here before the second week of August."

Roth frowned. Jeff shook his head. "Be realistic, Morris. It's more than three hundred miles from Krakow to Kassa."

"Yes, I know. I figure it at three hundred and thirty."

"We got no motorized transport, and it wouldn't do us much good if we did because the roads in this part of Europe start with 'they suck' and go downhill from there. Plus, most of the guard is infantry. If we can go three hundred and thirty miles in less than two months, we're doing okay."

The commander of the Grand Army of the Sunrise glowered at the map. "So much for blitzkrieg."

Jeff laughed. "Hell, that 'blitzkrieg' stuff was bullshit even in the Second World War. Most of the German army moved by foot or horseback, no different from the Roman army two thousand years earlier. They just never showed that in the movies."

He leaned over the map again and tapped his finger on the spot marked "Satu Mare." The map Morris was using was an up-time road map of Romania, and that was the modern name for the town. Almost all the names on the map were different from the ones being used in the year 1637. In the here and now, Hungarian place names still predominated. Košice was Kassa, Satu Mare was Szatmár, Baia Mare was Nagybánya, and the large provincial city of Cluj was Kolozsvár. The capital of Transylvania, which on the map bore the Latin name of Alba Iulia, still went by the name Gyulafehérvár—at least for people of Hungarian origin. For the Saxons, as Germans were called, the city was Weyssenburg; those of Ruthenian extraction called it Bilhorod; and there were still some folk who used the original Slavic name of Bălgrad.

"Is there a place for an airfield here?" he asked.

Morris nodded. "I would think so. The descriptions I've gotten say that is just on the edge of where elevations begin to ascend to the Transylvanian plateau. The town itself is on a lowland plain created by the Szamos, which is a pretty good-sized river."

"So we should be okay—at least, as long as the ground isn't too waterlogged." Jeff straightened back up. "That would help. The one little piece of 'blitzkrieg' we can lay claim to is that we've got an air force."

"Of sorts," said Morris, sounding a bit grumpy.

Jeff smiled. "I grant you, the Dauntless I flew on to get here—much less a Dvorak—isn't up to the dive-bombing standards of a Stuka. But it's more than what the OpForce has. For them, 'aviation' means carrier pigeons."

In a field outside Timișoara

The *Chaldiran* descended through low clouds and into a field where Usan Hussein's Janissary orta awaited. The airship flew over the full length of the orta, and Hussein's heart filled with pride as he surveyed the perfect rows of white, long-tailed bork hats atop the heads of a thousand men. Their bright red tunics fluttered in the breeze created by the airship rushing overhead. New muskets rested on their shoulders. Their cloth belts held their powder horns and yataghan swords. Many also possessed khanjar daggers. They were ready, and they were waiting for their *corbaci*.

Waiting for me . . .

Not so long ago, he had been saving night soil women from

the privations of his own men. Now he was at the head of a Janissary orta, a regiment. What more could he have asked for from Sultan Murad? From Allah? He had been given a second chance, and he wasn't going to waste it.

"Remember your orders, Usan," Moshe Mizrahi said as the *Chaldiran* slowed and touched down on a small spot of barren field. "Your orta is to accompany the army into Wallachia and there, you are to serve Voivode Basarab as the hammer of his infantry corps. You are to serve as his liaison to the Sultan, as his—"

"I understand my duty to the Sultan, Moshe," Hussein said as he put his left leg over the lip of the gondola and stepped out. "The Sultan wishes to keep eyes upon Voivode Basarab to ensure his fealty, his loyalty. Do not worry. It shall be done."

Moshe gave a curt bow. "Then I bid you farewell and safe travels, Usan. Mordechai and I shall be off."

"Wait!" Hussein said, adjusting his own uniform. "You are not coming with us?"

Moshe pointed to the horizon. "We're moving on to Moldavia in haste. Voivode Lupu has specifically requested this airship. He is paying in full for our usage."

Hussein knew exactly what usage that would be. "Then go with Allah," he said, bidding them a final farewell. "My orta awaits."

He walked slowly toward his men, trying to exude a confidence that he knew they expected from their commander. They were even more resplendent now that he was on the ground with them. Their ranks were deep and disappeared from his view as he grew closer. They were absolutely beautiful, and he adored them already.

But they were not frontline Janissaries, despite their new clothing. Moshe had reminded Hussein of that often on their trip, as if he were trying to insult him, as if Sultan Murad himself had wanted it hammered into his head. The men before him comprised a new orta. They were *jemaat*, frontier troops, eager and willing, but young. And Hussein would have to beat them into shape on the way.

As he approached, the field swelled with the rest of the force marching to Transylvania. Akinji and conscript infantry formed round the Janissary. Scores and scores of sipahi roared across the field, more cavalry in one place than Hussein had ever seen in his life. And far behind his ranks, he saw the billows of smoke and fire produced by the Sultan's war wagons—"tanks," they were calling them now. Sappers and katyusha rocket launchers, and a long, long line of supply. The field shook as the Sultan's army coalesced around his men.

Am I to lead this entire army? A foolish notion for sure. How could he possibly even imagine that he would be given such an honor after being told repeatedly, by a kafir no less, that he was only worthy of leading conscripts? No. Usan Hussein was not the commander of the entire force. But he was *corbaci*, and it was clear that his men would, at least, lead the army out of this field.

He inspected the entire first rank, accepted each of their muskets in turn. Clean and in full working order. They were each well-equipped with a bag of Murad mini-balls, their powder horns full, swords and daggers sharp and ready. Within an hour of the march, their red uniforms would darken with sweat, he knew, and some would remove their borks for a bit of fresh air, loosen their tunics and perhaps even remove them. He would let them for now, until he had a better sense of who these men were and what they were capable of. But eventually, discipline would have to be administered, and harshly, if necessary. For Usan Hussein knew that somewhere beyond this field, beyond the hazy horizon, high hills, and dense forests, many of these men would see their last day. And on that day, he wanted them all to greet Allah wearing proudly their uniforms, a bloody sword in one hand, and the bleeding head of a heretic in the other.

Usan Hussein drew his sword, turned on his heels. He waited until the entire army was in place. Then he raised his sword to the powerful beating of drums, shouted, *"Transilvanya'ya doğru!"* and led his janissaries out of the field.

Kassa (Košice)
Grand Army of the Sunrise communications tent

New radios had been distributed to the cavalry and to two regiments of the Joshua Corps. Training had gone well, and yesterday's test with the new frequencies had gone, what Ellie might call, "reasonably well." Only three of the radio controllers in the field (and all from infantry units) had fucked up their frequency switches and acknowledgement protocols. But by the end of the third trial, everything was running smoothly. Ellie was feeling good.

Then her husband walked into the tent and ruined the whole damned day.

"What's Morris want now?" she asked. "More radios smuggled out of Prague? Maybe he can get his budding air force to drop them by parachute into—"

"No, Ellie," Len said, removing his coat and hat and placing them on a wooden chair they had sequestered from the burgomaster's home. "We're on to Transylvania."

"I know," she said, flicking off her radio to ensure no one could eavesdrop. It was unlikely, but better safe than sorry. Spooks in the wire, and all that. "We've known that all along."

Len shook his head. "No, you don't understand. We're going... tonight."

Ellie stood. "What are you talking about?"

"Morris is sending von Mercy in with an advance force right now."

Len gave her all the details he knew, then finished with the bad news. "One of us must go in with them. Von Mercy needs a good radio op so that he can keep contact with Morris until such a time as the entire army can follow."

Ellie felt her heart sink. "Only one of us? Who?"

Len shrugged and walked to her. He held out his hands. She took them. "We have to decide."

"Why that sorry-ass, lousy son of a—"

"Ellie," Len interrupted, "come on now. We've no time for that. We've got to decide right now. In three hours, they're gone."

Ellie pulled him close and stifled her tears. She hadn't been apart from Len for more than a day since they had moved to Prague. And now, they were being asked to decide who would go into a completely foreign and unknown part of the world. Bohemia and Germany were like her backyard. She understood those countries well. But Transylvania? Skirted by a mountain range that, for lack of a better definition, scared the shit out of her. How effective would radio communication be in the rises and dips of all those Carpathian gaps and valleys? Just how far would they be able to transmit a signal? Not only that, but Transylvania was a land of vampires! Isn't that what all the up-time stories said?

"I'll go," she said, pulling him closer and pushing her face into his sweaty shirt.

Len cleared his throat. "I was thinking we'd toss a coin to decide."

She pulled back. "What?"

"Ellie, you can't just say, 'I'll go,' and that's that. That puts all the burden on you. No. We need to share the risk. Fifty-fifty. We flip a coin, and let it decide."

Len was willing to allow a thaler to decide their fate. *What kind of fucking man is my husband?*

"But you need to stay behind to keep Morris company," she said, pulling away and wiping her face. "Play chess with him."

"He didn't bring a board. Neither did I."

"What kind of goddamned man are you, who doesn't bring his chess board?"

"Enough, Ellie, enough!" Len said, anger rising in his voice. "Stop busting my balls. I don't like this anymore than you do, but we made a commitment to Morris and to . . . whatever it is he's doing here. And let's be perfectly honest: with the money he's paying us, once all this is over, we can retire back to Prague or wherever we choose, and never work another day of our lives. Let's make this decision now so that we have some time together before saying goodbye."

Her heart said no; her mind knew better. She turned away to collect her emotions. She didn't like this one bit, but at the end of the day, it was probably the best method. They were both equally qualified to serve von Mercy as his chief radio operator. One had to go; one had to stay behind.

She turned back to Len. "Okay, buster. Flip your damn coin."

Len fished a thaler out of his pants pocket. He showed her one side. "Heads." He showed her the other. "Tails. You call it."

Ellie breathed deeply, held it, exhaled, and said, "Heads."

Len flipped the coin. They both took a step back and let it turn and turn as Len had thrown it up farther than she had expected. It seemed to never stop turning and ascending. Then it peaked and began to fall. Another lifetime flashed before her, and she squeezed her eyes shut. The coin hit the ground, and both of them moved to see the result.

They looked at each other at the same time and said the exact same thing.

"Fuck!"

Chapter 19

Kassa (Košice)
Medical encampment

Isaac felt the table quake beneath him. He jerked his head up and heard Rabbi Gotkin's anxious voice. "Wake up, Isaac. Wake up. Time to go!"

"Where—" Falling asleep in a chair, with one's head resting on medical supply sheets, was not ideal. But in truth, it had been one of the most gratifying sleeps Isaac had gotten since he had spoken to and prayed with Morris and Jason.

He rubbed his face, shook his head. "What?"

"We're leaving," Jason said, "for Transylvania. Right now."

Isaac rubbed his face again and stood. "What are you talking about?" He reflexively looked at his wrist like he had seen up-timers do in Grantville and Magdeburg many times; sometimes checking a watch that was there, sometimes not. Isaac didn't have a watch. "We're not supposed to leave in another day, two days? What's going on?"

"We're getting the jump on Murad," Jason said, opening the flap of the tent and pointing outside. "Or so that's what I've been told. Move and countermove. All a game of chess. Let's go!"

Fighting grogginess, Isaac grabbed his white coat and stethoscope, put the coat on, wrapped the stethoscope around his neck, and stepped out.

The encampment was stirring. Men moved quickly everywhere. Isaac could hear officers shouting orders in the distance. Horses were moving. Columns were moving. Doctor Oberheuser waited.

"You got everything you need, bo—Doctor?" He asked, nearly stumbling into old habits. "You ready to go?"

Isaac breathed deeply, nodded. "Yes. Ahh"—he scratched his head—"four wagons of supplies."

"Got enough canvas for a med tent?"

"Yes. That's in the fourth wagon. PPE, suture material, poultices, scalpels, tweezers, drills, saws, three pressure cookers. Iodine—what little there is—bandages, some gauze. Needles. I'm set on supply. My staff requests?"

The old doctor handed him a clipboard. "Approved. I removed one nurse and one field medic. I need them here with me. Now, get the rest ready to go." He put his hand on Isaac's shoulder. "Do your duty. Do it well. Don't embarrass me. Good luck."

Doctor Oberheuser stepped away. "Thank you, Doctor," Isaac said as he looked at the roster. "I'll do my best."

The names were *good, good, good...damn!*

Nope, never, nada!

He cursed, slapped the clipboard across his thigh, and walked, through dim lantern and moonlight, across the field to the nurses' tent.

Devorah was waiting there at the flap. "I'm sorry, Isaac. I tried to get the old man to let me go, but—"

"Forget what he wants," Isaac said. "You're coming with me."

"But—"

He leaned into her and whispered, "Shhh...do as I say. Get your personals and go to the tent wagon. Quickly, now."

A mischievous smile spread across her face. She winked. "Ja, Herr Doctor."

Isaac spent the next thirty minutes making sure his staff was up and ready to go. He instructed them to collect all their personal belongings, including any personal medical equipment, and then meet him at the wagons.

Doctor Oberheuser had also rejected his request for young Tobias, but Isaac could live with that. The young medic was inquisitive and a quick study, indeed, but there were other medics accepted who were just as studious. His medical staff could manage without Tobias. Not without Devorah.

He met her at the tent wagon. He pulled up some canvas. "Climb up under here and keep quiet. I don't know if *Herr Doctor* will be around again, but we'll play it safe."

Devorah gave him a gentle kiss on the cheek. "Bless you, Isaac. There is no other doctor I wish to serve but you."

"Thank you, Devorah," he said, feeling the warm rush of blood to his face. "Now, get in and keep quiet."

Isaac laid the canvas over her gently and then proceeded with his inspection.

All four wagons were fully loaded and ready to go. The horses and driver for each wagon were set and waiting. His staff arrived piecemeal, and as they did, he marked their names off the roster and then had them climb in and find a seat in the wagons wherever possible. He wanted staff spread across all four wagons, so that they could keep an eye on the contents therein. Three of the four wagons were covered, so that was good. It would not do to have medical supplies and equipment getting damaged and soiled by rain and whatever else they might encounter. The fourth wagon, the one he would ride to ensure Devorah's continued safety, was not covered, but the entire bed was heaped with canvas and poles and rope and everything needed to construct a good, sturdy medical tent once they got to Transylvania.

Rabbi Gotkin and the rest of the chaplain corps moved their wagons into place behind the fourth wagon. Behind them would come the rest of the baggage train; not as long as the one that had pulled out of Krakow, but long enough: a sizable detachment of the Sunrise was moving out.

Isaac climbed into the seat next to the Brethren teamster, got as comfortable as possible, and waited for the signal to move to be trumpeted.

Len Tanner and a wagonload of communications equipment passed by on the left. Isaac gave a small nod and wave. Len tipped his hat. Men from the First Regiment of the Joshua Corps moved by in column, singing a Yiddish song about strife and war. They all wore their yarmulkes.

Isaac fished into his coat pocket, pulled his cap out and fastened it to his hair.

Be a proud Jew.

General Mercy and his sizable staff passed on horseback. Then came Colonel Renz's Second Cavalry Regiment.

Callenberk's company of heavy cavalry, mostly dragoons, followed Kinsky's "Wild Elite" to the front of the column. Truckmuller and Horst followed them, line after line after line of horses making the ground shake. Their collective rumble drowned out any other sounds that Isaac might hear in a roused camp. All he could see and hear was a wave of brown, gray, white, black, and rust-colored horses, on and on and on as they passed by. The light cavalry was to protect the baggage train and serve as flankers. There was no anticipation of meeting any serious resistance on their march to Transylvania, but General Mercy was not about to have his column interrupted by any unforeseen foe, Ottoman or otherwise. They would be moving through the narrow defile between two hostile entities: the magnates on one side and potentially the Ottomans on the other, assuming that Murad would move so far northeast to catch them unawares. If the supply train was hit before they arrived in Transylvania, the entire operation might be slowed, or come to a halt altogether.

Isaac waited until the rush of cavalry subsided. He turned his head up toward the moonlight, caught the strong whiff of horse hide and dung, torn up ground, and heavy dust. The dust settled and Christian von Jori appeared.

Sitting atop his beautiful dark brown Hanoverian, Christian was not dressed in full battle garb. This was a march, not a fight. He wore a light tan shirt loosely collected at his waist with a small leather belt. He wore thick canvas leggings and spurs, and riding gloves. He also wore a hat, though Isaac remembered Christian complaining about its fit. Was it new? Hard to tell in the faint light and with his horse caught up in the energy of the moment. It was all Christian could do to keep the beast from sprinting off. But he held the reins tightly and maneuvered his control back and forth to keep the horse as still as possible.

"Isn't it glorious, Isaac?" Christian asked, his voice high and louder than normal. "We're off to war."

"Yes, yes, very glorious," Isaac answered lazily. "But it's too early for all this. In the middle of the night? Couldn't they let us sleep a while longer?"

Christian laughed. "We're going to beat that son of a bitch to Transylvania, and he'll wish he'd stayed in Lenz."

Isaac nodded, realizing that his pessimism, his overly cautious "all business and no play" attitude would not serve him now. Like the horse, Christian's blood was running hot, his excitement, his emotions pulling on the slips. Isaac liked seeing the captain so excited, so driven in the moment. It was a far cry better than when they had first met in the tent months ago when Christian seemed on the verge of deep depression.

Isaac couldn't help himself. "How's your eye?"

Christian seemed to have forgotten the eye patch still in place over his face. He reached up, took off his hat, and then pulled the patch off. "It's perfect, Herr Doctor. I don't need this anymore."

He handed it over. Isaac paused and then reluctantly accepted it. He tucked it into his coat pocket. "How far can you see?"

Christian shrugged. "Far enough to slash a Janissary in two." He thumbed toward the saber at his belt.

Isaac nodded and spared a slight smile. "Let us hope it never comes to that."

A trumpet sounded far up the column. It was time to go.

"I'm glad you're coming with us, Isaac," Christian said. "They tell me you're a good doctor."

Isaac chuckled. "So I've been told."

Christian turned his horse up the column. "See you on the march."

Isaac saluted quickly. "Be safe, Captain, and go with God."

Christian spurred his horse, and he was gone.

They waited another ten minutes before the mass of men, horses, and wagons began to move in front of them. The teamster sitting beside Isaac called to the horses by name, snapped his reins, and the wagon rolled forward.

Part Four

July 1637

Low and muffled, like an angry bull
—Sophocles, *Ajax*

Chapter 20

Moldavian army headquarters
Twenty miles east of Csíkszereda

Vasile Lupu was glad to be out of the saddle and into a tent. Since his Moldavian forces had crossed the Transylvanian border and engaged a small, hastily conscripted Székely peasant force near the town of Csíkszereda, it seemed all he ever did these days was sit a horse. His rear end and spine were begging for relief. To have his boots touch solid ground was enough for now. Tomorrow, well, he'd see what the sunrise gave him.

The thought of the sunrise turned his attention back to the matter at hand. "Is Matei certain of this?" he asked Stroe Leurdeanu, who had come at Voivode Basarab's behest to deliver both good and bad news. "Is that Jew's army in full march toward the plateau?"

Stroe shook his head. "Not in full, my lord. Our Lithuanian contacts near the upper Eastern Carpathians indicate seeing a sizable force, but not, they suspect, his full army. Just a wing, if you will, a vanguard. A screening force for the inevitable move of the entire army from Kassa. They report seeing infantry, cavalry, and some cannon in the advance column. And it would seem that they are moving toward—"

"Szatmár," Vasile interrupted. "Yes, for it is a logical place to march to before entering the plateau." He leaned over the map on the makeshift table in his tent, scratched his beard, cleared his throat. "I suspect, then, that they would move from there into Transylvania and on to...where, do you suspect?"

Vasile already had his suspicions, but he wanted to see what Matei's golden child might say on the matter. Stroe's answer could reveal a lot about how serious Matei Basarab and his Wallachian court viewed the Bohemian threat.

Stroe shrugged his round shoulders. "It is hard to say, my lord. Turning their column south from Szatmár could force them to move through this gap here"—he pointed to a valley cutting through a southern portion of the Eastern Carpathians—"or they could move around the ridgeline altogether and follow a more southerly direction."

"I am concerned about their next move from Szatmár, yes. Right now, however, I want to know where you, where Matei, thinks this advance force will ultimately end its march."

"Kolozsvár, my lord. And then, of course, Gyulafehérvár."

"I am pleased to hear that, Stroe." Vasile moved to the other side of the table so that Matei's prized advisor could see the agitation in his eyes. "Most pleased. You and yours seem to have a fundamental grasp on where this Army of the Sunrise is headed.

"Yet, I am concerned as to why Voivode Basarab is moving so slowly to put his Wallachians into the field. At our last meeting, we agreed that he would move in haste against the Saxon See of Sibiu Hermannstadt, and yet I hear that your forces have *just* crossed the border into that See, a delay of at least a full seven days. What is the reason for the delay?"

The expression on Stroe's face suggested that he was personally insulted by the question. Vasile did not care. As much as he admired the young man and wished he were one of his own advisors, the matter at hand was far too important to worry right now about being kind and accommodating to a potential future confidant. Moldavian forces were currently engaged and dying near Csíkszereda. Voivode Basarab needed to marshal his forces and get them moving.

Stroe breathed deeply, exhaled slowly, and said, "My lord, there have been unavoidable delays in mustering men along the southern border with Transylvania. The Wallachian populations along that border hold as much allegiance to their Transylvanian brethren as they do Voivode Basarab. They have been slow to support our cause."

Vasile was about to interject, but Stroe continued. "However, the matter has been rectified for the most part by Hungarian and Polish mercenaries who have arrived over the past two weeks. Our numbers continue to swell. Soon, a column of Serbians will arrive along with the forces promised by Sultan Murad. At that point, we will be ready to move, and in force."

The only thing that kept Vasile from reaching over the table, yanking Stroe Leurdeanu's beard, and slamming his tattooed bald pate into the map was the fact that the Sultan had agreed to give him an airship. A Serbian messenger from the Sultan had arrived recently stating that the ship was en route and would likely arrive within a day or two. The question that remained, though, was what ground forces would arrive with the airship. The messenger from the Sultan had not been specific about that. *He better gift me with Janissaries*, Vasile thought as he calmed down and rejoined Stroe Leurdeanu on the same side of the table. *I know how to use them.*

"Does Matei understand what kind of army we are dealing with?" Vasile asked. "I am not speaking about Prince Rákóczi's army; they are of little concern. I speak now of this so-called Army of the Sunrise. It is a construct of the United States of Europe, and as such, it has modern capabilities that Voivode Basarab and I do not possess. Capabilities that we do not even fully understand. In the name of God and Christ his son, they might have a way to convey all of their soldiers by air and drop their entire army into Gyulafehérvár before we can blink our eyes. Time is critical, Stroe. It is important that you convey that message to Matei Basarab.

"Tell him," Vasile said, moving away from the map and table toward a pallet of fat pillows, "that I *insist* that he marshal his forces—in whatever numbers they may be right now—and move them to Hermannstadt immediately. Murad's forces, and those Serbians you speak of, can follow in thereafter."

"My lord," Stroe said, and Vasile could see the young man trying to contain his anger and impatience, "Voivode Basarab is a man, and the prince of his own country. It is imperative that you convey your messages to him in a manner befitting his position and status. I can assure you, my lord, that a harsh insistence of action on your part would be met with... resistance."

Impressive, Vasile thought. *The man is young, but he is willing to risk himself, in a foreign land, by snapping back at me, just to defend his voivode from insult. Impressive indeed.*

Vasile found a comfortable repose amidst his pillows. He unbuttoned his coat collar, leaned back into the soft plush, and closed his eyes. "Forgive me, Stroe. I misspoke. The day has been long, my army fights and dies just a few miles up the road, and I am hungry. Please convey my compliments to Voivode Basarab, and tell him that I humbly recommend that he consider moving as soon as possible to Hermannstadt in order to achieve what Sultan Murad wishes from us: the destruction of this Grand Army of the Sunrise that threatens not only Transylvania, but Wallachia as well. If it is not stopped before it reaches the capital, I fear for *all* of our futures.

"Thank you, young man, for your report. You may go now."

Stroe Leurdeanu bowed and left quickly. Vasile dozed. Twenty minutes later, he was awakened by an assistant with an urgent message.

"Yes, what is it?" he asked.

The humble boy nodded and said, "Sergiu Botnari is waiting to see you, my lord."

Vasile rolled out of his pillows, collected himself, and said, "Very well. Prepare my dinner table, and bring us food and wine."

It was rumored that Sergiu Botnari was the product of a Turkish cavalry officer and a Bessarabian whore. He certainly played the part. His clothing was decidedly Arabic in its color and fit. His beard was thick and black and reached down to the center of his chest. His head was shaved, but he covered it well with a scarf—sometimes blue, sometimes red—that hid numerous scars from sword slashes. At first glance, one might mistake him for a Black Sea pirate. He had the physical carriage and temperament of one. He worshipped Allah. He was thin, but not skinny. He was fluent in many languages. He was good at killing.

Vasile watched as Sergiu cracked the spine of the cooked pheasant and sucked juices from the marrow within its frail bones. Not all of a pheasant's bones had marrow, so his efforts seemed futile to Vasile. Why bother? And yet, the fact that he'd take the time to find what little there was told the voivode of Moldavia everything he needed to know: Sergiu Botnari was thorough, and that was what one needed in a killer.

"I'm pleased that you find the pheasant to your liking, Sergiu."
Vasile finished his last morsel of cabbage roll and downed his
wine. "I will be sure to have my cook give you another on your
way out of camp. Of course, you must pluck and prepare it on
your own, but that's a small price to pay for such succulent meat."

Sergiu nodded, fished around in his mouth with a dirty finger to dislodge a piece of that pheasant from an upper molar,
coughed, and swallowed it down with a swish of red wine. He
burped, and Vasile noticed that the man looked embarrassed at
doing so. He laughed. "Do not worry, Sergiu. It is well that you
eat, and completely, before you leave. Your service to me is just
beginning."

Before Sergiu had a chance to respond to that, a robed and
stooped man entered the tent and whispered into Vasile's ear.
Vasile took the man's news with raised eyebrows and a smile.
The man bowed again and departed in haste.

"Good news at the front," Vasile said with a lilt in his voice.
He poured himself another wine and offered one to Sergiu, who
accepted it humbly. "Those pesky peasants have surrendered near
Csíkszereda. The town is ours. Thank you for your assistance in
that."

Sergiu's assistance had been to ensure that strategic structures
within Csíkszereda and its surrounding countryside had been
razed to the ground and that leaders within the local Székely See
found their deaths in any way necessary to sow fear, indecision,
and compliance.

Sergiu took a sip which turned into a swig, then a gulp. His
fresh goblet of wine was gone. "You are welcome, Voivode. But I
would caution you to take care moving farther into Transylvania.
It is one thing to terrorize and defeat a peasant force near your
border. It will be another to face Rákóczi's full army as you move
toward Gyulafehérvár. He'll have Hajdu infantry, cavalry, his court
guard. The prince of Transylvania is foolish in many ways, but he
is no military fool. He has been on campaigns more than once.
I suspect his strategy will rely on castles and fortresses along the
route to the capital to maintain a ring of defense that will be
very difficult to overcome. Castles and rock fortresses, my lord,
are more difficult to burn than peasant towns."

Vasile nodded, but his patience with Sergiu's gruff demeanor
and blunt honesty was beginning to wane. "I'm aware of Prince

Rákóczi's reputation as a military leader, Sergiu. Do not presume to lecture me on that score. I and Voivode Basarab will take care of anything Rákóczi will send our way, once Sultan Murad's assistance arrives, which will be any day now. We will handle all military concerns as we move forward.

"Your services to me and to your country now must turn to greater matters." Vasile rose from the table and moved to the map that he and Stroe Leurdeanu had reviewed earlier. He waved Sergiu over. "You must send your Impalers northwest, above the capital, toward Kolozsvár, Déj, Zilah, Doboka, and any other route that that Jew's army might travel. Even as far north as Szatmár if necessary." He sighed. "Because our Wallachian brothers are moving slower than I had anticipated, it is even doubly important that he be stopped; or, at least, slowed down such that we can reach the capital before he gets there. In defense, I'm confident that we can hold against his *Grand Army of the Sunrise*."

Vasile said that last part with the appropriate amount of derision. *How absurd for an army to be called that; what arrogance!* On the other hand, calling Sergiu Botnari's irregular troops "Impalers" seemed most appropriate.

The Székely along the Moldavian border had begun calling them that when the first home had been razed, and when the first man was found with his throat cut, the moniker solidified. The only thing Vasile did not like about it was that, indeed, the moniker's namesake, Vlad Dracul, often called Vlad the Impaler, had been a Wallachian Voivode more than once. Vasile had no desire to give Matei Basarab and Wallachia credit for this most important work. Over time, people might forget that it was he, a Moldavian voivode, who had deployed the Impalers. It was imperative right now for the Transylvanian people to know who this terror squad was and who had sent them. History mattered, Vasile knew.

Sergiu studied the map, ran his fingers across the long line of towns and villages between the northern border of Transylvania and down to Kolozsvár. He nodded. "And you are certain that he will move in this direction."

"As certain as my faith in God."

Vasile waited to see how the declaration of his faith might affect this Muslim before him, but Sergiu took it in stride, ran his hand back up to the northern border near the Eastern Carpathians, and said, "I will dispatch men immediately, my lord. And how far can they take their activities?"

Vasile considered. He rubbed his beard and felt the alcohol in the wine tingle his face. His eyelids grew heavy. He was ready for a full night's sleep. "Despite his frustrating lack of speed, I'm duty bound to respect Matei Basarab's request that we treat lightly with the Transylvanian citizenry."

"We have already violated that request many times over, my lord," Sergiu said, baring his notorious evil grin.

"Nevertheless, I ask that you show patience and respect to them all." Vasile paused, then said under his breath, "However, if it is necessary to violate that request to secure victory, then I don't need to know about it. Do you hear me, Sergiu? And we don't need to extend any mercy to foreign invaders."

"Loudly, my lord. And what kind of activities would you like my men to conduct against this Sunrise army?"

Vasile smiled. "Everything you and they can think of. Everything necessary to stop them in their march. Force them to stack up and hold in place. If this is achieved, then we can beat them into Gyulafehérvár." He placed his hand on Sergiu's shoulder. "And if you do this for me and succeed, my friend, the reward that you will receive will make what you have already received look like a peasant's wage."

Sergiu stepped away from the map, stood straight. "Very well, my lord. When shall I send them?"

Vasile moved away from the map. He resisted the urge to return to his pillows and lie down. "Now that we have secured Csíkszereda," he said, "I will send a portion of our army to Kolozsvár. It will be a long, challenging march, but if your men do their duty, we may, by God's grace, get there quickly and hold it, thus completely cutting off the Sunrise's approach. You will move ahead of our army and lay the needed groundwork for such an action. You've done it before. See that it is done again."

Sergiu looked as if he were going to argue the point, but then thought better of it. Vasile was relieved. The day was over for him. It was time to rest. It was time for this killer to leave his sight.

"I will advise my men to follow your columns into Kolozsvár." He turned to leave. "And do not worry, my lord. The Impalers will do their duty. We will make the Sunrise bleed."

Now, silence. What a joy to hear nothing, Vasile thought, as he removed his clothing and fell back into his pillows. He was happy. Everything that he had had to do up to this moment had been accomplished. Things were going well, despite Matei's lack of speed. And soon, his airship would arrive. Tomorrow, or the next day. Murad's ground forces would arrive shortly thereafter, and then he would have everything he needed to achieve the throne of Transylvania. In time, he would have to eliminate Matei Basarab and that Bessarabian monster that had just left. In time, others might need to be eliminated as well, but for now, everything was unfolding as planned.

Vasile closed his eyes, fell asleep, and dreamed of flying through the clouds, like a bird, on his airship.

Chapter 21

Szatmár (Satu Mare)

They marched across the Hernád and onward east-southeast to the Tarca, which was, to their great joy, running low. Fording was easy, and they made good progress. Then they marched through all the small villages along the way with little to no resistance. Then they reached the Tisza, and the sky exploded with rain.

Its banks were overflowing such that fording was nearly impossible. Thus, most of the cavalrymen had to cross the river individually, holding onto a rope tied to both banks, while guiding and swimming alongside their horses burdened with saddles, firearms and accoutrements, satchels, and knapsacks. A couple horses spooked, broke away from their riders, and were found drowned a mile downstream.

The infantry fared better, moving in constant lines from one side of the bank to the other, holding a series of ropes and pulleys that brought them and their personal equipment across wet and disheveled, but in relatively good form. The baggage train, however, was not so lucky.

There was simply no way for the wagons to cross the Tisza where General von Mercy had decided to take his army. Thus, the train was diverted several miles downriver to a small village with adequate fords. Even then, the river was too high in most places for a safe crossing. So, the supplies were taken off the wagons and placed on boats that, if the citizenry refused to loan them, they simply confiscated. A makeshift pontoon bridge using three boats and warped slats was hastily bound together just to get the empty wagons across.

In the end, one wagon and one teamster were lost. The wagon tipped and broke apart in the rushing water; the teamster was crushed under the weight of his own wagon as it slipped through the warped slats of the pontoon bridge and pinned him against the damaged boat beneath.

Crossing the Tisza took two days for the army, five days for the baggage train. But now they had reached the northern town of Szatmár by following the relatively straight and calm Szamos River. The rain was still falling, but lightly, and nothing and no one else, had been lost.

General Franz von Mercy was glad to be out of the rain and into his tent. "I apologize for the accommodations, Herr Veres," he said, taking a moment to remove his coat, belt, and sword. He placed all on the small table near the back of the tent. "But I cannot, in good conscience, commandeer better accommodations for your visit, nor would I ask that you do so for me in the name of your prince. We won't be staying here in Szatmár for long."

The man bowed humbly. "Then allow me to officially introduce myself in the name of George I Rákóczi, prince of Transylvania.

"My name is Gáspár Bojthi Veres. I serve as a member of my master's court, and I and my small entourage have been sent here to officially welcome you to our humble garden. I apologize that the prince himself could not attend you, but..." He paused, and von Mercy saw a twitch of concern cross the man's face. "... for the prince to travel from the capital beyond the border of our northern country would be dangerous. We have just recently learned that there is a terror group comprised of Moldavians, Turks, and Bessarabians conducting strikes against our beloved country and its citizenry. The 'Impalers' it is called, harkening back to a darker period in our history. If this group were to learn that the prince travels north, I'm certain that these monsters would not hesitate to find and seize, if not kill, him.

"So, I have come to you as his liaison. I am here to welcome you and to guide you on your march to the capital...if that is still General Morris Roth's intention. As his field general, will you fulfill his and Prince Rákóczi's agreement to provide military aid to our country?"

Von Mercy could hear the anxiety in Herr Veres' voice. Obviously, communication between Morris Roth and the prince—or his brother Pál—had been nonexistent since they had agreed to the alliance back in Prague. Transylvania did not have radio communication, so they had no idea when, or if, the Grand Army of the Sunrise would arrive. The fact that this liaison had appeared so quickly here in Szatmár to welcome them meant that he was already bending the truth. Herr Gáspár Bojthi Veres hadn't traveled from the capital in lieu of the prince: he had already been stationed here, waiting.

"General Roth wishes to convey his apology for not arriving in full," von Mercy said. "Various issues—mostly related to supply and aerial resources—has forced him and the rest of the Sunrise to remain in Kassa until such a time as those matters can be resolved. In the meantime, he has sent me in with an advance force to make it clear that we will fulfill our agreement. We've agreed to render military assistance to Transylvania, and that is what we will do. Please, take a seat."

Von Mercy had acquired a few up-time aluminum folding chairs, so he grabbed one, opened it, and set it near the table. The liaison seemed reluctant at first to sit down. Then he relented and sat with a leery, but excited, grin on his face.

"Compliments of the future, Herr Veres," von Mercy said. "The up-timers have designed a lot of clever things on which to sit. You like?"

Gáspár wiggled his backside into the fibrous, plastic straps. "Comfortable. Very comfortable."

"Far better than a three-legged wooden stool, at least." Von Mercy grabbed another for himself and took a seat across the table. "Now, let's have a discussion. What is your military situation?"

Gáspár rubbed his Vandyke and sniffed loudly. He seemed congested. His eyes were watery, his nose runny. *I wonder if he has a cold? I'll call in Doctor Kohen afterward.*

"As anticipated, Moldavian and Wallachian forces are on the move," Gáspár said. He lowered his face and sighed deeply. "Csíkszereda has fallen in the east near the Moldavian border. Voivode Lupu's army, perhaps seven, eight thousand strong, moves toward the capital. Wallachian forces are prepared to march to Hermannstadt in the south. This will be a difficult endeavor for Voivode Basarab, but not impossible, especially now that Ottoman forces have arrived."

"They have arrived?" von Mercy asked, not liking the sound of that. "Have they been deployed?"

Gáspár shook his head. "Not as far as we can see. For now, the fighting east and south of Gyulafehérvár are of matching armies. Prince Rákóczi has put into the field his personal guard comprised of elite cavalry and artillery. Székely infantry and cavalry from Sees along the Moldavian border. Saxons from Sees south. And thousands of Hajdus from the Partium."

"Only Hajdus? No other mercenaries?"

"No, General," Gáspár said, again looking despondent. "It would seem that all other good mercenaries are fighting against us."

"Can you be more specific about troop types and numbers?"

"Alas, I cannot, General. I am a scholar, not a warrior."

Wonderful! They send me a teacher... "I see. And what is the state of your forces here in the north?"

"Not as well armed or equipped as those south and east of the capital, I'm afraid," Gáspár said, adjusting his position on the up-time chair. Von Mercy could hear the embarrassing squeak and groan of the chair as the man shifted his position. It seemed as if Gáspár heard it too and immediately stopped moving.

Von Mercy gave a small chuckle. "Don't worry about it, Herr Veres. I've heard much worse with other up-time chairs. You get used to it."

Gáspár accepted the general's assurance, nodded, and continued, "Many from our northern towns have answered Prince Rákóczi's call and have gone to the capital to help defend it against the invaders. This did not seem like a problem when the order was given, for we were expecting General Roth's entire army to arrive."

Von Mercy could hear the rebuke in Herr Veres' words. He let it go. If he were in the man's boots, he might say and feel the same thing. Transylvania was, in effect, under heavy siege. Von Mercy couldn't blame the man for being a little—how did the up-timers say it?—*miffed* about the situation and the slow pace under which aid had arrived.

"When can we expect the entire Grand Army of the Sunrise to arrive, General?"

Good question... but do I tell the truth? I don't know. "General Roth will be moving within a week, two weeks at the most. And they will follow the same path toward the capital that we will take."

"I see," Gáspár said and again, clearly unhappy with the answer. "And what route will that be?"

Von Mercy rose from his chair and rummaged through his sizable stack of maps bundled together with cord. He pulled out one and rolled it across the table. Gáspár assisted in holding down one side of the map to give von Mercy ample room to indicate the route.

"From here," von Mercy said, moving his hand south along a series of trails and dirt roads hastily sketched onto the rough surface of the map, "we move to Erdőd, to Zilah, and into Kolozsvár. Once there, I'm to await further orders."

Gáspár looked at the route carefully and sighed from time to time, which proved most annoying. "Is there a problem with this route, Herr Veres?"

"No, General," he said, "not at all. It is the most logical route for an army to take. It is a move straight into the plateau and it avoids the most egregious peaks and valleys of the Carpathians. It is a wise course. However, I do not believe that it will suffice under the current circumstances."

"Oh? And what circumstances are those?"

Gáspár stepped away from the map, sniffled again, seemed to suppress a sneeze, and said, "That terror group I spoke about? Those damnable Impalers? They are screening a sizable Moldavian force that has broken off from Voivode Lupu's main army and is moving to get behind the capital and, perhaps, take Kolozsvár. I do not know their exact destination, but that would be the most prudent thing for them to do under the circumstances."

Von Mercy nodded. "Thus establishing a defensive position along the most likely road into the capital, and thus evening the odds a little in their fight against a more modern army."

Gáspár nodded. "You see the truth of it, General. I've been told that you are a most excellent commander. It is a delight to see how your mind works."

Von Mercy appreciated the compliment, but he proceeded nonplussed. "Do you think this Moldavian force can actually seize Kolozsvár?"

Gáspár shrugged. "By itself, no. Kolozsvár is close to the capital. Prince Rákóczi will defend it as well as he defends his own home. But, it is clear that the Impalers are having an impact on the population as they screen the advancing force. They are calling the Grand Army of the Sunrise a heathen army, filled with godless Jews, whose true purpose is to kill and rape the country and turn Transylvania into a Jewish nation. They have killed Jews and Sabbatarians and have threatened to spit their babies up onto pikes to warn the rest of the peasants in that area not to support the *Jew's* army or suffer the consequences. Already, there are reports of scores of Transylvanians joining the ranks of the Moldavian force. If they are allowed to persist in this campaign of fear, General von Mercy, they may well have enough in the end to take Kolozsvár. If they do..."

The man did not need to finish his statement. Von Mercy knew the answer. "Then what direction to Kolozsvár, Herr Veres, do you recommend?"

Gáspár leaned over the map again and pointed in a more southeasterly direction. "From here, I recommend Nagybánya, then Déj, then Szamosújvár. I will guide you personally. It is in this direction that we believe the Moldavian force is headed."

Von Mercy nodded. "In order to get above Kolozsvár and cut us off before we arrive." He ran his finger along the entire route. "This will take us through more hazardous terrain, Herr Veres. Put us closer to the Eastern Carpathian range."

Gáspár nodded. "As I say, I will be your guide. I know the way. And, as Prince Rákóczi's liaison, I can settle nerves and the apprehension of the citizenry as we go along. And it may be that I can convince many of them to join your cause." He looked up and smiled. "That area is filled with Sabbatarians and Jews, General. You should find allies along the way."

Von Mercy had no desire to gather up peasants as he marched, regardless of their political or religious affiliations. Right now, his army was lean and mean, as up-timers might say, and with good up-time weaponry, it was an elite force, capable of holding its own against an army twice its size. Adding more mouths to feed, more bodies to train, was not part of the plan. Then again, if the Moldavian force was gobbling up recruits along the way, it would not hurt to add a little fat around the midriff to absorb some of their gunfire. *A brutal thought*, von Mercy admitted to himself, but then again, war was brutal.

The key to pulling off this change of route would be good intelligence, both on land and in the air. If at least one Dvorak plane could be put on reconnaissance duty, and if at least a few good cavalry companies could move ahead of the column and scout the way forward, then this relatively minor change of direction would go smoothly.

Von Mercy was less concerned about this reported Moldavian army trying to outflank him than he was these Impalers. Irregular warfare was aggravating, debilitating, and if allowed to continue, could break down the cohesion of an army in good time. One important purpose of such military tactics was to buy time, and like General Roth was fond of saying on occasion, time was not on their side.

"Then that is how it will be," he said, returning to his chair. "We will spend a couple days here. My men need a little time to recover, to get their bearings, and then we will strike out to Nagybánya, with you as our guide. I will radio General Roth and tell him of our plans."

"Radio?"

"You have never seen a radio, Herr Veres?"

The man shook his head and finally, in one large, tent-shaking breath, sneezed. He produced a handkerchief and wiped his nose and mouth. "My apologies for that, General. This weather has brought me down. I've heard of radios, but have never seen one in action."

"Ah," von Mercy said, "then I invite you to accompany me while I send a message. My communications chief is an expert. He can answer any questions you may have. In the meantime, I will ask my personal surgeon to take a look at you. He's trained in up-time medicine. He might be able to knock that cold right out."

Gáspár nodded. "Many thanks, General. But it may be that the only thing that can knock out this affliction is a mallet."

Chapter 22

Matei Basarab's headquarters, north of Târgovişte

Matei Basarab was awakened by a clamor of competing sounds before Stroe Leurdeanu poked his head into the tent and gave him the good news.

"The Sultan's forces have arrived, my lord."

Matei nodded and rubbed his sleepy eyes. "Thank you, Stroe. I'll greet them directly."

This news was much better than the demand that the young advisor had given him a few days ago upon his return from the Moldavian army camp. *Vasile commands* me *to move forward?* Stroe had not phrased the command so directly, but Matei knew the voivode of Moldavia well enough to know that, underneath Stroe's more muted and complimentary recommendation, was a direct order for action. Which fell on deaf ears, for Matei had already ordered his army forward to Hermannstadt. Soon, he figured, as he rolled out of bed to prepare for the day, his forces would reach the Olt River. Soon, they would cross it and engage Prince Rákóczi's Saxon forces. Who would win that engagement? Yesterday, Matei had been worried that his army would be routed from the field. Now that the Turks had arrived, he felt better about his chances...assuming they could get to his army in time.

He donned a doublet of dark red with gold buttons and embroidered gold leaflet chains. The gray shirt beneath revealed matching silver buttons and chains. His hat was a mixture of black-and-red-dyed bear fur, tall and thick, suited more for winter months, but more than appropriate for the occasion. A blue-black feather was tucked in on the side of the hat and it fluttered in the breeze that blew into the tent. He checked himself in the mirror. He had better attire, clothing more opulent and befitting a man of his stature. But he was a military man now, a general. The cleaner and more prepared look of a statesman would have to wait.

He stepped outside his tent into a morass of Turkish faces.

The valley before him was filled with Janissaries and cavalry both elite and light. Beyond the sea of bodies lay wagons fat with supplies, and beyond them, a strange device of tubes that he had never seen before. Beyond them, more cavalry. Matei smiled.

Not only had Sultan Murad delivered on his promise—albeit a little late—but Serbians had arrived as well.

"Is this all?" Matei asked the wind, in jest. The man stepping forward from the first rank of Janissaries apparently didn't get, or hear, the joke.

"Voivode Basarab," he said with a bow, "my name is Usan Hussein, and I am the *corbaci* of this orta. I greet you in the name of Sultan Murad IV."

The eye patch that covered the man's eye and the scar running across his face indicated a person of some experience. The men behind him, however, all arrayed in their tidy rows, looked like children. Most of them, if not all, had seen no battle whatsoever, and it was clear to Matei immediately that the Sultan, for all his good intentions, had sent nothing but conscripts.

And in fact, now that he had more time to look them over, there actually weren't that many Turkish regiments present. He asked his question again, and this time, with sincerity. "This is all Sultan Murad has sent me?"

Usan Hussein looked left and right and behind him. He rumpled his brow and seemed annoyed. "Sultan Murad is honoring you with the lion's share of forces, Voivode Basarab. A regiment of sipahi; a regiment of Akinji; two katyusha rocket launchers; all three tanks; and my orta. A sizable number of Serbian cavalry joined us in our march."

Matei leaned up on tiptoes and tried to get a better look beyond the Janissaries. He put his hand over his eyes to keep the sun's glare from obscuring his view. "I only see normal wagons. Where are these so-called tanks?"

Usan Hussein cleared his throat. "They are five, perhaps six, days behind us. They will arrive soon."

Which meant ten to twelve days in truth. Matei was no military man, indeed, but he understood well how men like Usan Hussein, under the extreme pressures of the Sultan, exaggerated their numbers to shed the best light on a situation. "And did Sultan Murad send Vasile Lupu his requested airship?"

"Yes, and all the rest of our forces."

Perhaps, Matei considered, *once Vasile receives his silly little air toy, he'll be less inclined to play with his terror group.*

Stroe had said that these evil men were being called the "Impalers." Upon hearing this, Matei had taken a kind of morbid pride in the label: associating these men with a previous—and very formidable—Wallachian prince should, indeed, fill the Transylvanian countryside with terror, and perhaps that alone would keep the citizenry heeled.

Once Stroe explained, however, that this group was violating—in the most hideous ways—the agreement Matei had made with Vasile on the matter, the novelty and nostalgia of the term waned. Matei was furious about it, but not at Vasile. Against himself. *I should have refused right off*, he thought, eyeing Usan Hussein carefully. *And if I catch any of these Impalers doing the devil's work on my battlefield, I'll feed them to the sword of the man in front of me.*

"I welcome you, Usan Hussein," Matei said, deciding not to argue numbers any longer. "I look forward to our service together in this endeavor."

The man nodded. "Thank you, Voivode. I am also charged with serving you personally as an advisor and in taking command of your infantry if necessary."

"As advisor or as a spy?"

The *corbaci* seemed thrown by the bluntness of the question. He pulled himself away as if he had smelled a foul odor. Then he stilled, calmed his eyeless face, and said, "Voivode Basarab, I serve the Sultan in the capacity that he commands. Let us not quibble over—"

Matei raised his hand, shook his head. "No need to explain further, Usan Hussein. I understand my *place* is this matter." He turned and motioned the man to follow. "Come. Let us speak in private."

Usan Hussein turned and barked an order to his men. They stood at ease.

Matei took Usan around his tent and toward a clear view of the Southern Carpathian mountain range. There, he stopped and let the man see the high, splendid, snow-covered peaks through the distant morning fog. "There," he said, "is my gift from God, Usan Hussein. The gift he has given all Wallachians and Transylvanians. A gift he has given the world. It is the most miraculous mountain range in all of Europe in my opinion, and it will be utterly impossible for your armored tanks to move through it, if the image I have of them in my mind is correct. It would have been more prudent to give me the airship and Vasile Lupu the tanks. Now, they will arrive here in your five to six days, and here, they will sit."

"We will find a way to move them forward, Voivode," Usan Hussein said. "Their crews are skilled men, and their presence on the battlefield can make all the difference in a fight."

"Perhaps," Matei said, "but in the meantime, you will have to navigate through those gaps alone to reach my army—which I have already moved forward. It marches through those gaps and toward the Olt River. It has a four-day head start."

"And what is beyond this Olt River?"

"Hermannstadt, which is, in effect, the capital of the southern Saxon Sees of Transylvania. Take Hermannstadt, and we take southern Transylvania." Matei paused and turned to face the *corbaci*. "You have to reach them before they reach the Olt. If they do, their standing order is to attack and lay siege to the city. I have faith in my army, but now that you are here, I see no reason to delay your involvement. Do you agree?"

Usan Hussein nodded. "We shall send riders immediately and tell them of our advance."

"Very good."

With regret, Matei turned from the wonderful view of God's gift and began walking away. "I must now greet our Serbian cousins and welcome them into my camp. Make your preparations, Usan Hussein, and I will meet with you again later to help finalize your departure."

Before he turned the corner of his tent, the *corbaci* shouted, "You will be coming with us, Voivode Basarab. You do understand that?"

Matei paused, turned, and with as humble a smile and bow as he could muster without losing his temper, said, "Of course. I serve at the pleasure of the Sultan."

Communications tent
Grand Army of the Sunrise
Kassa (Košice)

"Len! Len! Can you hear me? Can you hear me...*goddammit!*"

Ellie slammed the receiver down on the desk. More expletives escaped her mouth. Morris Roth ignored them and asked his question.

"What did he say? Did you get anything from him?"

Ellie breathed deeply and tried calming herself. It didn't work. "I hate this fucking mountain range, Morris. The Carpathians are a pain in the ass. I keep losing the signal." She fiddled with dials on the radio. "I'll try to get him back, but—"

"What did he say before you *lost* him?"

"I don't know. He said something about von Mercy changing his direction and heading east-northeast toward some town starting with an 'N.' Something about a Moldavian something out there." She stopped turning dials. "Morris, you got to get a plane in the sky to give me a signal boost. Or, let's get our asses in saddles and on to the plateau."

Morris nodded. Putting a plane up for a signal boost was no problem, but moving the entire army: they were close, very close. Three, maybe four, days away from making that decision. The APCs that they were awaiting had all arrived and with only minor mechanical problems; medical issues revolving around the fitness of the infantry regiments were well under control; training was going well. He was just waiting for...for what?

Morris waved his hand at Ellie. "Forget about trying to get Len back right now. We'll deal with that later. Contact Eddie Junker or Denise Beasley. Tell them to get a plane in the sky with a radio and fly along the route that von Mercy took to Szatmár; once you get your boost from that, try again. Understand?"

Ellie nodded. "Fine. But I ain't waiting for the boost. I'm going to keep trying."

Morris said nothing about that. If she wanted to keep trying to contact Len, that was fine. Trying wouldn't hurt anything, and she might get lucky. But they had been trying for over twenty-four hours and they'd acquired very little intelligence on what was going on—literally—at the front. Morris fully understood why Ellie was so frustrated. In truth, she could hardly care about where von Mercy was leading his men. What did it matter to her? What she wanted was to hear her husband's voice, even in crackle or through frequency garble. She just needed to hear his voice to know that he was alive and well.

He left the tent. Ellie didn't need him hovering over her like an overbearing parent. Ellie would do her job. Through fits of rage and tears, perhaps, but she'd do it. That's why Morris had brought her and Len back under his service. They were professionals. Rough around the edges, yes, but certified pros.

He stepped out of the tent and into the waiting mass of Doctor Oberheuser.

Morris rolled his eyes and said under his breath, "Oy vey."

"I need to speak to you, General," Oberheuser said with a curt snap. "I have a problem."

Of course you do. You kvetch *all the time.* Morris smiled. "What can I do for you today, Doctor?"

"It's Isaac, sir. He's stolen my best nurse."

Morris pushed past Oberheuser and continued walking. He screwed up his face, shook his head. "What are you talking about?"

"Devorah Bayer. She's gone. I forbade him to take her with him, and she's gone."

"You're just finding out about this now, Doctor? They've been gone a long time."

Oberheuser seemed insulted. "I'm a busy man, sir. I don't have time to check, every day, the whereabouts of my staff."

That is your weakness, Karl. "Okay, so she's gone. What can I do about it? They're well over a hundred miles away."

"I want her brought back."

Morris stopped and stared the old coot in the eyes. "How do you propose we get her back, Doctor?"

Oberheuser pointed his thumb over his shoulder to the east. "Send one of those infernal up-time planes and bring her back."

Morris stopped himself from laughing out loud. This couldn't be a serious request, but nothing in Oberheuser's eyes suggested otherwise. He shook his head. "No, sir. That is not going to happen. We don't have the time or the resources for that. We don't have a landing strip established in Transylvania yet, and even if we did, I wouldn't waste time hauling a nurse back to Kassa. Besides, what makes you think Isaac 'stole' her? I presume she's a grown woman. She might have decided all on her own to join him. And, I would suggest that her presence there is more valuable than back here. If she's the best, as you claim, then she's right where she needs to be."

That shut Oberheuser's mouth. Morris could see the rage welling up behind the man's eyes. He looked like a stick of dynamite ready to blow. Morris wondered who would win in a curse-out: Ellie Anderson or Karl Oberheuser? *I'd pay* real *money to see that.*

The doctor finally calmed and nodded. "Fine. At least allow me to reprimand him for insubordination."

"Fine, fine," Morris said just to get this ridiculous conversation over. "When next you two meet, you have my permission to give him a stern tongue-lashing."

Oberheuser nodded roughly and stalked away.

Morris paused. Finally, silence. Silence, save for the normal hustle and bustle of camp. That never-ending drone was welcome at the moment. He shut his eyes and breathed deeply.

His next crisis of the day was to meet with Colonel Velvel Schiff, commander of Second Regiment, Joshua Corps. Then, Provost Marshal Luthor Lange. Then, Colonel Burkenfeld. The meetings were never-ending, but all necessary, of course, if he wanted to get his army in the "saddle" as Ellie would say, to get them moving toward Transylvania and toward von Mercy's advance force, which had apparently shifted its move somewhere farther east than the planned route toward Kolozsvár. But where exactly, and what might he meet on that diverted course? Ellie had mentioned a "Moldavian something," and that could only mean one thing: von Mercy was hunting for a Moldavian army. To find it, he'd need more than a signal boost.

Morris turned back to the communications tent and poked his head through the flap.

"Ellie," he said, "when you get Eddie on the line, let me talk to him. I've got an idea."

Chapter 23

Inside the Chaldiran, *high above East Transylvania*

Moshe Mizrahi could not read Mordechai Pesach's mind, but he knew they were thinking the same thing: grab the legs of this howling buffoon at the head of their airship and toss him overboard. The *Chaldiran* had already been used as an execution platform for the crew of the *Esztergom*. There was certainly no reason why it couldn't be used again for that purpose. And it would be easy too. The man had come onto their airship with no protection, no guard. One nod to the Janissary guard who stood nearby, and over the edge the buffoon would go. But no, not now, not yet. Perhaps not ever. As much as the idea appealed to them both, it would not do to kill the voivode of Moldavia on the first day.

The buffoon stood there at the front of the gondola, leaning into the cool wind, letting it blow through his unkempt black hair and beard. He was grinning like a madman and howling like a wolf. "Whooooo! I've never felt anything like this. Feel that cold air. I feel like a bird. I feel like a god!"

What blasphemy! Then again, Moshe had heard that their new lord did suffer from delusions of grandeur. "My lord," he said, taking a step closer to the voivode, "my I ask that you step away from the front of the gondola? It is far, far forward, as you see." He swallowed. "With your weight, plus the weight of the extra

Kalkan shields that have been put in place for your protection, you are causing the nose of the craft to dip. Please, I beg you, come back to the center of the gondola."

Those extra Kalkan shields were bulky enough that the *Chaldiran* had to dispense with its radio. Signal flags would have to be used instead, but the prince of Moldavia didn't seem to care a wit about the technical details of his new weapon.

"I hate the up-timers!" Vasile said, shouting through the whistling wind and stretching his arms out wide as if he were praising God. Sunlight spread across his broad face. "I wish to see them all dead. But I do love their weapons of war."

"This is Sultan Murad's airship, my lord," Mordechai Pesach said as he guided the ship to the left and down. "His own design."

Vasile turned. His boyish delight was gone, now replaced with a look that Moshe could only describe as confusion. "On the contrary, kafir. It is mine. The *Chaldiran* is mine. I paid for it. Therefore, I paid for you. You are mine. You and everyone on this ship. Do you understand?"

Both Mordechai and Moshe bowed humbly. "Yes, my lord," they said almost in unison, then Moshe thought, *No, Voivode, it is not yours. You may think what you like, but if the Sultan wishes it back, he will get it back.*

"My lord," Moshe said, nodding to Mordechai, "will you allow our engineer to show you how the *Chaldiran* works, how its armaments work?"

Vasile Lupu deflated before them as if he were a child whose toy had been taken away. "Oh, very well. Let's get on with it."

Mordechai spent the next several minutes explaining how the airship worked. He then explained how ballasts were used to either lower or lift the airship to the desired height. The voivode of Moldavia accepted these demonstrations in a manner befitting his station: with a quiet interest that indicated clearly that he was bored. His attitude, however, changed when Mordechai hefted a jar bomb and began explaining its use.

"Oooh, can I throw it?"

Moshe and Mordechai exchanged exasperated glances. Moshe cleared his throat. "My lord, these bombs are very volatile. One error in its use, and the gondola, and yourself, could burst into flames."

Vasile grunted, grabbed the jar, and walked to the front of the gondola. "I want to throw it."

"Very well, my lord."

Mordechai readied the jar. "Toss it forward, my lord. Release the jar as soon as your arm is fully extended, like this." He extended his own arm in a throwing motion, opening his hand at the precise moment.

Vasile waited, waited, until they were flying over a farm. A Székely shepherd and his herd of Hungarian gray cattle moved like tiny ants below. The shepherd looked up, saw the monstrous airship, and began running, slapping his cattle on the rump to get them moving. Vasile cackled like a chicken.

He dropped the bomb. It struck the herd off-center, igniting across the ground and through the legs of the terrified beasts. Three were burned. The shepherd was untouched.

"Curse the sky!" Vasile said, wagging his fist in the air. "I missed him."

"My lord," Moshe said, again thinking about tossing this buffoon to the rolling hills below, "only two wagons of munitions resupply followed the *Chaldiran* into the field, many of which are larger bombs than the one you just tossed and are more appropriate for a battle. But nevertheless, it is important that we preserve our bombs, both large and small, to support your army as it moves—"

"Do not worry, Moshe Mizrahi," Vasile said, using his name for the first time since they had met. "I understand the need to preserve supply for the true battle. That was just for fun...and practice."

He rejoined them in the center of the gondola. "Now, let's turn this ship toward my army. We will fly ahead of my men and provide them with intelligence to ensure our victory over Prince Rákóczi as we march toward his capital. Forward!"

Moshe and Mordechai looked at each other, rolled their eyes out of Voivode Lupu's view, and said, "Yes, my lord."

Chapter 24

Nagybánya (Baia Mare)

A day before leaving Szatmár, Len Tanner finally got his radio signal boost. Effective communication was, once again, established with the main body of the Sunrise.

Eddie Junker had taken his Dauntless—*My Steady Girl*, he called it—and had flown it roughly half the distance from Kassa to Szatmár. That was enough to boost the signal and bring General Roth up to speed on von Mercy's plans. Since no effective landing site had been established yet in Szatmár, Eddie was forced to turn around and head back to Kassa after the boost. But Morris Roth made it perfectly clear how things would be going forward: before General von Mercy left Szatmár, he was to establish a landing site for the Dauntless and the Dvoraks there, and then along the march, establish others so that those ultralights could be used for his reconnaissance needs. The Dvoraks were small, lightweight, nimble. They only required an open field or a relatively flat, well-maintained dirt road on which to land. Even in such hilly terrain as the Transylvania plateau, landing sites could be found.

Finding good landing sites was not the problem, von Mercy had told Morris. "The problem is protecting and maintaining them once I pull out. I don't have enough men to establish garrisons to protect the sites, General Roth. If that Moldavian force is out there, I need every—how do you up-timers say it—swinging dick in the field? I can't afford to lose any man to such tasks."

Morris sighed at the other end of the radio. "We'll figure something out, General."

He, Gáspár, and Len Tanner were now in Nagybánya, waiting in a short field lined by trees on the approach from Szatmár and end-capped with a short stone wall. Denise Beasley would have to do some fancy maneuvering to land properly. The field was too small for Eddie to land his Dauntless safely.

"I don't see it," Gáspár said, stretching his neck to gaze through dwindling tendrils of fog. It was going to be a nice, sunny day. Von Mercy was glad of that.

"She's coming," he said. "Keep watching."

They heard the plane's engine first, and then, like a tiny crow, saw the plane dip out of a line of fog. It wobbled on approach, its wings dipping as its pilot brought the craft down until its landing gear nearly scraped the tree line.

"It's so fast," Gáspár said.

Len smiled. "That's slow for some planes."

Denise brought the plane into the field, touched its wheels to the ground, and took off again.

"What's the matter?" Gáspár asked.

"She was going too fast," von Mercy said, knowing enough about up-time planes now to make himself sound competent. "She'd have hit the wall. She'll circle back around and try again."

Denise did exactly that, taking the plane up again into the fog and then circling back until she was dropping the plane into its landing pattern. This time, thankfully, she was going slower.

The wheels touched again, the brakes were applied, and the pilot brought the craft to a halt about twenty feet from the wall.

They took a few steps into the field. Denise taxied the plane to their position.

Gáspár stood back a few paces as Denise drove the plane up, stopped, and killed the engine. A minute later, she was out of the cockpit and greeting them with a generous smile.

"I love this plane," she said, removing her leather helmet and stepping in front of General von Mercy. She saluted while maintaining her smile. "Pilot Denise Beasley reporting for duty, sir."

He returned her salute. "Good morning, Fräulein Beasley. I hope your trip was pleasant."

She nodded. "Pleasant enough, if you take away the wind shear and fog."

"I'd like to check out your radio," Len said.

"Have at it."

There wasn't much to it, von Mercy noted as he stepped up to the cockpit and looked inside. A delicate frame with canvas skin. No doors, although it looked like some additional canvas was tucked in behind the pilot seat which could be used as such. There was a second seat, but no additional crew. Instead, two metal tanks were strapped into the chair.

"No copilot?" von Mercy asked.

"Nope, sorry," Denise said, as she stepped into the cockpit and wriggled into the seat. She did not bother strapping herself in. "The original plan, General, as you well know, was to have the Dvoraks follow the main body of the army into Transylvania. But since you *deemed* it necessary to divert from the original marching order, we have to put one of us into the air now to support your approach to the capital. But since we don't really know what to expect from the Carpathians—wind and weather-wise—we can't afford to commit all three aircraft to this, or we risk losing them all."

She pointed a thumb to the metal tanks. "You didn't bring any fuel with you in your train. That's all the extra fuel we've got, General, so I hope you are not expecting me to conduct long flights."

Von Mercy shook his head. "No. I've sent elements of my second cavalry ahead to Déj for reconnaissance and to find another adequate landing site for you. From there, we are very close to Kolozsvár. As requested, each landing site is no more than fifty miles from another. So, from here to Déj is roughly thirty-seven miles; from Déj to Kolozsvár is roughly thirty."

"Good," Denise said, moving her legs out of the way so Len could lean into the cockpit and check out the radio. "I need secure landing sites, as many as you can find. That way, if I get into some nasty weather, I can make an emergency landing." Denise raised her hand and struck the roof of the cockpit twice. That made no sound, because the roof was also canvas. Except for the metal and wood framework, the whole fuselage of the plane was made of fabric. "She's a good plane. Well-constructed, good motor, and, thank God, good brakes. But she ain't invincible." She looked at Len. "How's my radio?"

Len nodded. "Good. I reset your frequency so you can talk

to me now. But I'm not making any promises on perfect communication. You're right about these mountains: they can play havoc with our radios with all these hills and valleys."

"Yep," Denise said. "Transylvania looks both beautiful and terrifying. Dracula chose well."

The two up-timers shared a laugh. Von Mercy had heard of the fictitious character based on the late Wallachian prince, Vlad Tepes. He had never read the book, however, and had no interest in doing so.

At his side, Gáspár seemed to struggle with the reference, as if he had a notion what they were speaking about, and yet, couldn't quite place it.

Von Mercy continued, "What can this Dvorak do for us, Denise?"

She stopped laughing and turned serious. "Yes, well, her official designation is Dvorak One, or DV-1, as the maintenance crew likes to call her. I call her the *Dixie Chick*. She's modeled after an up-time ultralight called the Hawk Arrow Two. She's five hundred pounds empty. I add another hundred and thirty. That leaves plenty of room for another passenger, if you or someone on your staff needs to get somewhere quickly."

Denise held up a cautioning finger. "*But*—don't ever forget this—every pound of people subtracts a pound from the fuel we can carry."

She lowered the finger and thought for a moment. Then added: "She has a service ceiling of a little more than two miles. I usually fly low, however, although I'd like to maintain a certain height to avoid snipers and punks who might get lucky with a shot. Her primary role is for scouting, reconnaissance. That's what I'm charged to do for you. As I said, she's not an attack plane, although you could, I suppose, put a rifleman in the back seat and take potshots. I'd advise against it, though, unless you have a real sniper like Julie McKay with a good rifle."

"I'm afraid we've no Julie McKays here, Denise," von Mercy said. "Your service to me will be primarily reconnaissance. We need you to help us find that Moldavian army. That's the reason I've shifted farther east, as I've explained it to General Roth."

Denise nodded and climbed out of the cockpit again. "No problem, General. I understand. What's that up-time expression: 'No plan survives first contact with the enemy'? You made a decision based on changing circumstances. Morris understands. He doesn't like it, for it could pose other problems down the line, but he understands." She looked at Gáspár. "Any sign yet of this Moldavian force you speak of?"

"Just rumor so far," Gáspár said. "They are somewhere east-southeast of Déj, Fräulein. The city itself is in the Szamos River Valley. It lies at an important crossroad, but it is surrounded by forests and hills and other, smaller valleys that lead into it. A Moldavian army, even a large one, can easily hide its movements as it makes its way there."

"That is why I have sent my cavalry forward," von Mercy said, "so that we can try, at least, to ascertain its whereabouts. I've ordered them to go no farther than Déj. But now that you're here, perhaps we'll have better luck in finding that...needle in a haystack?"

Denise nodded. "Well, then, let's get to work. As soon as your men have a landing site for me in Déj, I'll be off. In the meantime, General, can you provide me with breakfast and find me a tub? I don't want to think what I must smell like by now."

They left the field as the men von Mercy had designated to protect the Dvorak surrounded the plane and stood guard. Denise's flight over Nagybánya after her first attempt at landing had roused interest. Now, the citizenry began to assemble near the field, trying to catch a glimpse of the strange flying machine that had invaded their air space and landed in their field. *Perhaps I should let them draw closer*, von Mercy considered as they walked past a group of children craning their necks to get a better view. It would be good to start allowing the Transylvanian population to see what the up-timers had brought to their lives, what the future might hold for them. But not yet. The risk of damage to this aircraft, even inadvertently, was too great right now. The plane needed to be kept safe and in good condition.

As they walked into Nagybánya, von Mercy tugged at Denise's jacket sleeve and whispered, "Denise, can you find that army?"

She looked as if she was going to say something snide or sarcastic. She seemed to change her mind when she saw von Mercy's face. "Don't worry, General. If there's an army to be found, I'll find it."

Moldavian army encampment
Bistriz (Bistriţa)

Sergiu Botnari stared into the flames as his dinner sizzled at the end of a stick. The piece of chicken on its pointy end was small consolation to the rumble in his stomach. He preferred red meat, a nice slab of Hungarian Grey. His men had slaughtered one just this morning as they led Lupu's flanking army toward Déj, but by the time Sergiu had arrived for the feast, the bovine carcass had been picked clean. He considered ordering another killed, but doing so, even for a man in his position and authority, seemed... excessive. He'd settle for chicken now, but once Lupu rewarded him with his promised coin, Sergiu would dine on only the choicest meats. Dine on anything he liked.

Could he trust the voivode to fulfill his promise? That was a question. No, probably not. There were few men of Lupu's stature and breeding who could be trusted fully. A man like Lupu had his own agenda, and a cutthroat like Sergiu served a purpose in that agenda, but then, what afterward? In time, Lupu would probably order Sergiu's throat cut in order to tie up "loose ends," as they say. The key to his survival, then, was to do his duty for as long as he could, collect as many coins as possible, and then disappear. Sergiu was good at disappearing. Even sitting beside this roaring fire, he was difficult to notice.

Sergiu rather liked working in Bistriz. There were a lot of Jews and Sabbatarians in the area to terrorize. Terrorize, yes, but not kill. At least not yet. He was trying to abide by Lupu's directive to be somewhat civil in his march toward the up-time army. Total civility was impossible, of course. That's not how a terror campaign worked. One couldn't terrorize a population if one didn't use terrifying tactics: a murder here or there; beating up an elder or two; raping a daughter or two. But going too far in that endeavor was ultimately self-defeating. Sergiu had learned long ago that you had to always give a population a chance to meet your demands. Apply too much pain and punishment, and the citizenry would have no choice but to fight against you, even if it meant death to them all. There was only so much suffering a community would endure before it snapped. So far, his "Impalers" were doing quite well at convincing the locals to side with Vasile Lupu.

Some Székelys, even Sabbatarians, had joined the ranks of the Moldavian force, despite knowing that the up-time army heading their way was led by an Ashkenazi Jew. But that, too, Sergiu understood quite well. Jews could turn on Jews. Muslims on Muslims. Christians on Christians. There was no true loyalty to one's clan, tribe, country, or family. One could only be loyal to oneself. "To thine own self be true." Sergiu liked that line from the English poet. Sergiu couldn't argue with that bit of philosophy.

He managed to gulp down three bites of his chicken when a rider burst into camp. The horseman slid to a stop, spraying the campfire with dirt. "What's the meaning of this interruption?" Sergiu asked. "Can't you see I'm having a meal?"

"My apologies, sir," the boy said. "But I have important news."

"What is it?"

"Cavalry has been spotted moving toward Déj."

Sergiu raised his brow. "Cavalry? I was just told that the army is in Nagybánya and will likely not move for several days."

"Just a few cavalry companies from the main force," the boy said, eyeing the chicken as if it were a jewel. "Not a full regiment. Maybe a day, two days away."

Sergiu snorted and shook his head. "What arrogance. They're brave enough to send a pittance forward, even though they know we're out here? They march into *Jahannam* with no fear? So be it. We will show them fear."

Sergiu took a final bite and flung the remains into the fire. "Get my horse ready. We'll beat them into Déj. And inform General Radu that we're moving. He'll want to head out at first light."

The boy nodded, turned his horse, and left. Sergiu took a moment to reflect.

He was happy, despite the bad news. Von Mercy had gotten the jump on the Impalers, but that was, in fact, good news.

I may have to show restraint toward Székelys and Sabbatarians, but I don't have to do so against arrogant enemy cavalry.

Chapter 25

Déj

Christian saw the black pillars of smoke as they approached the town. Von Mercy's orders were clear: go no farther than Déj. But it looked as if someone had arrived already. And even more alarming were the column of citizens steaming out of the town and away from the evening's devastation.

"Impalers," Lieutenant Karl Enkefort whispered as they rode together at the head of their company.

Christian nodded. Could be, though they had not encountered any terror group since they had entered the Transylvania plateau. Christian was beginning to think the rumors of such men were false. Apparently, he was wrong.

He heard the rumble of horses behind him. He turned in the saddle and saw Colonel Renz approaching with his aide-de-camp. He saluted. "Sir."

The colonel reined his horse to a stop. "Captain von Jori. Move your men into Déj and determine the source of that smoke. Provide aid as you are able and as needed. We want to make it clear to these people that we are here to help, not harm. You understand me?"

"Yes, sir, I will do so, but it appears as if everyone is leaving." Christian pointed to the line of women, children, carts and mules, leaving Déj. "A lot of them, at least."

"Which is a bad sign, Captain. You know as well as I do

that the common man has an inherent sense when it comes to danger. Those people were obviously hit hard last night. They see a battle coming." Colonel Renz cleared his throat. "But not everyone leaves their homes, Captain. Some will stay out of pride if not arrogance. See to their needs, if any, and start looking for a field or road flat enough, smooth enough, for a plane."

"A plane, sir?"

Colonel Renz nodded. "Von Mercy had just informed me that one of his Dvoraks has arrived in Nagybánya, but it can't fly any farther unless we find a place for her to land."

"Her, sir?"

"Yes, Captain. Apparently, there's a woman flying it. She needs at least two hundred feet of flat field or road to land the infernal thing. The more feet, the better, he said. We're in a river valley. You'll find something near Déj for sure. Now, get going."

"What about the rest of the regiment?"

"I've sent flankers out to scout the area. I don't want a Moldavian army jumping up our backside and pinning us against the Szamos. Go, and report back to me immediately."

Christian saluted again. "Yes, sir."

Colonel Renz left and Christian turned to Lieutenant Enkefort. "You hear all that?"

"I did."

"You have your radio?"

Enkefort nodded and tugged on a leather satchel buckled to the side of his saddle. "Ready."

"And you know how to use it?"

The lieutenant flashed a modest smile. "If Len Tanner taught me correctly, I do."

Christian returned the smile. "Very good. Then move us out, Lieutenant Enkefort, and at the trot."

Communications tent
Nagybánya (Baia Mare)

Len Tanner wrote down as much information as he could ascertain from the spotty radio communiqué from Colonel Renz. He was annoyed. He couldn't tell whether the interference was because of weather, elevation, or from human error at the other end. Once taught, down-timers were quite competent at working a radio, but like everyone, using a radio under pressure could have a person making all kinds of mistakes. And it would appear that the enemy was closing in.

"Let me speak to him," von Mercy said, almost pushing Len out of the way. Len slid over and gave the general room.

"Push this button and speak, General," Len told him.

Von Mercy pushed the button. "Colonel Renz, tell me again your status."

There was a pause, then, "...have moved into Déj...several buildings razed overnight...deaths...citizenry remaining non-cooperative...requesting further instructions."

"Have you determined the location of the Moldavian army?" Von Mercy practically screamed the words.

"...no sighting as of...Impalers burned the...searching for landing site for..."

"Screw it!" Denise said from behind them. She had come into the tent as quiet as a mouse, wearing her flight gear, holding her leather helmet. "Let's not wait for a site. If I have to, I'll land in the middle of the town, so long as someone on that side can guide me down and it's got a street long enough and wide enough."

"It's a risky move, Denise," Len said.

"Not really," she said, moving forward. "If I haven't got a place to land, I'll just turn around and come back. At least with me in the sky, you'll get a signal boost and not have to mess around with these garbled transmissions."

Len looked at von Mercy. "What do you say, General?"

Von Mercy ignored the question and pushed the button again. "Colonel Renz...is Déj secure?"

Garble, then, "Yes, sir, for now, but the Moldavians must be near..."

The general nodded, which Len found amusing. Though, perhaps it wasn't as odd as it appeared. Colonel Renz was not standing a few feet away. He was nearly forty miles away. But his voice, though garbled, must sound to any down-timer like he was right in the tent.

"Stay put, Colonel," von Mercy said. "Hold that city and keep your radio open. I'm sending in the *Dixie Chick* immediately, and we'll be on the march soon." He looked as if he wasn't sure how to finish the conversation, then seemed to remember. "Von Mercy...out."

He turned to Denise, but she was already gone. Von Mercy shook his head. "Impetuous woman."

Chapter 26

Déj

Denise had to circle above the city three times before she found a landing site suitable to her needs. Her first option was a cobbled street that cut through the town's central square. She dipped low enough to get a good view of the cobbles. They looked adequately uniform and smooth enough to warrant a try, but would she be able to slow the craft down soon enough to avoid slamming into a narrower passage at the end of the strip? A twenty-foot passage and a thirty-foot wingspan did not mix.

She opted for option two: a small dirt road running alongside a stone wall butted against a field where a large amount of cavalry mingled about. The wagon tracks on the road provided some challenge for the Dvorak's tires, but Denise managed well enough. A lieutenant by the name of Enkefort guided her down.

A small group of officers approached. She did not bother climbing out of the cockpit to meet them. She left the motor running and motioned them forward. "Come on, gentlemen!" she shouted over the noise of the engine. "It won't bite you."

One advantage to a pusher design was that the propeller was safely in the rear where no one could bump into it accidentally. So, the men came forward without much hesitation.

"Welcome to Déj, Fräulein Beasley," said the man in the forefront, who seemed to be in charge. "I am Colonel Renz." He was just about to salute, then perhaps thought better of it. Denise had to keep herself from smiling. The man had probably never saluted a woman in his life.

Instead, he offered her a short bow of greeting, then turned and introduced the others. "This is my aide-de-camp, Major Schmidt. This is Captain von Jori, Second Cavalry Regiment. And this is Lieutenant Karl Enkefort, Captain von Jori's aide. He's the gentleman who found this road."

Denise removed her goggles, blinked, and looked at Enkefort. "You the radio man, too?"

The lieutenant nodded.

"You're pretty good with that thing," she complimented him, before turning back to Colonel Renz. "I'm Denise Beasley."

"Yes," Colonel Renz said, "and we are glad to have you here. What can we do for you?"

She pointed into the back of the cockpit. "First thing, you can remove those fuel tanks. They're all I have, and that's all the fuel I'm going to have until the rest of the air force arrives with General Roth. Find a nice, dry, safe place for them and keep them secure. If we lose those, I'll be grounded."

Colonel Renz nodded. "Major Schmidt, see to the removal and protection of those tanks."

"Yes, sir." Schmidt trotted off.

"Before I land for the night, I want to do some scouting for you. Let me get up there and have a look around, get a good feel for the lay of the land. You got a map?"

Captain von Jori stepped forward. He touched his coat as if he were looking for a pen, then pulled a satchel around hanging from his shoulder and produced a piece of neatly folded parchment. He unfolded it and handed it to Denise.

"Déj sits at the crossroads of two valleys," he said, pointing to the town sketched in the center of the parchment, "one from the east, one from the south. If a Moldavian army is moving this way, it'll be coming up one of those gaps, or both."

"Where are we on this map?" Denise asked.

Von Jori stepped forward and touched the map near mid-center. He was wearing his riding gloves so his touch was imprecise. "On the west side of the city. A small road just about there, which, as you can see looking this way, leads out of the city and south. We thought it best to place your landing site away from the two most logical approaches the Moldavian army may take into Déj."

"Good thinking," Denise said, nodding. She studied the map further. "Can I keep this?"

Von Jori nodded. "Certainly, sir. Ah...madam."

She smiled. "Just call me Denise."

The captain nodded. "As you wish."

"What's the weather been around here?" she asked.

"Some clouds, some wind," Colonel Renz said. "The air has been cool, but ample sunlight, praise God. No rain, but I don't know what it's going to be like tomorrow." He pointed to the *Dixie Chick*. "Can this thing predict the weather?"

Was that a joke? Denise wondered. She couldn't tell from the colonel's expression. "No, sir. We up-timers have a lot of fancy machines, but I'm afraid predicting the weather is out of my skill set. If it rains tomorrow, it rains. We'll deal with weather when the time comes."

Major Schmidt returned with four men. Denise coordinated their efforts in removing the tanks. They were a little too quick in pulling them free of their bindings, and one of them almost fell to the road. "Careful!" she snapped and flashed a stern look. "Handle them like babies, or, new foals, if you prefer. Gently now!" They slowed down and got both tanks out and away from the road.

Denise laid the map on her lap and leaned back into her seat. "Okay, gentleman, if you'll excuse me, I'm off. I'll scout east and then turn back south. About fifteen miles both ways." She pointed to Enkefort. "Keep that radio on. I'll contact you every ten minutes or so with updates."

Denise replaced her goggles and waited until the men stepped off the road. "And keep those tanks secure!" she shouted, then taxied the plane forward about fifty feet, turned it around, and gunned it.

It felt so, so good, to be back in the air.

"She needs wide open spaces—"

"This should give us an advantage," Christian said as he and Colonel Renz and Lieutenant Enkefort returned to the nearby field where the lion's share of cavalry awaited.

"Yes, it should," Colonel Renz said. "But I don't care what the up-timers say about the quality of their machines. Nothing will replace, in my mind anyway, good, on-the-ground reconnaissance. We need to keep up *our* scouting."

"What can I do for you, Colonel?" Christian asked.

Colonel Renz cleared his throat, looked around at his cavalry companies. "I'm ordering Neuneck and Keller to keep up their patrols day and night. I want them moving up those valley roads and rivers as far as they can go. I want you and Kinsky to pull your cavalry back into Déj and protect those people from another attack from those goddamned *Impalers*."

"The townspeople will not like that, Colonel," Christian said. "Their mayor has already said they don't want us here."

"I don't care what he says," Colonel Renz said, pausing to turn and look at Christian directly. "You and Kinsky will move into town and take charge of the situation. You understand my orders?"

Christian nodded. "Yes, sir. We'll take care of it."

"Good." Colonel Renz began walking again. "Now, another thing I'd like to you do is—"

A loud, high-pitched voice squelched out of Lieutenant Enkefort's radio.

"What the hell is that?" Colonel Renz asked.

Enkefort turned his radio around and pointed it toward the colonel and his captain so that they may hear it better. "It's Denise, sir. She's singing."

"I'm walking on sunshine... whoa... and don't it feel good?"

In truth, she was walking or rather, flying, under sunshine. But the air was cool with no appreciable wind shear. A few low clouds, but no rain. Denise could not have asked for better conditions for her first official reconnaissance mission. Thus, it was a good time to try out some new singing material.

She had always loved that song, and minus a radio station that she could tune into and sing along with, she tried to recall the video of Katrina and the Waves belting out their signature tune, as they enjoyed a rather gloomy day in London. The song was released before she had even been born, but somehow, it still mattered, resonated, as a lot of songs did with her. It seemed to Denise that music, perhaps more than any other human endeavor, endured. What was that biblical passage? *Men come and go, but Earth abides?* Add music to that list as well.

"... I feel alive, I feel the love, I feel the love that's really real..."

She certainly felt love for Eddie, with his big... airplane.

She chuckled to herself and hoped that she hadn't spoken any of that out loud; sometimes, in the midst of musical ecstasy, she would forget herself, and sometimes even forget that her radio was on. Lieutenant Enkefort and his superior officers were listening in, and she had no problem with those men hearing her sing. In fact, perhaps it was best. Let them laugh at the little up-time girl and her silly ways and fancy pusher plane. *Give them all the joy of music before the battle begins.*

She loved singing. It took away her stress and reminded her that what mattered most in her life was Eddie, all her old up-time friends, and all her new down-time friends as well.

She glanced at her fuel gauge and dipped lower, bringing *Dixie Chick* down another three hundred feet. From this height, she could see nearly everything, save for what lurked under the canopy of trees. A Dvorak did have its limitations, after all. But if anything—especially a large army—was moving down the valley toward Déj, she'd see it. Her height and speed was such that she had little concern for snipers, and besides, what kinds of weapons did the Moldavians really have? Matchlocks? Wheellocks? Flint? A good shooter could perhaps give her pause, but not now, not today. She was walking on sunshine.

She spoke clearly into her radio. "*Dixie Chick* now out about fifteen miles east, following the river. No sign of Moldavian forces, over."

Lieutenant Enkefort responded. "We hear you, *Dixie Chick*, over."

"Will now turn south and scout in that direction. *Dixie Chick* out!"

She steered right and gave her engine a little punch of speed. Sun glare off the sloped windshield bothered her a little, but it always had, and she had gotten somewhat used to it. She drew her goggles down and set them over her eyes while she braced against the inertia of the turn. "Woo-hoo!...I love this plane!"

The *Dixie Chick* straightened, and Denise settled in for the final leg of her mission.

The only blemish on her day was that she wouldn't be see-ing Eddie again for a while—possibly quite a while. Morris had been trying to get one or (preferably) two Jupiter V cargo planes from Markgraf & Smith Aeronautics in the Netherlands, and apparently he'd been able to get one. Markgraf & Smith would provide a pilot and a flight engineer to get the plane to Prague, but the provision was that Eddie would have to be part of the flight so he could learn the ropes. The Jupiter was a four-engine plane, much bigger and more complex than anything Eddie had even flown before.

It would be up to him to get the plane from Prague to wherever Morris wanted it. Markgraf & Smith weren't willing to let their employees go any farther. From Prague, there were plenty of commercial flights they could use to get back to the Netherlands. From Transylvania? That was not a gamble they were prepared to take.

Eddie would also need to provide himself with a copilot and flight engineer, after he reached Prague. Who? How?

Eddie would figure it out. Denise had a lot of confidence in her boyfriend to handle most anything.

That reassuring thought was enough to start her singing again. *"...walking on sunshine..."*

Sergiu Botnari stepped behind the protection of a tree and watched as the up-time plane flew by overhead. To him, it almost looked like a crow or a hawk, save for the sound of its engine. It suddenly dropped lower, and now, he could see it better, get a better sense of its size and speed. God, it was moving fast. *But can it see like a bird?* That was his question. *Whoever is flying that machine, can he see* me?

One of his men came up beside him and leveled a musket in the aircraft's direction. Sergiu pushed the barrel down. "Don't waste a shot, you fool. You'll never hit it, and it might see the puff of smoke."

"Can it fire at us?" the man asked.

Sergiu shook his head. "I don't know. Maybe. Let it fly past us."

"It might find General Radu and his army!"

Sergiu worked the muscles in his jaw. Indeed, it might, but what could it do when it found them? If it had long-range weapons of some kind, like the Sultan's airships, or like one of the USE airships that he had heard about, it could possibly do some damage to the Moldavian force before it reached Déj. But there was nothing he or any of his men could do about it right now. "Let it pass."

They dared to step out into the clear as the plane flew farther and farther away. Sergiu's heart began to race, and he began to feel real anger, the kind he often felt before he killed someone, the kind he relied upon most often to give him the courage to pull that trigger or draw a knife across a windpipe. Anger because it just didn't seem fair: the enemy using such a weapon against his countrymen. What an unfair advantage did the USE have on its down-time enemies! A very, very unholy advantage.

Sultan Murad had sent his own up-time-inspired weapons into the engagement, true, but they were hundreds of miles away in service to Lupu's and Basarab's armies. How was he, Sergiu Botnari, supposed to fulfill Lupu's demands of beating these people if they could see everything marching toward them from a bird's-eye view?

"It's turning."

Sergiu looked up from his despondence.

The plane had turned sharply right and was now flying south over the wooded ridgeline, away from the Szamos River Valley. "Idiot!" Sergiu barked. "Another five miles, and it would have found the whole army."

"Maybe it can see that far away," the man said.

Sergiu shook his head. "The Carpathians have never given up its secrets that easily. No way that *bird* can see through its canopy of trees five miles away. Whoever is in that thing has made a mistake...a big mistake, changing its direction."

Sergiu tucked his pistol away and said, "Is everything in place for later?"

The man nodded. "Yes, sir. We lay in wait."

"Good. Afterward, we will return to Déj and have a closer look at this flying machine."

"Do you think it'll be there?"

Sergiu nodded, surprised at the question. "I know it will." He smiled. "Even birds need to rest."

Chapter 27

Déj

"I don't understand these people!" Captain Josef Kinsky said—practically spit—into Christian's face. "How in hell can we defend them if they refuse to help us? If their mayor refuses to meet with us?"

Valid questions, indeed, but Christian knew his partner in defense of Déj would not like the answer.

Josef Kinsky hailed from a prominent Bohemian family, one that had risen recently from minor noble status to comital prior to the Ring of Fire. But he was an outcast, a black sheep, if you will, of the family, one who wore the Kinsky name, but didn't abide by it. He was a mercenary and the captain of perhaps the best dragoons in the regiment, though Captain Callenberk might take umbrage with that characterization. The so-called Wild Elite were tough, experienced, and well-suited to defend the town from an advancing enemy force. But only if the citizenry cooperated.

"They're scared, Josef," Christian said. "The Impalers came through last night and burned a good number of their homes, killed some of their officials. One woman told me that she thinks those bastards are still in town, waiting for any civilian to lend us a hand. And off their hands will go."

"And they can't tell the difference between terrorists and their own people?"

Christian shook his head. "I guess not." He waved his hands through the air, motioning to the few townsfolk moving about as if it were a normal day. "Can you tell the difference? Who is German? Who is Hungarian? Wallachian? Moldavian? I saw a man a moment ago with very dark skin. Another who looked like an Arab. Where is *he* from? I can't tell the difference between friend and foe."

"But we don't live here, Christian," Josef said, raising his voice to uncomfortable levels. "Surely these people can tell the difference between their neighbors and interlopers."

Or maybe they choose not to. Christian shrugged. "All I know is what I've been told: we can neither retreat, nor expect civilian help. At least not yet." He leaned in so that anyone walking by could not easily hear the rest. "But trust me, Josef, when bullets begin to fly, when they see which side is shooting at them and which one is not, those that remain will change their minds. You're no green recruit. You've seen it happen before."

Captain Kinsky nodded. "But what do we do in the meantime? In my *learned* opinion, Déj isn't defendable. Not with our numbers, anyway." He looked up into the wooded ridgelines that surrounded the city. "Blockading the roads east and south isn't going to stop infantry from moving into those hills and firing down upon us. And," he said, not waiting for a response, "our ZBs are short-range weapons, Christian. Maybe fifty, sixty yards at best. The kill range is much shorter."

"True, but they're more powerful than anything the Moldavians will muster against us. More accurate, too. When we put a man down at the right distance, he stays down."

Captain Kinsky sighed, shook his head. He removed his felt hat and scratched his scalp. "I wish the Brethren were here. They know how to defend a town."

"I wish they were here too," Christian said, "but without Brethren help, I think we stick with Colonel Renz's plan. We gather up anything we can to blockade all roads leading into the city—crates, barrels, wagons, furniture. We find wood planks and posts and stitch it all together in palisades. We then man those defensive walls with our best shooters. Pepper the ground with caltrops and sharp stakes in places we cannot defend so easily. That'll keep the cavalry at bay, at least for the most part. The infantry? Well, we don't know how much they have."

"We must assume a lot."

"Agreed," Christian said, "but Fräulein Denise did not spot any movement east or south. Neuneck and Keller are scouting in those directions. If they're coming, I'm sure we'll know soon enough, and we'll be able to adjust our defense accordingly."

Josef rubbed his beard, deep in thought. "Very well," he said. "We'll do as our commanding officer requests and pray to God that he is right. I'll defend the eastern approaches. You defend the southern ones. Let's just hope that, at the end of the day, our pay is commiserate with our success."

Christian nodded and almost smiled. "What about north and west?"

Captain Josef Kinsky shook his head. "Those roads, my friend, are in God's hands."

On the march to Déj

"I *am* worried about being outflanked, ambushed," General von Mercy said as he, his staff, and the rest of his army marched up the Szamos River Valley toward Déj. What they were marching on could hardly be called a road. Fit for cows and small carts, perhaps. Cavalry could navigate through it just fine. Infantry fine, though slow and spread thin in column. But cannons? Wagons? It felt like they were standing in place more often than not just to allow the supply train and the guns to keep up.

"I know the history of warfare in this part of the world. That is why we are moving slowly and in force, Herr Veres, so that we can keep our supply train protected in the event of such an attack. That is why I have ordered Ulfsparre and Hanau to send some of their men forward as flankers. I want to keep this army tight and in good order, and well-informed. Otherwise, we'll get cut to pieces and be less than useful when we reach our destination."

Gáspár Bojthi Veres nodded respectfully from his saddle. He was managing the march well, but it was clear to von Mercy that the prince's representative did not care for horses, and they apparently didn't care for him either. "Yes, General, and I apologize again for my ignorance of your battle plan. But Colonel Renz's latest assessment of the situation in Déj is worrisome. As he reports, many are leaving the city, deciding to wait it out in the hills. It is imperative that I attend to their concerns, allay any fears that they may have about you and the Sunrise, so that they may return to their homes and defend them in the name of their prince. If you would allow me to go forward with a small guard for protection, I can try to convince them that—"

"When the time comes, sir, I will send you forward. I've already instructed Callenberk and his dragoons to prepare to head out. But we need to get clear of this part of the valley. Too many gaps leading into this area, both east and west. Gaps are ripe for ambushes, and now that we know that these Impalers are in action, I'll be damned to hell if I allow them to strike my train and destroy our supplies.

"We're not going to make Déj today. Once we get clear of these gaps, we'll bivouac, and then I'll send you and Callenberk ahead. That is the end of it."

Gáspár nodded, but it was clear that he was angry. *Let him be,* von Mercy thought as he worked over in his mind the details that Colonel Renz had radioed to Len Tanner a moment ago. *I'm not going to allow this army to be routed. And I'm certainly not going to allow the representative of Prince Rákóczi to come to his death under my care. How would that sit with the citizenry of Transylvania or the prince?*

Chapter 28

Szamos River Valley
East of Déj

Sergiu Botnari watched as ten horsemen from the enemy army came into view. Light cavalry. Scouts. They were moving slowly, not even a trot. They seemed tired, bored. The one behind the lead horse was speaking German into a wooden box attached to the side of his saddle. He wasn't even trying to be quiet or discreet. His voice echoed through the river valley.

Beyond the cavalrymen ran the Szamos River, moving slowly but surely at the edge of the road, bright and sparkling as it caught light from the setting sun. The world was growing dark. Sergiu smiled. He couldn't have asked for a better tableau.

Sergiu did not speak. He was not as foolish or arrogant as the cavalryman down the ridgeline, speaking so loudly into that wooden box that it frightened birds in their passing. Sergiu raised his hand instead, and the twelve men lying in wait readied their muskets. He held his hand up, up, then dropped it.

The blast of their musket fire echoed through the valley. The first three riders and their horses in the patrol line dropped. Smoke obscured what had happened to the remaining horsemen down the line, but judging from the terrified screams of their horses, they too had been hit, to some extent at least. Sergiu wasted no time waiting for the smoke to clear.

He drew his sword and ran down the wooden hill. He and his men had already picked ideal spots to fire and then charge. They followed, their swords raised and so too their voices, no longer under strict noise discipline.

Sergiu took advantage of the confusion and ran right up to a cavalryman who was trying to regain control of his steed. Sergiu slashed at the saddle, trying to cut the girth straps and thus toss the rider. Instead, he cut the horse, which was almost as effective. It reared up on its powerful hind legs. Its rider tried keeping his balance, but Sergiu's sword strike had pushed the horse closer to the river. It lost its footing and toppled down the muddy bank as the rider released the reins. He tried breaking free from the horse, but he could not get his boots out of the stirrups. Both horse and rider hit the water and disappeared.

Sergiu turned toward the rear of the ambushed column. Three of the riders there had apparently not been hit at all in the first volley. One held a pistol that Sergiu had never seen before. It looked similar to the one tucked away at his belt, but it was thicker, heavier, longer. It was no wheellock. The man kept control of his horse, pointed the strange pistol at one of Sergiu's charging men, and pulled the trigger.

The man toppled over, a large hole blown through his chest and out his back.

For a moment, Sergiu balked, expressing a bit of fear at the marvelous wound from the up-time weapon, for that's what it must be, this pistol that he had never seen before. And for scout cavalry to be carrying such lethal firepower... well, it was marvelous and terrifying to witness.

A musket shot near his head brought Sergiu back to the matter at hand. He turned toward the firing man. He had a good notion to draw his knife and put it through the man's throat. "Don't fire so close to my head, you fool! I can't hear a goddamn thing now!"

The man tried to apologize. Sergiu pushed him out of the way as his ears began to recover from the blast. He drew his pistol and raced toward the remaining three scouts.

Another one of those marvelous pistols rang out, and another of Sergiu's men fell, this time with a point-blank shot in his face. The man receiving the shot dropped immediately, his hand catching in the horse's stirrup. The scout who had fired brought his horse under control and took off with Sergiu's dead man dragging at its side.

Sergiu stopped, raised his pistol, and aimed it at the scout as he tried to flee. The two other scouts who had not suffered wounds turned their horses and fled as well.

"Fire!" Sergiu shouted to three men still holding their muskets. One was trying to load, the other was confused. The third fired on command, but his shot was off. Sergiu followed that inaccurate shot with his own.

Sergiu cast down his pistol and screamed. "Aaaaaa! They got away! Three got away! You sons of whores. I said to get them all!"

His surviving men said nothing. They stood there, seemingly in shock, the whole affair over in just a few seconds.

Sergiu went to one of his men, writhing in pain on the ground. He had suffered a shoulder wound from one of those powerful pistols. He was still alive. Barely.

"Did you get your man?" Sergiu asked, kneeling and placing a comforting hand on the man's forehead. "It's okay. You can tell the truth."

The man shook his head, tears of pain running down his face. "No, sir...I—I missed the shot. Got his horse. Darius finished him."

"But Darius is dead too, isn't he?"

They both looked at the man lying nearby, facedown, his back blown out and pulsing blood.

"I'm sorry, sir...I...I..."

"It's okay," Sergiu said again as he pulled his knife from his belt, jammed it under the man's rib cage, then waited until the thrashing stopped. "You did your best."

Sergiu wiped his blade clean on the man's shirt, stood, and walked away.

He found the scout who had been talking into the wooden box. The man was dead. The box lay underneath him. Sergiu pulled it free and studied it.

A strange, buzzing sound emanated from the box. *Is this a radio?* Sergiu wondered. Probably so. He had heard of them, but had never seen one. The Ottomans apparently used them just like the USE. It was a way to communicate long distances. He wondered if he could use it. It didn't seem all that complicated.

Perhaps he could, but he had no time for such things now.

Sergiu stood and tossed the radio into the river and watched it slowly sink and disappear. Perhaps that was a foolish thing to do, since getting hands on up-time equipment was probably the best course of action. But he could not be burdened with such a bulky device. Besides, could his movements be tracked with it? If he kept it, would they know his whereabouts? He shook his head. The enemy could not know his movements. Never.

But a mistake had been made. Three scouts had escaped, and without doubt, they would return to Déj and report what had happened.

Colonel Renz's headquarters
Déj

"Three got away, sir," Captain Neuneck said in Colonel Renz's rather crowded headquarters. All four cavalry captains were in attendance, including Denise Beasley. "They were ambushed about ten miles east, men firing from the ridgeline, then charging."

"Do they have an indication of how many attacked them?" Colonel Renz asked.

Captain Neuneck shook his head. "Twelve, thirteen, fifteen. More than ten, for sure."

"Impalers?"

"That's what they assumed. They were not wearing uniforms. A mix of different kinds of people, different clothing."

"Could it have been Transylvanian citizens?" Captain Kinsky asked. "We've heard reports of Székelys joining the Moldavian army to drive out the 'Jew invader.'"

Captain Neuneck shook his head. "The attack was too coordinated, too well-conceived. These were professionals."

"Not professional enough," Colonel Renz said. "Three got away."

"Yes, sir."

Denise Beasley let out a big sigh. She'd been standing listening to these men talk for too long. "Colonel, if you want me to scout any more today, I need to go *now*, while we still have some daylight. I can fly east again. There and back, and it's going to be dicey anyway. Sun's setting fast. We got, maybe, an hour of good daylight left, and then it's gone. I've never tried to land the *Dixie Chick* in the dark. I don't plan on trying it tonight."

Colonel Renz nodded. "Keller? What have you seen on your flank?"

Captain Keller stepped forward, shook his head. "It's clear so far, sir. Nothing. I think we can say with some confidence that the main body of the Moldavian force is approaching from the east. It's clear to me that Neuneck's patrol was attacked to keep it from discovering the enemy's advance."

"Perhaps," Colonel Renz agreed, "though we cannot know that for sure. You keep your patrols running south, Captain Keller. Report back every fifteen minutes."

"Yes, sir," Captain Keller said, saluted, and left the room.

"Colonel," Denise said with a clear hint of frustration in her voice. She tapped her wrist even though nothing was there. "Times a'wasting."

Colonel Renz turned and faced Denise. "Can you take someone up with you?"

The question took her by surprise. Then she nodded. "I suppose so. Might be best, anyway. I can tell you, 'Oh, look, an army,' but I can't give you details." She turned to the other three captains standing nearby. "Which one of you wants to take a ride?"

No one volunteered. Denise could see serious trepidation on all of their faces, but time and daylight were running out. Someone needed to step up.

"Captain von Jori," Colonel Renz said. "You'll accompany Fräulein Beasley."

"Me, sir?"

"Yes. Do you have a problem with that, Captain?"

Christian swallowed. "Well, it's just that, with the recent injury to my eye, perhaps it's best to—"

"We can't send Captain Kinsky because he's commanding the defense of the approach that will most likely take the brunt of the attack when it comes. We need him to get his defenses in order before nightfall; every minute counts. We can't send Keller or Neuneck. Despite recent events, I still need them both scouting forward. That leaves you. The southern approaches appear to be quiet right now. I think we can afford to have you missing from the field for an hour or two.

"Go with her, and if you find anything, I want as many details as you can provide: numbers, weapons, dispositions. How many cavalry? Infantry? Cannon?"

Denise grabbed Christian by the shoulders and turned him to face her. She looked him up and down as if she were measuring him for a suit. "Well...he's a little big for the cockpit. He'll burn some serious fuel. But I'll take him." She popped him on the shoulder with a smile. "Saddle up, Captain. We fly!"

The Dixie Chick
East of Déj

"Feel that wind, Christian!" Denise shouted as they cruised at about eight hundred feet above the Szamos River Valley. "Isn't it wonderful?"

Christian nodded, though his true feelings on the matter were not quite as definitive. The wind felt good. His stomach did not.

He wasn't going to vomit. He wasn't that sick. It was more of a sickness brought on by anxiety, a churning in his stomach like he had felt when he had first charged into battle, or when he had killed his first man. Both life-changing events had been a few years ago, and he'd never forget those moments, nor would he ever forget what he was doing right now: he, Christian von Jori, the son of a prominent blacksmith and farrier from Zurich, Switzerland, was flying hundreds of feet above the ground, moving at a speed that he had never moved at before. How many people in all the world could claim that they had flown in an up-time plane?

The wind was cool with a touch of moisture. It felt good. His eye, however, did not.

Ever since Isaac had released him from care, Christian had suffered blurriness in his right eye. A kind of squiggly line right in the corner, which would grow and grow until he couldn't see much at all. It would, in time, go away. It had persisted, however, and one could never predict when it might reappear. His vision was fine right now, but it was difficult to see anything from their current height.

"Okay," Denise said, "We're ten miles out. You see anything?"

Christian leaned over and stuck his head out the canvas-covered cockpit. He was thankful that Denise had strapped him in thoroughly before they had launched. Otherwise, he'd be tumbling out the door and falling to his death. It was still scary, however, to hang into the wind like this. Christian gripped his seat as tightly as he could and tried to focus his eyes on the ground.

"Can we go lower?" he asked, shouting through the wind, speaking a half-truth. "The sun glare behind us is affecting my line of sight."

"How far can a musket fire?" Denise asked.

Christian considered. He was less experienced with rifles than with pistols, but a Moldavian army would likely be using less efficient down-time match and flintlock muskets. Unless, of course, the Ottomans had given them more modern weaponry. "Tactics dictate an optimal firing range of a volley up to fifty yards, but they can fire farther. Pistols are shorter range than that."

Denise paused, then said, "So, if I take it down to, say, four hundred feet, we'd be safe, with room to spare?"

Christian nodded. "I would think so, yes."

"Okay, brace yourself. Here we go."

The dip was faster than he expected, and his stomach reacted poorly. Christian suppressed a burp. With his head out the window, he could easily open his mouth and expel the meager scraps of his supper. But he held his mouth shut, opened his eyes wide, and searched the valley below for an army.

Nothing. Nothing at all, save for a small Székely village with a few tendrils of smoke rolling out of chimneys. A herd of cattle behind a stone fence. The Szamos River flowing gently along. The ground below him moved by quickly, almost to the point of making him dizzy. Christian blinked, sniffed the air, and caught the strong scent of smoke. A smell he knew well.

Campfires.

"Okay, look," Denise said, checking the gauges on her dashboard. "I'll take us another five miles or so, but then we'll have to turn around and—*holy shit!*"

Below them, across the entire river valley, were hundreds upon hundreds of tiny campfires, all scattered through the forest. Strong lines of smoke rose from them, and Denise had to pull the *Dixie Chick* up another fifty feet to keep from flying through the smoke. On the quick, Christian looked through the pall and saw infantry, cavalry, a few cannon, and even the beginning of the supply train, though the tail of it disappeared farther down the valley.

"Denise?" Christian said, sitting back in his chair. The queasiness of his stomach was gone. In its place, relief. "Please send word to Colonel Renz. We've found them."

Doctor Isaac Kohen's medical tent

Colonel Renz had radioed that a Moldavian army had been found encamped about twelve miles east of Déj. As sure as the sun would rise tomorrow, that army would attack by morning, and how many men would die? How many would die simply because Isaac and his entire staff were not present to assist in the care of the wounded?

It was a question that had burdened Isaac's thoughts ever since General von Mercy had ordered Colonel Renz and four of his cavalry companies forward to Déj. Now, those companies had been ordered to defend the city until the entire force had arrived. Cavalry defending a city? Not unheard of, but certainly not ideal. Casualties would be high.

Captain Callenberk's dragoons had been ordered to ride through the night to reach Déj by morning. Isaac had asked to be sent forward with them. General von Mercy had refused. "I'm not risking my chief surgeon on a night march through a foreign territory. We don't know where these Impalers are working. They could strike at any time, anywhere. Send others."

As ordered, Isaac sent in his place Devorah and an older surgeon that they had acquired in Kassa. The best nurse; not so much the best doctor. At least with Devorah, the embattled would have a professional nurse in their midst. But their medical supplies were so low, and based on radio reports, the citizenry of Déj were being less than helpful in the army's preparations for the attack. Not outright hostile, for what could mostly unarmed townspeople do against four hundred heavily armed cavalry in their streets? "Passively resisting" was what they were doing, and how foolish was that?

Part of the problem was that the eventual political fate of Déj was still unclear. The basic provisions of the agreement Prince Rákóczi had made with Bohemia were that he would exchange some of northern Transylvanian territory for Bohemian military assistance. That was widely known by now, at least among Transylvania's nobility and its Saxon and Székely notables.

But exactly where would that territory be? It seemed fairly well established that the three towns of Szatmár, Nagybánya, and Bistriţa would become Bohemian territory, but that Kolozsvár would remain in Transylvania. What then of Déj, which lay between them?

On some level, Isaac could understand the citizenry's desire not to get involved. Help one army, and potentially suffer reprisals from the other. Help the other, and suffer the same fate. But now was not the time for such inaction. Lives were at stake here, both family and friends.

Len Tanner poked his head into the tent. "Hey, Isaac. Sorry to disturb you so late, but there's someone on the radio who wants to talk to you."

Inside the Dixie Chick

Thank God for the Dixie Chick, *thank God for Denise Beasley, and thank God for Dvorak planes.*

Christian shared Colonel Renz's concern about relying strictly on up-time technology for reconnaissance, but no cavalry patrol could have flown over the breadth of the Moldavian army and given him the opportunity to ascertain the strength of the full force arrayed against them. He could not see every horse or every man; the forest canopy and the dips and wild elevation switches of the Carpathian foothills were an impediment indeed. But from high above, he could give Colonel Renz much more reliable numbers than any patrol on horseback.

By his numbers, he estimated an enemy force of at least thirty-five hundred to four thousand men. More infantry than cavalry, and not all of them were Moldavian. Denise had dangerously dipped to about two hundred feet on their last pass-over just to allow him to get a good look at the mercenaries in their midst: Tatars, and others whom he couldn't identify. It was a sizable force, and it outnumbered them in Déj almost ten to one. Until, of course, General von Mercy arrived with the rest of the army.

It was going to get deadly in the morning. The only questions remaining now were: when would they attack, and would the combination of defensive position and up-time weaponry be enough to hold them off long enough for reinforcements to arrive?

With the *Dixie Chick* powered off and standing still on its landing site, Denise's radio squelched into life. "Christian? Are you there?"

He sat upright in the pilot's seat. He pressed the button and spoke into the transmitter. "Hello, Isaac. Can you hear me?"

"I can here you, Captain. How are you? Where are you?"

"You wouldn't believe it, but I am sitting in the *Dixie Chick*, compliments of Denise Beasley and the Bohemian air force. I don't have very long. I have to finish my defensive preparations. We've got a Moldavian army that's going to hit us hard in the morning. But I just wanted to say good luck, God speed, and I hope to see you soon."

There was a pause at the other end, and Christian thought the signal had dropped. Then his friend's voice came through loudly. "Thank you, Christian. You too, my friend. I have sent Devorah in with Captain Callenberk's dragoons. She'll be there soon, God willing."

"I look forward to seeing her."

There was another pause, then Isaac asked, "How's your eye?"

Christian swallowed, said, "Fine, just fine. No concerns."

"Good...I hope...we have a..."

"Isaac? Isaac? Can you hear me? Can you..."

The signal was gone.

Christian placed the transmitter back into its holster. He didn't turn the radio off, however, because he wasn't sure how to do it. He'd leave that to Denise.

Chapter 29

The hour of ghosts (midnight)

The hour was late, the fog off the Carpathians was thickening, and Sergiu Botnari was tired. It had been a long, long day, and the days forthcoming would be just as long, just as tiresome. His war against the Jew's army had just begun, and it would continue for however long Allah demanded. Yes, he served Vasile Lupu, but Allah was guiding him now, this night, against the horrors brought to Transylvania. He had tossed one horror into the Szamos River. Through a thicket of brambles and dense leaves, he stared at another.

Twelve men guarded the aircraft: three on its left side; three on its right; three in front; three in back. They formed a tight, defensive square around the wooden-and-canvas bird. They talked amongst themselves, laughing at idiotic Gentile jokes that Sergiu couldn't, nor wouldn't, care to understand. Their defensive position was lighted by two lanterns, both sitting on the ground near the plane. Their buff coats, hard leather boots, and gloves cast shadows on the object, rousing images in Sergiu's mind of jinns, *Ifrits*, the kinds of monsters his mama used to speak of when she bothered to care for him. Their weapons were pistols, two per man holstered at their sides, and a sword on their backs. The same kind of pistol he had taken off one of the dead scouts; the same kind of sword as well.

The hypocrisy was not lost on him. Here he waited, alongside his men, carrying up-time weaponry with the intention of using them, while castigating similar weaponry sitting before his eyes. But a pistol in hand was different. A pistol, he understood. It might be a little more powerful, a little more efficient, in the attack, but it was one of many different kinds of pistols a soldier might find on a field of battle. Matchlocks, flintlocks, wheellocks...a veritable soup of firing mechanisms that, when all mixed together, hardly mattered when men fell and gaps were filled with fresh soldiers.

The weapon before him, being guarded so diligently by cavalrymen, had to be destroyed.

One of his men appeared through the thick foliage. He whispered, "There are no good approaches, Sergiu. Even through darkness, we'd be spotted in time for them to draw pistols and fire."

Sergiu nodded. "I know. I've been looking at the same position you have been for the past hour. We've not got enough men to assault it."

"Perhaps we should reconsider. Move into town and cause as much trouble as we can before morning."

It was a good idea, perhaps even ideal. But what could they do now so close to the fight? Destroy a few more buildings? Kill a few more townsfolk? What good would it do now that armies were arrayed for battle? No. The key to it all was this plane. Sergiu was convinced of that. Perhaps there were other flying air machines coming, but every one destroyed counted. The answer to the prayers that he had lifted up to Allah was simple: destroy this up-time monstrosity, and do it now.

But his man was correct. They could not attack it outright. They had neither the numbers, nor the position. The only option left for them now was what they were good at doing anyway.

"Bring up Dorel with his bow," Sergiu said, "and bring him now. Let's cause a little chaos."

The Dixie Chick

Colonel Renz had offered her more comfortable sleeping accommodations and for the Dvorak to be moved into the town itself, but Denise refused. Until the matter with this Moldavian army was resolved, she'd stay with the *Dixie Chick* on its landing strip and deal with less than comfortable accommodations. The cockpit chairs weren't horribly uncomfortable, but they had not been designed for sleeping. Their backs were a little too rigid for her tastes; their cushions on the seats a little too thin. But such was life. Living in the seventeenth century had its plusses and minuses.

The biggest minus was lack of air-conditioning. Oh, how she longed to feel cool air on her sweaty skin. The air around her wasn't too muggy, and a light breeze coming through the open doors was a relief. But it was different than AC. Nothing could beat AC, except perhaps ice cubes.

How she longed for those as well. Colonel Renz had been kind enough to send his aide-de-camp Major Schmidt to her with food and drink. She had accepted them both humbly, had her fill, and had given the rest to the fellows defending her and her Dvorak. The drink he had offered, however, some kind of heavily diluted wine, would have benefitted from a couple ice cubes. She couldn't complain, she supposed. Well, she could, but who was listening?

She had trouble sleeping because her guards kept speaking in what seemed like a million different languages. She had been living down-time long enough now that she could recognize many of them, and understand several up to a point. Aside from English and Amideutsch, she was by now reasonably fluent in German, although she had a rather pronounced accent that many Germans found hard to comprehend.

Among her guards, she could detect Scandinavian words—she spoke some Swedish and Danish herself—as well as Polish and Spanish. She could even pick out a word or two of Hungarian.

What struck her the most, and not for the first time, was the way they all seemed to speak their own languages, and at least one other person within their ranks understood what someone else was saying. Then again, these were mercenaries. Denise had been told that a company of mercenary cavalry could, over its service to an army, take on new recruits from all different countries, all different walks of life. It made sense.

She dozed, trying to drown out the guards' crude jokes and laughter. She had a good mind to lean out the cockpit and tell them to *shut the hell up, I'm trying to sleep here*, but she refrained.

These men were serving her, defending her with their lives. Let them have their banter. It looked like the evening would pass quietly anyway. No reason to rock the boat.

She dozed, woke up, dozed again. On the third try, a flaming arrow struck the cockpit canvas.

She barely felt it, the canvas and light frame absorbing the shock. She heard it, however, like a mighty tear of paper. She heard the flame bursting on the canvas itself, spreading around the hole where the arrow had struck. It took her a moment to come out of sleep, to come to a clear understanding about what was happening: the *Dixie Chick* was being attacked.

The guards outside were just as shocked as she was, perhaps never imagining that an attack would come from such an antiquated weapon. In their minds, she supposed, arrows were medieval. But such an attack had come, and it struck again. This time, luckily, the arrow missed the plane and hit the road.

The guards began firing back toward the direction where the arrows had come. Denise's only concern was the fire.

She raised out of her chair, grabbed her leather helmet, leaned out of the cockpit, and began slapping the puncture wound. Thank God the flames hadn't spread too far; the kind of canvas that they had used on the Dvoraks weren't flameproof, but they wouldn't go up like paper either. She slapped the flames with her leather helmet while the guards continued to return fire.

Another arrow struck the ground beneath the *Dixie Chick*. Another struck the wing.

Denise screamed, "Goddamn, the wing!"

She tried jumping out of the cockpit to address the burning wing, but one of the guards pushed her back. "*Nein! Bleib hier. Bleib sicher!*"

"We can't let that fire hit the tank!" she shouted, trying again to leave the cockpit, but the man was too strong. He held her down in the seat with one hand, while firing his pistol into the darkness.

Denise struggled to free herself, opened her mouth to bite the man's hand, when he suddenly went stiff and fell from a wound that sprayed her face with his blood.

"Shit!"

She straightened in the seat, tried collecting her nerves, and reached for the ignition. *Got to get away, got to get away...*

Another arrow struck the cockpit right above her. The arrow sliced a huge gap in the canvas, but luckily the flame went out. She reached up, ripped the arrow free, tossed it aside, and tried starting the engine.

A hand reached in, grabbed her hair, and pulled. She screamed again, clawing, pushing, and punching at the arm, but he was too strong, whoever he was. No guard, for sure. Pistol fire still reported nearby. Men howled, screamed, fell, and here she was, getting her hair ripped out by some beast who wanted her dead, or worse.

My pistol!

She had forgotten it. She so rarely needed it. Had never needed it, in fact.

She struggled with one hand to keep the wolf at bay and reached underneath her seat with the other. She felt around and found the gun—but the man pulled so hard this time that he dragged her partially out the cockpit door. She gripped her weapon, an up-time Smith & Wesson 442, a small, blunt nose .38 caliber revolver with five rounds.

The man yanked her out of the plane and onto the ground. Denise raised her pistol to his chest and fired.

He fell dead immediately on top of her. He was heavy, sweaty, smelly. Denise almost vomited. She held her bile, pushed free from the lout, and sat there.

Several of her guards were down. Another flaming arrow struck the propeller and spanged off harmlessly. Before her, a man crawled up the ditch, saw her, paused, and tried to raise his pistol. Denise fired, missed her first shot, got him on the second.

Another man came up behind him and tried to be quicker on his draw. But his cumbersome down-time pistol couldn't fire at the speed of her 442. She almost felt sorry for him as she put her penultimate round into his belly, and he fell dead beside his comrade.

There was a pause. Denise climbed up and got back into the cockpit. She was shaking so badly she almost dropped the pistol. But she managed to hold onto it, like it was a jewel or some favorite child's toy.

A hand reached into the cockpit. Denise flinched away from it, turned, fired—and missed.

Now she was out of bullets, and the man stood there, grinning like a mad clown, staring at her like she was a joke. He was sweaty too, but his bald head was covered with a blue scarf, his thin white shirt disheveled, the scars of previous fights roped across his face like ugly white worms. The pistol he held toward her was no down-time weapon; it was the exact same pistol her guards carried.

Desperately, she flung herself out of the cockpit onto his feet and then rolled back under the plane's fuselage. She heard him fire but wasn't struck by a bullet. The son of a bitch had probably expected her to cower. Fat chance of that happening! Denise was more scared than she'd ever been in her life, but she reacted to fear with belligerence.

She kept rolling until she was no longer under the fuselage. Then, she rose in a crouch and ran off as fast as she could manage. She was surprised that he didn't fire again. That might be because he wasn't familiar with aircraft and didn't realize that his bullets would pass right through the thin fabric of the fuselage.

If true, that meant—

She dodged to one side. An instant later she felt her leg struck by something. If it was a bullet, though, it had just been a grazing blow. The bastard was probably now crouched down and firing at her from underneath the fuselage.

If so—

She straightened up from her crouch and started doing her best to mimic the broken field running she'd seen football players do.

It worked! She heard two more shots fire but neither struck her—and then she reached the tree line and passed out of her enemy's sight.

She paused just long enough to catch her breath and then penetrated still deeper into the woods. Walking quickly, not running. The last thing she needed was to trip over a root and break a leg or sprain an ankle.

She didn't go very far, though, before the sound of galloping horses brought her out of her state of terror. That was cavalry coming. Whose, though?

Sergiu heard the same rumbling—but he knew exactly whose cavalry was coming.

Not his, that was for sure. He uncocked his up-time pistol, tucked it behind his belt, and disappeared into the night. Trying to decide whether he was more furious with the girl for outwitting him or more impressed.

More impressed. Sergiu had been in far too many battles, large and small, not to appreciate a capable enemy. And a girl that young!

Next time he met her, if he ever did, he'd make sure to fire instantly.

Once Denise was sure the cavalry that had arrived was on the side of the angels, she came back out of the woods.

Hobbling a little. That damn bastard *had* shot her, after all. The weirdest gunshot wound she'd ever heard of. The bullet hadn't even broken the skin, just barely grazed the limb and gone off into the distance.

She might wind up with one hell of a bruise, though.

Colonel Renz's headquarters, at dawn

"We're lucky that her radio was on," Christian said to Colonel Renz the next morning. "We heard the attack almost from the beginning. I don't think she remembered that I had just used it, and I hadn't turned it off."

Colonel Renz nodded. "Her status?"

"She's resting in my camp. After she was calm enough to taxi the plane into town, I didn't give her an option. She's fine physically, except for a small bruise on her left leg. Mentally, well, it'll take a little while for the shock to wear off. But most girls her age—most boys, for that matter—would probably still be shaking."

At that moment, Christian wished Isaac were here. He'd be the better judge of both Denise's physical and mental condition.

"And the plane?" Colonel Renz asked.

Christian shrugged. "Not destroyed, thankfully. The canvas on the left wing is badly damaged, however. We managed to douse the fire before it ignited the gas tank. The cockpit itself is in pretty good condition. Some small burn damage, some tears. Otherwise, it's fine. But Denise is grounded, sir. She and the *Dixie Chick* won't be helping us today. We don't have the kind of canvas they used to construct the wings, not in great abundance anyway. We could strip some of the wagon covers and use that cloth for the time being, but I don't think there are many among us who could make such repairs efficiently, not without Denise's guidance anyway, and I don't think she's up to that right now. Besides, and unfortunately, we have other matters to attend to this morning."

Colonel Renz nodded. "And I wouldn't think she'd be much help to us now anyway. The enemy will come, and men on the *ground* will engage it."

Christian wanted to correct the colonel's misguided notions. He wanted to tell him about what he had experienced being up there among the clouds, how valuable such visibility was to the overall understanding of how the battle was unfolding and how it might unfold in the hours to come. But he refrained. There was no time to argue the issue. No matter what Colonel Renz's attitude was, he was right: the enemy was near and, sometime today, it would attack.

Captain Neuneck, out of breath, stepped into the room. He didn't bother to salute. "They're here, Colonel."

"Who? Callenberk?"

"No, sir. The Moldavians."

Chapter 30

At the southern approaches into Déj

Crimean Tatars!!

A force perhaps two hundred, two hundred fifty strong, had attacked his fortifications by first light shortly after he had returned from Colonel Renz's headquarters. They wasted no time striking, regardless of his deployment of what up-timers called *area-denial weaponry*. Caltrops peppered the ground on both ends of the make-shift palisade that he and his men had constructed to slow down, if not prevent, cavalry and infantry charges. Sharp wooden spikes had been driven into the ground beyond those for additional protection. By doing all this, Christian had hoped that the Moldavian commanders would dispense with any cavalry charge at all. And they had, indeed, done so, but not in the manner he had hoped.

The Crimean Tatars were semi-independent vassals of the Ottomans and had firearms—and plenty of them. But they'd been mounted archers for centuries and still used their bows regularly. In this instance, realizing that the defenses would make a direct cavalry charge too costly, they were simply showering the fortifications with arrows. Some were using muskets for the purpose, but most weren't.

He ducked his head back behind a wagonload of barrels as an arrow *thunked* into wood above his head. He waited until the volley subsided, then said to Lieutenant Enkefort, who crouched nearby, hugging his radio close, "They're hitting us in caracole."

"How much longer can we hold, Captain?" Enkefort asked, keeping low.

Christian shook his head. "With the kind of constant barrage they're placing on us, I don't know. Thank God it isn't cannon fire. How are we doing on ammunition?"

"Fine, so far, sir," Enkefort said, brushing splintered wood off his shoulders. "Your order to fire single barrel was a sound one."

Christian shrugged as he finished loading that single barrel. "Well, it stretches out the ammunition, but our kill power has been reduced. War seems to be all about balancing choices, eh, Lieutenant?"

The ZB-2 Santee was a modification of the up-time Pedersoli Howdah 58-caliber hunting pistol, a breechloader that used paper cartridges. It was what up-timers called, in effect, a sawed-off double-barreled shotgun. At roughly a foot long, a cavalryman could either fire both barrels in a single shot or one at a time. On horseback, it was ideal to fire only one barrel at a time, thus giving the rider two shots in relatively quick succession. Firing both simultaneously could, in contrast, be dangerous because of its powerful recoil. In his short time as a cavalryman, Christian had seen men fire both barrels at full charge and have their pistols torn right out of their hands. One man had been knocked clean off his horse when the pistol kicked back and smacked his face.

Another Tatar volley struck the wooden defenses. A man at the head of the wagon he and Enkefort were in fell screaming with a wound to his shoulder. Christian grimaced, waited until the volley subsided, then fully cocked his ZB, stood up, and shouted, "Fire!"

His men, about ninety strong now, rose up along their hastily assembled palisade, and squeezed triggers.

The good thing about firing at Tatars was their light armor and paucity of helmets. A Tatar was a nice, meaty target if you could aim and shoot at him—or his horse—before he fired his bow and retreated, thus allowing another line of cavalry to move up and fire. Christian's men fired and dropped a half dozen before they had a chance to flee. *Good!* The road was becoming messy with dead horses, dead men, and pools of blood. *Good!*

"Reload!"

The idea of having cavalry defend a city was absurd. They were lucky that—so far, at least—they were only facing cavalry attackers. Captain Kinsky had been right to suggest that Colonel Renz was making a big mistake in ordering such a defense with men so unprepared for it. But as the morning's fight had raged, Christian saw the logic behind it.

Even firing one barrel at a time, the ZB was a powerful weapon, and its kill potential and accuracy was far superior to anything these Tatars were firing at them. Indeed, it wasn't a perfect weapon. It wounded or outright missed more than it struck, but what it struck, more often than not stayed down. A pile of dead men and horses were beginning to form along the enemy attack line. How much longer could the Tatars maintain their tactics before their horses couldn't maneuver around the piles? Mounted archery was deadly in the open field; much less so against fortified troops.

Christian reloaded his ZB and dared a moment to look toward the eastern approaches and Captain Kinsky's position. Large, dark plumes of smoke floated above his defensive lines, more so than Christian's line. According to initial radio reports, Captain Kinsky had been hit by a large block of pikemen who were nearly routed on first contact. A foolish tactic against a modern army such as the Sunrise, but the Moldavians obviously knew no better. Perhaps they should have known, being vassals of the Ottomans whose army was also relatively modern. The Ring of Fire hadn't just occurred, after all. But the Moldavians had recovered quickly and were now hitting Kinsky in the same caracole-style assault with additional Tatars and their own Hansari (or light) cavalry.

Another strong volley struck Christian's wagon. "Sir," Enkefort said, finishing the reload of his own pistol, "perhaps you should pull off the line for a bit. We can't afford to lose our commander."

"We can't afford to pull anyone right now," Christian said, rising up on his knees, and shouting, "Fire!"

A great volley, as a majority of the Tatars scattered before the wall of ZB fire. The road now was really beginning to get choked with wounded and dead men. Surely these tactics of theirs could not continue for much longer.

"Your spyglass," Christian said to Enkefort, who handed it over quickly and began reloading both their pistols.

The stack of planks and barrels in front of them now had plenty of gaps through which he could use the spyglass to have a good look. Christian made sure to use his good eye. The blurry one had been watery and uncomfortable all morning. He poked the lens of the spyglass through a hole and looked.

He didn't like what he saw.

At the eastern approaches into Déj

"I've got men in these houses now," Captain Kinsky said to Colonel Renz, pointing to the buildings near his defensive line. "My best shooters. Voinici infantry have moved up on the ridge-line, like I had predicted would happen, and are trying to rain shots down upon my rear. They're pretty damn good shots too, despite their antiquated weaponry. My men are returning fire. We're giving as good as we're getting right now. But right now is not forever, Colonel."

Colonel Renz was pleased. He nodded. "Can you hold?"

The dragoon captain shrugged. "A while longer, but as I say, not forever. We delivered a serious blow to them at first light. But they aren't stupid. They've adapted, and they know that their time is short. They're hitting us with everything they've got right now."

Ricochet musket fire from the ridgeline peppered the ground near their position. Captain Kinsky grabbed Colonel Renz's jacket and pulled him around the corner of a tannery. "See what I mean, Colonel? The streets of Déj aren't safe at the moment."

Colonel Renz breathed a sigh. "Understood. Hold as best as you can, Captain. Callenberk is about five miles out. He'll be here directly, and I've instructed him to add his men to your line."

"Thank you, Colonel," Kinsky said, not bothering to hide his relief and satisfaction with the decision. "That will be most helpful."

Major Schmidt scampered across the street from his defensive position behind a pile of crates. Shots along the ridgeline rang out, as if in response to his move, but no balls struck nearby or along the path that the colonel's aide-de-camp used to reach him.

Major Schmidt was out of breath, but he held the phone of his radio tightly in his hand. He held it out to Colonel Renz, who didn't like the look on his young aide's face. "It's Captain von Jori, sir."

At the southern approaches into Déj

Christian slammed the radio down. "Did you hear that?"

Lieutenant Enkefort nodded. "I did. Only half of Callenberk's men?"

Christian nodded. "I could hear Kinsky howling in the background. He wanted them all."

"Fifty dragoons *is* a decent number, sir."

"True, but it's not enough for what's coming."

He looked through his spyglass again to confirm. Yes, indeed: a full regiment of infantry with ample musket support, followed by another company of cavalry. The Tatars had pulled away to give them a clear line of approach.

Beyond that... hard to tell. The road turned, and the line of sight was blocked by trees, gun smoke, and dying white plumes of Carpathian fog. But surely, there was something more coming. Cannon?

God, give me strength!

"Reload... both barrels!" he screamed in the lull as the next Moldavian wave moved into place. He could hear their trumpets sounding, their commanders shouting orders, the shuffle of uncountable hooves. "Lieutenant, I want you to move up the line here and keep good order. The men will stand by your command or answer to me. We hold firm now, and hope by the grace of God that Callenberk arrives soon."

Lieutenant Enkefort scampered away. Christian looked through his spyglass again. The smoke from previous volleys had faded. He could now see the Moldavian lines forming. A sizable pike block, but in more modern fashion, a kind of hastily prepared tercio supported by rows of musketmen on all sides. The front block of musketeers was moving to form a three-row volley line. Roughly thirty muskets firing fresh and all at once. They were still too far away yet to hit even with powerful ZBs, but soon, very soon...

"Can I help?"

Despite all that had happened in the past two hours, Denise's voice startled him. He turned abruptly and saw her there, standing in the same clothing she had worn the night before when they had found her standing, shaking and in shock, near her Dvorak. "Denise! Why are you here?"

"I want to help."

Christian shook his head. "I don't think that's a good idea. Are you well? Have you recovered from last night?"

"What are you, my nurse?"

She asked the question with a smile on her face, as if in jest. Christian then realized just how much like Isaac he sounded. *I haven't released you from my care...* "Denise, with respect, I really don't think..."

She climbed into the wagon. "Too bad. I'm fine, I'm here to help. Give me a pistol. I know how to shoot."

"Where's that little pistol you had in your hand last night?" he asked.

She thumbed behind her. "I left it and my reload in the *Dixie Chick*. I ain't going to go get it. It wouldn't last long anyway, and besides, I won't be flying for a few days at least, and I'm bored sitting around in that tent of yours. The action is right here, right now. Give me a pistol."

Christian shook his head. "You can't fire a ZB Santee."

"Why, 'cause I'm a girl?"

"No," he said, checking the spyglass again to see the enemy progress. *Getting close...* "Not because of that, but because the kickback is too strong. With respect, Denise, your arm is too small, too thin." He hefted his pistol to show her its weight and size. "It's likely to damage your wrist for sure if you try to fire it."

"Why? The weight of the pistol will absorb most of the recoil."

"That's true. But look at the size of your hand. If you don't have a good grip on it..." He frowned. "It's hard to shoot that gun with a small hand without hurting yourself. I know. I've seen it happen. And that's all we need: a pilot with a broken wrist."

"Fine!" Denise said, crossing her arms in anger, just like his sister used to do when they were young. "Give me something else to do, then."

There was no further time to argue about it. Christian looked through the spyglass once more. "Ready arms!" he shouted, his voice cracking, his throat growing soar. "Wait for my command!

"Very well. Help the men bring ammunition to the line. They're going to hit us with everything they've got in about two minutes. Can you do that?"

Denise smiled and saluted. "Yes, sir, Captain, sir." She jumped off the wagon with clear excitement and sense of purpose on her face. And she began to sing.

"Every little thing she does is magic..."

Chapter 31

At the northern approaches into Déj

The sight of Captain Callenberk was most welcome. "Where the hell have you been, Captain?" Colonel Renz asked. "There's a war on!"

Callenberk reined his horse to a stop. He saluted quickly. "Orders, Colonel. Slow and steady, so sayeth the commanding officer."

It was a sound policy in a foreign land, especially in one as diverse as the Transylvanian plateau. So many places along the march to suffer ambushes, hazards. Move as one, consistent force, and keep from being divided and destroyed.

"Did you experience any problems en route, Captain?"

"Not a one."

"Good," Colonel Renz said, nodding, "then I want you to—"

A massive exchange of gunfire erupted near the southern approaches. Colonel Renz could not see what had just occurred, but he'd seen enough battle to know: volley against volley.

He pointed in that direction. "That's our killing field right now, Captain. Change of plans. Do not divide your men as previously ordered. Lead all your men there and help Captain von Jori beat those bastards back. You understand me?"

"Yes, Colonel," Captain Callenberk said. "Yaww!"

He was gone, and his company of dragoons followed.

Colonel Renz watched them pass with pride. He was beginning to feel much better about their situation.

At the southern approaches into Déj

Volley met volley, and the wooden fortifications around Christian weakened. The wagon he was on buckled to the ground, its rear axle splintering in two. The barrels in the wagon tumbled. The men standing alongside him lost their footing. He grabbed one before the man fell, held him tight, and said, "Reload! Double again!"

All up and down the line, the fortification that they had assembled began to weaken. Despite his urging and threats of discipline, a small number of the men had left their positions, had dropped off the back of the fortification, and were now milling about as if they didn't know what to do. Other men filled those gaps, but the number of those were dwindling. By raw count on fingers, Christian figured he'd lost a dozen, perhaps more. Pistols lay on the ground unclaimed.

Another lull. Behind his barrier, he could hear the death moans of men on both sides. It hurt him deeply to hear it, no matter which side, though he couldn't help but give deference to his men, those who still held their ground and fought as ordered. He understood the cowards; they were mercenaries. They fought for gold, for treasure. They would, if conditions warranted, turn at any time. That was the real price one paid for relying on mercenaries. But now was not the time, and here was not the place for such insubordination and cowardice.

"Fire!"

His fighting men rose and fired, full double barrels, into the lines of Moldavian musketmen who fired, fell back, fired, fell back, while the entire infantry block inched closer, closer. Bodies were still piling up in their path, and Christian allowed himself the notion that perhaps they were wavering, reconsidering this heavy assault against his position. Such tactics could not last forever. Indeed, Christian had far fewer men than the Moldavians, but they did not have an inexhaustible supply of fresh soldiers either. Their slow approach could not last much longer.

They'll charge...as sure as shit, they'll charge...

Denise crouched for protection behind a wagon wheel as the space above her erupted in splintered wood and whistling lead balls. When the madness stopped, she held up a box of paper carriages, and said, "Here, take it!"

Lieutenant Enkefort took the resupply and shouted down to her, "They're working up for a big charge, Fräulein. Time for you to leave!"

"Bite me!"

She waited a few seconds longer and then ran again to the three wagons that sat guarded about fifty feet behind the line. Luckily, the defensive wall itself had slowed down the enemy's massive volleys such that the supply wagons had not taken any hits. A steady stream of men moved back and forth across the space, delivering resupply to Captain von Jori's men still defending the battlements. It was a good system, but how long would it last? Lieutenant Enkefort was right. Denise knew next to nothing about war, but by God, anyone could hear and see that the enemy was drawing closer with every volley.

She grabbed another two boxes of cartridges, tucking one under each arm. They felt awkward, uncomfortable pushed up into her armpit, but she managed.

A shot ricocheted off a stone wall nearby, striking the runner down in front of her. Denise paused, stepped over the body carefully, and continued to the line.

"Reload!" Christian ordered. "Fire at will!"

He then jumped down from his damaged wagon and hefted his smoking pistol for the cowards to see. "What the hell are you doing back here? Turn, climb back to your positions, and defend the line."

One man huffed, shook his head. "I'm not an infantryman, Captain. I ride a horse. I did not sign up for this kind of work."

"Besides," another piped in, rubbing black powder residue out of his beard. "We can't hold this line forever. You know it."

"I know that!" Christian said, yelling louder than he intended. Loud enough for a number of the men on the wall to take notice. "But that is not our decision. Not yet, anyway. We can still hold, and so I'm ordering you to—"

"Captain!"

Christian answered the man's call by jumping back into his wagon and peeking through one of the many holes in the palisade.

The front lines of Moldavian musketmen had cleared away.

Behind them, dividing the block of infantry, were three crews moving their six-pounder cannons into position.

"Kill the crews!"

Denise heard Christian shout, "Kill the crews!" At first, she didn't know what that meant. *Kill the what?* Then she heard someone on the line say "cannon." Of course, now it made sense.

She dropped her boxes, and a man picked them up and carried them to his portion of the line. "What's going on, Lieutenant?" she asked, but Enkefort didn't respond. His attention was glued to a gap in the wall.

She climbed up beside him, keeping her head down. "Go away, Denise," he said, trepidation in his voice, his eyes red from smoke and anger. "This is no place for—"

"Yes, a woman, I know. But here I am. Give me a gun, damn you. You need all the shooters you can get!"

He cursed loudly and pushed a half-cocked ZB to her with his boot. "It's half-cocked. When I order, cock it fully and fire. You do know how to hold and fire a gun?"

Denise nodded. "I wouldn't have asked you for one if I didn't."

It was a lie, of course. Yes, she knew how to fire her little up-time pistol. But this? It was nearly a foot long, and heavy. *Maybe Christian is right*, she said to herself. She could barely wrap her hand around the handle and reach a finger out to the trigger. *Gretchen could fire this thing* . . . but Gretchen was not here, was she?

Denise looked up and down the line. Defending it were a bunch of determined but terrified cavalrymen, and a girl from West Virginia.

She smiled. *I like our odds* . . .

Christian's men were too far away for an effective shot, but they fired anyway and struck a couple in the advancing infantry block, a few retreating musketmen. Fire ricocheted off the gun barrels, but no crewmen were hit.

"Hold your positions!" Christian screamed, his voice cracking as he listened to the gun crews prepare to fire.

He prayed, something he rarely did. Not for himself, but for his men, even for the cowards. He looked back at them, but they were gone.

Orders from the officers of the gun crews rang out while his men, as required, fired at will. Every shot counted, Christian knew, even the ones that missed, for it created a wall of lead balls that would be difficult to navigate through.

At that moment, Christian wavered in his certainty. *Am I wise to stay here? Are those cowards the ones who are wiser? They're right: we're cavalry. We've no business defending a position like this. I've no business defending one. We can't hold. We've got to retreat... we've got to...*

He rose up to shout the order.

The Moldavian cannons fired, and the wagon to his right, the one tethered to his own, erupted in an explosion of splintered wood and broken bodies.

The wagon he was in toppled backward.

The wagons that erupted backward from the cannon fire were far enough away that neither Denise nor Enkefort were injured in the blast. They were, however, tossed backward off their wagons and to the ground.

Denise was surprised that she still gripped her pistol, had used it actually to support her fall. A soldier fell across her legs. His weight was painful, but she didn't hear any cracking or tearing. He rolled over her small body. She shielded her face from the pressure of his weight and waited until he was up and away.

Enemy infantry poured through the gap, their collective shouting making it difficult for her to concentrate. *Where's Enkefort?* she wondered. In the mass of men filing through the gap, she couldn't make out many details. The world was nothing but a swirl of confused men howling and running and firing and dying. Through the clamor, she could hear sword striking sword, and she looked toward the sound.

Enkefort and a Moldavian swordsman were engaged. The scene almost seemed comical to her. In the midst of all this chaos, here were two men trading sword blows like in a Hollywood movie. She almost imagined herself sitting in a dark theater, holding a bucket of popcorn, feeding her face while staring at the hero facing the villain.

Enkefort was good with a sword. But of course, he was a cavalry officer, probably better with a sword than a pistol. He parried everything the Moldavian soldier sent his way, and it seemed as if the villain was tiring. His shoulders were dropping, his thrusts and hacks weakening. The hero was ready to deliver the killing blow.

Then Enkefort was bumped by passing men and twisted to the left. He lost his footing, and the Moldavian swordsman popped the lieutenant on the back of his head with the hilt of his sword.

Enkefort fell on his face and lay still. The Moldavian raised the sword to thrust it into his back.

"NO!" Denise screamed. She cocked both barrels, raised her pistol, held it firmly with both hands to ensure no severe kick-back, and fired.

Christian could hear nothing, save for a ringing in his ears as a wave of Moldavian infantry poured through the gap created by the powerful cannon fire. For a moment, he did not move. The men pouring through the gap didn't notice or care about him. They held their pikes, swords, picks, and axes firmly, and rushed into the street. His men were still fighting, but now in full retreat.

The man lying on top of him was one of his own. The man wasn't dead, thankfully, just knocked cold from the focused cannon fire which had tossed him hard. Christian wanted to revive the man, but there was no time: enemy soldiers were flooding past them.

Christian pushed the man off and crawled backward, away from the shuffle of enemy infantry. He reached toward his holster to pull his pistol. It wasn't there. He groped around on the ground to find it. He found one, not his own. He cocked it, aimed it toward the mass of legs nearby, and pulled the trigger.

Nothing. He searched for another one, found it, cocked both hammers, and fired.

This time, the pistol sounded, and two Moldavian soldiers fell. The shots, however, didn't seem to affect the stream of enemy infantry. Men behind the fallen simply stepped over the writhing bodies and continued. Christian tried to find another discarded pistol. This time, he found an old ball-butt wheellock that appeared to be loaded, half-cocked, and ready. He paused, not because he was afraid, but because for a moment, he forgot how to use one. It had been so long. Then, memory flooded back. He cocked it, raised it, and fired.

Another man fell, and this time, two Moldavian soldiers took notice.

Christian was not injured; he didn't appear to be anyway, save for the small splinter cut on his cheek and the ringing in his ears that had diminished somewhat. He dropped the wheellock and scrambled backward, then used a broken crate to pull himself up. He was dizzy, but otherwise, whole. He drew his sword, and the two men who had noticed his wheellock fire pulled themselves out of the charging herd and raised their muskets to shoot him.

Christian did not give them time to aim. He raised his sword, screamed an obscenity, and charged.

The strong, high-pitched note of a trumpet sounded.

Reflexively, Christian dropped. One of the men fired over his head. Then they heard the blaring sound as well, turned back toward the breach in the wall, and ran for their lives.

Captain Callenberk's dragoons had arrived.

They did not bother to dismount. They simply charged into the Moldavian infantry as if they were nothing but a ripple of water, splitting them in two like a trowel through fresh spring soil. They were a little worn from their night ride, perhaps, but otherwise fresh, with unspotted cuirass armor glinting in the sun, long leather boots, long gauntlets. Each possessed two holstered ZBs and one sheathed ZB-1636 rifle on their saddles. On their backs—many now in their hands—were their much feared *Panzerstecher* heavy swords, hacking and hammering through the shocked Moldavians who, for their part, halted their charge and, instead, fled to the rear.

It was a beautiful thing to see. Not only the Moldavians falling dead or falling back, but by count, Christian was already up to sixty horses. He continued to count, and it became clear that Colonel Renz had changed the order. He had sent *all* of Captain Callenberk's dragoons to his position, not just half. Good decision. But why hadn't he heard of the order? Why hadn't Lieutenant Enkefort—

Then he remembered. Enkefort was on the other side of the breach. And where was he? Where was Denise? Christian tried looking through the mass of men and cavalry in front of him blocking his view of conditions on the other side. The other side constituted roughly half his men. How were they? Where were they?

A glut of bodies formed at the breach: Moldavian infantry that could not get through the gap quickly enough due to their panicked retreat; dragoons who were now using their pistols and rifles to kill as many as they could before the breach collapsed upon itself and cleared a path. Callenberk was giving no quarter. His men were firing at anything that moved. It became a slaughter, and Christian turned his eyes away.

The breach finally caved, and the Moldavian withdrawal became a total rout.

About a third of Callenberk's men pursued beyond the gap, continuing the slaughter until the trumpet sounded to order them back. Christian's line of sight to the other side of the breach now improved. He walked slowly through the mangle of bodies, pushing aside a dead man here, a wounded man there, searching for his lieutenant and Denise Beasley.

He found them, with Lieutenant Enkefort whole but apparently wounded. Denise held the man in her lap as they rested against a wagon wheel.

"Where are you wounded, Lieutenant?" Christian asked.

"A man clocked him on the back of the head," Denise said. "Looks like he's got a twisted knee as well."

Christian checked Enkefort's head. Yes, indeed: a right nasty bump on the back, near the neck. Swollen and bloody. "And what about you?" he asked Denise.

She shook her head. "I'm fine. The blood on my shirt is Enkefort's."

"I owe you my life, Fräulein," Enkefort said.

Denise waved it off with her good hand. "Don't worry about it. Buy me a drink when we get to Kolozsvár, and we'll call it even."

As his dragoons seized the breach, Captain Callenberk approached. He reined his horse to a stop and dismounted. Christian stood in greeting. "Captain Callenberk. Glad to see you."

"I'm sure you are," Callenberk said rather arrogantly, keeping an eye on his men as they began to take defensive positions along the much weakened fortifications. "How are you? Your men?"

Christian nodded. "Scattered. We'll have to re-form, collect our wounded." He pointed to Enkefort and Denise. "Lieutenant Enkefort will need to be taken to the medical tent."

Captain Callenberk nodded. "You take care of your company,

Captain. You can stand down. I claim the wall. Gather your men, take care of your wounded, and then I'd advise you to collect your horses and stand at the ready. We may have need of you later. I don't think the Moldavians are finished with us yet."

It was an unwritten rule in Colonel Renz's regiment that the captains of the dragoon companies held seniority over all other commanders, minus the colonel, of course. In effect, both Callenberk and Kinsky were Christian's superior officers. If they ordered him to do something, it was expected that he would. It wasn't binding, however, and amongst mercenary soldiers, trying to get them to take orders from a captain other than their own was difficult at best. But in this case, Christian was delighted to follow Callenberk's "advice."

"Very good, Captain," he said, "and I thank you."

Callenberk nodded, mounted his horse again, and joined his men.

"Come on," Christian said, offering his hand, "let's get you to the tent."

He and Denise helped Enkefort to his feet. The lieutenant winced under the pain of his twisted knee. "I think I'm going to throw up."

And he did, all over Christian's boot, which surprisingly was an improvement over the spattered Moldavian blood congealing on the blunt toe. "It's his head wound," Denise said. "I don't know much about blunt force trauma, but I know that much. He's got a concussion for sure."

General Andrian Radu's headquarters
East of Déj

General Radu took a final look at Sergiu Botnari's up-time pistol, then handed it back. "Nice pistol," he admitted, "but we've no time for this. You failed, Sergiu."

"On the contrary," the leader of the Impalers said, accepting his pistol back. "We damaged the plane. It has not flown since."

"Yes, but you did not kill its pilot. You had an opportunity to do so, or so you say. You did not fire. Why?"

Sergiu shrugged. "As I've explained, General, cavalry came to her aid before my men and I had the opportunity."

General Radu huffed. "Came too quickly to simply squeeze a trigger? That is inconsistent with everything I've learned about you."

Sergiu said nothing to that. He simply stood there, quietly, and let a smile draw across his face. "As I said, time ran out. As it appears to be doing for you, General. Your southern attack against the enemy cavalry did not end in success."

The general raged. "*You* are wrong, Sergiu. The attack did succeed. We breached those flimsy walls."

"Only to be pushed back."

"By fresh dragoons wielding those infernal up-time weapons," General Radu said, pointing at Sergiu's pistol. "All things considered, we've done well today. Our attack has depleted their men and materiel considerably. I do not need you lecturing me on field tactics."

"No, General, you do not. You served Voivode Lupu well at Csíkszereda. That is why he gave you this command. But there, you were fighting against conscripted peasants. Here, you are fighting against trained men, mercenaries, wielding these." Sergiu hefted his pistol.

"We still outnumber them eight to one."

Sergiu nodded. "Yes, but for how long? Von Mercy is coming, General. He is but a few hours away. When he arrives, that advantage will diminish considerably."

General Radu struck, in frustration, the makeshift table between them. The stones on the map in the center, representing units both friend and foe, toppled and shifted out of place.

"What are you proposing, sir?"

Sergiu cleared his throat. "I and mine are heading to Szamosújvár to continue to do what Voivode Lupu has charged me to do: burn fields, destroy homes—and kill if necessary—to ensure that von Mercy's army suffers as much as possible as they march to Kolozsvár. I'd advise you to do the same.

"Right now, despite our losses, your army is still in good order, and your wise decision to divert men and cannon to the southern attack gives you the march into Szamosújvár. If you pull your forces out now, you can be there by morning, entrenched, and ready when von Mercy arrives."

General Radu shook his head. "I have been informed that

Prince Rákóczi is sending an army to Szamosújvár. It might already be there."

Sergiu nodded. "You have proven yourself most capable of defeating a Transylvanian force, General. I don't doubt you can prove yourself again."

General Radu squinted, seemingly confused. "You're advising that I get myself caught between a hammer and an anvil?"

Sergiu was now losing patience with this man. He held his tongue and said, "I'm suggesting that you disengage from an army that you—that I—don't fully understand, and take your chances against one that you do. These up-time weapons—this pistol, their muskets—though not all that different in design from our own pistols and muskets, can make a force of four hundred fight like a thousand. When von Mercy arrives, there will be no chance to seize and control Déj. Fall back and fight another day, General. Our job, as required by Voivode Lupu, is to bide time."

General Radu huffed. "That's your job, Sergiu. Not mine."

Sergiu watched as Radu turned away from the table. He paced through the room, rubbing his ample chin and seemingly conducting a heated conversation with himself. It was disturbing to watch, but Sergiu let him pace and mumble, uninterrupted, for perhaps somewhere in that anxious mind, Radu would find the right decision.

"Thank you for your advice, Sergiu Botnari," General Radu said, turning back to the table. "Scurry off to Szamosújvár if you wish and do what you do best. My army will stay here. We will hit them on the eastern approach with everything we have, and we will bring Voivode Lupu his much deserved victory."

Chapter 32

Szatmár (Satu Mare)

A bit to her surprise, Gretchen and her wagon train arrived in Szatmár before Morris Roth and the main body of the Grand Army of the Sunrise. She knew she'd been making better time than he was, which wasn't surprising given the difference between an army numbering in the thousands, mostly infantry, and a wagon train with only six wagons. The fact that everyone in her expedition who wasn't riding in a wagon was on horseback made a difference also.

Still, from their last radio exchange a little over a week earlier, it had seemed they would arrive at roughly the same time. But they'd been traveling by different routes, neither of which had been scouted very thoroughly. The route taken by Gretchen and her wagon train had presented no significant problems. Perhaps the same hadn't been true for Morris' army.

It didn't really matter. Shortly after they arrived in Szatmár, they were able to resume radio contact with Morris, so they knew they wouldn't be on their own for very long. The main body of the Sunrise would arrive in Szatmár in four days.

And that didn't matter very much, either. There was no large military force in the town. Szatmár was not located near the battle lines that were forming, so most of its troops had been summoned south to defend the capital. The garrison that remained was small—about twenty men, more of a police force than anything else—and they were not what anyone, including themselves, would consider an elite unit.

There were almost that many armed men (and several women, including Gretchen herself) in the wagon train. And there were other differences as well. Most of the men assigned to the wagon train as a guard force were CoC militants, at least half of them military veterans. Several had been personally selected by Gunther Achterhof in Magdeburg. Gretchen had been one of the central founders of the Committees of Correspondence and was undoubtedly the best known. She was famous (or notorious) across most of Europe. The CoCs were not about to take chances with her life.

Then there was the disparity in weapons. Szatmár's garrison was armed with smoothbore muskets, many of which were still matchlocks and none of which were flintlocks. The best they had were snaphaunces, the predecessor of the flintlock. They might well have not even heard of percussion caps. They certainly didn't have any.

In contrast, every one of Gretchen's guards was equipped with the USE army's new rifle, the Hockenjoss & Klott Model C, shortened to H&KC but usually called by the nickname of "Hocklott." It was a .406 caliber breech-loading rifle and was probably the best rifle anywhere in the world, at least for the moment.

While on horseback, they were also armed with ZB-2 Santee pistols which they'd purchased in Bohemia on their way to Kassa.

Oh, yes—and they also had quite a few top-of-the-line grenades and even a small 2.5-inch mortar.

But what was probably most important was simply the difference between the men who would be involved in the event of an armed clash. The wagon train's guards didn't exactly exude savage belligerence and instant readiness to smite any and all foes, but...they came close enough that no one in Szatmár wanted to experiment with the possibility. Least of all the soldiers of the garrison.

Leaving all that aside, the current political status of Szatmár was in transition. It was part of the area that Prince Rákóczi had agreed to cede to Bohemia in exchange for an alliance.

As was true of many towns in the area, Szatmár was used to running its own affairs because it had changed hands so many times between various kingdoms over the centuries. The most recent overlord had been Transylvania, whose prince had taken advantage of the fuzziness surrounding the transfer of Royal Hungary (parts of it, anyway) from Habsburg to Bohemian hands. Rákóczi had sent in his own troops—most of whom had now been withdrawn to deal with the menace coming from Wallachia and Moldavia.

So, all remained tranquil. Gretchen tried to find whatever town authorities there might be to establish a modus vivendi, but her search proved fruitless. Word had already filtered into the area that it was going to be granted to Bohemia in exchange for Bohemian military support.

Transylvania was a more feudal region than the Germanies. Its power structure was complicated, though, because along with the feudal traditions there were also traditions produced by the principality's ethnic composition. There was really no such thing, in this time period, as a "Transylvanian," much less a "Romanian." The single largest component of Transylvania's population was of Hungarian origin—and they in turn were subdivided into groups. People of Hungarian extraction in the east were known as Székelys—the name derived from "frontier guards"—and were mostly Roman Catholics. Other Hungarians in Transylvania were as likely to be Calvinists as Catholics. But there was one sect of Székely Unitarians who had evolved in an unusual direction. They were known as Sabbatarians and, over time, had grown close to Judaism. (In their own opinion, at least. Most Jewish rabbis would not have agreed.)

They were being subjected to persecution now as "Judaizers," although as yet the persecution was not severe.

The other large and powerful ethnic group in Transylvania were the so-called Saxons, who were of German origin. They were almost all Lutherans, and, like the Szeklers, had a martial tradition. They'd been brought in starting in the twelfth century as border guards defending Transylvania's southeastern region. They also provided Transylvania with experienced miners and artisans of various kinds. These two ethnic groups in Transylvania were granted special recognition and each had a seat in the Transylvanian Diet along with the nobility.

Gretchen was able to make initial contact with a few leading figures in the Szekler and Saxon communities in Szatmár, but nothing much came out of her brief discussions. They were cordial but guarded in their responses.

As usual in Transylvania, everything was a linguistic mishmash. In the world of the future the Americans came from, Szatmár would become known as Satu Mare. But in the year 1637, most of its inhabitants used the Hungarian name of Szatmár, which was a shortening of the name Szatmárnémeti. Saxons, however, used the German variant of "Sathmar" and Jews used their own Yiddish variant of "Satmer."

Gretchen didn't speak Hungarian herself, but three of the people who came with her—two of the guards and one of the printers—were fluent in the language, so she was able to communicate with the Szeklers well enough. It was even easier with the Saxons. Despite the name, the ancestors of the Transylvanians of German origin came mostly from Franconia, and their dialect was easy for Gretchen to understand, just as hers was for them. In this time period, the German language was a constellation of closely related dialects, and people were accustomed to dealing with that.

Finding a place to establish themselves wasn't straightforward, so Gretchen decided to wait until Morris Roth arrived. She thought they'd probably be continuing to move south anyway. Kolozsvár or the capital city of Gyulafehérvár seemed more suitable places for her and her expedition to set themselves up. Probably Kolozsvár. It was the largest city in Transylvania—larger than the capital—and had a more diverse population. There were large concentrations of Saxons and Szeklers and a sizable number of Sabbatarians, all groups that Gretchen thought would be most receptive to the views of the Committees of Correspondence.

So, they'd be camping out for a few more days, which was no great hardship. It was one of the Saxon notables she spoke to who clarified where they should do so.

"Set yourselves up here," he said, indicating the town square they were standing in.

"Won't someone object?"

"Probably," he replied, smiling. "But you can just ignore them. There are no authorities left in Szatmár. Everyone knows by now that it won't be long before the Bohemians take over."

He pointed across the Szamos River, which bisected the town. "But if you prefer, you can set up your camp in a large meadow over there. It's just beyond the tree line." His finger shifted, pointing farther upriver. "You can't see it from here, but there's a good stone bridge about half a mile away. Be careful, though. There are rumors that the Moldavian Impalers, as they call themselves, are active in the area. Whether that's true or not, I don't know. But they are quite vicious."

"We'll use the meadow," Gretchen said.

After the Saxon left, Gretchen turned to the leader of her guard detachment, Werner Ruppel. "Let's hope these Impalers *are* present. We'll make an example of them."

Ruppel nodded. "Even if they're in the area, they won't arrive for another day or two, most likely. We'll set up a good and very obvious guard tonight and then appear to start slacking off." He glanced up at the broad-brimmed hat shading her from the sun. "And take that thing off and let your hair loose. We want that famous blonde hair as visible as possible."

Gretchen made a face but didn't object. The truth was, at least in the USE and Silesia and parts of Bohemia—not to mention such places as Dresden and Amsterdam—her long and bright yellow hair was indeed famous. It even figured in a painting by Rubens. She doubted that was true here on the Transylvanian border, but...

It might be. Even if it wasn't, it would certainly be visible by the light of a campfire. Having a young woman sitting in the middle of a camp was likely to lull the suspicions of any would-be assailant.

Almost by unconscious reflex, she reached under her vest to check that her 9mm pistol slid easily out of the shoulder holster.

Poor fools, them.

Fehérgyarmat

Morris had set up his temporary headquarters in an abandoned shop—a cobbler's shop, from the looks of it—in the town of Fehérgyarmat, situated on the Szatmár Plain, which was part of the Northern Great Plain region of eastern Hungary. It had the official status of a market town, although it looked more like a village to Morris.

As was true of Szatmár, the political future of Fehérgyarmat was quite clear. It had originally been owned by the Báthori family and later became the property of succeeding Transylvanian princely families. But apparently the town's inhabitants either hadn't learned of the new alliance Prince Rákóczi had made with

Bohemia, or didn't believe the rumor, or were simply guided by the ancient wisdom *put not your faith in princes*, because by the time the Grand Army of the Sunrise entered Fehérgyarmat, it was completely deserted.

They wouldn't be staying there more than a day, anyway, so Morris made no effort to find out where the population had fled to. They were probably huddled in the nearby woods.

Ellie Anderson strode into the headquarters with her usual lack of concern for military protocol. "Hey, Morris," she said, "I just got a message from Eddie. Clear as crystal, too—they must have finally gotten the antenna set up in Kassa. He's in the Jupiter you bought, and he estimates he'll reach Szatmár in three days."

Morris frowned. "Why so long? The distance between Kassa and Szatmár—as the crow flies, not the way we're doing it—isn't more than a hundred miles. In a Jupiter, he can do that in one hop in two hours."

"He says he needs to go back to Prague to escort Tuva and her Dvorak out here." She shrugged. "Why that would take three days, I don't know, and he didn't tell me. Prague's not more than five hundred miles flying distance from here."

Morris managed not to wince. He knew why it was going to take Eddie that long. In his flight to Kassa, he'd been carrying a very heavy cargo, so he hadn't been able to carry any passengers or other freight. In fact, he probably had to remove all the seats from the plane except the two he and his copilot used. For what he had to do now—set up refueling stops that were closely enough spaced that a Dvorak could make it all the way to Transylvania—at least a couple of days would be needed.

The reason for Morris' anxiety was that the cargo was heavy because it was gold and silver coins—ducats and thalers, to be precise—that he needed to pay his soldiers. The guard unit he'd left behind in Kassa was one he trusted, true. Still . . . that would be a lot of temptation.

"Any word from Brigadier Higgins?"

Ellie shook her head. "No, nothing. And why the formality? For Christ's sake, Morris, you've known Jeff Higgins since he was a toddler."

He didn't bother to explain. Ellie Anderson had as little understanding—not to mention lack of interest—of the logic of military protocol as a salamander did of the far side of the moon.

Mátészalka

The reason Ellie hadn't heard anything from Jeff was because he was preoccupied with cursing himself for being a dimwit and overseeing the task of getting his First Regiment across the Krasna River. The route he'd chosen to take was a few miles farther west than the one Morris had been using for his forces. It skirted the town of Mátészalka, which was a benefit. The problem was that it turned out they were skirting the river on the wrong bank—and there were no bridges in the area.

The Krasna wasn't a big river. In West Virginia, it would probably have been labeled a creek. The width ranged from twenty to thirty feet, and it wasn't more than a few feet deep. A ten-year-old child could have waded across it in less than a minute.

The problem was that a sizable military force found crossing *any* body of water a challenge, unless a bridge could be found or built. Ten-year-old kids don't have to get anything across a river except themselves. Jeff's First Regiment had to get volley guns across—not to mention supply wagons and, worst of all, artillery.

The artillery was on the modest size. Outside of the mortars, just a dozen four-pound cannons. But between the barrel, the carriage, and the limber, even that small a piece weighed about a ton. Getting a ton of an awkwardly designed (for this purpose) weapon across even a river as small as the Krasna was not easy, to say the least, much less a dozen of them.

The volley guns were much lighter, but they were still no piece of cake. And while the mortars were officially capable of being "carried by hand," that meant carried across reasonably dry and level ground—*not* across slippery stones covered in three or four feet of water.

They'd get it done, to be sure. Most likely, no one would be killed or even badly injured. But it was still a royal pain in the ass and more than enough to keep Jeff from even thinking about sending any radio messages.

Chapter 33

Déj

Isaac's wagon paused before moving into the central square to allow the First Regiment of the Joshua Corps time to move ahead and form ranks. First Alpha Company, then Baker, then Charlie. Two hundred men each in ranks of twenty-five. Their rifles were loaded and half-cocked; their swords ready at their belts. The regimental drums tapped staccato notes to a Yiddish song about bravery. Isaac had never heard the tune before, but as the men formed their lines, he couldn't help but feel a swell of pride. These men wore cuirasses over their white shirts, and helmets over their yarmulkes. Some had initially forgone wearing their helmets to show the enemy who they were, what they were, but sergeants within the ranks boxed their ears for such stupidity. "Wear your yarmulkes if you must," Isaac had heard one sergeant yell at his men, "but I'll beat you where you stand if you join battle without your helmets on!"

Isaac fished around in the pocket of his scrubs, pulled his own yarmulke out, and fixed it to his scalp. "What's going on?" he asked a sergeant of Baker Company passing by.

The man paused, said, "Enemy cavalry has breached the eastern fortifications. Tatars!"

Radio reports through Len Tanner had indicated a large enemy attack on the eastern side of the city, but Isaac had only gotten dribs and drabs of the reports, enough to know that he had to don his scrubs and get ready for the inevitable casualties. He watched as the Joshua Corps assembled and then, to the sound of drums, trumpets, and officers barking orders, began to move through the streets of Déj in one massive sea of humanity that terrified and excited him at the same time. His people, his brothers, marching to battle.

"Hello, Isaac."

Isaac turned in his wagon seat and smiled. "Hello, Christian. How have you been?"

Christian shrugged. "I've had better days, but I'm alive, so I guess that counts for something."

Isaac nodded, chuckled, and climbed out of the wagon. "When they are out of the way," he said to the driver, "move up to the tent and begin unloading." He turned back to Christian. "Is it safe here?"

"Not as safe as the northern approach, but safe enough. Assuming, of course, the corps prevails."

They paused a moment to listen to the sounds of gunfire echoing through the town. Isaac's instinct was to duck, to move out of the street and into a building, but the wagons passing by with the rest of his medical supplies gave him comfort.

He noticed the cut on Christian's cheek. "That's a nice cut. Are you wounded elsewhere?"

Christian shook his head. "Other than exhaustion, no. I was lucky. A lot of my men were not."

"How many did you lose?"

"Twelve, for sure, and it could well be more. I'm not entirely sure of the exact number yet; things are still a bit chaotic. A quarter or more wounded, but most of them superficially, like my cheek. Some men just threw down their arms and fled. Not many, but a few. The regimental provost marshal is out looking for them."

"Why bother?" Isaac asked, taking hold of Christian's arm and guiding him toward the medical tent. "What are a few fleeing men?"

"And allow even more to abandon the company later? I understand the nature of mercenaries, Isaac, but I cannot allow such insubordination to fester. A captain who cannot maintain good order is not a captain for long."

"Yes, but—" Isaac didn't say the rest out loud... *push too hard, and you'll lose them anyway.* There was no point in arguing. Now was certainly not the time. Instead, he said, "May I have a look at that cut?"

Christian nodded. "Certainly." He pointed around the square. "By the way, I have my company guarding all the approaches to the medical tent."

Indeed he did. With all the Ashkenazi soldiers moving through the streets, Isaac had not seen the cavalry in a tight ring around the plaza. "Thank you, Isaac."

Before they stepped into the tent, Christian said, "Oh, one thing. Before you tend to me, I have one groggy patient who needs your attention."

Distant cannon and musket fire sounded. General von Mercy had set up his guns on a ridgeline on the western side of the town and was answering Moldavian cannon fire with his own. The sound of clashing steel and shouting men seemed closer.

"Don't worry, Isaac," Christian said. "Those sounds are not as close as they seem. We're safe here."

Isaac wasn't so sure. He wouldn't feel safe until all guns stopped firing, all swords stopped striking, and men stopped dying.

The first casualties from the Joshua Corps' assault against the Tatars began arriving.

Isaac did a quick check of the wound on the back of Lieutenant Enkefort's head. "We'll need to shave the area around the wound to check it completely. He'll probably need stitches. I'll have Devorah do that as soon as possible. How do you feel, Lieutenant?"

Enkefort nodded. "I'm fine, Isaac."

"Good. You know my name. Do you know yours?"

Isaac went through a few concussion protocols with the lieutenant, then laid his head back down. "Devorah! Get someone to shave this man's head, and then when you are able, please stitch his wound. And have someone look at Christian's face."

A badly wounded man stumbled through the flap and fell to the ground. "I'm sorry, Christian," Isaac said, standing and turning away. "I can't take care of you right now."

Corps casualties began arriving in clusters of twos and threes, but in truth, Christian liked those numbers. There weren't as many as he had feared. He figured that the wave of fire being delivered by the corps' ZB-1636 rifles must be keeping casualties low. Casualties on their side of the battle line, anyway.

He turned to his lieutenant, but Enkefort had fallen asleep. "Well, Denise, it looks like it's just you and me. Why don't we—"

She was gone, and he figured she'd probably run off to check on her plane. Christian shook his head and sighed deeply. *She could have at least allowed me to escort her there safely.* The *Dixie Chick* wasn't too far away. Captain Keller had taken up its security, but still: the streets of Déj were not safe right now and wouldn't be until the last ball was fired.

He turned toward the flap to go out and check on his men. A young lady blocked his path.

"Excuse me, Fräulein, I didn't see you—"

"My name is Andreea Hatmanu. Frau Devorah has asked me to look at your face. Come," she said, motioning toward the flap. "Let us go outside. We are in their way."

Christian followed her. "I don't recall ever seeing you before," he said, stepping out. The sun was high, the smell of drifting black powder strong. Cannons and muskets were still firing. Wounded men were still arriving. "Did you join the army on the march?"

Andreea shook her head. "No, I live here. I felt it my duty to assist in the care of wounded."

Christian nodded, impressed.

"You speak excellent German." He took to a chair she pointed to, then raised his face and closed his eyes. The sunlight was warm and welcoming on his skin.

"That surprises you?" Andreea asked. "Székelys know a lot of languages. We've had many...visitors...come through our lands, Herr von Jori. I know Yiddish and some Turkish as well, if you'd prefer—"

"No, thank you. German will be just fine."

She pushed on his chin to raise his head higher. She then pressed a wet cloth against his cut and began to wipe gently. "Ah, not so bad. I do not think you will even need stitches." She paused, then: "But I see that you have other wounds, fresh scars."

Christian nodded. "Yes. Many months ago, from a different fight. Doctor Kohen can tell you all about those if you're interested in knowing."

She finished cleaning his wound and let his head down. He opened his eyes, and he spent several seconds looking at her face.

Her dark hair was tucked underneath a green bonnet. Errant strands of it covered her smooth cheeks. She was sweating, of course, with a bit of odor about her of both blood and bile, though it wasn't unbearable or unpleasant to him. Her eyes were brown and large. Her mouth thin and pale. She was in her twenties, Christian assumed, though he couldn't figure her exact age. Older than he was, by a few years at least. She was thin, but not skinny or malnourished. He found himself very attracted to her, as much by her obvious skill and intelligence as her appearance.

"You may go now," she said to him finally, nodding and flashing a quick smile. "I wish you good health and safety, Captain von Jori. May God bless you."

She turned to reenter the tent. "Thank you, Andreea," he said. "I hope to see you again."

She nodded and disappeared into the tent.

Don't be foolish, Christian, he said to himself. *You've no time for this right now. She isn't Young Greta.*

And yet, Christian couldn't help himself from stepping to the flap and pulling it aside to take another long look at Andreea Hatmanu as she joined Isaac and Devorah to save a patient.

At the eastern approaches into Déj

The Joshua Corps had broken the back of the Tatar charge and had reinforced Captain Kinsky's much beleaguered eastern defenses. The Moldavian attack had breached Kinsky's wall in three places and then hit an immovable wall itself when the Ashkenazi soldiers countercharged with fixed bayonets. They were still pushing the Tatars back down the valley when the trumpets called to halt, fall back, and defend the wall. There wasn't much of a wall left to defend, but General von Mercy was pleased. The Moldavians had hit them with everything, and with a much larger force, and still couldn't tip the scales. A good sign of things to come.

"I must attend to the dying, General," Rabbi Gotkin said as he rode beside von Mercy. He pointed to the casualty collection site that the corps' medics had created about fifty feet behind the wall. There, a line of dead lay alongside a gathering of wounded. Some of them, von Mercy could see, were *very* badly wounded. Expectant, in fact.

"Of course, Rabbi," von Mercy said. "Do your service."

The rabbi climbed off his horse and joined a group of Ashkenazim who were huddled near a wounded fellow soldier. The wounded man was crying, begging for prayer. Rabbi Gotkin knelt beside him and began speaking to him in Yiddish. Von Mercy had no idea what he was saying, but the boy calmed immediately, began reciting what Rabbi Gotkin had said to him. A couple of minutes later, he died.

Colonel Renz and his staff rode into view. The colonel reined his horse, saluted, and said, "Congratulations, General. It would appear that Déj is yours."

Von Mercy turned his ear to the wind. Distant cannon fire still erupted, errant muskets sounded near the southern approach, but otherwise, all was quiet, save for the commotion around them as the Joshua Corps began redressing its lines and gathering wounded. "How are Callenberk's men doing?"

Colonel Renz nodded. "Well, sir. He'd like to get them back in the saddle and give pursuit."

Von Mercy shook his head. "No, Colonel. He will withdraw from those defenses, reconstitute, and gather in the field near the Dvorak landing strip. I want all cavalry to do so. The Brethren will take command of the southern approaches. Our infantry will hold this town, not the cavalry."

"Sir, the Moldavians are in full retreat. If we strike them now, we could deliver a serious blow from which they will have difficulty recovering." Colonel Renz pulled a small map from his satchel, rolled it out, looked at it, and said, "Szamosújvár is the next town along the march. They will most certainly reconstitute there to try to hold the line."

Von Mercy nodded. "It's our understanding that a Transylvanian force marches to Szamosújvár right now. They may already be there."

"Yes, General, but if we strike them hard on retreat, we could annihilate them. Hammer and anvil."

Von Mercy considered. It was a sound strategy. Callenberk's men were certainly capable of delivering such a blow, and they weren't completely worn out from the fight. *But...*

"Fine, Colonel. But not Callenberk. I'm not going to push my finest dragoons out into a salient that could collapse on them at any moment. Send Hanau's company, or Ulfsparre's. They're light, but far more capable of pulling out of a scrap than our heavies. Our Dvorak isn't in the air, Colonel. We don't really know what's out there. We don't know where the Impalers are, who, by the way, are the ones who grounded our pilot. Let us not be lethargic, but let us not be rash either. A little prudence right now is beneficial, Colonel. You have permission to send your lights, but Callenberk pulls back."

"Yes, sir."

Colonel Renz was gone. Von Mercy continued to pick his way through the remnants of Kinsky's eastern defenses.

A shot fired from the ridgeline overlooking the city. The ball hit the cobbles near the left hoof of von Mercy's horse.

Corps soldiers returned fire, and the ridgeline quieted.

"General," Rabbi Gotkin said, "I beg you: please return to headquarters. It isn't safe for you and your staff to be here."

His aide-de-camp grabbed the reins of von Mercy's horse and guided them into an alley away from any further opportunistic assassination attempts. Von Mercy removed his hat and wiped his brow, letting his heart slow its pace.

Here I am speaking of prudence with my ass hanging in the wind, he thought as he allowed his staff to guide him through the narrow street and out of harm's way. *Wake up, General. Or you'll be dead before you reach the capital.*

Déj

Two of the four deserters from Captain von Jori's company were found. The regimental provost marshal recommended that they "ride the donkey" to set an example, not only for the company, but for the entire regiment. And then they would be hanged by the neck until death.

Colonel Renz had no objection with either punishment but left the decision to Christian. "They're your men, Captain," he had said. "Do as you will."

Christian overruled the first recommendation. The second, however, would stand.

Thus, ropes were strung into trees, and nooses placed around their necks, as they sat with hands tied behind their backs on their own horses. The Catholic chaplain gave the condemned their last rites and took their confessions. Christian then slapped his own hand against the hind quarters of each horse to make them bolt and watched until the deed was done.

"Are you okay?" Denise asked as they broke bread together in the regimental field kitchen hours later. She had come by to have supper with Christian's company, the fourth time in as many days.

"I'm fine," he said, stabbing a piece of horse meat and placing it on his tongue. A little tough, but it tasted wonderful, especially peppered with local seasoning. "I did not enjoy the sentence, but it was necessary. They had abandoned their company, their brothers, putting us all at risk."

"Isn't that what mercenaries do? Leave the battle when it gets too hot or switch sides when a better deal comes along?"

He nodded. "Sometimes, yes, and when unengaged, such conduct can be expected. Mercenaries most often desert for lack of pay, which, in our line of work, is paramount for our services. But in the middle of a fight? At the height of the battle? Abandoning their posts was tantamount to treason. They put my life—*your* life—at risk. That was unacceptable."

Denise said nothing, but Christian could see that she was trying to reconcile her up-time sensibilities with down-time reality. Clearly, she did not like the idea of execution. Neither did he. But the alternative was even worse: losing his company altogether for his lack of leadership. His men had defended the southern fortifications well, but they had taken a beating, had suffered losses, and losses that could not be replaced until the full Sunrise gathered at Kolozsvár. Morale was low. They had not been paid since departing Kassa, and soon, they would saddle up and head to the next town. They needed to see that their captain was strong and capable, and not burdened with excessive sensitivity. Christian's previous captain, Tideman, had taught him that, and it was advice worth respecting.

Christian finished his meal, then waited for Denise. His long, deliberate stare obviously made her uncomfortable. "Why are you looking at me like that?" She smiled. "Don't get any ideas, Captain von Jori. I have a boyfriend."

"No, no, no," he said, waving her off. "I have no desire for that. Trust me: my eyes are for someone else."

He stood and brushed himself off. "But, if you are finished, there is something we must do." He offered his hand. "Will you accompany me to the *Dixie Chick*, my up-time friend?"

✧   ✧   ✧

"I thought you were going to tell me that story tonight."

Christian nodded as the *Dixie Chick* came into view. "I will. I will. But first, Lieutenant Enkefort and I have a surprise for you."

The *Dixie Chick* had been fully repaired. Or, at least as well repaired as it could be, given the fact that no one in town possessed the kind of canvas used in its construction or the exact skills necessary to do the work. A more flexible but thinner fabric had been found for the wing, and all the minor tears had been sewn shut. Denise knew about all this. She had coordinated the repairs herself and was scheduled to leave in the morning to return to Nagybánya. What she didn't know about was waiting inside the cockpit.

"Okay, what's the surprise?"

"Don't worry. You'll see."

He brought them to a stop behind the plane's tail. He dismounted and then helped her down. Together, they walked to the front of the plane. Lieutenant Enkefort stepped out of the cockpit.

"Hate to break it to you, Christian," Denise said sarcastically, "but Enkefort is no surprise. Nice fellow. Injured knee. A little woozy with a big bump on his head, but good with a radio."

Christian sighed and motioned to the cockpit. "Look inside."

She did so. At first, she didn't see it, and then her gaze went to the canopy. Her mouth dropped open.

"I was able to find some quills and ink in town," Christian said, moving up. "All the men in the company have signed their names. Those who can't write marked themselves with an X or a scribble of some sort. But everyone in the company has signed it in appreciation for your service to us and for saving Lieutenant Enkefort in the line of duty.

"Denise Beasley!" he said, almost shouting her name. "Stand at attention!"

Shocked at the abruptness of his order, Denise turned and stood straight, allowing one tear to roll down her cheek. "For showing unfaltering courage in the face of the enemy and for saving Karl Enkefort's life, you are hereby given honorary membership in Captain Christian von Jori's cavalry company, Second Regiment."

Lieutenant Enkefort unbuckled the sword on his back and handed it to her. "Denise Beasley," he said. "Please accept this sword as the symbol of your status in the company. Keep it with you at all times, and may God keep you safe in the air and on the ground."

Denise stood there silently, holding the scabbarded sword in her trembling hands. She let another tear fall down her face, and Christian could see that she was fighting the strong emotion to break down and cry. Finally, she couldn't hold it in any longer.

She dropped the sword, cried like a baby, then pulled Lieutenant Enkefort forward in a strong embrace.

"How about a hug for me?" Christian finally said, hands on his hips. "I'm the one who's actually bestowing the honor."

Chapter 34

Kisvárda
Political status in transition

"There it is, Eddie," said Minnie Hugelmair, leaning out the open cockpit window far enough to point to a feature in the landscape below. From his vantage point at the plane's controls, Eddie couldn't see for himself what she was pointing at, but knew that it had to be the small lake they'd been told about. "White Lake," the local residents called it. It was part of the wetlands created by the Tisza River in this far northeastern corner of the Great Hungarian Plain.

The plan was to create a small fuel and supply depot on the shores of the lake, which was only a few miles from the nearby town of Kisvárda. A small unit of the Grand Army of the Sunrise was supposed to be in place already. Whether that was true or not remained to be discovered, since the unit had no radio. Eddie would provide them with one in a later trip, along with a radio operator—who were in shorter supply than the radios themselves.

They'd chosen that location for a fuel and supply depot for several reasons. First, it was approximately halfway between Kassa and Szatmár, roughly fifty miles either way, which was well within the range of a Dvorak aircraft. Secondly, the lake provided a good landing area for a Jupiter, with its air cushion landing gear; and there was a good area to create a short airstrip next to the lake

259

for either a Dvorak or a Dauntless. Thirdly, Kisvárda and the area around it were definitely included in that portion of Royal Hungary that Austria had ceded to Bohemia. And finally, because the town had a large Jewish population which could be counted on to be friendly to Bohemia and the Grand Army of the Sunrise.

Eddie circled back around and brought the Jupiter to a landing on the lake, and then did the water equivalent of taxiing to bring the aircraft to the place on the shore indicated by the small group of men he could see waving their arms. He wasn't concerned about their identity since all but two of them were wearing GAS uniforms, and one of the soldiers was holding a Bohemian standard aloft.

The location had been well chosen. This stretch of the lake shore sloped up gently, which enabled Eddie, using the air cushion landing gear, to move smoothly from traveling across water to traveling up onto the adjacent land. It had taken him a while to get accustomed to the ACLG, but the more he used it, the more he liked it.

As soon as he brought the Jupiter to a stop, Minnie Hugelmair and Tuva Dreyzl hopped out. That was from habit, not because there was any need for them to do their usual routine of chocking the wheels. Once the plane came to a halt, the skirt of the landing gear did a fine job of securing itself to the patch of land it rested on.

By the time Eddie clambered out of the aircraft, the propellers had stopped spinning, and the small group awaiting them felt confident enough to approach—although they kept a wary eye on the propellers. They weren't accustomed yet to dealing with aircraft, but they knew enough to know that a propeller was quite capable of lopping off an arm or a head—and this plane had four of them.

The man in the lead was a civilian. When he reached Eddie, he made a small bow and said: "Greetings. I am Matej Došek, the newly appointed administrator of Kisvárda district. We will be establishing your depot here"—he waved his hand about—"if you find that suitable."

"Quite suitable," said Eddie. "If some of your people will help me, we can unload the fuel and other supplies quickly, and we'll be on our way."

That took no more than ten minutes. When they were done,

there was enough fuel in place to supply a Dvorak for at least a week.

"And now," Eddie said, "we'll return to Prague to get the second Dvorak. Tuva'll be flying it, of course."

"Yes," said Tuva. Minnie made a face. She was still grouchy that Eddie had peremptorily disqualified her as a solo pilot.

"You've only got one eye, Minnie," he'd said. "Dammit, face facts. You've got no depth perception—which is the last thing you want in a pilot trying to land a plane. You'll be the flight engineer for the Jupiter, and you can double as a relief pilot once you're up in the air."

"I can do takeoffs, too!"

Eddie nodded. "Yeah, that'll be okay. Just no landings."

Eddie gestured toward the cockpit of the big, four-engine aircraft. "In fact, you can do this takeoff. You need to get used to a Jupiter."

Despite her naturally self-confident disposition, Minnie was a bit apprehensive as she took her seat. Eddie had let her fly the plane once they were aloft, but this would be her first takeoff.

She looked in both directions at the wings. The Jupiter was a biplane, unlike either a Dvorak or a Dauntless or a Belle. What made her more nervous was simply the sheer size of the aircraft. The Jupiter was sixty feet long, and the wingspan of the upper wing was one hundred feet. It was powered by four 110-horsepower radial engines suspended from the wider, upper wing. A Dvorak looked like a moth if it were placed next to it. Even a Dauntless was a little puny looking.

On the positive side, the four engines were a source of comfort. If one or two of them failed, the plane was quite capable of flying on only two engines—probably on only one engine, in fact, if it weren't too heavily loaded.

Camp of the Grand Army of the Sunrise
Five miles northwest of Szatmár

Morris had hoped the main body of the Grand Army of the Sunrise would be able to reach Szatmár before sundown, but it was not to be. He'd once heard Mike Stearns grousing about the plodding nature of army "marches" in the here and now. He hadn't

thought much of it at the time; he'd probably just written it off
as Mike having a grumpy day. But since he'd been in command
of a large military force himself, he'd come to realize just how
much truth there'd been in what Stearns had said.

The problem for an up-timer was that even now, more than
six years after the Ring of Fire, their subconscious minds still
had a notion of what "roads" were that derived from the universe
they'd come from.

Roads were:

Wide.

Flat.

Smooth.

Firm.

Uniform.

Graded.

Everything, in short, that roads were *not* in the year 1637.

Oh, yes—and roads had bridges over moving bodies of water
and over steep-walled gullies and ravines.

The terrain southwest of Fehérgyarmat had been particularly
bad, even by the standards of eastern Europe. At one point, the
day before, the army had been delayed for almost six hours by
the need to lay down a corduroy road through what amounted
to a swamp.

Morris could remember reading, in a history of the American
Civil War, about one of the Union armies progressing by the use
of corduroy roads. Sherman's army in the Carolinas, if he remembered correctly. It had seemed very simple and straightforward
in the pages of a book—even a bit romantic.

The reality was miserable for the men who had to build it
and miserable when they had to cross a swamp afterward. It was
far worse for horses. They'd had to put down four horses who'd
suffered broken legs from logs that had shifted or rolled under
their weight.

By now, though, Morris had gotten philosophical about such
things. As exhausted as the army was, at least most of the men
would sleep well tonight. When they weren't on sentry duty, at
least.

Szatmár

"I'd be happier if the lighting was better," said Werner Ruppel. He glanced up at the evening sky. There was a moon out, but it wasn't much of one—crescent, not gibbous, and a very slender crescent at that. Once the twilight faded away in an hour or so, the meadow where they'd set up their camp would become very dark.

Gretchen glanced at the moon herself. "Yes, so would I. But I think the big campfires we set up around the perimeter will make up for most of it."

The campfires she was referring to had been set up at least thirty yards away from the camp. None of them had been lit yet because they wanted to conserve the wood. Hopefully, the fires would last through the night. Once all of them were lit, anyone attacking the camp would be silhouetted against the light they cast—but the campfires wouldn't cast enough light to make the camp itself very visible except in rough outlines.

From the distance of the meadow's edge, the camp looked pretty simple. The wagons had been drawn up in a circle, with about twenty feet of space between one wagon and the next. Those gaps had been filled with enough posts and crossbars to turn the camp into a corral—a crude one, but sufficient to keep the expedition's livestock penned in and protected. The rough fencing wouldn't prevent attackers from breaking into the corral, but it would slow them down quite a bit.

And that should be enough, unless their assailants turned out to be a much larger force than anyone expected. By all accounts, Vasile Lupu's force of so-called "Impalers"—terrorists, to call them by their right name—operated in bands of one to two dozen men. If there were two dozen, they would outnumber the defenders of the camp, but not by all that much. To compensate for that, the defenders were better armed and would be fighting from behind well-built defensive positions.

There would only be a few visible sentries—three, each standing atop one of the wagons. In the event of an attack, they were to sound the alarm and take shelter immediately in the rough fortifications that had been placed on those wagons—nothing much, just logs big enough and thick enough to stop a bullet.

Most of the shooting wouldn't be coming from them. Hidden out of sight beneath each of the wagons were shallow trenches, also protected by logs. There would be two shooters under each wagon and a third person to reload the guns. In the darkness, with no light except a slim crescent moon and whatever illumination came from campfires dozens of yards away, they would be all but invisible to attackers—who would themselves be out in the open, being fired upon by powerful breech-loading rifles.

Gretchen would be a distraction also. She and another woman were perched atop a fourth wagon. If an attack came, they would also take immediate shelter in the same sort of log fortifications that defended the other wagon guards. Between her reputation and her long blonde hair, the attention of attackers was more likely to be on her than trying to peer into the dark recesses below the wagons.

That reputation would work in another way as well—for the defenders, not the attackers. By now, after the sieges of Amsterdam and Dresden and everything else Gretchen had done—Lady Protector of two provinces, Saxony and Silesia—her reputation among CoC members had assumed near-mythic proportions. Knowing that she was leading the defense would bolster their confidence and determination immensely. Every one of them, starting with Gretchen herself, would fight to the death—and not one of them doubted it of any other.

As her up-timer husband would put it, Gretchen Richter was a very tough nut to crack. Of course, they still didn't know if any of the Impalers were actually in the area or if that was just a wild rumor. They'd never appeared in the Szatmár region. Their depredations had so far been confined to areas farther south. So, all of these defensive measures might well just turn out to be wasted labor. But...not so. That question was settled a little past three o'clock in the morning, when nineteen men burst into the clearing, firing as they came.

The weapons they were using were wheellock pistols, the kind favored by cavalrymen. Each assailant was carrying three of the pieces, one in each hand and one in a holster.

They had two holsters, actually, into one of which they stuffed the now-fired pistol. This required them to shift their second pistol from one hand to the other, while they drew out the loaded pistol in the holster.

Clearly enough, the purpose of that initial volley, coming in the dead of night, was to spread panic and disorder among their intended victims. Used against caravans camped for the night, it was probably quite effective. But used against enemies such as the ones they faced here, it was a bad mistake. First, because all the shots were wasted. Secondly, and worse, because carrying out a complicated maneuver like shifting pistols from hand to hand in the middle of the night on uncertain, dimly visible footing, required them to slow down or even stop.

Right at the point when the riflemen hidden under the wagons had come fully alert and had time to aim their weapons. The three sentries atop the wagons had made no attempt to aim their rifles when they spotted the Impalers charging out of the woods. They simply fired a shot in the air and dove for cover into the prepared fortifications. That was enough to arouse whichever of the guards under the wagons had dozed off—about half of them—and give them just enough time to get ready.

The result was devastating. At this short range, Hocklott rifles were very accurate. Five of the Impalers were killed instantly, three were mortally wounded, and two were injured badly enough to knock them down and render them *hors de combat*. Two others were lightly wounded. One turned and ran away immediately. The other brought up his second pistol and fired a wild shot into the air. As he fumbled to get his third and last pistol out of its holster, Gretchen rose up a bit from the fortifications atop her wagon and shot him three times with her 9mm pistol.

The first shot missed because she hurried it. She was furious with herself for having dozed off at some point. But she settled down, and the next two shots inflicted fatal wounds. One struck the man in his throat, and the other squarely in his chest. He was wearing a leather cuirass, but it was cheaply made and not enough to keep the bullet from penetrating his heart.

Two more of the Impalers ran off, but the rest stood their ground and fired their second pistol. At which point, they made another mistake, because four out of the five men who fired were aiming at Gretchen—who had already ducked behind the log shelter she was perched in.

The one Impaler who had the presence of mind to fire at a rifleman under the wagons inflicted the only damage the assailants managed to do that night—and that was minor. His bullet struck the ground a few feet ahead of the wagons and off to the side by a foot or two, sending dirt and pebbles flying into the face of his target. But the man had time to close his eyes, so the injuries were painful but not permanent.

That Impaler and all but one of the five who'd stood their ground were killed in the ensuing volley. The one survivor turned to run, but didn't get more than two strides away before Gretchen brought him down.

As she rose back up and aimed, she was shouting: "*He's mine! He's mine! Nobody else shoot at him!*" She aimed for his legs and brought him down with six more shots. Only three of them hit the man, but that was enough.

She felt a little guilty, then. Dan Frost had taught her to shoot, and one of his firmest rules was *always aim for center mass*. But she wanted at least one survivor, and she didn't know if that was true of any of the other Impalers who'd been brought down.

In any event, she wound up with three survivors. She didn't bother providing them with medical treatment because, within less than four hours, dawn had arrived. By then, she and her guards had hauled all of the corpses, as well as the three still-living Impalers, across the bridge to the town square on the other side of the river.

The day before, a couple of the CoC guards had found what Gretchen had sent them looking for—a sawed-off section of log big enough to serve as a headsman's chopping block. They spent the early morning in somewhat more pleasant work than hauling corpses across the Szamos: setting up and stabilizing the block in the middle of the town square.

The three still-alive Impalers were the first ones Gretchen sent to the block—and she did the headsman's work herself. She was a big woman, a very strong one, had grown up a printer's daughter, so she was no stranger to manual labor and had learned how to use an axe during the time she'd spent as a mercenary army's camp follower. And as far as temperament went, for this sort of thing, she would have gained the approval of Attila the Hun or Tamerlane.

The only Impaler who put up resistance was the one Gretchen had shot herself, who went first. She settled that by clubbing him with the flat of the ax blade. Then two of the CoC guards man-handled him into position. *Whack!* And that was done. One of them dragged away the now headless corpse toward a mass grave being dug in a vacant lot—unhallowed ground, needless to say—while the other undertook the lighter duty of fitting the head onto one of the stakes that other CoC people were erecting nearby.

The other two surviving Impalers were brought up—*whack! and whack! again*—after which Gretchen passed the ax over to a former logger to handle the rest. He'd deal with the remaining thirteen of the sixteen heads that soon decorated Szatmár's town square. By the time he finished, signs had been erected that identified those who'd been decapitated:

Lupu's Impalers, now impaled.

By then, a large crowd had gathered. Some were disapproving, but didn't say much. A larger number approved, and several of them were quite vociferous about it. The Szekler priest and Saxon pastor just wanted assurances that the corpses wouldn't be reburied on the grounds of their nearby churches.

As for Ignaz Honterus, the Saxon notable who'd given his advice to Gretchen the day she and her wagon train arrived, he summoned two other Saxon notables and a couple of their Szekler counterparts to a meeting in a nearby tavern.

"We need to make some plans and some decisions," he said. He raised his mug of ale in what amounted to a toast. "Things are looking up."

"I'm not clear what you mean by that, Ignaz," said his fellow Saxon, Christian Sommerus.

"Neither am I," said one of the Szeklers, Janos Corvinus.

Honterus looked around the table. "I take it that none of you have pondered the presence of Gretchen Richter in Transylvania—along with a sizable and very capable body of confederates. What is she doing here? On the face of it, her presence doesn't make a lot of sense."

His companions all had frowns on their faces—which were expressions of puzzlement, not disagreement or disapproval.

"I'm still not following you," said Sommerus.

"Why is the Bohemian army here?" asked Ignaz. "And the smaller force sent by the USE?"

The other men at the table looked around at each other, still with frowns of puzzlement on their faces.

"Well, that's all clear enough," said Corvinus. "Prince Rákóczi—for better or ill—made a pact with Bohemia. In exchange for

Bohemia's military support for ending our vassalage to the Ottomans, Rákóczi will grant a strip of land in northern Transylvania
to Bohemia. The involvement of the USE forces is a bit murkier,
since they're not getting any direct benefit from also backing Transylvania, but their motives are clear enough. All they're investing
is three thousand troops from one of their poorest provinces, in
exchange for which they open up a new front against Murad."

"But that doesn't explain why *Richter* came as well. She's not
a military leader. Her reputation was built on political organizing,
at which she's supposed to be something of a genius."

"Reputations like that are widely overblown," sneered Corvinus.

Ignaz gave him a sarcastic glance. *And your own reputation
in that field is what? Zero?*

But he left the words unsaid. It would be pointless to start a
feud with a Szekler of Corvinus' stature, grossly overblown that
it be among his own people.

Happily, deflating the pompous ass was done by his fellow
Szekler, Elek Ferenc.

"I suppose you think her reputation for decisive and often
ruthless action is overblown as well," he said. "But you might
want to consult the thirteen Impalers in the town square before
coming to any definite conclusions on the matter."

A snicker went around the table. Ferenc turned to Ignaz and
said, "Why don't you just ask her?"

"I plan to."

The Grand Army of the Sunrise started arriving in Szatmár
less than an hour after the heads went up in the town square.
Morris Roth rode at the forefront along with several of his officers
and aides, as well as Ellie Anderson.

When he saw the display in the town square, he sucked in a
deep breath—luckily, the heads hadn't started to stink yet—and
let it out.

"I see Gretchen's already arrived."

"What tipped you off?" asked Ellie.

The lead elements of the Silesian Guard's First Regiment—the
one which still called itself the Hangman, damn what the regula-
tions said—arrived early in the afternoon.

When they saw the decorations, the soldiers started cheering.

Except for one malcontent, who loudly insisted Gretchen should have hung them.

Jeff just smiled. He hadn't seen his wife in weeks. Hell, *months.*

Thoughts of Lady Macbeth didn't cross his mind once. Why would they?

Out, damn spot!

All the perfumes of Arabia will not sweeten this little hand.

Yet who would have thought the old man to have had so much blood in him?

Were not words anyone would ever, ever, ever hear coming out of Gretchen Richter's mouth.

Tuva flew in late in the afternoon. She overflew the town square, to see if it would be suitable for a landing place, and decided there was enough room as long as she steered clear of the obstacles in the center.

She didn't give the obstacles themselves much thought. She and Minnie shared a self-assured—indeed, downright sanguine—temperament, although they came from very different backgrounds. Minnie had grown up as poor as the proverbial church mouse and had lost her eye to a brick thrown by a religious zealot. And now she was pregnant by a young Austrian archduke of whom she'd grown surprisingly fond. If there were two phrases that described Minnie Hugelmair to a T, they were:

Takes things in stride.

Seventeenth century, through and through.

Tuva, on the other hand, came from the upper crust of Prague's Jewish community. Her father was a well-to-do merchant and her mother was a *firzogerin.* The literal meaning of the term was "fore-sayer" and was bestowed on learned Jewish women in the synagogue whose role was to lead women in prayer in the gender-segregated women's gallery.

She gave the heads impaled on stakes no more than a glance. Tuva approved of Gretchen Richter and had no more use than she did for the bullies and thugs of royalty and aristocracy. As was true of Gretchen—not to mention Minnie and her best friend, Denise Beasley—*good riddance* were words that came trippingly off her tongue.

Morris Roth greeted her on landing. Tuva was a little surprised at that. Shouldn't a man of his stature have "people" for such a task?

"Good day, General," she said, removing her leather helmet to better greet him.

"I'm very glad you're here, Tuva. We need ya!"

She was delighted to hear that, and ready and willing to work.

"But," he said, not allowing her to respond to his greeting with more than a smile, "don't kick your boots up for too long. I'm sending you back up at first light."

"Oh? What's the occasion?"

"A good friend needs your help."

Chapter 35

Nagybánya

Denise was surprised by her anxiety. It wasn't from flying in a half-repaired, ready-to-fall-out-of-the-sky-at-any-moment pusher plane, nor was it from her near-death experiences at the Battle of Déj. Her anxiety stemmed from the other little pusher plane that had just cleared the tree line and now maneuvered to land.

"Come on, girlie," she whispered to herself, "land that mother."

She resisted the urge to wave lest it distract Tuva from her task. The Dvorak sputtered, dipped, shifted about ten feet to the right from the persistent wind shear that had threatened Denise's landing a few days ago. By God's grace, the weather had turned pleasant overnight. The sun was rising. Landing conditions were good. But could the newly trained pilot from Prague do it? Tuva was a Jewish girl from the Josefov—the first in history who had ever tried to become a pilot.

Without a hitch, as it turned out. Her little Dvorak bumped twice upon landing and came to a nice, pleasant stop twenty feet from the short rock wall on the edge of the field.

Denise's hand shot into the air and she waved vigorously as Tuva brought her plane to a full stop. She then walked up to the little ultralight. Tuva stepped out. They hugged each other. "Good to see you, sweetie!" Denise said with an ear-to-ear smile.

"You too, Denise. I've missed you."

Denise looked into the cockpit, pointed a thumb to the second seat. "Who's your passenger?"

Tuva looked at the man sitting in the passenger seat unbuckling his strap. "That's Lukas Cerny. He's a member of our repair crew. He's come to do a proper fixing of your damage." She winked. "They don't trust me with the tools."

Denise nodded. "Did you bring canvas?"

Lukas nodded and motioned to his feet. There, a nice pile of canvas covered his boots. "Good," she said. "The folk in Déj managed to patch up the wing pretty well, but the short trip from there to here loosened the cloth quite a bit. Some of the stitching has torn open. I considered risking a flight back to Szatmár, but the people here are so nice, they actually urged me to stay and wait." She smiled. "I'm like a celebrity. The lady from the sky."

"Now, they have two of us," Tuva chirped.

"Fräulein Beasley," Lukas said, "where is the *Dixie Chick* now?"

She motioned behind her with a stiff thumb. "It's hidden in a barn up the path here. It was necessary to do so. As nice as these people have been to me, there have been concerns about those fucking Impalers moving into the area."

Tuva's face grew still, concerned. "Have you been attacked?"

"No. Not yet, anyway."

"Gretchen did a number on them near Szatmár," Tuva said while running her index finger across her throat. "Lopped their heads clean off. We've not had an incident there since."

Denise shook her head and huffed. "I love that woman, but she scares the shit out of me."

Tuva laughed. "You and everyone else. Especially our enemies."

"But there have been some suspicious folk moving in and out of town," Denise continued, "asking unusual questions, then leaving abruptly. Not many, but enough to cause concern. Something's in the works."

"Morris is giving Lukas twenty-four hours to get you up and running," Tuva said. "We have to DD by first light."

Denise suppressed a chuckle and a smile. Minnie's grasp of American slang was that of a native, by now. Tuva was still learning her way, using it as best as she could. This time, she'd used it correctly. *So cute.*

Denise leaned into the cockpit. "We don't have that much

time. Lukas, can you get me all patched up by, say, three this afternoon?"

Lukas stepped out with the canvas slung over his shoulder. He reached back into the cockpit and grabbed a satchel of tools. "That depends on the extent of the damage. If it is just wing repair, that should be possible. But if there is damage to the frame, especially fire damage, it will take longer. I also want to check your engine, landing gear, tail. I need to go over the entire craft."

"As far as I can tell, it's just wing damage." Denise moved out of the way to give Lukas ample room to climb out and adjust his portage. "I'll take you there now."

As they walked toward the barn where the *Dixie Chick* lay under guard, Denise asked: "You name it yet?"

Tuva frowned. "Named what?"

"Your plane, of course."

"Oh." Tuva had that inquisitive look as if she hadn't given the notion much thought. "No, I haven't, actually."

"Don't worry. We'll find a good name for it before you take her into action."

They reached the barn, and Denise could see Tuva's surprise at how small the structure was. "How in the world did you cram the *Dixie Chick* into that?"

"Very carefully."

The guards assigned to its security opened the doors. "As you can see," Denise said, as the Dvorak came into view, "packed tight like a sardine can."

"It'll have to be rolled out before I can work on it," Lukas said, dropping his satchel and the canvas to the ground.

Erdőd (Ardud)

Two days after Tuva and Denise returned from Nagybánya, General Roth ordered the Grand Army of the Sunrise to march into Transylvania. Jeff Higgins and his Silesian Guard, and Gretchen Richter and her CoC militants, followed.

Eddie Junker and his air force would stay behind until such a time as they could find level ground on which to land. For the Dvoraks, that would be simple. For the Jupiter and the Dauntless, Morris figured they'd have to wait until reaching Kolozsvár, which was just as well. By their maps, the distance between Szatmár and Kolozsvár was roughly eighty miles. A relatively easy distance to travel for the larger craft and quite honestly, given their cargo, made better sense. As much impact as Gretchen's brutal display of impaled Impaler heads had caused, Morris didn't want to take any chances of losing so much mercenary pay at the hands of Moldavian and Wallachian thugs. Lose the gold, lose the mercenaries. Then lose the war.

There was some debate as to who would lead the army onto the plateau. Flankers were sent forward, of course, to screen the army's march and to provide information as to the conditions of the roads and trails. The honor of leading the main body of the Sunrise forward ultimately fell to the Second and Third Regiments of the Joshua Corps, under the command of Colonel's Velvel Schiff and Getzel Zelikovich. Green men, every one, but they were now all healthy, well-trained, and ready to fight. The best of the Joshua Corps was far up the road and heading to Kolozsvár with von Mercy. Morris would be glad to have his entire army back together again.

The first day of the march went well, though slow. Morris insisted that they maintain tight control over the baggage train, the cannons, and the APCs as they moved onto the plateau, lest these elements trail behind at unacceptable distances. Once the army had a better sense of the country and its people, they could perhaps allow more flexibility, move a little faster, open the formations up and let men walk at a more relaxed pace. But on this first day, they moved slow and tight and made only ten miles.

They bivouacked near the small town of Erdőd in sight of an old, weatherworn fortress that looked down upon them like a weary eye. Morris didn't care about its eye. He cared more for the eyes of the townsfolk. Upon arrival, some packed up and left. Those who stayed behind to receive the Sunrise either stayed locked in their homes or greeted them warily as regiment after regiment traipsed through their roads, paths, and set up camp wherever they could. From this behavior, Morris could tell that the Impalers had paid a visit.

But the march went well, and no harm came to the Sunrise. Until they awoke at first light.

✧   ✧   ✧

"Who the *fuck* allowed an entire herd of cattle to be stolen?"

Colonel Reznik Makovec was the commander of all the Brethren. They were organized in what they called the Zizka Brigade, which was more like two-thirds of a brigade, since—so far—they only had a little under two thousand men under arms. He stood like stolid granite in front of General Roth in his tent, trying to look cool and calm under the heavy gaze of his commanding officer, Brigadier Higgins, and Gretchen Richter. "It wasn't the entire herd, General. Only half."

"Only half!" Morris threw his arms up in exasperation. He wanted to spit further expletives in response to that ridiculous statement. Instead, he said, "That herd is nearly our whole meat supply, Colonel. You understand that, don't you?"

"Yes, sir, I do."

"And you also understand that with half that herd gone, we'll be marching on empty stomachs by the time we reach Kolozsvár."

"Yes, sir."

"So, what are you going to do about the matter?"

"The men in charge of guarding the herd have been taken into custody by Marshal Lange. They will be disciplined, General, I can assure you."

Morris had spoken and dealt with Provost Marshal Luthor Lange on several occasions. Assigned to the position by von Mercy, he seemed a decent enough fellow. Though, on the march, what would he do exactly to a group of men at least some of whom must have been paid off by the Impalers to look the other way? Morris made a mental note to speak with Lange before any serious punishments were ladled out.

"And what about your missing cattle?"

Colonel Makovec cleared his throat. "Our cattle are of a different breed than the Hungarian Grey that you find in this area, General. They will be easy to recover."

"That's assuming, of course, that they can be found alive," Morris said, sharing a glance with Gretchen Richter, who rolled her eyes in response, "and if the Impalers haven't moved them in several different directions, which is most likely."

Oh, what's the point of continuing this conversation? Morris sighed. "Very well, Colonel. Do what you can to try to recover our missing herd. But we're moving forward, and I don't want the Brethren falling behind. Search for the cattle, but you get your men ready to move out."

"Yes, sir."

Colonel Makovec saluted and hurried out of the tent.

"You know they'll never be found, don't you?" Gretchen asked. "They'll scatter them everywhere, and I will bet you all the ducats on the Jupiter that they got local support to pull it off."

"That goes without saying." Morris sank into his chair, closed his eyes, and let out a frustrated breath. "It would seem that your tough actions in Szatmár met with limited success."

"Hell, Morris," Jeff said, coming to the defense of his wife, "what did you expect? We're moving into a country without radios. Word of mouth, horseman to horseman...that's how the word of Gretchen's wrath is going to spread, and that's going to take a while."

"I need to keep up the pressure," Gretchen said as she nodded agreement. She moved forward to stand next to her husband. "I need to concentrate right now on eliminating—well, it'll be more like diminishing—the Impaler threat, but also begin to get this country in full on our side. Our goal is Kolozsvár, yes, but we've a lot of ground to cover before we get there."

Morris wasn't married to Gretchen—Thank you, God!—but he knew as well as Jeff that once she had decided on a course of action, trying to recommend caution was nearly impossible. Her blood was up, as was said of up-time American generals who often acted rashly in the face of danger. Neither Morris nor Jeff was going to change her mind. And besides, she was making a good point. They couldn't afford to allow these Impalers to work unfettered against the Sunrise whilst on the march. And it was abundantly clear now that these thugs, these Moldavian terrorists, were getting local support. Their numbers would continue to grow and grow, and like he always said, "Success breeds success." A few more successful attacks against the Sunrise, and the Impalers would stop being a nuisance and become a major threat.

There was no one better suited to putting an end to that and convincing the local population to turn its support toward the Sunrise than Gretchen Richter. She was even better at organizing supporters and allies than she was at terrorizing enemies.

Morris stood. "Very well, Gretchen. You do your worst... and your best. But I don't want you moving too far into the countryside without screening support. You're tough as nails, Lady Protector, and so are your men, but I want at least a company of cavalry working as escort for you."

He turned to Jeff. "Would you be so kind, sir, as to speak with Colonel Burkenfeld of First Cavalry and see if he can spare a company?"

Jeff nodded. "Yes, I will do so."

"Good. Once all that's in place, Gretchen, do your best to keep us free of Impaler entanglements. Now, let's turn our attention to Zilah."

Chapter 36

Zilah (Zalău)

"I've got it!" Denise shouted into her radio.

"Got what?" Tuva asked as they both flew, side by side, over the Grand Army of the Sunrise as it made its slow, deliberate way into Zilah.

"The name for your plane. How's about..."

"How's about what?"

The answer hung on the tip of Denise's tongue. She bit it back as they both flew their little pushers up and over a crest of wooded hills skirting the field on which they were required to land. The weather had been pleasant, but now, Denise eyed a low rolling series of nimbus clouds moving quickly into the area.

"Five thalers says I land better than you."

The name she was going to propose was now completely out of her mind as Denise turned her attention toward the challenge. "You're on."

Denise couldn't recall if she had ever seen a Blue Angels routine up-time. Probably not, save for glimpses of them on the TV. She imagined now that she and Tuva were pilots in that distinguished group. Sure, their Dvoraks lacked the speed, performance, and sheer strength of those up-time jets, but in the here and now, no one would make the comparison.

She shifted farther right, moving away from Tuva a tad to give them both ample room for the landing and for the possible need to pull up and have another go at it if necessary. Tuva increased her speed, and Denise considered signaling caution, as the field below was short, and who the hell forgot to remove their cattle? Instead, she increased her own speed as she now understood why Tuva had done so: to avoid slamming into that same herd.

"If my landing gear gets all funky with cow shit, I'm—"

"Don't worry, Denise," Tuva said. "I'll guide you in."

Guide me in? Who does she think she is? Better than me?

Tuva had grown extremely competent in piloting the Dvorak, much to Denise's chagrin and delight. Any more time behind the stick, and the young girl would replace her as the premier pusher pilot of the Sunrise.

Denise slowed the *Dixie Chick* and maneuvered to fall behind Tuva. It didn't matter who landed first; what mattered was the manner in which they landed. And besides, let Tuva hit all the cow patties.

The first droplets of rain struck Denise's windshield, and a burst of wind pushed the *Dixie Chick* left. She considered ditching her plan to follow Tuva down, but managed to regain control and slide back into place.

Down, down, down, both planes dropped to align themselves with the hastily assigned landing crew who, waving dirty cloth flags, guided them in.

Tuva touched down first, bouncing three times before her landing gear found the proper purchase. Denise waited for that third bounce before she too set down.

Their speeds were such that it was difficult to know at a glance whether or not Tuva was plowing through cattle waste. Denise couldn't help but laugh.

"Are you laughing at me?" Tuva asked over the radio.

Denise followed her lead and slowly set on the brakes to bring the *Dixie Chick* to a complete halt, just ten feet behind her.

"Not at all," Denise said as she ran a quick check of the cockpit and then killed the engine. "I thank you for clearing a path for my perfect landing."

Tuva huffed. "Mine was better!"

Denise climbed out of the cockpit, removed her leather helmet, tossed it on the pilot seat, and met Tuva in the middle. "You did good, girlie. You did good. Pretty soon, you'll be as good a pilot as me."

"Already am." Tuva winked. "It took you four bounces to settle. I got it in three."

Denise shrugged. "Three, four. What does it really matter? I tell you what: you buy me lunch before we meet with the boss, and we'll call it a draw."

Denise almost burst out laughing as she saw Tuva struggle with whether or not that was a fair deal. Finally, she snorted and wrapped her arm around Tuva's shoulders. "Oh, never mind. It's on me."

Tuva blew Denise a raspberry, bumped her with her hip, and allowed herself to be led from the field. A large number of soldiers took up guard around the Dvoraks. That was good, Denise thought. There'd been a lot of Impaler activity during the march, though Gretchen had lowered the boom on much of that. Still, security around all aircraft was essential now that they were farther into Transylvania than they had ever been. How long they might stay in Zilah was a question that might or might not be decided later today at their meeting with Morris. Right now, however, sustenance called.

"Say," Tuva said as they walked from the field, stepping carefully through the cow patties, "what's the name you were going to say?"

"Name?"

"For my plane."

"Oh yes. How about..." Denise groaned and scratched her head. "*Damn.* I plumb forgot."

"So what do they want?" asked Werner Ruppel, after Gretchen returned from her discussion with the small group of people who had been awaiting them in front of the wooden church that was more or less the center of the small town of Zilah. The church was fairly good-sized. Its most notable feature was a narrow conical steeple topped by a crucifix.

"It seems this area, including Zilah itself, is governed by a council of elected officials they call 'senators.'" She nodded her head back in the direction of the church. "The short, plump one with the plumed hat is the mayor. This group of five senators has been given the authority to negotiate with us."

Werner squinted in their direction. "Negotiate with us? About what?"

"The Impalers have been terrorizing the area for the past couple of weeks. They heard about what we did at Szatmár and would like us to do the same for them."

Werner sniffed. "And what help do they offer us?"

Gretchen smiled thinly. "They will cheer us on most loudly and fervently. After we succeed, they might even give us a parade."

Werner sniffed again. "As long as we cover the cost, I presume."

Gretchen's smile turned into a genuine grin. "As it stands, their proposal is ridiculous. But there might be something useful we could do, given that we do now have official sanction and approval."

Gretchen looked around the open space that served Zilah as a "town square." There appeared to be no Rathaus that would have a convenient cellar restaurant and tavern, but down the street a ways and across from the church, she saw a large two-story building—made of wood, like the church—which was probably a local substitute for a Rathaus. They could get some food and perhaps even some lodgings for the night, at least for some of their group.

"Down there," Gretchen said, pointing.

Happily, it did turn out to be a tavern with some rooms available. The tavern was spacious enough for all of them to eat together and even had a few rooms available. Most of them would have to make camp in the square—no, better make that all of them. The dilapidated nature of the tavern made Gretchen think that the bedding would already be well-inhabited with small multilegged wildlife.

Once her eyes got accustomed to the dim interior of the tavern, she saw that it already had three people sitting at a table toward one side—all of whom she recognized.

"Well, that's interesting," she said, heading their way. "A coincidence running into them here? I doubt it."

After she and Werner took a seat at the same table, they ordered ale but no food. All the tavern was serving was a stew of some sort, and judging from the only half-eaten bowls in front of their three new companions, she thought they'd all do better to have lunch prepared by the CoC expedition's two cooks.

"I assume meeting you here is not accidental," she said, after ordering the steins of ale.

The Saxon "notable" they'd first met in Szatmár, Ignaz Honterus, smiled and shook his head. "Not entirely, no. As it happens, my friends and I had been planning to make a trip to Kolozsvár in the near future. We arrived here in Zilah the day before yesterday and decided to stay until you appeared. There are things we'd like to talk about."

"Are you the ones who persuaded this delegation of senators to ask us for our help against the Impalers—which amounted to us doing it alone?" asked Werner, his tone bordering on belligerence.

The answer came from one of the two men accompanying Honterus. "No—in fact, we told them you'd insist on an alliance. You're not mercenaries."

Unlike Honterus, for whom German was his native tongue, this fellow's was heavily accented. Gretchen assumed he was a Szekler, who grew up speaking Hungarian.

"We haven't been introduced," she said.

"My oversight," said Honterus apologetically. "This is Elek Ferenc, one of my Székely associates." He nodded toward the third man. "And this is a fellow Saxon, Christian Sommerus."

"We're willing to help," said Gretchen, "but only under certain conditions.

"First, we can only leave four of our people here. We will need the rest for our operations in Kolozsvár." Here, she smiled. "I will leave unsaid the precise nature of those operations, at least for the moment. We can also leave behind ten of our Hocklott rifles, and..."

She looked at Werner. "A thousand rounds," he said. "More later, if we can prevail upon Morris Roth to lend us the use of one of the Jupiters."

Now she looked back at Honterus. "The Hocklott is the USE army's newest rifle, a .406 caliber breechloader, and probably the best rifle anywhere in the world, at least for the moment. You'll be far better armed than the Impalers."

She paused for a moment. "We will require at least ten, preferably fifteen or twenty, of your own people. All of them should have some military experience—and all of them must be willing to accept the direction and orders of our people. The man we will leave behind in command is Heinz Anckermann. He was a platoon leader in the USE army and fought at the battle of Ahrensbök. Perhaps more useful was that he later led one of the

CoC columns during Operation Krystalnacht which scoured the Rhineland of anti-Semites. There's not much difference between such folk and Moldavian Impalers."

Honterus and his two companions looked at each other.

"Given the preponderance of Szeklers in this area, it might make sense for me to remain behind," said Ferenc.

Honterus shook his head. "No, I'll need you to deal with the Szeklers in Kolozsvár." Here he bestowed a thin smile upon Gretchen. "I will leave unsaid the precise nature of those dealings, at least for the moment."

Gretchen laughed.

"I think Christian can handle the situation here," he added. "Don't forget that there are now a lot more Saxons here than usual, who fled from the Wallachian invasion."

"And many of whom are furious about the situation," said Christian. "Some of them are bound to find the prospect of killing Moldavian invaders appealing. I don't think we'll have much trouble getting recruits."

Gretchen rose from the table. "We're done, then. Heinz will introduce himself later today. Tomorrow, the rest of us will be on our way to Kolozsvár."

Part Five

August 1637

At the mercy of compelling fortune
—Sophocles, *Ajax*

Chapter 37

Kolozsvár (Cluj)

The defeated Moldavian army in Déj had withdrawn to Szamosújvár. Upon arrival, they were greeted by a small but potent Transylvanian force comprised of Prince Rákóczi's personal court corps, Hajdu mercenaries from the Partium, and two Székely infantry companies. A force smaller than General von Mercy's vanguard, to be sure, but large and dangerous enough to convince General Radu that retreat was the best course of action. The Moldavians, stuck between a hammer and an anvil, withdrew back toward the Eastern Carpathians, leaving the road to Kolozsvár wide open.

Some of the officers in the ranks wanted to pursue the Moldavians to the grave, as Captain Kinsky had said, to finish the job, but neither Colonel Renz nor General von Mercy agreed to such a fruitless endeavor. Instead, they stuck to the original plan: move to Kolozsvár and await the arrival of General Roth and the rest of the Grand Army of the Sunrise, which was already in-country, on its way, and only one, maybe two weeks out, weather and road conditions permitting.

Isaac Kohen and his staff had assembled their hospital tent and were tending to patients still recovering from wounds received at the Battle of Déj, when General von Mercy wanted to see him.

Headquarters was mad with activity. Nearly all senior officers were in attendance, with their aide-de-camps, personal servants,

287

and staff. Officers of the baggage train were there as well, including the quartermaster and his staff. Isaac assumed that they had all been assembled for a meeting. Such was not the case.

"Ah, Doctor Kohen," von Mercy said, waving him through the forest of officers. "Come, come."

"You wanted to see me, General?"

The general handed the quartermaster a signed document, then said with a wipe of his sweaty and much receded hairline, "How are you and yours set with medical supplies?"

Isaac nodded. "Adequate, although it's never enough. We had to use a lot of our supply in Déj, as you know. I'm glad we're here in Kolozsvár now. It'll be nice to reassemble the full medical corps when General Roth arrives."

Von Mercy pulled a rueful face. "Yes, well, that's why I've called you here. Don't get too comfortable, Doctor. We're heading to the capital tomorrow first light."

"Sir?"

"Gáspár has just received a request from Prince George Rákóczi that we attend him immediately. I've discussed the matter with Morris, and he's agreed to it. We're leaving just enough of the Brethren behind to find, assemble, and secure a landing site for the planes. Morris is bringing the air force with him. So, get your people to pack it all up and be ready to depart."

He went back to other business, as if the matter was done and closed.

"No, sir."

At first, von Mercy didn't seem to hear Isaac's refusal. He did the second time.

"Say again?" the general asked, pausing his conversation with Colonel Renz.

Isaac took a deep breath. "Sir, we just assembled the hospital tent a few hours ago. Wounded have been transferred from wagons to beds. I can't ask my people, who've been working nonstop since Déj, to 'pack it all up' again. No, sir. We'll stay here until General Roth arrives."

Von Mercy shook his head. "No, Doctor. We're heading to the capital. I need my entire senior staff with me, including you. We're only leaving a large enough force behind to secure a landing site. Not enough to protect and support a medical operation. I don't have to remind you, Doctor, that we are in hostile territory.

Granted, we've more support here in Kolozsvár than in Déj, but the Impalers are still out there, despite Gretchen's fearful display of their severed heads. Perhaps their bands are a little smaller now, a little less prominent than they might have been prior to such a display, but they're still in the field. By God, they cut the throats of three of our sleeping soldiers just the other day. Shot one of our company commanders."

"Yes," Isaac said, "and I lost four patients from Szamosújvár to here simply because we packed them onto wagons. I can't afford to lose any other patients, sir. No, as senior medical officer of this endeavor, I refuse to move and thus endanger any further patients. We'll risk staying."

By now, the activity in the room had fallen silent. Some were still talking to each other, but in muted tones. All their attention had turned toward Isaac and General von Mercy's red face.

"Your patients? Your patients, Doctor, are my soldiers. *My* men. Perhaps you've forgotten that?"

Isaac shook his head. "No, sir. I've not forgotten. But you are not a doctor, and you can't possibly know how severely wounded some of my patients—your soldiers—are. I'm telling it to you straight: they cannot be moved, or you risk losing them all."

"Now look here," von Mercy said, coming out from behind his desk, anger accentuating his red cheeks. "Don't you come into my headquarters and refuse an order from me, Doctor Kohen. You serve at my pleasure. You will pack up the tent, and you will come follow us to the capital."

At his sides, Isaac's hands were shaking. He felt faint, light-headed. He wanted to throw up, but he swallowed down the bile rising in his throat and said, "No, sir. I will not."

"If you do not, then I will relieve you of your service."

"You may do so. That is your prerogative. But as long as I am chief medical officer of your army, I will not move my patients one more mile until I deem them able to travel."

Von Mercy nodded. "Very well. Then I relieve you of—"

"General von Mercy!" Colonel Renz stepped forward to put his body between them. "Please...if I may..."

Isaac took a breath and stepped back. He hadn't realized that he had been holding his breath. Von Mercy stepped back as well, his face still colored in anger.

"Doctor Kohen," Colonel Renz said, stepping out of their way, "it is inappropriate for you to challenge General von Mercy's authority in such a manner. However"—he shot a wary glance at von Mercy—"General, couldn't we find a compromise on this matter?"

Von Mercy looked at his officer. "What do you mean?"

"Sir Veres," Colonel Renz said, looking past them to Prince Rákóczi's liaison. "General von Mercy's concern is the safety of his men and medical team if they stay here in Kolozsvár. Could you perhaps ask one of the commanders of the two Székely companies that escorted us from Szamosújvár to leave some of his men behind to garrison and protect Doctor Kohen's staff and supplies?"

Gáspár Bojthi Veres seemed out of breath from watching the argument unfold. "Yes, yes. I'm sure they would accommodate your needs." He cleared his throat. "I'll take care of it."

"Sir," Colonel Renz said, "will that satisfy your safety concerns?"

Von Mercy was silent for a grueling moment. He glanced around the room, then nodded. "That will be fine."

Isaac saw Colonel Renz staring him down, nodding subtly toward the general with eyes wide open. He got the hint. "Yes, I'm fine with that as well, General. I thank you. And I apologize for my outburst. It's been a stressful several weeks."

Von Mercy nodded. "I can attest to that." He moved back to the other side of the table as the conversation and activity in the room returned to its brisk pace. "That's the end of it. We'll miss you in the capital, Doctor. While here, you will maintain good order amongst your staff and ensure that your patients—my men—are properly cared for as you await General Roth's arrival. But I want a written report from you about the status of each of your patients by nightfall. Understood?"

Isaac nodded. "Yes, sir."

"You may go now."

Isaac turned to Colonel Renz and mouthed a silent "Thank you." The colonel didn't respond; he just continued with his duties as if nothing had happened. As did seemingly everyone else in the room. It was as if the argument hadn't occurred.

Isaac left. Once outside, he found a tree and leaned against it. He let the bile of his stomach rise into his throat and then leaned over and vomited all over its exposed roots.

✦　　　✦　　　✦

It was late, near midnight, and Christian von Jori stepped into the hospital tent. Lighting was poor, but he found Devorah Bayer tending to the infected leg of a Joshua Corps infantryman. He stepped quietly between the rows of sleeping men—some snoring, some moaning in restless pain, some wide awake.

Devorah saw him and smiled. "*Guten abend*, Christian."

"*Guten abend*, Devorah. Is Isaac on duty?"

She wrung out a bloody washcloth and said quietly, "He stepped outside for a breath of fresh air." She shook her head and twisted the cloth as if she were trying to strangle it. Christian could feel and see her agitation.

"Is there something wrong? Something with Isaac?"

Devorah kept wringing the cloth. She stopped, snapped the cloth out, laid it gently on the soldier's wound, and applied firm pressure. She pointed toward the back wall of the tent. "Go see for yourself."

Christian nodded. He turned, then remembered. "Oh, yes. Is Andreea Hatmanu working tonight?"

Devorah's agitation was gone. In its place, a thin smile. "I'm sorry to say, no. She's been summoned to the capital."

"The capital? Why?"

She shrugged. "I don't know. She left this morning."

"She's still a member of your nursing staff, isn't she?"

Again, Devorah shrugged.

He wanted to say more but left it alone. Saying anything else would, perhaps, reveal his feelings. Then again, just asking if Andreea was working probably had done just that, though judging from Devorah's sly smile, she already had an inkling of his feelings. How? He had never confided in Devorah anything. How could she know?

"*Danke*, Devorah," he said with a short bow. "I hope you have a pleasant evening."

He found Isaac sitting on a rock overlooking Kolozsvár. Flickering lantern light captured the expanse of the city beautifully. Though near midnight, the whinny of horses, the far-off moan of cattle, the howls of dogs all gathered in the dark to give Christian a sense of peace and comfort. These, he was happy to note, were not the sounds of war.

"*Guten abend*, Isaac," Christian said, finding a rock beside him.

The abrupt greeting shook Isaac from his euphoric stare

across the city. He nearly fell off his rock. He collected himself and offered Christian a bottle. "Ah, Captain von Jori. Please sit. Have some wine."

Christian took his hat off and laid it aside. "Very well," he said, grabbing the bottle and taking a drink. The warm, red liquid felt like heaven on his lips and in his dry throat. He wished he could down the whole thing, and perhaps it was best to get rid of it, judging from how the good doctor was swaying so aggressively to and fro in the light breeze.

Reluctantly, he handed the bottle back. "Thank you, but maybe you should go easy on that." He chuckled. "Can Jews even drink alcohol?"

Isaac took a big swig and snorted. "Of course we can. In moderation. Wine is perfectly permissible, especially for ceremonial purposes."

"Are you conducting a ceremony right now?"

Isaac took another drink. He raised the bottle in salute. "The ceremony of the spirit, Christian! To keep my spirits up . . . in the midst of all this death."

The bottle dropped from Isaac's hand. Christian tried catching it, but it slipped past him and shattered on the smaller rocks at his feet. Isaac mumbled a curse and tried grabbing a shard of glass out of the growing puddle of red liquid. Christian stopped him.

"Steady, my friend, steady. Don't make me call Devorah out here."

"I'm sorry, Christian," Isaac said, allowing himself to be stopped and held. "I apologize for my behavior. I've had a bad, bad day."

Christian moved Isaac off the rock and placed him on firm ground. "That's all right. Tell me, what's wrong?"

Isaac settled, drew his sleeve across his face to wipe wine from his lips, breathed deeply. "I thought I'd never say this, but I'm looking forward to seeing Oberheuser again."

"Is the work becoming too much?" Christian asked. "I admit: it's been a long march."

Isaac held up his hand. In the faint light, it was hard to see it, but Christian could detect modest shaking. Isaac grabbed it with his other hand and held it in his lap. "I refused a direct order from the commanding officer today. I told General von Mercy that I would resign before I would pack up the hospital again and move to Gyula . . . Gyulafe—"

"Gyulafehérvár," Christian said with a slight chuckle. "It's a difficult name to pronounce."

Isaac nodded. "I told him that I would not lose one more patient simply by moving them from one town to another." He paused, cleared his throat. "We lost four yesterday on the road from Szamosújvár simply because I packed them in a goddamned wagon!"

He was near tears. Christian leaned Isaac into him, letting his head rest on his shoulder. "Yes, I know what you said to the general."

"Who told you?"

"Colonel Renz. That's why I'm here. He wanted me to check in on you, make sure that you were all right."

"It was a stupid thing to do, snapping at him in his own headquarters. But I just wasn't going to do it, Christian. I was not going to allow them to be moved again."

Christian patted him on the back. "Don't worry about it. Yes, it was unwise for you to challenge von Mercy's authority in his own headquarters, but he's a smart man, a rational man. He'll come around to your way of thinking. In a week, it'll all be forgotten, especially once the next fight is on."

"It's not just that," Isaac said, pulling away. "It's all of it. All of this. Before we left Kassa, I told Morris that I was unqualified to be a chief surgeon, and he assigned me anyway. He made a mistake."

"Nonsense. You're every bit as good as Oberheuser. You saved my sight, my life. You've saved countless lives. You're a hero to many."

Isaac sniffled. *Is he crying?* It was hard for Christian to know for sure, the light being so poor.

"I was a stupid boy on that bridge in Prague," Isaac said, kicking his left leg out and pushing away the bottle shards. "When I decided on that day to become a physician, I set my expectations on what that would mean based upon my experiences there. So foolish. Since then, all the war I've seen is ten times worse than on that bridge. I'm not prepared for so much . . . death."

Christian laid his hand on the back of Isaac's neck and squeezed gently. "Come on, friend, don't say such things. You are far better than that cursing buffoon—"

"You know," Isaac said, "maybe Oberheuser has the right of it.

He curses and rants and yells and wears his anger on his sleeve. Everyone thinks he's a son of a bitch, but maybe it's his way of dealing with all the pain and suffering. Don't hold anything back. Wear it all on your sleeve, leave it all on the operating room floor. Then maybe, just maybe, you can sleep at night."

Christian shook his head. "You're not sleeping?"

Isaac shrugged. "A little, but who has time, right?"

"Doctor Kohen, I order you to get some sleep," Christian said, "or I'll tell Devorah."

They both laughed at that. It was good hearing Isaac laugh; it had been so long.

"Look," Christian said, "Oberheuser's a swine. He may be a good doctor, but he's a swine. When I look into his eyes, I don't see a man who cares. He doesn't look upon his patients like you do. They watch you as you work the tent. They respond to you. You walk past their beds, and they look upon you with reverence, as if you're Jesus."

"Don't say that, Christian," Isaac said, giving his friend a little push. "I don't need God's wrath brought down upon me as well as everything else."

Christian chuckled and pushed Isaac back. "But it's true. You're the one they care about. And it's not just your patients. It's your nurses, too. All of them. Why do you think Devorah risked her service to the Sunrise by defying Oberheuser's demand to stay behind? Because she wants to work with you. She *has* to work with you. You matter, Isaac, and we need you."

He pulled Isaac close again, gave him a tight hug around the shoulders. "Stick with it, Isaac. It'll all be over soon. The capital is near. We've not much longer to go. And I want you to be there at the end, so that I can buy you a new bottle of wine. And on that day, we'll drink in real celebration."

"Am I disturbing you?"

Both Christian and Isaac started and turned abruptly.

"Rabbi Gotkin," Christian said, standing. "Nice to see you again. It's been a while."

"Yes," Gotkin said, nodding. "I'm glad to see you again, too, Captain." He motioned to Isaac. "May I have some time alone with Isaac, please, sir?"

Christian fixed his uniform, grabbed his hat, and placed it back on his head. "Of course." He turned back to Isaac and smiled. "I'll check in on you again before we head out in the morning to the capital."

"That will be fine," Isaac said. "And thank you, Christian, for sharing your time with me and my wine."

"Doctor . . . Rabbi." Christian bid them both goodbye and walked away.

It was nearly one in the morning now, and Christian had to find some of that elusive sleep for himself before he and his company struck camp and headed toward Gyulafehérvár with the rest of General von Mercy's army. He hoped that what he had told Isaac was true, that all the fighting, the war, would end soon. But now he wasn't so sure.

Word from the Transylvanian capital was that the Wallachian and Moldavian armies were moving fast. A fight was coming, and right soon.

Christian paused and looked back toward the hospital tent, listening to the soft, quiet prayer being shared between Isaac and Rabbi Gotkin. He said a prayer for himself, and then turned and walked away.

Chapter 38

Hermannstadt (Sibiu)
Southern Transylvania

Rockets from the two katyusha launchers fired on the *mülazım's* command. The walls of Hermannstadt were too thick and strong for the rockets to do any damage, so their trajectories had been set to fly over them and into the city itself. From his position behind the Ottoman tanks, Usan Hussein listened to the rockets whistle madly across the sky, land, and explode inside the city, followed by the shouts and screams of the anxious Saxon citizen defense inside. Whether the rockets were doing much damage, he could not say. That hardly mattered. What mattered was the fear, the terror, that they inflicted, and on that score, Usan knew they were working.

The *mülazım awal* in command of the tanks stood upright next to Usan, as if he were impervious to the large hackbut muskets being fired from the ramparts. All day, the Saxon defenders had tried killing the cannon and rocket crews with those large muskets. So far, they had been unsuccessful.

"I beg you, Great Effendi," Usan said, ducking another ricochet of gunfire off the tire rim of the tank. "Please crouch for safety. Spare us the ignominy of your death before our assault on the gate."

The Turkish lieutenant scoffed and waved off Usan's concern.

"I am perfectly safe here, *corbaci*. Those are antiquated weapons. Useless muskets from a useless age. They couldn't so much as hit the broadside of a seraglio than a—"

A hackbut round struck the lieutenant's chest.

He fell atop Usan, who used his body to absorb another dedicated volley of hackbut fire, then flung him aside with spit curses.

Now what do we do? Who orders the tanks forward?

It had taken a whole regiment of Wallachian infantry to push, pull, drag, and prod the fire tanks through the narrow gaps of the southern Carpathian range, and there had been times when, down to the man, everyone wanted to quit and just leave the smoky hulks to rust in the mud. But they had made it, they were here, and they now needed a commander.

Usan's Janissary orta waited patiently under the protection of the three tanks arrayed in echelon for the assault, waiting for Usan's order to attack. Serbian cavalry had swept around the city and now held all roads leading in and out. Wallachian infantry were lined up just behind the ridgeline, and from that ridgeline, cannons barked continually, peppering the burning gate with punishing volleys. But so far, it had held.

Not for long...

As he had seen the lieutenant do numerous times, he went from tank to tank and smacked its iron hull hard with the butt of his musket. Three quick strikes to denote the order to move.

With violent belches of steam, the Sultan's fire tanks came to life. The steam, combined with the smoke from the flamethrowers, was a blessing and a curse. It was nearly impossible to breathe when in its thick, combined cloud, but it also made it difficult for the enemy to see his advancing Janissaries.

Musket and cannon fire erupted along the city wall. Neither could do much damage to the tanks, but like the arrogant and now dead effendi had proven, men were still men, made of flesh, and could be easily killed with new or old weapons alike. Usan's men followed slowly, taking care to keep their bodies low to the ground.

Like the katyusha rockets, the tanks' flamethrowers could not penetrate Hermannstadt's walls. But the gate was vulnerable, and so were the men defending the ramparts.

For an hour now, it had burned consistently from flamethrower shots from the tanks, despite the defenders' hurried efforts to douse the fire. Burn, burn, burn! It was a sight that fascinated and terrified Usan in equal measures. It was like witnessing the work of an *Ifrit*—the tanks were often called such—a swirling dervish of flame, relentless and mad with power. The gate burned, and there seemed to be nothing the defenders of the city could do about it.

Another volley of cannon fire from the ridgeline struck the gate as the tanks halted a mere dozen *kulaçs* from their target. Saxons along the wall now fired everything they had at the tanks despite their low visibility from the smoke and steam. Usan heard the final death cries of some of his men as hackbut rounds found victims. Most of his men now huddled very close to the rear of the tanks for more protection, waiting for his order to charge, but there were too many for all of them to be well-protected.

With the butt of his musket, he tapped out the order for the tanks to charge the gate. Each tank had a short but strong and heavy battering ram protruding forward. The machines couldn't move very fast, but their engines were powerful and the gate was badly weakened from the flamethrowers. In succession, each tank rammed the gate. The third time the lead tank did so, the gate on the left came off its hinges. The second tank immediately rammed it and knocked it completely off. It fell, tearing in two, its wrought iron bands twisting in the final cannonball strikes. The rest of the gate fell inward. Some of the wood was still burning.

Usan wasted no time. "Attack!" he shouted through choking smoke.

In a wave of whirling swords and muskets, Usan led his Janissaries out from behind the tanks—a sea of screaming, howling warriors aching for a fight. The small skirmishes that they had encountered along the march had done little to satiate their need for battle. This assault, Usan knew, would cure that malady.

Some of his men were injured by the flames, but within a few minutes the stamping boots of the charging Janissaries extinguished them. The Saxon defenders had hastily assembled additional wooden fortifications behind the gate, hoping to slow the assault. The Janissaries smashed into those, knocking them aside, and giving battle to the Saxon infantry desperately trying to hold the line.

Usan struck the first Saxon in the throat with the butt of his musket. As the man fell choking, he slung the musket behind him and drew his sword.

The rush of his men pushed Usan forward. A Saxon man's face smashed into his own, their lips nearly touching as the weight of both forces pushed against each other. Usan spit and knocked the Saxon soldier away by smacking him down with the hilt of his sword. He then ducked a spear thrust from his right as a Janissary stepped up and protected his *corbaci* from a sword slash to his left. Usan fell back a pace, collected himself, and continued the fight.

Hackbuts fired from the ramparts. Small cannonades sent grapeshot into the swarming Janissaries. His men began to fall in handfuls, and Usan was suddenly unsure of his rash charge. He wondered if he should sound the retreat; or, at the least, fall back to the gate and re-form his lines.

Another volley of rockets struck inside the city, spreading its thick, murderous shrapnel through screaming ranks of Saxons. Then, the lead tank pushed its way through the gate and opened fire with its flamethrower.

Some of his Janissaries were caught in the stream of fire, but it was the Saxons who took the brunt of the strike. They ignited like dry kindling, a nice steady line of men turning black in the flame. The sight of it made Usan's stomach turn. The sight of it routed the Saxons.

"Follow them!" Usan shouted, refreshing his blade by swiping it through the air. "Follow them to the square. Let no one escape!"

An hour later, with a third of his city burning and his defenders routed, the burgomaster of Hermannstadt surrendered.

Voivode Basarab found Usan Hussein in the town square, standing with his men. His orta had taken losses. They were battered and bloody, but intact and ready for further orders.

"Congratulations, Usan," Matei Basarab said, a satisfied smile on his face. "You've won the city."

Usan bowed humbly, though he knew the truth of it. "Thank you, Voivode Basarab. But I will give all the credit to the tanks... and the rockets."

"You took command of the tanks," Matei said. "You took the initiative and won the city. This is your victory."

Usan was pleased with the voivode's humility, something he often did not get from Ottoman leaders and higher-ranking officers who respected the Janissary corps for their fighting prowess, but who also resented them and saw them as a threat. It was quite refreshing to hear a leader of a country—albeit a vassal state—give humble praise.

"I thank you again, sir." Usan bowed even lower this time. "I'm sure that once Sultan Murad hears of this, he will be most pleased. With Hermannstadt in your hands, the Saxon Sees will not likely give their men and materiel to Prince Rákóczi, lest they suffer more death and desolation from our tanks and rockets. They are heeled, as is said, and you now have control of southern Transylvania. The part that matters, anyway."

Matei nodded and looked over the cleanup and regroupment that was going on around him. "The question *now* becomes: when do we march to Gyulafehérvár?"

"What is the situation with Voivode Lupu?" Usan asked.

"Pushing slowly through the Carpathians, though he has had fewer engagements than we." Matei chuckled. "Ironically, it is now *his* army that is the slowest in this affair. We will remain here and regroup, refit, until I've sent word to Vasile, and he has responded in kind. By his previous requests, we will march together, in coordination, to Gyulafehérvár."

A sound decision, though Usan wondered if moving sooner than that might not be the better plan, even if it meant reaching the capital before the Moldavians. According to maps he had seen, Gyulafehérvár was only thirty-five to forty miles away. A three-day march, perhaps four depending upon weather, ground conditions, and the speed, mobility, and health of the tanks.

"Very well," Usan said. "Then I and my men will gather provisions and conduct a refit for that inevitable march."

Matei nodded. "That is well." He stepped up to Usan, his gaze hard. "But I wish to make it clear to you and to your men. Do not harm these people. If I hear of random killings and rapes, I will execute on the spot. And do not vandalize or take more than we absolutely need for our march to Gyulafehérvár. I do not want these Saxons rising up behind us and cutting off our baggage train. We need the roads from Hermannstadt to the capital left open and in good condition to maintain proper supply."

Another sound decision. Usan nodded. "I will keep my men in line, Voivode Basarab. I cannot speak for anyone else."

"They'll stay in line," Basarab said. "Or they will answer to me."

Schäßburg (Sighişoara)

With measured impatience, Vasile Lupu looked out the window of his headquarters at the tethered airship. The weather had been foul, the winds strong. He had not had the opportunity to ride the *Chaldiran* in days. But that would change soon. Very soon.

Those two kafirs, Moshe and Mordechai, were conducting a very thorough check of the ship, ensuring its viability and safety. Despite their religious differences, Vasile approved of them both. They did not speak much to him, but they were courteous and did what they were told. A good quality in servants.

"General Radu," Vasile said, finally acknowledging the man's presence. "I thank you for your devotion to Moldavia and to your prince. Your efforts in Déj did not bear the kind of fruit that I had desired. Kolozsvár is no longer obtainable, which is a setback. But you bought us time, time that we can now spend planning our final march to Gyulafehérvár."

Radu bowed low. "Thank you, My Voivode. I did my best. I attacked them with everything I had. I attacked twice. I breached both of their fortifications. I—"

Vasile put up his hand. "I'm aware of your battle plan and the decisions that you made." He glanced over at Sergiu Botnari sitting nearby, waiting with arms crossed. "I don't wish to hear them again. Despite your failings, General, I've decided to keep you on my staff. You may bring your army forward and bivouac alongside General Mardare's force. Then join us tonight for a final discussion about our march to the capital."

"Yes, My Voivode," Radu said, bowing lower as he stepped backward toward the door. "I will serve you, this army, and God well."

General Radu was escorted out as Vasile waved him away.

"That was generous, my lord," Sergiu Botnari said. "His loss at Déj was far more serious than you let on. I was expecting you to relieve him of duty; or possibly of his head."

Vasile stared again out the window toward the *Chaldiran*. "General Radu is the only member of my staff who has actually faced up-time weaponry. That alone is reason enough to keep him active. I need that experience on the field."

"I faced those weapons as well, my lord."

Vasile nodded and turned away from the window. "Yes, you have. And you have shown me the kinds of muskets and pistols that they wield. Not all that dissimilar to those Sultan Murad has graciously given us. But I'm not simply interested in the differences or similarities of our weapons versus theirs, Sergiu. I need to know what the strategic and tactical ramifications are as well. I especially want to know more about that aircraft you spoke about." Vasile leaned over, grunted, and found a seat among his plush pillows. "Tell me more."

Sergiu cleared his throat. "It's a fragile machine, my lord. Frankly, I'm surprised it can fly. It's made of wood and canvas and metal. As I said, the canvas burns well enough, so it's vulnerable to attack. On the ground, at least. In flight, I can't see it being vulnerable to much of anything, save for wind and weather."

"The *Chaldiran* has capabilities," Vasile said, thumbing to the window.

"Yes, and perhaps it could strike one of them and bring it down. But they move much faster than your airship. I think it would be difficult to do."

"Men with rifles can be placed on the airship."

Sergiu nodded. "Yes, and that would be wise to do. But I'm sure that those who fly the enemy's planes are experienced enough not to give you an easy target."

"Speaking of their pilots," Vasile said, grunting, standing up again. "It's my understanding that you failed to capture or kill the pilot in the craft that you attacked, even though you had the chance. Why?"

Vasile leaned in close until his nose was mere inches from Sergiu's dirty face. "You spoke harshly of General Radu's failures on the battlefield. How do you explain yours?"

Sergiu glanced around at the men standing guard at the door, near the window, and behind him in the far corner. "She surprised me, that's all. There aren't many girls—or men—who could have reacted as quickly and cleverly as she did. Plus, I was not familiar with the machine she hid behind. Looking back on it, I think I could have shot right through it, which might possibly have killed her."

He shrugged. "Or possibly not. She was very quick and it was dark. And don't forget that this same girl also killed three of us who went for the plane. She's not someone to be taken lightly."

Vasile was not altogether satisfied by the answer, but...

The truth was, he needed Sergiu Botnari's services as much as he did General Radu's. And there was this much consolation to be taken from the affair—at least the chief of his Impalers now had a much better understanding of the enemy's planes. And of their pilots.

The door opened, and a messenger begged admittance. Vasile waved him forward.

The man bowed and offered a note. "From the capital, my lord."

Vasile took the note and read it. He read it again and then a third time. "The birds in Gyulafehérvár are chirping, Sergiu, and they tell me that General von Mercy has arrived. I have need of your services."

Sergiu nodded. "What can I do for you, my lord?"

Vasile folded the note and tucked it into the pocket of his long, fur-lined dolman.

"For now, just stay in camp and wait. But soon, I may ask you to help me do something I promised Basarab I would not do."

Chapter 39

The Collegium Academicum
Gyulafehérvár

Gyulafehérvár was smaller than Kolozsvár, but it was the political and cultural center of Transylvania. Set comfortably upon a hill, it rested beside the Maros River, in view of the Carpathian Alps, and von Mercy was glad to see that it was on the right bank of the river, the side where, if an invading force was coming from either the south or the east, they'd have to cross the Maros to lay siege.

He entered the city with only his personal staff, deciding to keep his army and its officers outside the walls. It was best not to fill the city streets with mercenary cavalry and highly motivated Ashkenazi infantry, lest his army be seen as an invading force.

Why he was meeting Prince Rákóczi in a college, von Mercy could not say. He had been told by Gáspár Bojthi Veres that the so-called Princely Palace, where George and his family lived whilst in the city, was a splendid domicile, one to rival any castle in Germany. So, why not there? The general had his suspicions but kept them to himself.

The prince of Transylvania greeted him warmly at the front gate of the Collegium Academicum. Only a translator was at his side, a man whom Gáspár knew well, apparently. They greeted each other with a similar measure of warmth. The prince was the first to speak, in Hungarian, through his man.

"I welcome you, General Franz von Mercy, to Gabriel Bethlen's greatest achievement. Well, one of his greatest. There were so many." He motioned for them all to follow. "Come in. Let me show you the finest university in the world."

"Thank you for welcoming us into your city, Prince Rákóczi," von Mercy said, following. "I regret that Morris Roth could not be here to greet you in person. But I assure you... he and the rest of our army will be arriving in Kolozsvár soon."

The prince brushed off von Mercy's apology with a wave. "Let us not worry about that right now. First, allow me to show you the grounds."

They walked through the entire campus. Still under construction, it was indeed an impressive compound, though von Mercy doubted that it quite met the standard of universities in Germany or Italy. Young men were nestled into corners, studying, talking, debating. The students and teachers that they met were very respectful in the presence of their prince. They greeted von Mercy with kindness, but with a kind of polite hesitation. Polite, but wary, as if they were happy to make his acquaintance, but not sure if it was the right thing to do. Clearly, the apprehension of the citizenry of Déj to the Sunrise's presence in their country had made its way to the capital.

As the tour proceeded, through a maze of study rooms, living quarters, kitchen, and dining hall, von Mercy wondered if the reason for the tour was simply to show him that Transylvania was not the barbaric, uneducated Eastern European vassal state that many in the west assumed. For his part, von Mercy had never held those opinions. Being a general for so many years, having to treat with mercenaries from all over Europe, he knew that intelligence—and stupidity—was universal. One was not a barbarian simply because he hailed from Hungary—Prince Rákóczi's country of birth—or a learned man because he lived in Prague or Magdeburg. A tour like this would better serve Morris Roth, not a soldier like him. Yet, he endured and applied all the proper nods and impressive acknowledgements of this statue and that ancient tome and that bit of history that the prince seemed quite anxious to provide.

The tour ended in the library. It was, indeed, an impressive room, with walls of books and scrolls and lovely paintings that hung proudly on each wall. What impressed von Mercy the most about it was the long table in the center covered in maps. Detailed maps. War maps.

He understood now why they were here and not at the palace.

"Would you care for a drink, General?" Gáspár asked, pointing to a tray of four goblets and a bottle of light red wine.

Von Mercy shook his head. "No, thank you. I'm fine."

"Then please sit," Prince Rákóczi said, pulling a chair out for himself at the table. "We have a lot to discuss."

Von Mercy accepted a chair from Gáspár. He sat humbly, unbuckling his belt and laying it and his sword and scabbard on the floor at his feet. He laid his hat over them and leaned back, wiggled a little for comfort, and then waited.

The prince stared at him across the table. Von Mercy stared back, taking the measure of the man.

George Rákóczi was middle-aged, at least a few years older than von Mercy. His face was long, his nose Hunnic in its prominence. His hair was pitch black and curly. It hugged his face and cascaded down and across his shoulders in a swirl of over-combed split ends. His chin was bare save for a small tuft of black whiskers that looked like a hastily prepared Vandyke. His mustache was nothing more than a whisk of hair that seemed rather juvenile resting above a pair of thin lips that he pressed together tightly as if he were holding words back.

Finally, he spoke. "I must say, General von Mercy, that your reputation on the battlefield precedes you."

Von Mercy nodded. "Thank you, Prince Rákóczi. As does yours, though I admit my knowledge of your service is, at best, spotty. I'd like to know more."

"I'd be happy to share the stories of my time as a soldier for the great Gabriel Bethlen at tonight's reception."

Von Mercy cocked his head. "Reception?"

"Yes. At my palace. There will be a dinner and entertainment in honor of your arrival. I'm expecting you and your staff to attend."

Von Mercy moved to kindly refuse the offer. He wasn't sure if he had the proper attire to attend such a feast. For that matter, none of his staff probably did. Surely they all had fresh clothing of some kind tucked away in their travel lockers, but nothing as appropriate as royal dress. He looked at Gáspár and knew immediately that such an invite could not be refused. Von Mercy sighed.

"We'd be delighted to attend."

Prince Rákóczi nodded. "Let's turn then to more pressing, important matters." He held his breath, then let it out slowly. "You served the Imperial army, did you not, sir?"

Von Mercy felt like falling out of his chair, as if the man sitting before him had pulled the trigger of a pistol and had sent a ball through his chest. Such an abrupt switch of topic and tone surprised him, though he kept his poise and nodded truthfully. "Yes."

"And therefore, you served the Habsburgs."

"Yes."

"And now, you serve the Bohemians, General Morris Roth, and this so-called Grand Army of the Sunrise."

Von Mercy smiled. "Yes."

He could tell that his lack of elaboration on each point rankled the prince.

"Then you should know, sir, that I have, my whole professional life, fought against the Habsburgs."

"Yes, I am aware of that," von Mercy said, keeping calm. "My service to the Imperial army and to the Habsburgs is, as they say, ancient history. I serve a better cause now, Prince Rákóczi. A better man."

Rákóczi nodded, sighed, and leaned up in his chair until his elbows were perched on the table's edge. "Why should I, or my countrymen, trust a general who so readily switches sides?"

Von Mercy pursed his lips, gritted his teeth. "I could ask the same of you, Prince Rákóczi. You most recently served Sultan Murad and the Ottomans as a vassal state, but you have now signed an alliance with Bohemia and with Herr Roth. Could that not be seen as 'readily switching sides'?"

"Those two matters are entirely different, General," Rákóczi said, his jaw muscles now moving fast. He flashed a speck of tongue between his pale lips, said, "You made conscious decisions in your alliances. My countrymen had little or no choice but to serve Murad, lest they be absorbed by the Ottomans in full. In Transylvania, we serve and worship God, General von Mercy. Not Allah."

Von Mercy couldn't decide if the prince was just being—as the up-timers might say—a *dick* or if he were playing to a larger audience. There were three doors that led out of the room. Could curious ears be pressed against those doors, or could it possibly be for an audience of one: for the translator who sat at his side changing his Hungarian words into perfect German for the benefit of his guest? The truth of it was not written on Rákóczi's face. His expression was closed, foreign.

"You must understand, General," he said, striking a less adversarial tone. "There are many in my court, in the Transylvanian Diet, who think I have made a terrible mistake putting my trust and alliance behind a"—he leaned forward and whispered—"a Jewish army." He continued to whisper. "The Lutherans and Calvinists fear that, with your arrival, the Sabbatarians and Unitarians will be given too much power... not to mention the Jews. I, myself, like many of my predecessors, have always tried to be tolerant of the cultural and religious diversity of Transylvania, though I will admit to some disdain for Sabbatarians. Be a Jew or a Christian, I say. Not both! Many are wondering if your arrival will tip the scales in favor of our Jewish citizens and, indirectly, the Sabbatarians. Despite what I may or may not feel about it, it is a valid concern."

Whether it was a valid concern or not, it was not something von Mercy wished to discuss. "My good sir," he said, suddenly feeling uncomfortable and quite annoyed in his seat. "I am no politician. I am a soldier. Your concerns are best laid at the feet of General Roth, with whom your brother signed the alliance. He understands matters of state better than I.

"But what I can tell you is that those Jews you, or whoever, are concerned about... They died in dozens at the Battle of Déj defending your country from a Moldavian force that, if left unattended, could have easily seized the town and others. They are still dying, in fact. My personal surgeon, who is a Jew himself by the way, is working himself half to death trying to keep men alive so that they may take up arms once more and, again, fight for your country. I cannot speak eloquently about your political and religious concerns, as valid as they may be. Again, I am a soldier, a general, and my duty is to serve the army to which I have pledged my service.

"So I say again, please, in good faith, discuss these matters with Herr Roth upon his arrival, and let us turn toward any military concerns that you may have."

Von Mercy found it odd that he would vigorously defend Doctor Kohen with whom he had so recently argued. He was still angry with the young physician. *How dare he come into my tent and refuse my orders so publicly?* A general's authority could not be challenged so readily, lest others try the same. But he wasn't about to let this...*prince*...impugn the integrity or intent of any of his soldiers, including the Jews. Whatever von Mercy thought of Morris Roth's objectives, or the end goal of the Anaconda Project, he was not about to allow his soldiers' motives to be questioned, or be accused of an agenda they did not have.

The room was quiet, too quiet, as if no one could speak, as if God himself had waved His hand and denied everyone a voice. Finally, Gáspár cleared his throat, and said, "My Prince, if I may?"

He waited until Rákóczi nodded, then, "I have seen General von Mercy and his army in action, and I can say with certainty: they are not the conquerors of our history. They treated the citizens of Déj very kindly, despite their reluctance to assist against the Moldavians."

Rákóczi huffed, looking straight at von Mercy. "It is my understanding that you ransacked their homes, their farms, and took every scrap of wood you could find."

Von Mercy nodded. "Yes, in order to construct fortifications to protect the eastern and southern roads from attack. Otherwise, Déj would be under Moldavian control right now."

"Do you intend on paying them back for their contributions?"

Von Mercy closed his eyes to slits. "A small price for them to pay for their safety."

Rákóczi huffed again. "Well, my good man Gáspár, that sounds like a conquering army to me."

Von Mercy had had enough. "Sir, are you withdrawing from your agreement with Bohemia? Shall I pull my forces back to Kolozsvár?"

"What's done is done!" Rákóczi flew out of his chair and threw up his arms as if he were swatting away flies. "You are here, your army is here. The agreement has been signed. I cannot rescind it even if I wanted to. The die has been cast, isn't that what your up-time friends say? Pieces on the chess board are moving to check. Hermannstadt has fallen to the Wallachian army. The Moldavians march west. Soon, they will link arms and come for the capital."

What Prince Rákóczi was really saying through his frustrated rant was that the enemy had moved faster and had seized territory more efficiently than he had anticipated. Because of that, his own forces were ill-prepared to face them, especially against forces in possession of Murad's up-time-inspired weaponry. Von Mercy could hardly blame the prince or the citizens of Transylvania for their concerns and frustrations. If he had never experienced the working end of a ZB-1636 rifle or a ZB-2 Santee, he'd be shitting his breeches as well. But it did no good to accuse the army that had come to save them of being conquerors.

Von Mercy let the silence in the room linger a moment more, then he stood up and said, "Then I would say, Prince Rákóczi, that the next move in this chess game is yours. What do you want to do?"

The prince of Transylvania stood there, silently, rubbing his poorly groomed chin, staring out a window that cast bright light across the room. Finally, he turned toward von Mercy, and nodded. "Let us discuss the coming battle."

Prince Rákóczi's mood improved a little once the discussion turned to war. He allowed General von Mercy to bring in his staff, who picked his personal aide-de-camp, Colonel Shalit, Colonel Renz, and some of their subordinates to take copious notes of the conversation. Likewise, the prince invited his brother Pál, one cavalry officer, a Hajdu mercenary captain, Colonel Marius Hatmanu, the leader of the prince's red trabant Szekler infantry corps, and additional staff. The room, as large as it was, now felt cramped.

Before they started, von Mercy made it perfectly clear to the prince that this would not be the final word on the matter. "Everything we discuss here, I must impart to General Roth, you understand," he said, taking his place near the table bearing the maps. "We will have other meetings to discuss a final battle plan once he arrives."

Prince Rákóczi nodded. "Of course, General. But we do not have a lot of time to debate. As I have said, Hermannstadt has fallen. The Wallachians are now ready to move against our capital."

"Why do they hesitate?" Colonel Shalit asked.

The prince seemed a little put out by the question, as if the answer were so obvious. "Matei Basarab would be a fool to face us alone. No. He awaits the arrival of Vasile Lupu and his Moldavians." He placed his finger on the map where Gyulafehérvár sat atop a hill, then ran it south along the Maros River. "Our belief is that Basarab, now in possession of the most important Saxon See, will move as soon as the Moldavians link their forces with his. At which point, they will march up the valley in this direction and try to seize the city."

Von Mercy much preferred large, open battlefields to all this valley fighting. One couldn't get away from mountains in this blasted country! Everywhere you looked... mountains, mountains, mountains. Although it was difficult to get a clear sense of the exact elevations of the valley floor versus the Carpathian ranges both east and west, moving an army up the river valley toward the capital was the soundest tactic, but also the most obvious.

"We have the good fortune of the Maros River between them and us," von Mercy said, running his finger up the river to the capital. "Though, I'm sure it's possible for the Moldavians, at least, to swing around behind us and attack from here." He pointed to the roads running south from Kolozsvár.

"It would be foolish for them to do so," Colonel Marius Hatmanu said, standing as erect as a statue. "My Székelys would destroy them easily."

"I have recommended to my lieutenants, General von Mercy," Prince Rákóczi said, "that their best role in the battle to come is defensive. The bulk of our county forces will defend the capital while your more modern, up-time army will meet the enemy in the field."

"Why not just hold position along the Maros River?" Colonel Renz asked, pointing to various spots at the bends. "Force them to push across. Stack them up in critical places. Cut them to pieces."

"Surely you aren't suggesting that we allow them to lay siege?" Colonel Hatmanu asked.

"I did not bring my men all the way from the Partium to lie in winter camp," Lazlo Guth, leader of the Hajdus, said. "I will turn my columns around and head home if such an idea takes root."

Prince Rákóczi eyed the mercenary captain with a wry smile. "Perhaps, General von Mercy, you can find a place in your battle line for this brave, yet impetuous man and his hearty soldiers."

It seemed as if Captain Guth was about to object to being called impetuous, but von Mercy spoke before it came to that. "Colonel Renz is not necessarily suggesting a siege, Captain Guth.

There's ample space between the Maros and the edge of the city. We could place the army here, here, and here, and force them to strike first."

"That's assuming, of course," Pál Rákóczi said, "they decide to cross the river and engage. Neither Voivode Basarab, nor Lupu, are skilled tacticians, General, but they aren't stupid."

Von Mercy had to agree. "They've certainly done well for themselves so far. Despite their lack of military experience, they're practically at your doorstep."

Prince Rákóczi shrugged the comment off. "Only with the aid of Murad's forces. Trust me, General. If they had to advance without armored tanks, screaming rockets, and Janissaries at the point of the spear, we would have crushed them already."

Von Mercy nodded, though he wasn't so sure. The Transylvanian troops that the prince had been able to muster prior to their arrival had, at least, slowed down Wallachia's and Moldavia's inexorable march toward Gyulafehérvár, giving them some time to meet and plan their defense, but he had yet to see the Transylvanian forces in action.

"With Gyulafehérvár on a hill," Colonel Shalit said, "it should be relatively easy to defend against a direct assault. A siege, if it came to that, should be as easy to endure."

Laughter broke out on the Transylvanian side of the table. "Please forgive me, gentlemen. Did I say something funny?" Colonel Shalit asked.

"Sir," Colonel Hatmanu asked, "have you ever endured a Carpathian winter?"

"No. But I've endured a Krakow winter."

Now it was von Mercy's side of the table to laugh.

"I'm well aware that Polish winters are brutal," Prince Rákóczi said, "but there is nothing like a Carpathian winter. Though the temperatures may not fall as swiftly as they do in your country, Colonel Shalit, the snows and blistering winds that howl through the Maros River Valley can freeze fat men solid where they lay. Before it is all over with, you'd beg for death. The Wallachians know this; the Moldavians know this. My countrymen know this. We would endure. You?" The prince gestured with his hand as if he were tossing snowflakes into the wind. "Well, I don't think a siege is the right approach. And I don't think General Roth, like Captain Guth here, brought the Sunrise all this way just to lie in winter quarters."

That much was true, von Mercy had to admit. Though there the prince went again, impugning the resolve of his soldiers. Von Mercy had a good mind to pack up and leave with Captain Guth and his Partium mercenaries.

Instead, he took a deep breath, and said, "Well, there are many options before us. We'll need to know a lot more about the composition of the Wallachian and Moldavian armies before we commit to a plan. We'll need to know more about what forces you, Prince Rákóczi, can put into the field in full, whether they be gathered in defensive circles around the city or share our battle line. And I'll need to see the lay of the land before I commit to anything. While these maps are excellent, I cannot get a good sense of all the different elevations. I need to see the ground."

"We can take you out at first light," Pál Rákóczi said, "and show you everything you'd like." He turned to his brother, nodded. "With your permission, of course."

"Of course," Prince Rákóczi nodded. He looked at von Mercy and winked. "Assuming that you and your officers do not over-indulge at tonight's party."

Von Mercy gritted his teeth. "No problem on that, Prince Rákóczi. My men are always prepared for duty."

Chapter 40

General von Mercy's encampment
Gyulafehérvár

"There's one thing you can say about George Rákóczi," von Mercy said via radio to Morris Roth. "He's not the most pleasant man in the world."

General Roth's chuckle crackled over the connection, though von Mercy was pleased that, for the most part, radio contact had been better since they had arrived in the capital. The fact that a good portion of Gyulafehérvár was at a higher elevation didn't hurt. "He must be under a lot of internal pressure to give a show of force to the 'invaders,' as I'm sure many in his close circle consider us to be. Don't worry about the prince's contrariness, General. I'll have a good sit-down with him when I arrive. We'll hash it all out."

"He can show whatever outward bluster he requires to satisfy his detractors in the Diet, but if this endeavor is going to succeed, his army—whatever army that may be—is going to have to fight hard in the battle that's coming."

There was a pause, then: "When do you expect the Wallachians and Moldavians to arrive?"

Von Mercy shook his head, still not quite used to speaking to someone so effortlessly, so far away. "Hard to know. The prince claims to have spies along their most likely routes of ingress. If so, we should be able to keep apprised of their movements. If not..."

General Roth cleared his throat. It sounded like a cork popping out of a bottle. "Have you considered training at least one of these spies on a radio?"

"If we had one to spare, I'd consider it. But we lost a few at Déj. One went missing, two were damaged beyond repair. But I'll have Len check to see what we can do." He paused, deciding whether or not to be so forward with his next comment.

"What would really help, General, is for you to get in the saddle and double-time it to Kolozsvár and then on to the capital. Having the whole army back together, sir, will make the biggest difference and allow me more reconnaissance options than I have right now. We beat the Moldavians back at Déj but expended a lot of supplies doing so. Lost more men that I would have expected too."

Von Mercy could hear Morris sigh deeply on the other end. "Three days. Possibly four, depending on weather. We're in Zilah now which, according to our maps, is a little under forty miles from Kolozsvár. We've had to deal with rain squalls for the last couple days, causing all sorts of havoc on these meager little roads we're marching. Hell, Franz, it's not easy getting our APCs and cannons through the mud. Not to mention being harried at every step by those goddamned Impalers. The Zizka Brigade had nearly half of their cattle herd stolen by those bastards. Those sneaky little shits are like hornets without a nest. Gretchen's aggressive tactics—and that's putting it mildly—are beginning to have an effect. They're becoming less active, less bloodthirsty, I guess you could say. But information travels slow in a country with no radios, so a lot of their field operatives don't quite yet understand the reality of her message: Don't fuck with the Sunrise. We'll get there, though, and soon. I promise.

"In the meantime, I want you to be careful tomorrow on your survey of the field. I'm sure the prince will have a large security detail tagging along, but take one of your own as well...just to be prudent."

"No worries, General. We'll have sufficient security."

"Oh, and take Len with you tomorrow. I'll have Ellie keep contact with you during your tour in case anything immediate comes up that requires my attention."

Von Mercy nodded again. "Yes, I've already assigned him to my team."

"And finally...have fun tonight. Relax. Eat a good meal. Have a drink for me."

The Princely Palace
Gyulafehérvár

The complex was impressive, but to say that it rivaled any castle in Western Europe was, to put it mildly, hyperbole. In his mind, von Mercy let the comparison go, as he, his staff, regimental and company commanders, Len, Rabbi Gotkin, and Gáspár were led into the dining hall to greet many members of Prince Rákóczi's court, Diet, and the leading families of the various Transylvanian counties. The room was, quite literally, packed.

"I must show you the grounds, General von Mercy," Gáspár said as they were led to their seats. "Perhaps tonight, after the feast."

Von Mercy nodded. "Thank you, Gáspár. I would like that."

Three tables had been set up in the center of the room, creating a U-shape with the top table of the U reserved for the prince, his family, and close advisors. All others in attendance were guided to seats at the remaining two. Von Mercy and his entourage were honored with positions closest to the royal table.

Von Mercy was impressed with the opulent clothing on display. Most everyone wore what he could only surmise as traditional Hungarian attire: the men in red, green, silver, and gold fur-lined dolmans, held together in the front by gold and silver buttons. Some had *mente* dress coats over their dolmans. Some carried walking sticks. Some wore felt caps with feathers. Some wore modest chains of gold affixed to crosses.

For the ladies, their dresses were just as resplendent and similar in color to the men. Many wore outer dresses of red and green with modest white shifts beneath. Some wore traditional bodices laced in full display across their pressed cleavage. Their head-dresses were a mixture of scarfs, felt hats, feathers, and various long pins that held their dark, flowing hair up in stylish buns.

Everyone was courteous. Everyone smiled. Everyone greeted von Mercy and his staff with polite bows, broad smiles. Some even dared give him a hug. Their attitudes were better than what he had experienced so far with the prince. They would be, he admitted, as he accepted a golden goblet of wine from a girl in a modest shift of red and white. It was their homes, their lands, their families being threatened by the Wallachians, Moldavians, and—for all intents and purposes—the Ottomans. So far, the enemy had confined itself to attacking Saxon areas of southern Transylvania. It was a sound move: eliminate the Saxon threat—some of it, at least—and lessen the threat of an enemy army rising behind you. Whether it would play out that way in the end was to be determined. But the enemy was coming, with Ottoman support, and these people knew it.

Von Mercy looked around the dining hall, trying to see who among them might be representatives from the much beleaguered Saxon Sees. It was difficult to tell in the ocean of pressing colors. Some were wearing more traditional German garb, but the entire ensemble was a mixture of local, Hungarian, German, and indeed, Ottoman attire.

A small troupe of musicians behind the royal table began to play a pleasant tune that von Mercy did not recognize but, based on the reaction to it around the room, was a signal for quiet.

Shortly afterward, a man wearing a gold, flowing dolman and a felt hat with black feathers walked up the space between the two facing tables. He paused in front of the royal table, struck the floor three times with the foot of his walking stick, and then proclaimed loudly, "Prince Rákóczi and the royal family!"

Everyone stood and began to cheer and applaud loudly. Von Mercy's own clapping was drowned out by the ruckus, including the pleasant music still playing behind the prince.

Von Mercy leaned over to Colonel Renz and said in a muted tone, "This is going to be interesting!"

The order to attend the reception had taken Christian by surprise. He expected only General von Mercy's top lieutenants to be required. When he got the word from Colonel Renz to get ready, he scrambled to get a good bath and find suitable attire.

The bath was less than desirable. By the time he reached the tub, it had already been used by a couple of other officers, including Captain Kinsky, who never failed to make a mess. The water was cloudy, dirty, and lukewarm. Still, it was one of the best baths he had had since entering Transylvania. The hard-bristled scrub brush did its job well, although Christian's skin was a bit red and sore afterward.

As far as clothing was concerned, he had nothing but his

battle uniform, which these days was little more than a worn tan buffcoat, a ragged plain white shirt, torn breeches, and dusty black boots. Lieutenant Enkefort loaned him a heavily worn red doublet and a clean black felt hat that, when all assembled on his person, made Christian look almost presentable. Good enough for a simple sit-down meal, anyway.

The meal, he had to admit, was most excellent. He hadn't had such delicious and filling food since they had entered the country. He particularly liked the *lepény* and the marzipan cakes. A dozen of those were rolled out and distributed among the tables. Prince Rákóczi himself brought the dinner to a momentary pause to present them "in honor of Gabriel Bethlen. May God bless his name." Christian did not know who this Bethlen fellow was, but he sure liked his cakes.

Geese and pheasant and boiled partridge eggs. Roast pig, beef, lamb, and fish from the nearby river. Potato soup and wine... God, the wine! By the end of the meal, Christian had already drunk a full bottle.

Now, he stumbled through the three courtyards of the complex—greeting with kindness everyone who bothered to pause and give him notice—and watching musicians and dancing troupes entertaining the prince's guests.

The most appealing dance to him was an ensemble of men and women facing each other across the courtyard, clapping and shouting to one another to the feverish pace of the music. The men were dressed head to toe in a modest white dolman tied at the waist with a black belt. To Christian, their costumes resembled a woman's shift. The men wore a hat that a lady standing next to Christian said was a *clopuri*. To him, it resembled a Turkish fez.

Similarly, the ladies wore white dresses, but with red-and-yellow aprons tied at their waists to give themselves a little color. Their heads were wrapped in matching red-and-yellow scarfs.

Everyone looked clean, fresh, well-groomed, and common. Christian liked it.

He stood and watched as the dancers began to shout "Hey... hey... hey" and clap to the music. Then, the ladies gathered round and formed a huddle, as if deciding which men they would choose. Shortly thereafter, they broke the huddle and paired off.

Christian found himself swaying back and forth to the music as the male dancers stood like statues and let their partners dance around them like hovering birds. Then each pairing joined hands again and continued to dance.

"You like the dance?"

Christian started. He stumbled back but kept his balance and looked at the beautiful woman standing next to him. He almost didn't recognize her, because of the apparel she wore—a long, red gown, very unlike what she'd worn while working as a nurse.

"Andreea Hatmanu," he said, bowing. "Nice to see you again."

She nodded. The hint of a smile spread across her red lips. "Nice to see you as well, Captain von Jori."

"You are welcome to call me Christian."

"Very well. Then simply call me Andreea."

They stood there a moment in awkward silence, then Christian said, pointing to the dancers, "I would ask you to dance, but I don't think they have room in their line for us."

Andreea nodded. "I don't think you would like my dancing anyway, Christian. Especially in this dress. How is your face?"

Christian put his hand up to his cheek. Only a scar remained where a large splinter had struck him during the Battle of Déj. "Healing well, thank you. You did a wonderful job on it. I was in good hands that day."

Andreea smiled and nodded, but said nothing. Another pause of awkward silence passed between them. Christian then asked the big question. "I was sorry to learn from Devorah that you had been 'summoned,' as she called it, to the capital. I came by the hospital to say goodbye to you before we left Kolozsvár." He chuckled. "Summoned to the capital. A confidant of the prince, eh?"

Andreea smiled, shook her head. "No, not at all. The prince hardly cares about what I think of politics or matters of war."

"Then I take it your nursing skills are known far and wide here in Transylvania, and that—"

"No, Christian," she said, cutting him off. She cast her eyes to her slippers, which were just as red and beautiful as her dress. "I...came here because my husband summoned me."

"Oh? And who is your husband?"

Von Mercy was watching a dance troupe comprised entirely of men dressed in white shirts, black vests, and black hats, when Pál Rákóczi pulled him aside.

"I must apologize for my brother's behavior, General von Mercy," he whispered to ensure the guests walking by could not hear. "But you must understand the enormous pressure he is under. Many in the Diet are ready to call off the alliance with Bohemia and beg Sultan Murad for forgiveness. Some never liked the idea of an alliance in the first place. And now, with the Saxon Sees all but conquered, many are wondering if a mostly Jewish army can defend Gyulafehérvár. And some are opposed to the idea itself, anyway." He looked left, right. "It's a delicate time."

Von Mercy nodded. "I appreciate your brother's situation, but he himself suggested that time was running thin. I agree with that. If the alliance were to fall now, if Morris Roth were to order me to fall back to Kolozsvár now, I guarantee, this city *will* fall. Your army is not prepared to face up-time weaponry alone. So, please persuade your brother to set aside any concerns or animosities that he may have. Convince your court to do the same. You're going to need my army—yes, including the Jews, Pál Rákóczi—if you have any hope to beat back the wolves that are coming."

"I know that," Pál hissed, more forcefully than perhaps he wanted. He backed away a pace, held up his hand. "My brother knows that, and whether they wish to admit it or not, the people of Transylvania know it as well. Most of them, at least. But there is danger in this capital, General, and my brother must navigate through it carefully. He'll be there with you in the end." He smiled. "A victory against the Wallachians and Moldavians and, in truth, against Sultan Murad, will solve so many problems."

Von Mercy nodded, but glanced left and right as if he suddenly felt a thousand distrusting eyes upon him. "On that, Herr Rákóczi, we can agree."

"I am her husband, sir." Marius Hatmanu said, stepping forward as a group of guests passed by. "Colonel Hatmanu, commander of Prince Rákóczi's red trabants."

Christian turned abruptly toward the colonel, bowed sharply. "Nice to meet you, sir. Captain von Jori."

Hatmanu eyed him wearily. "Are you enjoying the reception, Captain?"

"Yes," Christian said, nodding. "Very much. I was asking your lovely wife why she was summoned to the capital. Her service as a nurse for the Sunrise has been most welcome. It would be disappointing to lose her services."

"Yes," Andreea said, "and I was about to explain to him why—"

"You need not explain anything to anyone, Andreea," Hatmanu said, loud enough such that those nearby threw an uncomfortable glance their way. "The fact that I, your husband, summoned you, is *reason* enough."

Christian was just as shocked as Andreea at the outburst. Their expressions matched. But Andreea put her head down and fell silent under her husband's glare, as if she had done so many times before. Christian was about to say something, anything, when the princess consort appeared beside him.

"Captain von Jori," Zsuzsanna Lorántffy said. "Colonel Renz has told me that you are a Calvinist. Is this true?"

She was dressed in a modest black-and-white gown. Her soft, round face was cupped in a simple white scarf wrapped around her head. To Christian, she looked like a nun. A far, far cry from all the other royal ladies in attendance.

"Well...yes," he said, trying to recover his bearings and focus on the princess's question. "I am a Calvinist. But I must confess, Princess Lorántffy, I do not practice my faith as much as I—"

"That is no problem, Captain." She extended her left arm to invite Christian to take it. He did, and she obliged, wrapping it with her own until Christian couldn't pull away if he wanted to. "Come. Let us find Minster Alsted and have a frank discussion."

Prince Rákóczi rolled his eyes and shook his head, letting a small grin cross his mouth. "God, give us strength! Captain, you have many hours of grueling religious debate ahead of you tonight. Good luck!" He turned toward Colonel Hatmanu. "Come, Colonel. Let us find General von Mercy and further discuss our survey of the field tomorrow."

"Yes, My Prince."

As he was pulled away, with Zsuzsanna Lorántffy's voice droning in his ear about John Calvin and Huldrych Zwingli, Christian looked back at Andreea standing alone, despondent, humiliated by her husband's sharp rebuke, abandoned by everyone. But then her eyes caught his. She smiled and from her waist where her hands were cupped together, she allowed two fingers to wiggle in his direction.

Schäßburg (Sighișoara)

The *Chaldiran* hovered above Sergiu Botnari like a floating mountain. Up close, it was even more formidable. His heart raced as the airship pulled on its tethers like a dog straining on its leash, its engine belching hydrogen into its expanding envelope.

Vasile Lupu popped his head up out of the gondola. He waved at Sergiu. "Morning, my murderous little friend. Isn't she lovely?"

In a way Sergiu could not describe. Early morning fog curled around the ship's wicker gondola, obscuring what the voivode had in his hand. It looked like a musket; it could be a walking stick.

"Come," Vasile said, tossing a rope ladder over the side. "Welcome aboard."

Sergiu took the ladder and climbed slowly, making sure each foot was set before climbing to the next rung, and the next, and the next. Eight steps and he was at the lip of the gondola. The Janissary guard gave him a hand and pulled him over. The gondola wobbled slightly; Sergiu gained his balance before standing.

The crew comprised Voivode Lupu and the two kafirs, Moshe Mizrahi and Mordecai Pesach, one Janissary, and another man whom Sergiu did not recognize. They were all moving here and there in the gondola, as if in preparation for flight. Sergiu finally got a good look at Vasile Lupu's hands. He was definitely holding a musket.

He offered it to Sergiu. "Here," he said, "give it a try."

Sergiu accepted the weapon and looked it over. A muzzle-loading flintlock. Good heft. Decent balance. "Is it loaded?"

Vasile nodded. "Of course. With Sultan Murad's own mini-ball. A brilliant design. Smaller than the normal ball, with a flange that expands when fired, thus the bore as you may notice is rifled, making said mini-ball far more accurate on the shot than other muskets. Go ahead. Give it a try."

Vasile motioned to the larboard side of the gondola. Sergiu walked over to the edge, cocked the hammer, and raised the musket forward.

About one hundred yards away, a man stood in the dark with a torch. He waved it back and forth, catching in the light what Sergiu could only deduce was a circular target, a plate perhaps, attached to a post. The dim light of dawn, dispersed through the fog, made it very difficult to see the object in full.

"Go ahead," Vasile said, "fire it. See if you can hit the plate."

Sergiu was an excellent shot, especially with a rifle, but under these conditions? What purpose did all this serve, save to satiate the whims of a crazed voivode with delusions of grandeur? Sergiu's time would be best served with his men, in the field, preparing the way for the Moldavian army to move against the capital. His Impalers had ventured farther into Transylvania and were doing good work against the main body of the Sunrise; had done good work in Déj and Szamosújvár. He hadn't gotten a report yet from the detachment he'd sent to ambush the Silesian wagon train at Szatmár, but he was sure they'd done well also. They could do so much more if Sergiu was with them.

But... he worked for the voivode of Moldavia.

"Very well," he said, crouching.

He rested the musket on the lip of the larboard wall. He aimed down the barrel and waited as the torchlight moved into his sight, out, in, out, each time shedding light on the tiny plate so far away. He timed it: one, two, three...

He fired, catching the recoil against his shoulder. The musket fired true with a tiny spark off the frizzen, a burst of smoke from the pan and barrel. A nice, clean shot.

"Excellent," Vasile said. "Now, we wait."

A few seconds later, a horseman rode up from the target. He reined his horse to a stop and shouted up to the gondola. "Hit! Left side. Small crack. One inch chip."

"Wonderful!" Voivode Lupu could not contain his joy. "You will do wonderfully."

"Do what 'wonderfully'?" Sergiu asked.

Vasile ignored the question. He clapped his hands at the Janissary standing guard at the rope ladder. "Go, and get the rest of the rifles." He then turned to the kafir Mordecai Pesach. "When he returns, drop the tethers, and we'll be off."

Sergiu looked at Moshe and Mordecai, hoping to see a clue in their eyes, on their faces, as to what was happening. Moshe simply shrugged and got back to work; Mordecai looked away.

"My Voivode, if I may ask. What are we doing? Where are we going? With respect, I really must return to my men. We've work to do before—"

"You will return to your men soon, Sergiu. That is a promise. But right now, you will serve me." Vasile turned and placed his hand on Sergiu's shoulder. "Another report from Gyulafehérvár tells me of a great, great many things that we must look for, act upon, and quickly. You will be a part of that."

Sergiu shook his head. "What *things*, Voivode?"

Vasile winked and smiled. "Opportunities, my murderous little friend. Opportunities."

Chapter 41

The battlefield survey

Len Tanner hated riding a horse on his best day, especially with a cumbersome radio pack strapped to his shoulder. It was ten times worse with a hangover pounding Beethoven's Fifth in your brain with a ball-peen hammer. *God-god-god-damnnnn...* That, plus an incessant stream of Ellie's giggling, lecturing tone in his ear. "I told you not to drink so much... didn't I tell you not to drink so much?" She had, but how could one pass up all that free food and *free wine*. Hell, there was so much left at the end of the night that one of the good lady servants at the dinner allowed him to leave the palace with a full glass. *What a thoughtful person!*

Now, however, he wished he had begged off this little soiree to survey the battlefield. Trotting behind General von Mercy's horse, watching it drop shit with every step... well, he was ready to puke booze with every clop. But, he had been asked to attend, and he had agreed. Besides, the day always started well when he could hear Ellie's voice, even if she were cursing at him.

"Are you all right, Len?" Gáspár asked as they trotted down a narrow wagon path along the Maros River.

Len nodded and tried not to look up into the sky toward the rising sun. Though burning off quickly, there was still enough fog skirting the forest around them that he couldn't see much

325

of anything even if he wanted to. "I'm fine, Gáspár, thank you. I just have to make a mental note never to drink Transylvanian wine again."

Gáspár chuckled and patted Len on the back lightly. "It can be strong, my friend. Last night's was particularly strong, perhaps the strongest I've encountered in a long time. It'll wear off, trust me, and when it does, you'll remember the good flavor and not the aftermath."

In attendance were General von Mercy, his staff and security retinue, Colonel Renz, and Colonel Shalit. As promised, Prince Rákóczi rode amidst his own security and staff, his brother Pál, Colonel Hatmanu and a mercenary fellow named Guth. Len had greeted them all before they had let out, but his mind was in no mood to remember details right now.

The clump of officers in front of him halted. Prince Rákóczi sidled up to von Mercy to have a chat.

"This tree line would be good for skirmishers," von Mercy said, pointing down the trail. "We can have snipers lined up along the river, pickets farther down the line here to report any enemy movement, if they choose to cross the river a mile or two away and attack the capital in full."

"The Maros River here at Gyulafehérvár is wide, General," Prince Rákóczi said. "I don't think they would dare cross it, even farther down."

"With Ottoman engineers erecting a bridge, they might," von Mercy said. "We cannot discount the possibility. Plus, now that I've seen more of the ground, I realize that even though the capital is on a hill, it's not as steep an elevation as I first thought. The ground runs a nice, smooth slope to the valley floor. You've walls for protection, but they won't stop determined armies with Ottoman support."

"All the more reason," Colonel Shalit said at von Mercy's side, "to keep our forces on this side of the river and force them to attack. In my opinion, it's dependent upon them to seize ground, not the other way around. We set up a strong defense of the capital and let them attack...sir."

In the past few days, it had become clear to Len that von Mercy's lieutenants were in serious disagreement about how to conduct the coming battle. Obviously, Colonel Shalit preferred a defensive posture. Colonel Renz, however, judging from the hostile glare he was giving the infantry officer at the moment, disagreed. As did Captain Guth and Colonel Hatmanu, Len could see.

Colonel Renz's attitude surprised Len. Hadn't the good cavalry officer just thwarted a strong Moldavian army at Déj with a defensive stance? And with cavalry, no less. Now that Len thought about it, however, Colonel Renz's disagreement with the idea did make a bit of sense. He and his men were mercenaries. Mercenaries who had not been paid since they had entered Transylvania. Morris Roth was going to rectify that problem once he reached the capital, but how long could he keep mercenaries in winter quarters? Morris was rich, but his resources were finite. From Colonel Renz's point of view, victory needed to come before the first snows of winter hit the ground.

Len relayed their heated conversation in whispers to Ellie.

"Gentlemen," von Mercy said, raising his hand, "let us delay these arguments until we've seen the full field." He turned to the prince. "Is there a way to cross the river?"

Prince Rákóczi nodded. "Just a ways up the road is a ferry."

"Very good. Please guide us, sir."

"We're crossing the river now," Len whispered to Ellie as he nudged his horse forward.

"Don't fall off and drown," she replied with a chuckle.

Aboard the Chaldiran

As anxious as he was, Sergiu immediately understood Vasile Lupu's excitement being on the airship. The wind was wonderfully cool against his sweaty face, exhilarating, and life-affirming. The *Chaldiran* floated through low-hanging clouds and fog, and the sunlight was so brilliant, so white, it seemed that he had died and gone to heaven.

He dared release his white-knuckle grip on the gondola and walk over to the line of muskets leaning against the starboard side, waiting for use. He ran his hand over the stocks. Nice, clean, loaded muskets. "To do this right," he said, "I need to be as close as I can. How close to the ground can you fly?"

Mordecai Pesach shrugged. "Very low, if need be. But we must try to stay at an altitude outside their effective range. The bottom of the gondola is most vulnerable to gunfire."

Sergiu raised an eyebrow. "The most vulnerable part of the ship is the bottom of its gondola?"

Again, Mordecai shrugged. "I don't believe that our Sultan imagined them being vulnerable from the ground. He was more concerned about facing USE airships." And indeed, the rest of the gondola was well protected with shields.

Sergiu sighed. "Very well. That means, however, that we will not be able to fly low for long." He lifted one of the muskets, checked it, and put it back down. "First two or three shots, they will be disoriented, confused. After that, we'll start drawing fire."

"Then take only two, three shots," Vasile said from the stern. "I added additional guns just in case."

Sergiu tried not to imagine grabbing Vasile's legs and hoisting him overboard. He smiled instead. "As good as I am, Voivode Lupu, I will miss. We are not moving very fast, but a moving target is always difficult to hit. I will miss, so I'll need to take all six shots."

He cleared his throat and shivered at a cool gust of wind. He pulled his coat together at his chest and looked into the sky. No chance of rain, Allah be praised, but the seasons were changing. The air was growing colder, the days shorter. He shook the cold away and said, "So, just the prince?"

Vasile shrugged, then smiled. "He is our primary target, yes. But you have six guns. Kill as many around him as you can."

The battlefield survey

Len was beginning to enjoy Transylvania. It reminded him of up-time West Virginia, with its mountains, rolling hills, and river valleys. The sun was still trying to work its way over the Carpathians to the east, but the fog had burned off nicely. Now, he could see all the precious farmland and humble little homes that marked the ground he and the others were surveying. The people living on the land, though very different ethnically than those he had known up-time, were quite pleasant, nice. Toiling in their early-morning labors, they paused to greet their prince, gave directions, information, whatever was asked of them. A lady even came out of her home with a basket of bread and shared the loaves. Len took one bite and fell in love. He needed a full stomach to ward off the alcohol-laden pounding in his head.

He downed the bread quickly, then whispered more data to Ellie as von Mercy and the rest of the military men spoke. Now, they stood at a crossroad, debating about the viability of massing the infantry along the segmented stone walls lined up against the cart path winding its way over the hill.

"This would be a good defensive position, Colonel Shalit," von Mercy said. "If we pushed the army across the river and lined up the Joshua Corps here, guns forward. They'd have a hell of a time breaching your line."

Colonel Shalit nodded. "I would be concerned with the flanks."

"I'll protect the flanks," Colonel Hatmanu said, stepping his horse forward so that he was in everyone's line of sight. "My Székelys can hold and wheel into battle and crush them."

Len didn't like Colonel Hatmanu. He wasn't sure what he didn't like about the man. Pretty much everything, he supposed. His arrogance, for sure; his narcissistic need to attract attention; his face. Yep, pretty much everything.

"There will be plenty of infantry on both flanks," Prince Rákóczi said. "Ours and theirs, Colonel Hatmanu. The issue before us, though, is if we do wish to defend these walls, then we must capture the field before they do. Otherwise, they'll do exactly the same."

Von Mercy turned in his saddle and pointed to the rising slope of land up to the capital. "If we set our batteries up there, we can pound their approach." He turned to Len. "How's your radio working?"

Len nodded. "Not bad, not bad."

"You think you'll be able to maintain radio contact throughout the battle?"

Len shrugged. "This is as good a ground as any we've experienced in Transylvania to date." Len pointed to the capital. "If Ellie and I can set up our comm tent safely in the capital, away from cannon and rocket fire, we should be able to maintain contact with the companies."

"Herr Tanner," Colonel Hatmanu said, almost spitting. "May I have a radio for the battle?"

Len looked at von Mercy, who said nothing in return. "I'll check with my wife when she arrives and see what we can do, Colonel Hatmanu. If we have some to spare, we'll try to distribute them to other Transylvanian units as well. It'll require some training, but that shouldn't be a problem."

"Why the hell did you tell them you'd give them radios?" Ellie asked over the radio.

Len whispered, "I said 'if we have some to spare.' I didn't make promises."

"We ain't got a damn one to spare. Tell them that."

Aboard the Chaldiran

"Can you shut off the engine?" Sergiu asked. "It would be best to go in quietly."

Moshe Mizrahi looked at Mordecai Pesach, then shook his head. "We could, but that would be a mistake. If they do return fire shortly after your first few shots, then we need to accelerate fast, and we need the engine for that. The *Chaldiran* is slow, but she can pick up speed quickly for a better escape."

In truth, the engine wasn't too loud, and because they were sailing into the wind most of the sound wouldn't carry forward. Nor was he planning to fire from any closer distance than he needed to. Still, quiet was always preferred when sniping. If he didn't get his first shot off successfully, the sound of the airship's engine would indeed attract attention. Then, it might be impossible to finish the job. The first shot would have to be on point. The good news in all this: the first shot was always the most accurate. *Hit the main target and get his staff scrambling to save him.*

"We're here," Vasile Lupu said.

The *Chaldiran* dipped below the cloud it had been riding in for several minutes. Sergiu grabbed his spyglass and brought it into focus.

Tiny, yet colorful dots moved on horseback down a trail. Many, many colorful dots.

"That's George Rákóczi," Vasile said, pointing across Sergiu's line of sight. "The one with the long black hair, no hat."

Sergiu fixed his spyglass on the target. Near the front, sandwiched between two other riders, was the man Vasile pointed out. Sergiu smiled. Easy to see.

He put down the spyglass. "We cannot go in on the side, my lord. We must approach them from behind or from the front. From behind is preferred. If we approach from their side, I will have to fire and then run to the other side of the gondola as they pass underneath. That's too much time lost. We have to go in from behind."

Vasile sighed. "Very well." He pointed his thumb toward *Chaldiran*'s envelope. "Take us up and around and bring us down as he requests."

The battlefield survey

Len thought he heard something, looked up. Nothing but clouds. The sun was behind it now as well. The world grew darker.

"You hear anything?" he asked Ellie.

Her cracking voice said, "What are you talking about? All I hear is you, and not as well as I did a few minutes ago."

Indeed, they had traveled beyond the wall and fields and farmhouses and were now quite a ways away from the looming shadow of Gyulafehérvár. "Never mind," he said. "It's nothing."

Pál Rákóczi was pointing out a series of wagon trails leading out of the farmland and into foothills and forests. He was indicating that those paths were the most likely ones to be used by a Moldavian army upon its approach. Colonel Hatmanu was commenting that those pathways were very narrow and thus, could be easily defended by Székely skirmishers. Colonel Renz was discussing cavalry tactics with Captain Guth. Colonel Shalit was still talking about the defensive use of the walls with his staff. The conversation was chaotic and everywhere, a clear sign that the tour had gone on long enough. It was time to bring the matter to a close.

Len heard a *pop!* He almost missed it in the haze of voices. It sounded like a piece of wood snapping, but hollow, as if it were far away.

Then Prince Rákóczi fell off his horse, hard. His left leg caught in his stirrup. His head hit a stone near the pathway.

Another pop, and one of Colonel Hatmanu's aides grunted and slumped over in the saddle.

Len dropped from his horse, careful to keep his radio open and safe.

He dared look to the sky, and there it was.

"Airship!" he screamed, keeping his horse between him and the ship. "It's attacking!"

Another shot, and this time, Len could tell that it was gunfire. Len glanced quickly at those up the trail, the confused and chaotic mass of bodies scrambling to save the prince, save Hatmanu's man, save themselves.

Another, and this one seemed to miss. Four shots. *God*, he wondered, *how many more?*

Finally, the men who had gotten off their horses began to return fire, but the airship sped up and pulled away.

A fifth shot, and again, it seemed to miss.

"I'm hit!"

Von Mercy!

Len didn't care anymore about saving himself. He came out from the protection of his horse and ran to the general's side, catching him just before he fell from his horse.

"Where are you hit, General?" Len asked frantically as he and Colonel Renz helped the general down.

"My leg!"

Indeed. Blood covered his pant leg from his boot down. A lot of blood.

They laid him down carefully, and Len pulled off the general's boot. His eyes widened.

"Jesus Christ! Someone get a tourniquet...now!"

Aboard the Chaldiran

The bottom of the gondola suffered gunfire, and Mordechai Pesach had been hit in the thigh. Not life-threatening, but he was on the gondola floor being cared for by the Janissary guard, who looked like he too had taken a sharp scrape across his chest. Moshe Mizrahi manned the rudder. No one else seemed to have taken any wounds, including Vasile Lupu, who crouched like a coward at the stern.

Sergiu still had one musket to fire. It wasn't necessary. The mission had been a success. The prince had been hit. And yet, why not take that final shot?

With musket in hand, he stepped to the stern and stared through his spyglass. Chaos. Men scrambling over Prince Rákóczi's limp body. Men near General von Mercy...wait! *Who is that?*

A man crouching next to von Mercy held a radio. Sergiu

recognized its wooden box well from the ambush near the Szamos. He smiled.

He dropped his spyglass, raised his musket, cocked the hammer, and aimed.

The battlefield survey

At first, Len didn't feel much pain; just a pinching bee sting. Then his left shoulder began to bleed, and suddenly a wave of nausea overtook him.

He fell backward, reaching for his shoulder. Where his shoulder used to be. Now, it was a mangle of wool fabric and blood.

"Len's hit!" he heard someone say.

He reached with his bloody hand to retrieve his radio. Someone put the transmitter in his hand. He pressed the button and screamed, "Mayday, mayday! Send help!"

"What the fuck is going on, Len?"

Ellie's voice was sweet. Even when she was cussing, he loved her voice.

"I'm down! Von Mercy is down! The prince is down! WE'RE ALL FUCKING DOWN!"

Chapter 42

Grand Army of the Sunrise encampment
Zilah

"Ellie! Ellie! Wait!"

She left the radio mic swinging and was out the communications tent and moving toward Tuva's Dvorak before anyone could catch her. *Fuck them all*, she thought as she focused her attention on the small plane waiting in a wet field. Where Tuva was currently, Ellie didn't know. It didn't matter. By God, she was going to the capital to be with Len, to be with her husband, and that was that. If she had to fly there by her *damned* self, she'd do it, and no matter the poor weather.

She pulled open the cockpit door and tried climbing in. A hand from behind grabbed her shoulders and pulled her out.

She rounded on the person standing behind her and checked her swing when she saw Morris Roth's face. "Leave me alone, Morris. I'm going to Len. He needs me!"

He held her firmly. He was stronger than he appeared. "Let me go, *goddammit!*"

"Ellie...Ellie, please, hear me out!"

She wanted to *punch* him out, but suddenly all her emotional strength collapsed into his arms. Her face was soaked with tears. She leaned into his shoulder and buried her face into his coat. "He's going to die, Morris. I just know it."

She felt him move his head. "No," he said, "he isn't. He's going to be fine. They've stabilized him and moved him off the field. Don't worry, Ellie. We've got Denise in the air. She'll be picking up Isaac in Kolozsvár any minute now. Len's going to be just fine."

"But I need to be there, Morris. I need to be there to make sure. He's my whole world."

No matter how knowledgeable Doctor Kohen was about up-time medicine, he was still a young man, still inexperienced. And this was the seventeenth century, not up-time America. Len would get an infection for sure. He'd die in a deep coma, burned through with fever. "I have to be there."

"You will be, I promise." Morris pushed away but held her shoulders and stared into her face until she met his eyes. "But listen to me, Ellie. Listen. The weather right now is lousy. We try to launch this plane with the wind shear we have right now, it'll go down hard. Denise was already in the air giving us a signal boost to Len, and she's racing ahead of the storm. If I put you and Tuva in the air *right now*, I might lose you both."

To accentuate his point, the thick storm clouds above cracked with lightning. The wind surged.

"As soon as this squall passes, I promise I'll have Tuva get you there. Okay?"

She was stuck. She couldn't fly the damned plane; foolish for her to even imagine doing so. But Len . . . God, how could she go on without him? How could she navigate through this medieval century without her husband? Okay, it wasn't the Middle Ages, she knew, but still. She'd been able to bear it all at Len's side: the trauma of displacement through the Ring of Fire; the realization that she'd never again see everything and everyone she had left up-time; the loss of simple, day-to-day comforts taken for granted. All of it. Without Len?

"Okay, Morris, you win."

He shook his head. "It's not about me winning, Ellie. It's about keeping you and Tuva safe and providing the best care that we can to Len." He gave her an earnest shake. "You *will* see your husband again. I promise."

He hugged her once more and then he turned them back to the tent.

Kolozsvár

Isaac paused before approaching the *Dixie Chick*, knowing full well that doing so could mean the difference between Len's life and his death. Christian had regaled him with stories of his personal experience flying inside the up-time machine, but now it was his turn to fly. He didn't know if he could do it, especially in this foul weather.

Denise Beasley shocked him from his pause. "Come on," she shouted, waving violently. "No stalling. We've got to keep ahead of this weather!"

He took a deep breath and walked the last twenty feet to the craft, burdened by two large satchels of medical equipment and supplies, with rain soaking his yarmulke.

Denise took one look at his portage and shook her head. "We can't take all that."

Isaac set his satchels down. "I don't know what I'll be facing with Len, Denise. I won't have my medical staff or my best nurse. I need to take a lot of equipment to be prepared." He sighed, shook his head. "Or you go and get him and bring him to me."

Denise shook her head again. "Nah...radio chatter indicates he can't be moved. Too risky."

"What about General von Mercy and Prince Rákóczi?"

"From what I've heard, von Mercy isn't too bad off. Don't know about the prince. They won't speak his name. I guess they're worried about zips in the wire."

Isaac didn't know what that meant but said nothing. He pressed the issue. "I have to take these bags, Denise, or I can't go."

She sighed and cussed under her breath. "Okay. Give me a sec."

Denise climbed into the Dvorak and did something in the back compartment. He couldn't tell exactly what she was doing, but then a red canister dropped out of the cockpit. Then another. She climbed back out with a grunt.

"Okay, that'll free up enough weight to accommodate your bags." She wiped her hands and pointed her thumb to the craft. "Let's go. We gotta haul ass. We'll be running at top speed. The capital's about fifty miles or so from here. It'll be a short flight, all things considered, but damn bumpy. I hope you didn't eat anything today."

No such luck there. He'd dined on local bread and cheese and had washed it all down with a cup of wine. Preparing for the day when the desperate call came in from Ellie and General Roth. In that moment, the anxiety and doubt that Isaac had been able to control since his last conversation with Christian and Rabbi Gotkin came back tenfold. It dissipated as fast as it had erupted, thankfully, and he had girded his courage and packed his bags. Len Tanner needed him. Ellie needed him. Von Mercy, and maybe even the prince, needed him. Time to grow up, put away the self-doubt, and do his duty.

Denise helped him with the bags and got him strapped into the passenger seat. "Hold on tight, my friend," she said, giving him a confident smile and a pat on his cheek. "It's gonna be a rough takeoff."

Gyulafehérvár

Lieutenant Enkefort guided them into the capital via radio contact, onto a short, narrow, and relatively straight path that led alongside the Collegium Academicum. That was where the victims of the assassination attempt had been taken, including the prince.

Christian von Jori met them on the path as the Dvorak came to a halt. He greeted Isaac warmly, but with a clear mark of anxiety on his face. "Good to see you again, Christian," Isaac said as the cavalry officer helped with his bags. "Do you know the situation of our wounded?"

Christian nodded. "A little. The prince is in a...coma? I think that's what you call it."

Isaac nodded. "Yes, that's the term."

"Not so much from the shot as the fall. He struck his head on a rock. They say he has a fractured skull. He's alive, but I don't know much more than that. His wife and children are with him."

"The general?"

"He's sleeping. He lost a lot of blood, but he's well. They put a tourniquet on him in the field. I think it saved his life."

Isaac hesitated then, "And Len?"

"He's alive, praise God. The physicians here at the college put some kind of poultice on his wound; it's pretty bad. The mini-ball hit him in the shoulder. Not a full, deep strike. More of an indirect hit, but it tore him up badly. His shoulder is dislocated. The physicians here have stopped the bleeding, I think, but they haven't done anything to remove the mini-ball. He's in a lot of pain."

"Okay," Isaac said. "Thank you. Can you assist me today? I've no staff."

Christian nodded. "Absolutely. Whatever you need. Whatever I can do."

They were led into the college by Prince Rákóczi's personal guard. There was no argument as to whom Isaac had to see first.

The prince's wife Zsuzsanna and their two sons were at his side. When the princess consort saw Christian, she immediately began to cry and fell into his arms. That surprised Isaac. How in the world did they know each other? he wondered. It was a story Isaac wanted to hear, but not now. Now, the prince of Transylvania lay still in his bed, his head wrapped in bloody strips of wool.

Isaac felt immediate unease. Everyone in the room—and the number was substantial—was staring at him, and some in not a very positive way. Were they just worried about their prince, he wondered, or were they anxious that a Jew was about to administer care? It was hard to know, and it made him nervous. He wanted to tell everyone to leave the room, but did he have the authority to do so, and would they listen if he did?

Gáspár Bojthi Veres, who stood near the bed, seemed to detect Isaac's worry. He motioned to the door. "Okay, now. Everyone needs to leave. Please. Let's give Doctor Kohen some room and privacy to do his work."

The crowd hesitated, then slowly filed out, including the princess and her sons. Christian led them to the door.

Isaac sighed gratefully. "Thank you, Herr Veres."

But not everyone left the room. There were still guards in the corners and at the door. Two young medical students from the university begged to stay. Isaac let them. Christian returned to the prince's bedside. "What do we do?"

"I need to check his vitals first."

Isaac removed a stethoscope from his bag and checked the prince's pulse and heart rate. Thready pulse, irregular heartbeat. But based on the condition the prince was in, that was a positive sign. He then checked airflow. It was decent—for now. He checked for a fever; none. He then reached into his bag and pulled out a blood pressure cuff, one that he had gotten from the Leahy Medical Center. He wrapped the cuff around the prince's right arm.

"I suspect his blood pressure is quite low," he said, "but I want to make sure."

It was, and dangerously so. He removed the cuff and tucked it away in his bag. "He needs fluids to try to bring his BP up."

From the second bag, Isaac pulled out IV equipment and got the medical students to help him set it up and attach it to the prince's arm. "Fluids from this bag will drip into this line," he said, pointing out the mechanics of the device now hanging near the bed, "and then into his body. This will help increase his blood pressure. We need to watch the bag closely and replace it when it's empty. I only brought four."

Isaac then leaned over the prince. He reached for the woolen head wrappings. "Help me remove this bandage. Carefully now. We must take great care. I don't know what kind of trauma his neck might have suffered in the fall—if any."

Christian and the two medical students helped to stabilize the prince's body while Isaac slowly unraveled the bloody wool wrap. He nodded as the head wound was revealed. "I see that someone cleaned the wound well."

"That was me, Herr Kohen," one of the students in the room said.

Isaac nodded. "Well done. I'd like you to serve as Prince Rákóczi's personal attendant while he is in this condition. You keep me informed of his status by the hour. Understand?"

The students looked at each other and, again, Isaac wasn't sure if their apprehension to his order was because he was a Jew. Finally, the student nodded. "Of course, Herr Kohen. It would be an honor to serve the prince."

The prince's long hair hindered Isaac's examination. "Get someone to shave his head around the wound. We need full access to it for proper treatment."

"How does it look?" Christian asked, keeping his hands level and strong as he cradled the prince's head.

"The wound itself isn't too bad. Deep gash, yes, but see the minimal bruising? The young doctor here did a good job on its immediate care. But notice the bone?"

Christian shook his head. "I cannot see anything clearly."

Isaac winced, suddenly concerned about his friend's eyesight.

He let it go—for now. "This is a side trauma. The sphenoid and zygomatic bones are fractured." Isaac moved the prince's head so that Christian could see clearly. "There...and there. Very serious fractures." Isaac made room so that everyone could see.

"Yes, I see them," Christian said. "That's what put him in a coma?"

"The rock strike certainly knocked him out. As for the coma itself, I want to check one more thing..."

Isaac moved his hand underneath Christian's. He set his fingers along the cervical spine bones and carefully massaged upward toward the cranium. He halted, and his heart sank.

"Okay, let's wrap a new bandage around his head." Isaac looked at the students. "Can one of you do that for me while I examine his other wounds?"

"Yes, Herr Kohen."

While the students got to work on the next bandage, Isaac examined the gunshot wound that pierced Prince Rákóczi's side. "A clean shot right though the muscle tissue and out the back. Luckily, it missed his kidney, though it may have perforated his bowel."

"What does it mean if the shot perforated the bowel?" Christian asked.

Isaac reapplied the bandage over the wound, sighed, and said, "An infection like peritonitis and possibly sepsis. Someone's got to go in there and look. If the bowel is torn, infection can spread rapidly. I didn't smell anything foul, thankfully, but to know for sure, at some point I'll need to go in there and see."

The other wound was more of an injury, a simple ankle sprain when his boot got caught in the stirrup on the fall. His ankle was puffy, but not broken. Finally, some good news.

"What is his condition, Doctor?" Christian asked as Isaac washed his hands in a pot of clean water.

"Not here," he whispered. "Let's open the door and allow his family back in. Then let's speak to Gáspár privately."

The crowd rolled right back into their places in the room. Isaac spent a little time reassuring the princess consort and her children about their father's status. He smiled and put as positive a tone in his voice as he could, remembering the need for a good bedside manner. Then he and Christian pulled Gáspár out of the room and found a private corner in which to speak.

"I am no expert on the human nervous system," Isaac said. "I have a working knowledge, but it's one of the weaker parts of my training and study." He sighed, rubbed his forehead, and continued. "But he's in a bad condition, Gáspár. The fall severely cracked his skull. There may be brain damage, I don't know. The gunshot wound is manageable, assuming no infection develops. The ankle sprain is unimportant. But..."

He paused. They waited for him to continue. "The real problem is his spine. His cervical spine—the part in his neck that connects to the skull—it's pinched, badly, from the trauma and impact of the fall. It may be cracked somewhere between the C4 and C5 vertebrae. There's no doubt in my mind that his spinal cord is compressed...severely. If he survives everything else that he has suffered—and I'm not guaranteeing that—I suspect he'll be paralyzed. Again, I'm not an expert on the human nervous system, but that's my professional judgment."

The pause was palpable. Frightening, in fact, for the voices of the people in Prince Rákóczi's room nearby gave the silence of the hallway a ghostly quality, an echo of false hope. The man lying in the room was dying...and there was very little Doctor Isaac Kohen, junior surgeon for the Grand Army of the Sunrise, could do about it.

"We cannot release these details to the public," Gáspár said.

Christian shook his head. "They will get out there eventually." He pointed to the room. "Forgive me, Herr Veres. I am no politician, but who can you trust in that room? How many of them would keep a secret like this?"

"They will if I demand it," Gáspár said, almost spitting. "Do you understand what is happening, gentlemen? Two belligerent armies march on our capital. War is upon us, and you have no concerns about the truth of his condition getting out? Chaos will ensue if it does. No," he said, shaking his head furiously. "No, it cannot be done. We will say that he is in serious, but stable, condition. I've heard you use those very words, Doctor Kohen, on the march."

Isaac nodded. "Fine, fine. As Christian said, we're not politicians. You do what you feel is right. My duty here is to save lives. But Prince Rákóczi? He is in God's hands now, and I just pray that, in this matter, God is a better surgeon than I."

Isaac walked away. Christian followed. "He is foolish if he thinks the prince's condition will remain a secret."

"I know, Christian, I know."

"Someone in that room right now must have told whomever it was flying that airship that the prince would be in that field. There's no *way* that that ship would have been there at the time, at that moment, by accident."

Again, Christian would get no argument from Isaac. "You are right. But let's not worry about such things right now. Our duty *now* is to save Len."

What remained of the mini-ball that had struck Len Tanner was lodged about half an inch into the glenoid cavity between the scapula and the humerus. Upon entry, the ball had apparently struck both the humerus and scapula, leaving bone fragments everywhere. Some of those fragments now threatened to tear the axillary artery. The skin and muscle in that area were heavily damaged.

"It's worse than I had hoped," Isaac said as he and Christian prepared themselves for surgery, "but not as bad as I had feared."

A group of local physicians and ladies volunteering to assist had arrived. Isaac sent most of them away, save for four—two men, two women—who would assist, like Christian, in ensuring Len remained still and cooperative during the surgery. A small portion of morphine had been administered, giving Len some relief from hours of pain. In his stupor, however, he shouted Ellie's name and tried sitting up.

"Keep him still!" Isaac shouted to his volunteers. "We cannot allow those bone fragments to move even a millimeter, lest they puncture the artery."

And then it would be a mad scramble to try to keep him from spouting blood like a fountain. If that happened, there'd likely be no choice but to sever the arm and ligate the artery.

"I won't be able to use the magnet like I did with you, Christian," Isaac said through his mask as he approached Len lying on the makeshift surgery table. "I'm going to have to go in and pull each of those fragments out one by one." He checked Christian to ensure he was wearing his prophylaxis properly. "Keep close, keep the magnifying glass closer, and hand me my scalpels and tweezers when needed, and swiftly."

"I understand, Isaac," Christian said, holding up his hands to reveal he was wearing his gloves properly. "I want this to go well. For Len. For Ellie."

"*Ellie!*"

Len tried lifting himself off the table at the sound of his wife's name, but one of the ladies Isaac had picked to assist pressed her hands firmly into Len's chest, leaned over, and whispered softly against Len's sweaty forehead, "Shhh! I am here, my love. Please, be still."

The woman's lips grazed Len's balmy skin, and the touch of them with her words soothed him immediately. "Ellie? Ellie? Are you here?"

Through his morphine-induced stupor, he couldn't tell whether the woman was his wife or no. "Yes," the woman cooed again. She stroked his head with soft fingers. "I am here. Be still now. Be still."

Impressive, Isaac thought, as he selected tweezers from his array of medical tools and got to work.

Four fragments removed—the easiest ones—and Isaac paused and asked, "What is your name, young lady?"

"Oana Dalca," she said.

"And how old are you?"

She paused, then: "Eighteen."

He huffed. "You handled that problem well."

"Thank you," she said. She did not raise her head to acknowledge him. She kept her focus on Len and her hands on his chest, his other shoulder, to keep him still. "My mother used to assist our Rabbi, who was also a physician, when men were sick and high of fever. They too would call out for their mothers, their wives."

"Ah, so you are Jewish."

"No," she said, then paused as if she were embarrassed or afraid to continue. Finally, she sighed and said, "I am Sabbatarian."

"Should we really be having this conversation, Isaac?" Christian asked.

Isaac smiled and suppressed a laugh. "It is fine, my friend. What do the up-timers say? I've got this? Well . . . *I've got this.* I'm almost finished."

He had worked from the easiest fragments to the harder, and so far, he'd removed twenty. The last five were now waiting, and they were the most critical.

"I've got some blood seepage here," Isaac said, looking up at one of the physicians.

The man moved quickly to staunch the blood. The other physician and the two ladies held Len down firmly.

"Len," Isaac said, "you may not be able to hear me well, but I want to be honest with you. The next several minutes are going to be painful. But you can handle it, my friend. I have faith in you. Are you ready?"

Len gave a halfhearted nod, the effects of his morphine still working, though only partially.

"Okay," Isaac said. He waved Christian closer. "Hold the magnifying glass directly over the wound, and close."

Isaac breathed deeply, mouthed a silent Yiddish prayer for strength and courage, and then moved in toward the axillary artery with scalpel in one hand, tweezers in the other.

Three fragments down, two to go, as Isaac's back and neck ached from so much standing, stooping. And worry. His muscles were so tense, his heart racing such that it was difficult to breathe. Oana and one of the physicians helped to keep him upright, to alleviate some of the pain, by allowing him to put his weight into their hands as they held him in a semi-hug. He could feel Oana's breath on his neck. That, too, was distracting.

He pulled the penultimate fragment free of the swollen flesh around the axillary artery. It was a big one, the biggest yet, and its extraction created a pool of blood that seeped out of Len's shoulder. But not a spray or gush. Isaac breathed a sigh of relief. The artery was intact.

A student physician staunched the blood as Oana helped Isaac stand and catch his breath. "There's one more," he said, wiping his brow with a washcloth. "I can see the top of it, but I don't know how deep it rests or how fragmented it is. I may have to cut into the pectoral to get it out. I hate to do it; he's already suffered enough damage."

The guard outside the room started to shout something. There was a scuffle, more shouting, and the door burst open.

Ellie Anderson and Tuva came in. Tuva walked; Ellie stormed. She ran toward the table. "Len!"

Christian caught her before she reached her husband's side. "Let me go, goddammit! Let me—"

"He's just fine, Ellie!" Isaac put up his bloody, gloved hand. "Please, stand back, and let me do my work."

"Is he gonna live?" She strained against Christian's arms.

Isaac nodded. "Yes, if you let me do my work!"

She burst into tears. "Please, please, don't let my Len die. Please!"

Christian let her go, and Oana led her to a chair.

It was heartbreaking for everyone in the room. It added a level of anxiety and stress to Isaac that he did not need, but he didn't let it show. Christian grabbed his shaking hand. "It'll be all right, my friend. We'll get you through this."

The smile on Christian's face was enough. "Very well. Let's continue."

The last fragment turned into two. As Isaac pulled it carefully out of Len's pectoral muscle, it broke in half and the bottom portion slipped back into the muscle. Luckily, it wasn't anywhere near the axillary artery, so it was a simple matter of a small cut into the muscle tissue and then extraction. Pulling out that last piece of bone was almost the most satisfying thing Isaac had ever done in his short medical career.

He spoke loud enough for everyone in the room to hear, especially Ellie. "All the fragments are out. Now we address the mini-ball."

The shoulder was dislocated due to the impact of the mini-ball into the glenoid cavity. Getting the mini-ball out and then popping the humerus back into place was not the major concern. The damage to the humerus itself, and the articular cartilage, was the issue.

Compared to the time and care needed to extract the fragments, the surgery on Len's shoulder moved quickly. A careful cut around the mini-ball, a quick pluck with needle-nose pliers, and the ball was out. The heat of the shot had cauterized some of the flesh around the entry point, making bleeding less of a factor.

When finished, he spent some time stitching up the most egregious wounds along the mini-ball's entry point, and then they wrapped Len's shoulder tightly with a harness that Isaac had acquired from the Leahy Medical Center specifically designed for dislocated shoulders. It was the only one his medical team possessed, but hopefully, it'd do the job. The key was to completely immobilize Len's shoulder for . . . how long? That was hard to know for sure. Everyone's recovery rate was different, Isaac knew. Len, otherwise in reasonable shape with no chronic medical conditions, would probably recover quickly. But "probably" was not "for certain."

Isaac cleaned up, provided care instructions to his helpers, ordered another morphine shot despite low supply, and then met Oana and Ellie outside the room.

"How is he, Isaac?" Ellie said, exhaustion and sincere concern rimming her red, swollen eyes. "Will my husband live?"

"He's fine, Ellie," Isaac said. "For right now. The fragments have been removed, the mini-ball removed, and the shoulder snapped back in place and wrapped. I gave him another shot of morphine to keep him calm. But the next twenty-four to forty-eight hours will be critical. The short-term concern is infection. If we can keep him from getting an infection, he should be fine. Fine meaning, alive. Ellie, I don't want to lie to you. The wound he suffered was serious."

Isaac held up his arm as if he were pointing at the ceiling of the hallway in which they stood. "He must have been pointing into the sky—perhaps at the airship—when the ball struck. It hit his humerus up near the shoulder and scraped along the bone, lodging itself into the glenoid cavity. The cartilage in that area, Ellie, has been severely damaged."

"What does that mean?"

"The cartilage won't heal on its own. In time, it'll break down even further, at which point the underlying bone will react by creating bone spurs. This will eventually cause swelling, pain, and possibly immobility."

Ellie waved her hand. "Don't waste my time with medical details, Doc. Tell me straight: is Len going to be okay or not?"

"Yes, I believe he will. But he has a long, long road to recovery ahead. The next few days are critical, but the next several weeks will determine if he regains full motion in his arm and shoulder. I can't tell you yes or no, Ellie. What needs to happen is for him to be airlifted to Grantville or Magdeburg. He needs to recover fully in a facility that is superior to this, with doctors better trained than I."

Ellie shook her head. "Morris is never going to agree to that." She sniffled and rubbed a tear off her cheek. "He's not going to spare an entire plane for just one man."

"I'll talk to him about it," Isaac said. "But in the meantime, Len's here, he's safe, he's resting, and I will personally see to his recovery. On my honor."

"Thank you, Isaac." She hugged him, harder than he expected, and longer too. He hugged her back, patted her shoulder, and let her squeeze as long as she needed. She then pulled away. "Can I see him?"

"Yes, of course. He's heavily sedated right now, so he's not going to respond to you or talk."

Ellie huffed. "That'll be a first."

She burst into laughter, nervous laughter, the kind manifest from hours upon hours of stress. He laughed with her. "Now go...see your husband. Oana? You will accompany her?"

The young Sabbatarian nodded, took Ellie by the arm, and guided her into the room.

When they were alone, Christian said, "You did well in there, Isaac. The best I've ever seen."

"Thank you. God was with me today."

Christian nodded. "Why don't you get some rest, my friend. I can keep an eye on Len for you. If anything comes up, I'll let you know."

Isaac shook his head. "No, not yet. There's still one more patient to visit."

Isaac felt immediate guilt upon entering von Mercy's room. Not because the general's wound was worse than those suffered by his other two patients, but because of the result of their last meeting. Isaac had, in effect, publicly rebuked and embarrassed von Mercy in front of his staff. Isaac was expecting the general to refuse his treatment. He did nothing of the sort.

"*Guten abend, Herr Doctor.*" Von Mercy seemed in a good mood. Someone must have given him a sedative. Maybe opium. "Please, come in and give me a proper examination. These so-called physicians here cannot seem to settle on a proper diagnosis."

Isaac leaned into one of the local physicians in attendance and whispered, "Do you have a supply of opium here in the capital?"

The man nodded. "Yes. As a vassal state of Sultan Murad, opium is available. Not in large quantities necessarily, but enough for pain management."

Transylvania wasn't a vassal state any longer, though Isaac figured that it would take some time for the citizenry to come to that realization. And, if the battle to come ended badly for the Army of the Sunrise, the man in front of him wouldn't have to accept his country's political changes at all. "Let's talk after my examination of General von Mercy about what stores of opium are available."

Isaac turned to his patient. "So, General...what ails ya?"

The up-time idiom seemed lost on von Mercy for a second, then he understood. "The bastards shot me in the leg."

Von Mercy was lying on a bed with legs exposed. Isaac pulled on a clean pair of gloves and leaned over the left leg, taking hold of it carefully and turning it to see both sides of the wound. He nodded. "A clean shot right through." Then he winced. "Looks like it nicked the femur...but just a centimeter or so. Any pain?"

"Not right now."

Of course not, Isaac thought, rolling his eyes. All tanked up on opium, it was a wonder the general's speech wasn't slurred.

"Hand me my tweezers, please, Christian," he said, pointing to the bag.

"Ah, yes, Captain von Jori," von Mercy said. "Are your men ready for a fight?"

Christian reached into Isaac's satchel, pulled out the needed tweezers, and handed them over. "Yes, General. They're ready."

"Good. I'm going to need my cavalry to sweep the field of these cowards who attack from the sky."

"Who do you suspect they were, General?" Christian asked. "The ones who fired at you from the airship?"

Von Mercy shook his head. "I did not see the shot, young man. My attention was on Prince Rákóczi. But it's our understanding that it was Moldavians who acquired the airship from Murad. The Moldavians!" He shook his head. "I guess we didn't whip them hard enough at Déj."

"Gentlemen," Isaac said, leaning back from von Mercy's thrashing leg. "Can you please discuss military matters later? I'm trying to remove a couple fragments here."

The local physician now moved to settle von Mercy's leg. Isaac thanked him and proceeded.

Von Mercy chuckled. "You'll have to forgive my personal physician, Captain von Jori. He has a singular focus that can be...irritating."

"Sir," von Jori said, "Isaac Kohen is the finest physician I know."

How many do you know? Isaac wanted to ask, but that would be petty and unproductive. Besides, given the look on von Jori's face, he meant it.

The general mumbled something indecipherable and laid back down.

There were only two small fragments that Isaac found in his search. He plucked them out quickly and then helped the physician and the lone nurse given to von Mercy's care rewrap the wound and set his leg down carefully.

Isaac then made a quick check on the general's vitals, and said, "Okay, General von Mercy. You are a fortunate man. The shot went right through your leg, not striking any arteries. I'd say the tourniquet saved your life. A couple bone fragments off the femur. That alone will cause some significant pain for the next several days. But otherwise, you're going to be fine. You'll be off your feet, though, for weeks."

Von Mercy shook his head and moved as if he were going to get up. "No, that's not possible. There's a battle coming. I have to be with my men."

Isaac and Christian tried to hold him down. "No, sir," Isaac said with a grunt as they worked to keep von Mercy calm. "Trust your doctor on this. Whatever you need to do for the army, it'll have to be conducted from this room. And don't you go thinking you'll be riding a horse soon."

"You take orders from me, sir," von Mercy blurted, though the punch and potency of its authority was lacking due to the opium. "You take orders from—"

Isaac reached up and took von Mercy's face into his hands. He turned the general's head to look him in the eyes. "General… General. Look at me. Look at me!"

Von Mercy opened his droopy eyes. "You are on bed restriction until I say otherwise, sir. Your calf muscle was severely damaged. You've lost a lot of blood. You're weak, disoriented, and I suspect in a lot of pain, which is why they gave you so much opium. You stay put. That's an order from your physician. Please… trust your doctor."

They laid his head down carefully, and von Mercy tried again to argue the point, but his speech was slurred, his resistance minimal.

"Let him rest," Isaac said to the attending physician and nurse. "Do not give him so much opium again, is that clear? You check with me first on the dosage. And check his bandage hourly. Clean the wound in an hour, and apply a new bandage.

Keep everything clean. We don't want infection setting up in that wound. I'll be back around in a few hours to check his status. Understand?"

Isaac turned to leave the room.

"Isaac."

It was von Mercy's voice. Isaac turned. "Yes, General."

"I *do* trust my physician . . . completely."

Part Six

September 1637

A warrior brilliant among warriors
—Sophocles, *Ajax*

Chapter 43

Hermannstadt (Sibiu)
Southern Transylvania

The airship slipped through a large blanket of fog. It disappeared, reappeared, and disappeared again as Matei Basarab watched from the protection of his personal guard. He thanked God that Usan Hussein was not at his side. For this meeting, he did not need the roving eyes and ears of the Sultan passing judgment on his decisions. In truth, Matei didn't know what he was going to do. The knife in its sheath on his belt craved blood, Lupu's blood, and how easy would it be to have his guards seize that bumbling buffoon, cut his throat, and watch him bleed out? Then, perhaps, Matei could broker a peace with the Diet of Transylvania, with Bohemia. Perhaps, then, he could escape his terrible dreams.

The *Chaldiran* appeared again and, this time, descended in a slow, deliberate manner until mooring lines were tossed out of the gondola and tethered to the ground by men waiting below. When secure, a rope ladder was tossed out.

Matei stepped forward and waited as Vasile Lupu's round form was helped onto the ladder. Following him was a well-muscled, heavily armed Janissary. Matei had been around enough Janissaries now to know one when he saw one. But that was all. No other protection.

Bold, Matei thought. *Stupid.*

Matei gripped the hilt of his knife tightly as he approached his partner in this ill-advised endeavor. For his part, the voivode of Moldavia jumped off the ladder with an extra spring in his step, a contented smile on his puffy lips.

"You fool!"

It was not the planned initial response that Matei wanted to deliver, but it was either that or draw the knife. "How could you do it? After you *promised* no direct attack against George."

Vasile's joyful expression turned hard. Gone was his smile. In its place, a cold stare that told Matei that the man had changed, that he had tasted too much military success of late, despite word that the Moldavians and their mercenary allies had suffered a terrible defeat against the Sunrise near Déj.

"I did what had to be done," Vasile said. He paused to allow his Janissary guard to join him, then said, "In your heart, you know it had to be done."

"I should turn my columns back to Wallachia and leave you to the wolves!"

Vasile sighed. "The situation has not changed, my friend. When you retreat to the comfort of your court, please inform the Sultan of your decision and await his bloody response. There was never a choice here, Matei! The minute your man Stroe Leurdeanu read Murad's order, our fates were cast. Now, the only thing left for us is victory, and I have greatly improved our chances on that score by killing the prince of Transylvania."

"He is not dead."

"Not yet, which makes the matter even better for us. Chaos and confusion now rule their politics. Their prince's life hangs in the balance. Who will rule when he dies? His oldest son, George Junior? His wife? One of his brothers? A Jewish general from Bohemia? Confusion will lead to indecision. Indecision to inaction. Inaction to defeat.

"I have given us a real chance for victory. I. Not you or your Janissaries or your *Ifrit* fire tanks. *Me*. The only thing left now is for us to move onto Gyulafehérvár and quickly bring this matter to a conclusion. The capital is ours, Matei. Transylvania is ours...if we're man enough to take it."

At this moment, Matei wished that his mother, his father, had raised him to be more ruthless. This nagging sense of decency and fair play was an impediment. His best move was to agree with Vasile Lupu, put aside his doubt, his fear, and press forward. Life would be so much simpler if he saw the world through a more practical, financial lens as did Vasile. He'd certainly sleep better at night if he did.

Matei closed his eyes, shook his head, sighed, and said, "Where is your army now?"

"It awaits in Schäßburg."

"And these . . . Impalers of yours?"

Vasile smiled. "Everywhere."

Matei raised his brow. "It's my understanding—from my sources, Vasile—that their efforts have met with severe resistance north of the capital."

Again, the voivode of Moldavia shook his head vigorously. "Silly rumor and hearsay. I've been assured that whatever *resistance* they have experienced is minor and inconsequential. The citizenry of Transylvania is flocking to our ranks to help us defeat this Sunrise before it reaches the capital or, at least, cause it enough harm to make its effectiveness less so. Do not worry about unfounded rumors, my friend. The Impalers will do their job."

Worries? Matei had plenty. "Is your army ready to join ranks with mine?"

"Oh, yes indeed." Vasile seemed to relax. His belly now pushed against the gold cloth of his dolman. His shoulders relaxed and lowered. "I'm waiting on you to give the word, and then I'll order my men forward."

How clever he is to now shift the burden, the decision to march onto me, Matei thought. He nodded for show and ran through the operational situation in his mind. Hermannstadt had fallen relatively easily, but the citizenry was less than cooperative. Small pockets of resistance harried his army everywhere. Perhaps the citizenry of northern Transylvania was falling into line, but not the Saxons of the south. Like their Impaler counterparts, they were aggravating the Wallachian supply line at every turn, causing Usan Hussein all sorts of trouble. More bee stings than hammer blows, for sure, but still, a matter that would need to be addressed before moving forward to link arms with the Moldavians.

"I'll give the word soon, Vasile," Matei said. "Within days."

"I await your order," Vasile said, taking a step backward toward his airship. "Send it soon. The weather is beginning to turn. Fall is here. Winter will arrive soon. We do *not* want to lie in winter quarters. We must strike now. Now is our time, Matei, before the Grand Army of the Sunrise reaches the capital."

Vasile said nothing more and turned. Matei watched the fool reach the *Chaldiran* and climb aboard.

He turned from the field as well, his mind racing with myriad problems and tedious details. He burped and felt the sting of stomach acid in his throat, on his tongue. He spit.

Life was so much easier just six months ago.

Chapter 44

The Collegium Academicum
Gyulafehérvár

Isaac watched young Oana Dalca work with one of Prince Rákóczi's medical student caregivers as they began stitching up the incision that Isaac had made in the prince's abdomen. Some good news: no perforated bowel, no signs of peritonitis. The Murad mini-ball that had torn through the prince had partially cauterized the wound. The chance now of infection was slim. But the man was still in a coma, still clinging to life. His weight was down. He was dehydrated despite their efforts to provide liquids. He was dying, and how long could the man linger on the cusp of death before he finally succumbed?

Oana had a delicate touch, a soothing demeanor. Like a young Devorah Bayer. She was inexperienced with needles and stitching, but she was a quick study, and over the past several days while administering care to all three of Isaac's very important patients, she had learned a great deal.

They finished, and the student left the room to check on Len Tanner. Oana stayed behind to begin preparing Prince Rákóczi's soiled bedsheets for washing.

"I must compliment you, Oana," Isaac said. "You learn quickly. Your needlework is improving."

"Thank you, Doctor," she said, giving a small curtsey as she rolled a dirty sheet up and placed it in a basket. "You are a good teacher."

A moment of silence passed between them. Isaac then said, "Perhaps when all this is over, you can become a full-time nurse. Or even a doctor, like me."

Oana paused. She smiled, wiped her wrist on the green scarf around her head. "A woman doctor? I do not think that is possible."

Isaac shrugged. "In the USE, in Grantville, in Magdeburg, it is. If you are interested, I can speak with General Roth. With my recommendation, I'm sure he would be willing to send you."

She said nothing to that, kept her head down while filling her basket with additional linens and wet rags.

"May I ask you a question, Oana?"

"Certainly, Doc—Isaac."

He cleared his throat. "You are very young. Where are your parents?"

Oana paused, and Isaac immediately regretted asking the question. She continued packing her basket. "My mother died ten years ago. A fever. My father is in prison."

"Prison?"

She nodded. "He spoke out publicly against Prince Rákóczi's alliance with Bohemia. That, and the fact that he's an unrepentant Sabbatarian."

Isaac paused in his cleaning. To some extent, he could understand how a man might find a prison cell speaking out against his prince in public. He did not, however, understand the latter point. "I don't understand why his religious beliefs would—"

"Then you do not understand Transylvania," she said. Isaac could see her immediate regret at being so abrupt. She dropped her basket, bowed. "Forgive me, sir. I did not mean to—"

Isaac scoffed and waved it away. "That is quite all right, Oana. These are stressful times. Forgive me my excessive curiosity. I only wish to understand why a young lady like you would willingly provide medical aid to the man who, as you say, has thrown your father into prison." He lowered his head. "Were it me, I wonder if I would be so kind."

Oana smiled. "I am Sabbatarian as well, Isaac. My father says that Sabbatarians are like horsemen, with one stirrup in Unitarianism, one stirrup in Judaism. We straddle that delicate line between both religions, a line that terrifies some people... like the prince."

She motioned to Prince Rákóczi's still form, his pallid face, his shrinking body. "But the Bible teaches us that if we do not forgive others their sins, then how can our Father forgive us ours? My hope is that if I care for the prince, and if he survives, he will see how I have cared for him, and he will forgive my father his public transgressions. And perhaps he'll forgive us for being Sabbatarian."

Be a proud Jew . . .

Isaac smiled. He performed a few menial tasks with his scalpels, his tweezers, and then asked, "Would you care to join me tonight in Shabbos? Rabbi Gotkin will be holding a service for the First Regiment of the Joshua Corps. You can come as my guest."

The offer seemed to surprise her. She considered for a moment, then: "Yes, I would like to. But I must ask the family I am staying with. Would your Rabbi Gotkin approve of my attendance?"

Isaac shrugged. "Why wouldn't he?"

"Some Rabbis are not comfortable with Sabbatarians either."

Isaac waved her concern off with a pronounced huff. "Jason Gotkin is an up-timer. There will be no problem."

Her expression suggested she wasn't so sure, but Isaac said nothing further on the matter. He waited.

"Very well," she said. "Thank you, Isaac, for the offer. I will let you know."

The Collegium Academicum
Gyulafehérvár

Ellie had taken Len's radio and had set up a small communications desk in his room. Add to that a cot, and she had commandeered a corner as her personal living space. Isaac was against this at first, for the noise of the radio chatter would, without doubt, affect Len's sleep, and good sleep was what he needed the most right now. But in the end, he'd relented and allowed her to do so. It would have taken three Ashkenazim guards to drag her away. Maybe more.

Len's pain management was growing more difficult by the day. Like Prince Rákóczi's wound, the ball that had struck Len's shoulder had cauterized much of the flesh. They were beyond the concern for infection. Now, severe swelling had set in. The healing process had begun, thankfully, but his discomfort was constant.

Len called for pain medication hourly. Small doses of opium had been administered. That helped to calm him and allow him to sleep. But now, he was asking for larger doses.

"We need to keep his doses small, Ellie," Isaac said as they huddled outside the room for a brief chat. "I've no doubt that he's in a lot of pain. Increasing his dosage would be helpful, but we can't afford to allow him to become addicted."

"Your people are in control of those doses, Isaac," Ellie said, her hands on her hips, "not me. How can I be of help?"

He smiled and put his hand on her shoulder. "I cannot be with him around the clock, nor can my staff. There will be times where you will be alone with him, and I've seen it before, Ellie. A mother, sister, brother, seeing their loved ones in such pain. They will do almost anything to make that pain go away."

Ellie shrugged his hand off her shoulder and put up her own hand. "Hold up. Are you suggesting that I would try to—what— smuggle opium into his room when you're not looking?"

"I'm asking you to help me ensure that Len doesn't get his hands on any doses outside his normal regimen." He looked left, right, then leaned in close. He whispered, "Ellie, we are in a dangerous place, and you know as well as I do that someone here, in the capital, told the Moldavians that Len, the prince, von Mercy, and all the others would be on that field.

"I've assigned Ashkenazim from the Joshua Corps to guard their rooms, but I can't even guarantee that *they* may not succumb to bribery and allow someone to slip Len an extra dose nor can I absolutely guarantee that every student physician helping me is sincere in their care. I've seen nothing in their behavior to indicate otherwise, but I cannot be sure. The only one I trust completely is Oana Dalca, who, by the way, I'll be assigning to Len's care more often now that he's no longer bedridden."

"Is she the young lady who tricked Len into thinking she was me?"

Isaac nodded. "Don't be upset at her, Ellie. It was the only way to keep him calm during the surgery."

"I'm not upset," Ellie said, smiling. "I want to give her a big wet kiss."

Isaac laughed and nodded. "All I'm asking of you, Ellie, is to keep your eyes open. Make sure you know who's coming into the room to care for him. And try to distract him from his pain. If he can help you with radio work without using his shoulder and without moving around too much, give him work. That'll help take his mind off the pain."

"Incoming message!"

Len's voice echoed through the hallway.

Isaac followed Ellie into the room. With his good arm, Len pointed to the radio sitting on the table at the foot of his bed. "Morse code."

"Hmm." Ellie grunted. "Must be quite an important message to be in code."

Isaac had heard the clicks of Morse code before, but couldn't understand any of it. Ellie turned her chair around, sat, grabbed a piece of paper and an up-time pencil, and began scribbling out the message. It went on for quite some time. By the end, the page was almost filled with her dictation.

Ellie returned her reply in Morse code as well, then stood and winked. She didn't read the entire message, but Isaac and Len got the essence of it.

"Some good news, finally! The Sunrise is in Kolozsvár."

Chapter 45

The Collegium Academicum
Gyulafehérvár

General Franz von Mercy had a spring in his step. A proverbial one, of course, for his wounded leg was swollen like the envelope of an airship, and he could barely walk. But word that the Sunrise had finally arrived in Kolozsvár had put a smile on his face. One that was difficult for Colonel Renz not to notice.

"You are in a particularly good mood this morning, General," Renz said, standing alongside von Mercy's bed with a fistful of papers requiring the general's signature. "Surprising for a man in your condition."

"Our full army is only fifty miles away, Colonel," von Mercy said, accepting the papers and a quill. "The whole army, including Higgins' Silesian Guard, the new Brethren APCs, the Dauntless, and Jupiter. All of it, including our pay. Even if the Moldavians and Wallachians were to attack tomorrow, we could hold them off now for a few days knowing that reinforcements will arrive."

Colonel Renz nodded. "There are also a number of new Székely infantry companies that have entered the capital, answering Princess Zsuzsanna Lorántffy's call to defend their prince in this—*his*—hour of need."

"Green recruits, I assume."

"Yes, most of them, though Colonel Hatmanu has taken it upon himself to absorb them all under his direct command."

Colonel Renz rolled his eyes. "The man's at least wise enough to be putting them through drills."

Von Mercy wasn't sure of Colonel Hatmanu's wisdom at all. The man hadn't expressed much during their personal encounters. Hatmanu hadn't even bothered paying von Mercy a visit since the assassination attempt. Had he even bothered to pay the prince a visit, or was he so caught up in his own ambitions that he thought *he* was in charge of this whole affair?

"As I've indicated before," von Mercy said, scribbling his name on papers and handing them back to Renz one at a time, "the best use for our Transylvanian brothers is second-line defense. We'll set them up in a ring around the capital, position them in places considered ripe for breach. It's the Sunrise that needs to meet our enemies in the field. We've got the experience and the weapons that can face their Ottoman forces. If we allow Hatmanu and his men to push forward, they'll be slaughtered."

Colonel Renz huffed. "I don't think Lazlo Guth and his Hajdus would get slaughtered."

Von Mercy shook his head and handed over the last signed paper. "Neither do I. He's the exception. We'll need to form a battle plan with his men in a significant role."

"Yes, sir." Colonel Renz accepted the last paper and placed them all in a leather satchel hanging from his shoulder. "And when will we form that battle plan?"

Von Mercy shrugged. "Whenever General Roth arrives. I've asked him to fly in ahead of the Sunrise so that we can have those discussions right away. In a few days, hopefully."

A knock came to the door. It opened, and one of the general's aides peeked in. "General von Mercy. Sorry to disturb you, sir, but Princess Zsuzsanna Lorántffy is here to see you."

Von Mercy's aides took a few minutes to help him out of bed and to a chair, where he threw on a few modest pieces of clothing, touched up his hair, and set another chair nearby for the princess. It was the best they could do under the circumstances. A blanket covered his legs.

They let the princess consort in. She was dressed similarly to how she had presented at the reception: a modest white-and-black gown with matching scarf. Her eyes were weary, bloodshot. Von Mercy could tell that she had spent a lot of time the past several days crying, worrying about her husband, most certainly worrying about her country, her people. He felt sorry for her, despite his misgivings about her husband. The weight of the world had suddenly been thrust onto her shoulders and to the shoulders of her sons, no doubt.

"My lady Lorántffy," von Mercy said, nodding, "I thank you for paying a visit. I apologize for the sparse conditions. I've not had many opportunities to rise since ... well, the event. Forgive my appearance."

She waved him off. "That is quite all right, General. My husband's quarters are even less appealing than yours. And he lies naked under a sheet." She motioned to the chair. "May I sit?"

"Please."

She took a seat, fixed herself, folded her hands over her lap. "I've wanted to pay you a visit for some time, General, but of course my attention has been devoted to my husband and his recovery."

"May I ask," von Mercy said, "how is he doing?"

She shrugged. "Your Jewish doctor is doing his best, I suppose. He is taking a ... balanced approach to my husband's care. He smiles and nods and tells me that all that can be done is being done. But beneath his subdued optimism, I detect resignation. He believes my husband will die. But he doesn't understand Prince Rákóczi's strength. George is a fighter. He will recover, General von Mercy, and I will broach no argument to the contrary."

Von Mercy nodded, but even through her resolute facade, he could see a twinge of doubt in her swollen eyes. "I look forward to his recovery, my lady."

She smiled, a modest, unassuming curl of her lips. "It is a matter of the interim that I wish to speak to you about, General. Until my husband recovers, there is a need for someone to maintain the peace, the control, of the streets of the capital." She stared at him for a long moment, then sighed. "It has been said that that someone could be you."

Von Mercy leaned back, pointed to himself. "Me? I am just a general in the Grand Army of the Sunrise. I am not one of your countrymen. It would be impractical for me to assume any administrative duties here in the capital."

The princess nodded. "Indeed, and I would not expect you to take charge of the administrative matters of Transylvania, General. I and my oldest son and George's brother Pál, if necessary, can deal with those matters until my husband recovers. George is still alive, praise God, and therefore is still our prince, our leader. No thought on succession will be contemplated right now.

"But... the Diet is concerned with the growing number of Saxon refugees pouring into the capital and the county. They, being primarily German, are looking for a leader with whom they can feel comfortable. I have given full command of all Székely forces to Colonel Marius Hatmanu, but there is a growing dispute over who should be in overall command. That person would also oversee the direct security of the streets of Gyulafehérvár."

Von Mercy pushed his case. "My lady, I am convalescing." He pulled the blanket aside and hiked up his leg painfully to give her a look at its size. "Please forgive my immodesty, but as you can see, I am in no condition right now to assume a battlefield role, much less oversee the security of the capital. In fact, I shall be honest with you and say that it is uncertain whether or not I will remain a general in the Sunrise once Morris Roth arrives."

"Who do you think would take your place?"

Von Mercy shook his head. "I do not know. There are a number of qualified commanders in the Sunrise ready to become generals."

Princess Lorántffy huffed. "Please advise your General Roth not to give the command to Colonel Hatmanu, no matter how much he begs for it."

Von Mercy smiled and couldn't help but chuckle. "On that, my lady, we are in full agreement."

They sat a moment in silence, neither speaking, neither moving to continue the conversation. At one point, von Mercy thought the princess was about to get up and leave. Instead, she straightened the scarf wrapped around her head, leaned forward, and said, "I will be perfectly honest with you too, General. I do not like the idea of you being in overall command.

"You are a Catholic, and I have no love for Catholics and for their Vatican or their Pope. In fact, I have less respect for Catholicism than Judaism. I'm a Christian, a Calvinist, and I try very hard to forgive everyone their sins. There are many in the Diet that agree with me, and they are not happy I am here making this offer. But I have an obligation to the entirety of Transylvania. I am here for Pál and for the Saxon Sees."

"Why didn't Pál come to me and make the offer himself?" von Mercy asked. "We know each other."

She breathed deeply, then let it out in a long sigh. She smiled.

"He thought it best that I—a woman—make the offer. He thought that you might be more amenable to the idea if it came from the princess."

Unfortunately, Pál was wrong. The idea wasn't entirely out of sorts, von Mercy had to admit to himself, even though he didn't like the idea of playing nursemaid to political unrest in the streets of the capital. He certainly couldn't decline the offer out of hand, lest the Diet make the offer to the likes of Marius Hatmanu, who would agree without hesitation. His statement to the princess that Morris Roth might replace him as general of the Sunrise was, of course, a nonstarter, as up-timers might say. The last time he had made that offer, General Roth ripped him a new one. But he certainly couldn't put himself on a horse right now, couldn't assume a field command. Someone else in the Sunrise might have to assume that role.

It all came down to when the Moldavian and Wallachian armies arrived at the capital. And unfortunately, the enemy wasn't kind enough to provide their operational plans.

"I thank you for the offer, my lady," von Mercy said, adjusting his position in the chair, "but I cannot agree to your request today. I must speak with *my* commanding officer first. If he thinks it would be a good idea, then I will accept. Can you give me a day, at least, to make a decision?"

Princess Lorántffy nodded. "That is why many of our officers, and many in the Diet, want you over Hatmanu, General. You respect the chain of command."

She stood, straightened her gown. "I will leave you now. Thank you for your hospitality. Consult whomever you wish on the matter, General, but please make your decision soon. We do not have a lot of time, and the offer will not wait forever."

He watched her leave, as modestly as she had arrived.

Interesting woman, he thought. Rough around the edges like her husband, but certainly dedicated to her people. *I just hope that that dedication doesn't get her killed. Or her sons.*

Colonel Renz entered the room. "How did it go, General?"

Von Mercy nodded. "Fine, fine."

"What did she say?"

"We'll speak about that shortly. But first," Von Mercy said, pointing to the door, "get me to Len Tanner's room. I have to make a call."

Chapter 46

The Collegium Academicum
Gyulafehérvár

Morris preferred riding in a Dvorak with Tuva as the pilot. Like Denise, she was quite self-confident in the air, but her demeanor lacked Denise's bravura. And she didn't sing that damned song Denise was so fond of.

They landed near the Collegium Academicum, despite the capital having a more permanent, and better, landing site north of the city. The distance between there and here was small, Morris knew, but he didn't want to waste any time. He had to see his commanding general. He had to see all three of Isaac's patients.

Len first. Ellie wanted to discuss a few communications matters with Morris in person. A tower needed to be erected near the newly constructed airport, if the Sunrise was going to be in the capital for any length of time. Morris approved the request and made a mental note to get the machinery moving, so to speak, on that score. Having a tower would reduce their need to use the Dvoraks for signal boosts. That would make both Denise and Tuva—and Eddie—very happy.

"How are you feeling, Len?" Morris asked, daring to place a hand on the poor man's good shoulder. The other was wrapped tightly in gauze. Dried blood had seeped through the fabric. Morris winced at the sight of it.

"I feel like shit if you want to know the truth of it," Len said, apparently in a foul mood. Based on the look on Ellie's face, they had had an argument about something, and recently. Tempers were still on a knife's edge. "*El Doctor* never gives me enough pain meds, and my beloved wife here refuses to support me on the matter."

"That's all I need," Ellie snapped back. "A goddamned junkie for a husband. He gives you plenty, Len. You're knocked right out when they give it to you. And besides, you're already constipated. What do you want to do? Never take a shit again?"

It seemed as if the fight would blow right back up. Morris said nothing, subduing his inclination to jump into the fray. It'd be like jumping into the middle of a catfight.

To his surprise, the argument ended as quickly as it had started. Ellie turned away and went to her radio equipment. Len lay back into his pillow. "Sorry, boss. Things have been a little... hot around here for the past few days. It's my fault. I'm in a foul mood."

"As to be expected," Morris said. "Don't worry about it. And I must apologize for refusing your request to be airlifted back to Kassa. Trust me: riding in one of those Dvoraks would not be ideal and, quite honestly, perhaps suicidal. And we cannot afford using the Dauntless or the Jupiter for one man. I'm sorry, my friend."

Len shrugged and winced in pain when he seemed to forget that his shoulder and half his torso were wrapped solid. "Oww! That's okay, Morris. It wasn't my idea anyway. It was Isaac's and Ellie's. But I told them no. I'm not on a deathbed here. I hurt, but I'm alive, and by God, I can be useful in the battle that's coming."

"Can you do radio work?"

Len nodded and forced a chuckle as he adjusted himself on his bed and closed his eyes. "As much as my beloved wife and doctor will allow."

His visit with Prince Rákóczi was short. The prince was still in a coma. They had never met in person, and so Morris thought it best to simply step in, pay his proper respects, and leave. Isaac and a young lady named Oana Dalca were attending the patient.

"He has good days and bad days, Morris," Isaac said. "Today is a particularly bad one."

"What are his chances?" Morris asked.

Isaac took care to look around the room, at the guards, the prince's attending aides who did nothing but simply stand there and stare at their declining prince. There were clergy in the room as well, including a Calvinist minister who introduced himself as Johann Heinrich Alsted. Morris couldn't immediately identify the religious affiliations of the other two.

Isaac did not speak. Instead, he simply widened his eyes, glanced upward, and moved his head in a small, unassuming shake.

"I understand," Morris said, his mood worsening. "We'll speak later. Perhaps pray as well."

He then visited von Mercy who, despite his disheveled appearance and swollen leg, was in relatively good shape.

"The Sunrise will conduct a force march for the capital at first light," Morris said. "Along with Higgins' Silesian Guard."

"Not Richter?"

Morris shook his head. "She's decided to remain in Kolozsvár. It's really the ideal place for her to work because it has a bigger, more diverse population than the capital here. She'll have her personal guard for protection, as well as additional security from the Transylvanian forces already there. She'll be fine."

"Very good, sir. I don't know when the Wallachians and Moldavians will move against us, but I'm certain it'll be soon. If I were them, I wouldn't hesitate." There was a pause, then: "So, what have you decided about Princess Lorántffy's offer to me?"

"I think you should accept it."

Von Mercy adjusted the blanket over his legs. "The Diet is going to explode when I do."

"We'll deal with that problem when we get to it," Morris said, shooting a quick glance down the bed. "But I think you're right, General. You're in no shape for fieldwork. You'll coordinate the battle from here in the capital, via radio and runners. That'll allow you to keep a better handle on the security matters in the streets. But you'll need to assign someone to field command. You can't be allowed on a horse."

Von Mercy winced, from the pain in his leg, most likely, and not from the reality that he wouldn't lead the Sunrise into battle. In all the time the ex-Imperial general had served him, Morris had never gotten the impression that von Mercy was overly arrogant or self-absorbed. He had an ego for sure, and it could be bruised, but he seemed capable of keeping it under control...most of the time, at least. The fact that he had offered in Krakow to step down as field commander and give the Sunrise to an Ashkenazi commander was admirable.

"Brigadier Higgins?" von Mercy offered.

Morris shrugged. "Without doubt, Jeff is a fine field commander. But as far as I know, he's never commanded anyone other than his own Hangmen. And now, of course, the entire Silesian Guard. I worry that, at the height of the battle, he'd focus more on them than looking at the overall strategic situation. Besides, I don't think he'd accept the command anyway. He strikes me as more of a tactician than a strategist, at least at this stage of his military career. He's still quite young—twenty-five or twenty-six, I forget which."

Von Mercy nodded and rubbed his messy, overgrown beard. It had fallen out of clean and well-kept Vandyke status and was now just a nest of black-and-gray stubble. "Then I'd say let it be Colonel Gerhardt Renz. He's proven to be a good, reliable commander, and I am confident he can coordinate and execute an effective battle plan."

Morris smiled. "Colonel Burkenfeld might take offense, being as he is commander of First Cavalry Regiment."

"The decision to promote cannot be based upon the number designation of a regiment," von Mercy said, his more commanding, authoritative voice taking hold. "Burkenfeld is a fine regimental commander, but Renz would be, in my estimation, a better leader over all. With your permission, General, I will appoint him upon the army's arrival. I will also appoint Major General Luthor Lange as head of security for the capital."

Morris nodded. "I've said it many times—and to the annoyance of all concerned, I'm sure—I'm not a combat commander, General von Mercy. I shift supplies back and forth. It's your decision to make." He smiled and placed his hand atop the general's. He squeezed it. "And I'm glad to see you so well, sir. We can't do this without you."

Isaac was awakened from a short nap by Oana. "Come," she said such that Isaac thought her voice a dream, "it's Prince Rákóczi."

Isaac rubbed his tired eyes clear and got up, grabbed his stethoscope, and followed her into the hallway.

His steps were heavy. His head ached. A thousand issues clouded his mind. Since he had arrived in the capital, he had gotten, perhaps, four hours of sleep each day. He felt like collapsing, but Oana held his arm and guided him into the prince's room.

The guards were still there, though they lacked their rigid, statue-like visages. They leaned forward from their corners, their eyes fixed on the prince's limp, motionless body, like Princess Lorántffy, who sat at his side, gripping his left hand tightly. George II, his oldest son, was there, standing beside his mother, looking down at his father's cold, white face.

Gáspár stepped aside to give Isaac ample room and light. The oil lamp on the nightstand cast shadows across the bed. Isaac placed his fingers on the prince's throat. He pressed harder.

He then placed the stethoscope's earpieces into his ears and pressed the chest piece into the prince's chest. He moved it to another spot and another, and another.

He stood straight, removed the earpieces, and sighed. "I'm sorry, my lady, but he's gone."

Chapter 47

Hermannstadt (Sibiu)

"I am no general," Matei Basarab said, more animated than Usan Hussein had seen him in a long time, "but Lupu's request that we meet in Medwesch seems foolish to me."

Usan leaned over the map to study the route that the voivode of Moldavia had recommended—nay, demanded—that the Wallachian army take to link arms with his forces. Around him crowded most of the commanding officers of Matei's army, including Captain Andrej Dordevic, a Serbian mercenary commander who seemed most agitated.

"It is a preposterous route!" Dordevic barked, his accent heavy in Usan's ears. "We should march to Meinbach instead. The terrain is less obstructive and more manageable than working ourselves through those mountainous gaps to Medwesch. From Meinbach, we are only ten miles, at most, from the capital."

"My lord," Stroe Leurdeanu said, leaning over the map as well, but keeping his eyes fixed on his voivode, "I will remind you that you did promise Voivode Lupu to link arms with his army before moving against the capital."

"As he made promises to me that he did not keep!"

"Yes, my lord, you are correct. But"—Stroe traced his hand across the route proposed by Lupu—"a move to Medwesch is not much farther than a direct march to Meinbach, if this map is correctly scaled. An extra day, perhaps, at the most."

"Only an extra day," Dordevic said, "if the weather behaves, if there are no hazards to face through the gaps." He looked at Usan. "If the *Ifrit* fire tanks can make the journey at all."

Yes, of course, Usan sneered to himself, *place the burden of the decision on me.*

In truth, both plans had merit. A march directly through the Carpathians, albeit dangerous, would bring the armies together. Doing so would allow them to march down the Große Kokel River Valley, reach and cross the Maros River, and then attack the capital in force from the north. This would have the added benefit of cutting the Sunrise's supply lines from Kolozsvár.

The downside of the idea was that the Wallachians would be cut off from their supply lines altogether. The thought of that did not sit well with Usan, whose Janissaries had fought Saxon insurgents here in Hermannstadt to secure those lines. Many of his men had died for that cause. The Sultan's men—Janissaries that he would not be able to replace before the battle to come.

"A move to Medwesch," Matei said, "would actually be a march *away* from the capital, not a large distance, indeed, but a distance nonetheless. Then, we would have to march back *toward* the capital. Another thirty miles or so of rigorous marching through yet another river valley just to reach the battlefield. Another *long* delay."

That, too, was a sound point. Yet, it all depended upon whether the voivode of Wallachia was bold enough to attack the capital upon their arrival in Meinbach. Did Matei Basarab possess the courage to take on the up-time army by himself? Or, once reaching Meinbach, would he sit there and wait for the Moldavians to make their long, arduous journey through the Carpathians to their attack position above the capital?

Usan nodded. *Attacking from two separate directions has its positives as well.*

Everyone was looking at him, waiting.

"I'm forced to agree with my Serbian colleague," he said, pointing to a smudge on the map that represented Meinbach. "A march to Meinbach is a much better plan. Marching to Medwesch could place a heavy burden upon the *Ifrits*, and their crews *must* be fresh when we meet the enemy. We must match up-time weapons with up-time weapons wherever possible. Moving to Meinbach will also keep our supply line in stable condition." He looked at Matei and nodded. "I say we head to Meinbach, and soon."

"And I say we stick to the original plan and march to Med-wesch," Stroe said, reinforcing his opinion with a firm tap of the table with his fist. "We move together in one massive force to meet the enemy north of the capital. We strike them in one location, with everything we have. Our chance of a breakthrough and capture of the capital is far greater under those circumstances."

Now the burden fell to Matei Basarab, who looked at the map with eyes that, if able, would ignite the paper and burn it to ash. A nonmilitary man having to make such a critical operational decision. A decision that was, to Usan's mind at least, close to an even choice.

The voivode of Wallachia moved away from the map. He stared out the flap of his tent, letting the cool Carpathian breeze upset the tassels of his coat. He stared into the darkness for a long while as his lieutenants grew restless.

"Very well," he said with less force than Usan would have liked to hear, "we march to Meinbach."

Medwesch (Mediaş)

Day by day, Moshe Mizrahi found it exceedingly difficult to deal with the buffoon. The voivode of Moldavia's perpetual outrage was becoming tedious and, in truth, exhausting.

"Disgraceful," Vasile Lupu said as he balled up the message sent from Stroe Leurdeanu and tossed it to the ground. "The fool marches to Meinbach! Meinbach! Why would they do something so foolish?"

Moshe was about to offer an explanation when General Radu saved him. "Meinbach is just a few miles from Gyulafehérvár. They must have thought that by moving there instead of through the Carpathians, that they—"

"I know what they thought, General Radu," Vasile said, nearly spitting, "I just read the message. But now our armies will be split as we move to the capital. A foolish, foolish decision."

"There can be advantage in attacking from two different fronts, my Voivode," Radu continued, trying his best to soothe Vasile Lupu's angry feelings. "Doing so will require our enemy to divide his forces as well."

"Wonderful," Vasile said, throwing his arms up. "Now we can be destroyed piecemeal!"

"Or the enemy's army can be thus destroyed," Radu said.

"Be silent!" Vasile leered at Radu, his jaw muscles pumping hard. "Let me think!"

The voivode's lieutenants were assembled in an impromptu circle in the middle of the field wherein the *Chaldiran* waited to be boarded. Why Vasile had asked Moshe to be in attendance was anyone's guess. Then again, it was important for him and Mordechai to know the current operational planning of the army, so that they could provide the most practical, reliable service... whatever that service might be. Up to now, that service had been confined to nothing more than giving Vasile Lupu pleasure rides through the various river valleys down which the Moldavian army traveled. Except, of course, for the assassination attempt against Prince Rákóczi. That trip, according to the most recent intelligence, had proved quite successful.

"Where is Sergiu?" Vasile asked. "Get me Sergiu Botnari!"

"My lord," General Radu said, perplexed, "he is gone. He has rejoined the Impalers in the field, as planned."

"Plans, plans, plans! Everyone has a plan, and they are all incompatible with my own! No. I need him here, with me. General Radu, after we are done, you will send men to find him and bring him to me. He serves at my pleasure, not his own."

General Radu nodded. "Yes, My Voivode."

Moshe looked toward the *Chaldiran*, saw Mordechai's tiny head peeking over the ship's gondola. He fought the urge to simply walk away. General Radu and all the other Moldavian commanders, including three mercenary officers, looked just as uncomfortable as he in the midst of Lupu's temper tantrum.

Finally, a Tatar captain named Alim Ibragimov, spoke. "I am comfortable with the Wallachian voivode's decision. Like General Radu suggests, I will enjoy harassing the Jew's supply lines to Kolozsvár. As it is now, your army is well-manned, well-commanded, and in good balance. Adding another full army to your ranks... well, I'd have to contend with squabbling Serbians and those infernal Ottoman fire tanks that, I hear, can scare horses unfamiliar with their sounds. Let the Wallachians attack from the south. We will handle the Jew's army in the north."

"Yes, yes," Vasile said, turning back to his commanders, "but how do we coordinate the effort? We cannot hope to win if we attack individually. We *must* attack together."

"I agree," General Radu said quickly, trying to recover from his earlier upsetting comments. "We need to attack as one force. How do we accomplish that?"

"We do it the way we have always done it," Ibragimov said, "the way armies have communicated for centuries. By runner, by horse messenger."

Vasile shook his head. "Against an army with up-time radios? An army that can communicate with its commanders in the field in the blink of an eye? We'll be one, two steps behind every time." He threw his arms up again. "I should execute Sergiu Botnari for tossing that radio in the river."

One, two captured radios would not have made much of a dif-ference. Moshe wanted to say that out loud, but he knew that it could lead to his own punishment. Vasile and, in fact, everyone in attendance did not understand how radios worked and could not understand their usage even if they had them, in the short time before the coming battle.

"My Voivode," Moshe said instead, "the *Chaldiran* can help in this endeavor. As I have studied the maps of the fields around the capital, the distance between our armies will be no more than, perhaps, fifteen to eighteen miles. That distance will shrink, of course, as our respective columns move into the battlefield. But the *Chaldiran* can conduct reconnaissance missions during the battle and convey any messages deemed necessary to the Wallachians."

Ibragimov scowled. "One of my riders can move faster than your airship can fly."

"On the tactical level, I agree," Moshe said, nodding, "but a courier on horseback can be intercepted by enemy forces, or get lost, or his horse come up lame. The *Chaldiran* will suffer none of those maladies."

"Until you set down, or get shot down," Ibragimov said, his tone becoming agitated by the fact that a kafir was challenging his statements. "Then you are as vulnerable, and perhaps more so, than a man on horseback who can flee quicker and who is a much smaller target."

"We can remain aloft and convey the messages with signal flags."

"Who in their ranks knows your signals?" General Radu asked.

Moshe considered. "Usan Hussein, sir. The *corbaci* of their Janissaries."

"And what about their aircraft?" Vasile asked. "General Radu says that they are unarmed, but they do have two seats. Am I correct?" He looked to General Radu, who nodded. "They could place musketmen in those seats, and we would then be vulnerable."

"Not really, sir. An airship makes a good platform for a rifleman because we are moving slowly and he can fire straight ahead while we maintain a steady course on his target. An airplane is moving much faster and a rifleman can only shoot to the side. His chances of hitting anything are miniscule."

"They shot down several of the Sultan's airships at Linz, didn't they?"

"Yes, but their plane was specifically designed for that purpose. They weren't using a marksman firing a rifle; they had what they call a machine gun mounted in the nose of the plane so they could fire straight ahead—and they were using incendiary rounds, which we don't have."

The voivode's mulish expression made clear he was unconvinced, so Moshe hurried on. "And as you have stated in the past, you desire that the *Chaldiran* be used as an offensive weapon. Placing a couple of additional musketmen in the gondola, plus our Janissary guard, plus your own personal weapons, we can easily defend ourselves against any attack that they might attempt from the air. We can move back and forth over the battle line and perform attacks as you desire . . . and deliver important messages to the Wallachians at the same time."

Moshe waited as everyone considered his plan. The Tatar commander glared at him, as did others. It was clear to Moshe that they were not comfortable being lectured to by a mere kafir. But he wasn't lecturing them; he was giving them the right course of action. Couldn't they put aside their bigotry just for a moment to see the wisdom of his plan?

Vasile moved into the middle of the circle and nodded. "Moshe," he said, "return to the *Chaldiran* and prepare for launch. I will be with you shortly, and we will discuss this matter further."

Moshe nodded. He paid the proper respect and deference by nodding to each commander in turn, then walked away.

As he approached the *Chaldiran*, Mordechai dropped the rope ladder. Moshe grabbed it, secured himself on the first rung, and climbed slowly.

The Janissary guard helped him into the gondola. "What was that talk about?" Mordechai asked. "Lupu seemed angry."

Moshe was about to provide details, then reconsidered. He looked at the Janissary guard and then at the crew member checking the engine. Finally, he looked at Mordechai, flashed a smile, and asked, "My friend, do you ever wonder if perhaps we're fighting for the wrong side?"

Mordechai seemed shocked at the question. "To be honest, my friend, yes I do. Every day. Then I ask myself, 'What have Christians ever given us that Sultan Murad has not?' The Ottomans have been kinder to us, Moshe, than any Christian nation that I can recall."

Moshe nodded. "But this Grand Army of the Sunrise is not commanded by a Christian, Mordechai. Its commander is a Jew."

"A Jew who is, in effect, under the command of a Bohemian king. A Christian king. Remember our families, Moshe," Mordechai said, now seemingly annoyed by the conversation. He furrowed his brow and wagged his finger in clear warning. "Remember: we do this for them. We serve the Sultan for them."

As if we have a choice. "Of course," Moshe said, now feeling silly and a little embarrassed about even bringing the matter up. And yet, he could not shake the question from his mind.

Mordechai went about his business. Moshe walked to the larboard side of the gondola and watched as Vasile ended the meeting abruptly and then turned toward the *Chaldiran.*

We are fighting for the wrong side.

Chapter 48

Sunrise Airfield
Gyulafehérvár

Isaac waited patiently for the infantry columns of the Joshua Corps' Second and Third Regiments to pass, followed closely by cavalry, then more infantry, the Brethren's massive armored wagons and steam locomotives, and then, finally, the medical wagons and baggage train. He smiled, waved, and saluted along with everyone else, civilians and soldiers alike. To him, it felt like a military parade, with line after line of soldiers marching along the edge of the airfield and onward toward the capital and their designated encampments. It was good to see the whole army, the whole of the Sunrise, back together again.

"Doctor Isaac Kohen!"

His stomach churned as Karl Oberheuser's voice rang out over the belching steam of the locomotives. Isaac sighed. He'd been dreading this moment for months.

"I will speak with you now!"

The old, contrary doctor had at least the decency to take Isaac into a tent and chew him out in private. The number of foul words, hot air, and phlegm spewing from Oberheuser's mouth was more than Isaac had experienced in a long time, even in his sickest patients. Isaac let the old man spew as he worked hard to contain his mirth.

"Now...*is that clear?*"

Isaac nodded, "Yes, sir. My apologies. I'll never steal one of your nurses away again."

Steal, of course, was a ridiculous term to apply to Devorah. She had been, as they say, chomping at the bit to leave Kassa under a mound of canvas. A more appropriate term would be "liberate."

Doctor Oberheuser nodded, stepped back, and cleared his throat. "Good. And let that be a lesson to you. Now, you will give me a full assessment of the current medical situation, and you will then take me immediately to see Herr Tanner and General von Mercy."

Christian caught a glimpse of Isaac's white medical coat, hanging stethoscope, and yarmulke across the military procession. He was about to wave and shout his friend's name when old, cranky Oberheuser interrupted with a bellow of his own. Instead, he pulled back and stood quietly next to Lieutenant Enkefort while saluting as each company commander of First Cavalry Regiment passed by. Third Cavalry Regiment was somewhere near the rear, protecting the baggage train. Christian craned his neck to get a glimpse, hoping that he'd be able to pluck some of those men away to fill gaps in his own company. But the Brethren's armored field train blocked his view.

How impressive they were. Christian and Second Cavalry Regiment had pulled out of Kassa as part of von Mercy's vanguard before these up-time-inspired armored wagons had arrived. He'd never seen anything like them before. Sure, he was aware—at least moderately so—of the history of the Hussites and their well-fortified war wagons. But they had been mostly comprised of regular wooden wagons serving as mobile palisades. They were nothing like what was passing by him right now, pulled by steam locomotives, and in the shadow of their massive, armor-plated walls, he felt well-protected.

"I wish we had had some of those at Déj, eh?" Lieutenant Enkefort asked with a wink, elbowing his commander.

Christian nodded, but kept silent as the last armored locomotive and its two attached APCs passed. He looked again across the procession, but Isaac was gone.

The baggage train now rolled by. Christian tugged on Lieutenant

Enkefort's shoulder. "Come, let us get to camp and have a chat with the men."

"Yes, sir." Lieutenant Enkefort followed. "There's a rumor that General von Mercy will give field command to Colonel Renz."

"Yes, I've heard that."

"Who do you think he'll promote to regimental commander?"

Christian shrugged. "Callenberk, most likely."

"Kinsky will beg for it."

"Yes, but he's not qualified." Christian looked around to ensure the Wild Elite commander wasn't nearby. "He's a fine company commander. He's a friend, and I respect his courage. But, given his disposition, he'd likely lead us all into ruin."

Lieutenant Enkefort paused, then: "He could give you the command."

Christian huffed and shook his head. "Thank you for your faith in my abilities, Lieutenant, but like Kinsky, I'm unqualified. And I wouldn't accept if it were offered."

Chapter 49

In the skies above Gyulafehérvár

"*Dixie Chick,*" Tuva said over the radio, "this is... *Smooth Operator.* Come in, *Dixie Chick.*"

Tuva hesitated while repeating the name of her Dvorak. It was the name Denise had suggested, and she had accepted with a raised brow. It wasn't a bad name; in fact, it fit quite well. Many in her circle of friends and colleagues had commented upon how calm and collected Tuva was under stressful circumstances, just like Minnie. Eddie had even commented on her smooth demeanor more than once. So, Denise had sung several bars of the up-time song to her. Tuva didn't understand a lot of the context of the lyrics. There were references to places in the world the singer made that Tuva didn't know anything about. But the song had a positive message, and in a time of war, perhaps that's what mattered the most.

"*Dixie Chick* here," Denise's voice crackled over the radio. "Flying about five, six miles south toward, according to the map, a little spot called Meinbach. No sign of the enemy so far."

"All clear here as well," Tuva said. "Moving through some pretty heavy cloud cover right now. Will drop lower to get a better look at the ground."

"How far out are you?" Denise asked.

Tuva checked her gauges, her timer. "I estimate about ten miles, give or take."

"You be careful. This is your first real recon mission. Keep a clear eye, okay?"

"Roger that."

Well, it wasn't her first mission, per se, but the first that really mattered. Denise had taken the point on most of the Sunrise's scouting missions as the army had moved down the Transylvanian plateau toward Kolozsvár. Tuva had served as Denise's second in that regard, providing any support she could, radio signal boost, passenger transport (like delivering Ellie Anderson and Morris Roth to the capital), among other tasks. Those were important duties, but this was her first real solo scouting mission. It was important that she impress.

The massive gondola of an Ottoman airship exploded out of the low, gray clouds directly in her flight path. Tuva screamed at its sudden appearance and dove.

"Tuva, what's wrong? Respond!"

The sudden descent pressed her body against the chair, and for a moment, she lost control. She had no idea if this plane could handle a barrel roll nor was she going to find out right now. The nose of the *Smooth Operator* was pointed toward the ground. Tuva let the plane drop, drop, and then pulled up hard until her landing gear almost scraped treetops. Denise kept yelling in her ear.

"Dammit, Tuva...talk to me!"

"Can't right now," she said, accelerating until the Dvorak acquired some lift and began ascending. Her heart pounded in her chest; her stomach churned. She calmed her breathing. "Ottoman airship...we damn near collided. Circling around to take another look."

"Radio it in!" Denise shouted. "And get the hell out of there!"

She would do both, but not yet. She was back in control of the *Smooth Operator* and circling left under the airship. "Roger that."

My, but it was big! She knew little about them. The USE had them as well, but she had never flown in one nor, by her recollection, had she even been near one. It was beautiful and terrifying at the same time. The men in the gondola were pointing muskets at her.

She dipped again as the sound of rifled musket fire followed her dive. How much elevation-change pressure could her flimsy canvassed wings take? No bullets had come near her, and she knew those firing the guns would have to pause to reload. That gave her at least a few more seconds to fly up and take a better look at this ballooned monster.

Such a marvelous craft—but slow. It certainly couldn't match the Dvorak's speed and maneuverability. But it would be difficult to attack from the ground, and without offensive weaponry, the Dvoraks couldn't hope to bring it down either.

She dropped again, and this time, at her own pace and speed. Tuva heard the muskets fire again, but she didn't care. She was now too far away and moving too fast for it to be of any concern. She banked right and circled toward the capital.

"Woo-hoo!" Tuva shouted in the radio. "What a beautiful craft...without the musket fire, of course."

"Get your butt back to base, girl," Denise said, though Tuva could hear that her friend's anxiety was gone, "or I'll tell my boyfriend on you."

"Eddie won't care. He's already betrothed to a wild child." Tuva giggled.

"Don't bet on it." There was a pause, then: "If that airship is up and running this close to the capital, then you know what that means."

Tuva nodded, feeling silly doing so. "The Moldavians are here."

Where are the Wallachians? Denise wondered as she flew at a thousand feet, high and above the dense fog floating through the Maros River Valley. She checked her fuel gauge. Half a tank. She grunted. "Where's a service station when you need one?"

"What was that?"

Tuva's voice surprised her, though it shouldn't have. They were still connected. But Tuva's escape from the Ottoman airship had given Denise such relief that she had quite forgotten. "Sorry, *Smooth Operator.* An up-time joke."

Tuva chuckled. "You up-timers make too many jokes."

Perhaps that was true, Denise thought as she dropped a little lower, fighting against a headwind. *But look at it from our perspective. Pulled out of our time and dropped hundreds of years into the past? We crack wise just to stay sane.*

Living in the seventeenth century wasn't so bad, Denise had to admit. If the Ring of Fire hadn't happened, she would have never met Eddie, or Minnie, or Tuva, or Christian, or Enkefort, or any of her other good down-time friends. Hell, she'd probably be sitting at a desk somewhere in a boring job, or serving as some man's bored housewife, taking tequila shots in the afternoon just to drive away the blues. Nope. Life in 1637 was a bitch, a lot of the time, but at least it wasn't boring.

The horizon opened to her, and there it was, the town of Meinbach. And there, too, the Wallachian army, making its way through its narrow streets.

"*Smooth Operator*," she said, her excitement up, her heart racing, "tell the boss that we got an army sighting. And it's a big 'un!"

Part Seven

September 1637

Strong oath and iron intent come crashing down
—Sophocles, *Ajax*

Chapter 50

Nurses' tent
Grand Army of the Sunrise

"Andreea is the wife of Col—*General* Marius Hatmanu, Christian," said Devorah. "He's a courtier of the prince, and one of the highest-ranking officers among the Székelys."

"The prince is dead."

Devorah shook her head. "Be that as it may, Hatmanu is still a very important man in the Transylvanian Diet."

"That doesn't give him a right to demean his wife."

Devorah shook her head. "No, it doesn't. But this is not Grantville, Christian, nor the USE. In this part of the world the"—she searched for the right word—"*sensibilities* of the up-timers have not taken root. Not yet, anyway. To interfere in a domestic dispute between a man and his wife, especially a man of Hatmanu's station, could have serious repercussions."

"I know, I know," Christian said, throwing up his hands, waving her off, exasperated by the whole mess. "I just—I just can't let him verbally abuse her like that."

"Andreea claims that he has never struck her."

He turned to Devorah, an inquisitive look on his face. "She has spoken to you about this matter?"

She nodded. "Of course. I'm a woman, Christian, and one who has seen her fair share of abuse. My late husband was a

kind man. I thanked God every day for that. But my father...
well, let me just say that I understand what she is going through."

"He belittled and humiliated her," Christian said, blowing
out a long breath of air. "Right in front of everyone, including
the prince and princess. I'm sure they heard what he said. And I
just stood there, Devorah, and did nothing. Well, it won't happen
again. I won't allow him to harm her."

"Then what are you going to do?"

There was a pause as Christian moved away from Devorah
and found a quiet corner of the tent to stand and reflect upon
her question. There wasn't much to reflect on, in truth. He didn't
have an answer for her. Andreea was not his woman, his wife.
What could he really do to protect her, save to eventually draw
his sword and run her husband through? Devorah was right: doing
so would be foolish and could lead to his own death. *I may be
many things*, Christian thought as he heard Devorah rise from
her chair and walk to him across the tent, *but I'm no murderer.
Yet, I* must *do something.*

"Christian."

Devorah took his arm and turned him so that they were
facing each other. She took his face in her hands and smiled.
"You are a wonderful man, a wonderful person. And Isaac says
that you're a good soldier, though I pray to God every day that
you, in time, turn away from that occupation and find a good
woman like Andreea, make babies, and live a peaceful life. Until
that day, I hope you will tread lightly. Be careful. I do not know
the rules in this country, Christian, but I suppose they are like
everywhere else: take care when coming between a man and his
wife. Whatever you decide to do, my good friend, I hope you
will think twice before you commit. Promise me that."

He cupped her hands with his own, squeezed them, and took
them off his face. He smiled. "I promise, Devorah. I promise."

Andreea Hatmanu entered the tent. Christian backed away
from Devorah as if he were embarrassed by his closeness to her.
Devorah turned and acknowledged the girl with a faint smile and
a nod. She then turned back to Christian and whispered, "Good
luck, Captain. I wish you well."

Andreea curtsied as Devorah left the tent. Christian did not
know what to say, but he couldn't take his eyes off of her. She
was in a perfectly kept dress of green and red with a white head

scarf. Not a commoner's dress, but not overly opulent either. In a way, it reminded him of Princess Zsuzsanna's clothing, though not quite as humble or religious. Andreea's hair flowed down out of the scarf and across her shoulders. Christian forced conversation to keep from blushing.

"Will you assist Devorah and the other nurses again?" he asked.

Andreea nodded and stepped closer. "Yes. My husband will allow it."

Christian gnashed his jaw muscles, trying not to let his anger show. "That's very *graceful* of him."

"Yes. Marius loves his country... if nothing else."

"You still shouldn't have to endure such a... such a..."

"Such a man?"

To his surprise, she laughed. A short, sweet little laugh that warmed his heart, calmed him. "My father arranged the marriage, of course, and like many young girls, I was so honored. Marius was such a handsome, dashing fellow, and a confidant of the prince. How could I refuse? I couldn't refuse, of course, and at the time, I didn't want to." Her expression turned sour. "But, I didn't really know my husband then, how driven he was, how determined he still is to work his way into the Transylvanian court, to work himself into power. I think he honestly believes he can become prince of Transylvania someday. He will not let anyone... anyone... stand in his way of that goal. Including me."

She swallowed, cleared her throat, perhaps fighting back tears. "But I didn't come here to pour my troubles out to you, Christian. I came here to thank you."

"Thank me?"

"For not doing something so foolish as to confront my husband in such a place. I am glad you stayed your hand, said nothing."

"I wanted to," he said, "as God is my witness, I—"

Andreea chuckled, moved closer, reached for his neck, and pulled him close.

Through his shock, Christian tried meeting her lips with his, but instead, she turned his head with her thumb and kissed him on the cheek. His rough warrior's cheek, scarred by battle and uneven stubble. Oh, how he so wanted to turn his face just a little so that their lips could touch. Instead, he held firm and breathed in her scent. Perfume and sweat. The smell of her hair, the light fabric of her head scarf. Perfect... all of it.

She pulled away. She smiled again, reached up, and patted his cheek. "Perhaps in a different world, a different time, we might have met, and our lives might have been different. But God has set us on different paths, Christian von Jori, and so we must follow them."

Andreea stepped aside to allow him to depart. "Now go, Captain. Go to your men and fight your battle. I pray for your safety, and I hope you will come back to me, so that we may speak again."

He didn't want to leave. He wanted to stay in that tent forever, to be with her, to do what Devorah said: make babies and live a peaceful life forever in Andreea's arms, in her care. He was ready to throw off his uniform and put on scrubs and be a nurse right alongside her. That would make Isaac very happy. But no. She was right. He was a soldier, a captain. It was time to go and fight.

He said nothing as he stepped to the tent flap. Before he left, he turned, and said, "You are wrong, Andreea. We do live in a different world, a different time. I was raised a Calvinist, to believe in predestination. I no longer believe in such things. We live now in a world with a Ring of Fire. And in that world, my sweet lady, anything is possible."

Chapter 51

Headquarters
Grand Army of the Sunrise

General von Mercy's tiny room had been converted into a temporary HQ until a more permanent one could be constructed. Now, between his bed and the door was nothing but a steady stream of staff moving in and out with this request, that request, every kind of request one could imagine, and much of it having to do with supply, mercenary payment, and capital security. These matters were tangentially related to the impending battle, of course, but not directly. What he wanted was peace and quiet to consider the battle at hand, but from his bed or wheelchair—depending on the day—he greeted everyone with as much patience as his aching leg would allow.

General Renz burst into the room, followed by his aide-de-camp. They waited until Major General Luthor Lange, who had grudgingly accepted security of the streets of the capital, finished his business with von Mercy. When he was out the door, General Renz stepped up.

"Busy morning, eh, General?"

Von Mercy groaned, rolled his eyes. He pointed to the door. "The Impalers have been giving Lange hell. He lost two police last night from gunshot wounds. The night before, one was strung up by the neck. Perpetrators have been apprehended, but it's getting ugly out there."

General Renz nodded. "This is what happens when your prince has been murdered without a clear successor."

"There is a clear successor," von Mercy said. "His son, George Junior. But half the Diet believes he's too young to take charge in a time of war. The other half doesn't know *what* to do. Some of them want to see the late prince's brother Pál as prince; others want his brother Zsigmond to return from Hungary and take command." He rubbed his face. "It's a mess."

"Well, success on the battlefield can solve a lot of problems for these poor people. Allay a lot of their fears."

"Indeed." Von Mercy nodded. "That's why I've called you here, General. It's time to plan the battle. General Roth and Brigadier Higgins will arrive directly. We want to discuss what Morris calls 'the big picture' before we have a larger, more detailed, discussion with our regimental commanders about troop deployment and timetables."

So, they waited, and waited, and waited. Finally, Morris and Jeff arrived, alone, with Ellie following them in while bringing Morris up to speed on Len's progress. "He's ornery, complainy," she said, "but surviving." She looked at von Mercy. "He wants to get out of the room, General. Can I borrow your wheelchair and give him the dime tour of the college?"

Von Mercy nodded. "Of course. It's not the best chair in the world, Frau Ellie, but it'll do. Watch the right wheel. It's got a constant wobble. And take a guard or two with you. The building is pretty secure, but you never know."

Ellie grabbed the chair and wheeled it out. General Renz shut the door behind her, and they got to work.

"What's the status of General Hatmanu's delaying action against the Moldavians?" Morris asked.

Von Mercy shook his head. "No word yet. The Székelys aren't using the radio we gave them."

"Why not?" Morris asked. "Hatmanu was the one who requested it."

Von Mercy nodded. "I know, but they aren't responding. Ellie has tried all morning to rouse them, and no word. I've sent runners. We should know something soon, God willing."

"Why not send in one of the Dvoraks?" General Renz asked.

Morris shook his head. "That's why we gave him the radio, so we wouldn't have to constantly put them up and expend fuel.

Now that the Jupiter and Dauntless can fly in at any time, fuel issues have been lessened, but still: we're going to need Denise and Tuva in the air round the clock when the battle starts. Hatmanu just needs to use his damned radio, and problem solved."

Morris and Jeff took seats. Everyone was now huddled up close to the bed. Von Mercy felt a little self-conscious of their closeness. He was dressed; he made sure that his aides helped him in that regard before the meeting. But he didn't like lying in bed with everyone around him. It felt like they were waiting for his passing, like Prince Rákóczi on his last night. Well, he wasn't going to die; not today, anyway. He couldn't take to the field, but by God, he was still in overall charge of the Sunrise. Lying in front of them, propped up with several pillows, he felt weak. He now regretted allowing Ellie to seize his wheelchair.

Morris drew a map from his satchel and laid it out over von Mercy's covered legs. "Forgive me, General. You don't mind if we use you as a desk, do you?"

Von Mercy rolled his eyes and adjusted his legs to steady the map. "Oh, no, not at all. Be my guest... General."

Jeff Higgins chuckled. "Here's our battlefield, gentlemen. Roughly, a five-, six-mile stretch of hills, woods, and farmland in front of the Maros River."

"That's if we take an offensive posture," General Renz said, "and prepare to attack. There are still officers in the army, sir—Colonels Shalit and Makovec, specifically—that will continue to howl for a defensive posture. They want to set up a ring of defense around the capital and let the enemy come to us."

Morris shot a quick, wary glance at Brigadier Higgins, who chimed in with a shake of his head. "No, Morris and I have already discussed this. My Silesian Guard are not suited for a siege. We function best on a field of battle. My Hangman Regiment, specifically, are shock troopers. One of the most elite forces in the world. And that isn't hyperbole, gentlemen. They're damned good. Sitting in a siege is a waste of their talents, and quite frankly, I don't know just how long I can keep them in the field before Tata or Thorsten start screaming from Silesia to get them back."

"There's also a larger political issue to consider," Morris said. "The USE is under siege at Linz. I don't think we want to give Sultan Murad another 'siege' on which he can declare victory. Fighting two up-time armies to, in effect, a stalemate, is the kind of message he wants to give the world. The kind of message that says, 'See here, these sons of bitches aren't that tough; they can be stopped.' And it may well embolden other countries to try their hand at chipping away at what we've accomplished.

"Plus, as you've noted, General von Mercy, the Sunrise is primarily a mercenary army. And I'm not made of money, contrary to popular myth. My coffers will dry up under a long siege, I'll become a pauper, and Murad will just keep pouring more and more men into the theater until we can no longer hold them. No, we must meet them in the field and defeat them now."

"Then we have to cross the Maros," General Renz said, "and take control of the field before they arrive."

Brigadier Higgins shrugged. "Well, maybe, maybe not. Morris and I have some thoughts on that."

In turn, Jeff and Morris laid out their ideas one at a time. Von Mercy was grateful for General Renz's presence, for he wasn't shy about holding up his hand and playing devil's advocate to shoot down any ideas that seemed far-fetched or downright dangerous. There weren't many, von Mercy had to admit. General Roth wasn't much of a strategist when it came to war—and he'd be the first to admit it—but Jeff Higgins seemed to have a keen mind when it came to planning. There was, however, a kink in their plan.

Von Mercy raised his hand. "Brigadier, you are assuming that the enemy has decided to conduct a two-pronged attack: the Moldavians from the north, the Wallachians from the south. It's a fair notion, since we know from aerial reconnaissance that the Moldavians are now pushing to the Maros above the capital and the Wallachians are in Meinbach to the south." He raised off his pillows and pointed to the center of the proposed battlefield. "But you are leaving the center almost entirely empty, save for a few Szekler infantry companies and some Hajdu mercenaries."

Morris nodded. "Yes, we are. You've stated yourself that the Maros is difficult to cross there. One bridge and only a couple narrow fords, so we defend those to ensure any attempt to cross the river is difficult at best. Everyone else, we send north and south."

"Based on intelligence," General Renz said, "both the Moldavian and Wallachian armies have grown in their march to the capital. Not all, but some Transylvanian troops, even some Saxons, have joined their ranks, fearing more the reprisals of the

Ottomans than our Grand Army of the Sunrise. Both armies will, in time, regardless of our deployments, push across the Maros. Once they do that, there's nothing that will prevent them from pushing into our weak interior lines, linking arms, and marching into the capital as one force."

Morris smiled, winked at General Renz, and said, "That's where the Silesian Guard and the Zizka Brigade come in."

"Yes," Jeff said, "we're going to hold my men and the Brethren in reserve and then deploy them like Napoleon used to do his Old Guard."

"Napoleon, sir?" General Renz said.

Jeff nodded. "An up-time French general. One of the greatest in the history of the world."

"A Frenchman?"

Von Mercy was as surprised as General Renz, but he said nothing, and instead, allowed Jeff Higgins to explain who Napoleon was and how he deployed his so-called Old Guard, his finest soldiers, in a battle.

"So you see," Jeff said, continuing, "if the Wallachians break through in the south, I move my men and volley guns there in force. If the north suffers a breakthrough, the same. If both fronts begin to waver, I go south, the Zizka Brigade and its APCs go north, or vice versa. We'll be fresh and ready to go.

"And remember, we have aerial reconnaissance that can be in the sky pretty much all day if necessary. We'll be able to keep a good eye on their movements and be ready to act immediately."

"Don't forget, General," von Mercy said, adjusting his sore leg to relieve the pressure. The map slid a little to the left. "The enemy has its own aerial asset. It'll be up in the sky as well, assuming the weather behaves."

"Yes, I know," Morris said rather curtly, "and no plan ever survives first contact with the enemy. I know the adage, General von Mercy. But it *is* a plan, and I believe it's a good one. So, overall, what do you think of it?"

No plan ever survives first contact ... Von Mercy wasn't sure if he had ever heard that one, but it was quite appropriate. Morris' and Jeff's plan would not survive either. Von Mercy had already fought a battle in Transylvania, and although it had gone well, it could have gone *very* badly. The Transylvanian terrain, its cool, foggy weather, and with winter coming on, who knew what natural impediments they might face on the morning of the fight? Radio contact might be spotty; rain and wind might ground the Dvoraks; the APCs might get mired in mud. A million things could, and would, go wrong on the day of the battle. But, General Roth was correct. It was a plan, and honestly, a pretty good one given their current situation.

"Okay, General," he said, "I accept it. General Renz?"

The newly appointed field commander of the Sunrise scratched his hairy chin, cleared his throat, and said, "It's a good plan. But for it to work, we really must make a strong show of force both north and south. And soon. If we commit in a strong way, the enemy will be forced to do the same, and maybe we can stack them up before all their columns clear the river. That will buy us time, and if we're lucky, they may not be able to cross at all."

Morris nodded. "Then let's gather all the regimental commanders together tonight and talk deployments and timetables. Eight o'clock."

"We cannot meet in here, General," von Mercy said. "Not enough room."

"We'll move the meeting to the library," Morris said, "but this has to be a secure conversation."

General Renz nodded. "I'll ask Major General Lange to post guards inside and out—"

The door opened, and in walked a young cavalryman, out of breath, covered in splatters of mud and smelling of horse. His hard boots and stirrups clicked as he walked toward the bed. "General von Mercy, sir." He bowed and held out a scrap of paper. "A message for you, sir."

"Read it, General," von Mercy said.

General Renz took the message and unrolled it. He read it once to himself, and von Mercy could see the man's rather upbeat demeanor turn sour.

"What does it say, General?"

Renz rolled the message up and handed it to von Mercy. "It looks like our plan is already beginning to unravel."

Chapter 52

General Hatmanu's headquarters
North of Gyulafehérvár

Three regiments of Székely trabants had pushed across the Küküllő River to keep the Moldavians at bay until such time as a plan of attack was developed. But for some inexplicable reason, General Marius Hatmanu had retreated back across the river prematurely, thus giving the Moldavians full access to all routes leading to and across the Maros. Brigadier Higgins had given the message to Colonel Callenberk via radio in a tirade of up-time expletives that forced the newly minted regimental commander to pull the phone away from his ear. Standing nearby, Christian, who had been given the order to deliver that message, could hear every foul word and almost see Brigadier Higgins' spit flying through the receiver.

"What are you going to say to him, sir?" Lieutenant Enkefort asked.

Christian pulled on his reins to bring his horse to a slow, steady walk. He shrugged. "I'll do my duty. What else can I do?"

Two Székely soldiers came forward and grabbed the reins of their horses, bringing them to a halt. They said nothing, nor did they salute him as a superior officer. Christian didn't care. Now was not the time to *waste time* with formalities.

He climbed off his horse, fixed his coat, hat, belt, and said to the man holding Alphonse's reins, "We are here to see General Hatmanu."

Hatmanu stepped out of the tent. His uniform was the same bright red of his soldiers, but the accoutrements of command were prominent at his neck, on his lapel, on his hat, and without question, in his demeanor. If he preened any more, he'd break in two.

"Why are you here, *Captain*?"

Christian held his tongue, bit back the bile in his throat, and forced a salute. "General Hatmanu, I'm here to—"

"If you are here to relieve me of command, Captain, you've wasted your time. This is my country, my men, my command. I refuse to do so, and I do not recognize you as a—"

"I am not here to relieve you of command, sir," Christian said, interrupting and raising his tone over Hatmanu's petulant voice. "I am here to—"

"Tell your Jewish master that I withdrew because, had I not, the Moldavians would have crushed us against the Küküllő. I withdrew to save my brigade, damn you. They had rockets and that infernal flying machine dropping bombs, with fifteen thousand soldiers at their heels. I asked for more men. I didn't get them. Had we stayed, we'd have been annihilated."

"I am not here to relieve you of command, sir, nor am I here to listen to your reasons for withdrawal. I am here to escort you to a meeting with Generals Roth, von Mercy, Renz, Higgins, and all the regimental commanders of the Sunrise, so that a plan of attack can be immediately devised."

"The plan of attack is simple, Captain." Hatmanu widened his eyes and raised his hands. The image of this pitiful man raising his hand to his wife shot through Christian's mind. "Give me more men, and I can destroy the enemy."

Christian sighed, quickly growing annoyed with this delay. "Sir, Brigadier Higgins is sending one regiment of his Silesian Guard here in haste—with volley guns—to help secure your lines. They will be here within the hour and will take command of your defense while you are attending General Roth's meeting."

General Hatmanu placed his hands on his hips. "Why didn't the brigadier send me this message himself? Is he afraid to—"

"He attempted to rouse you by radio, sir. You did not respond."

The general lowered his gaze, looked almost embarrassed. "The radio's been...destroyed. Struck by gunfire."

Impalers. It had to be, mixed in with the advancing Moldavians.

They know what radios look like, and they know their value. "Sir, I will say again, you are required to attend me to the meeting."

General Hatmanu crossed his arms and locked his knees. He closed his eyes to slits. "And if I refuse...Captain?"

Christian paused. He hadn't considered what might happen if the cretin refused the request, nor had Colonel Callenberk given further instructions on what to do if so.

He cleared his throat. "Sir, you will accompany me to General Roth's headquarters. If you refuse, I'm quite certain that Brigadier Higgins will be *most* happy to compel you to do so."

They stood there, staring at each other. Christian's heart was beating madly, his confused emotions of anger, fear, rage, all converging to give him an anxiety he wasn't used to. He was comforted by Alphonse being so close. If things got out of hand, he knew that he could rely on Alphonse, on Lieutenant Enkefort, to get him out of danger. *If* things got out of hand.

The general's shoulders lowered. "Very well, Captain. If General Roth wishes to receive my counsel, I will gladly give it. Lead on, *boy*. Let's go see what a jeweler knows about war."

Wallachian Army encampment
Meinbach

Through thick morning fog, Usan Hussein read the signal flags from the *Chaldiran*. Its crew refused to land and, instead, made three circles over the Wallachian army encampment to give him enough time to decipher the message. He wasn't sure he had interpreted everything correctly; his skills with signal flags had waned by lack of use. He understood most of it. The parts of the message that mattered, anyway.

"General Hatmanu has fallen back beyond the Küküllő," he said to Matei Basarab as they watched the airship rise and disappear in a bank of clouds. "Voivode Lupu's way is open in the north. He will attempt to cross the Maros soon and attack shortly thereafter. He asks that we march on Gyulafehérvár immediately."

"Asking or demanding?" Matei asked.

Usan huffed. "Is there a difference when it comes to the man?"

Matei nodded. "None. We are but ten, perhaps twelve, miles from the capital. We can be there in half a day." He sighed deeply. "If we move too quickly, however, without knowing if he has successfully crossed the Maros, then we may be in the middle of a fight before he even engages. If he wants us to attack in unison, then we need to know his disposition beforehand. We need to know that he has crossed the Maros before we engage."

"If we wait too long, my lord," Usan said, "then we give the Sunrise the opportunity to seize the field. If we move now, even if we get there too soon, *we* can determine the ground on which to fight."

Matei stepped away, looked behind them, turned left, and walked over to Stroe Leurdeanu. They talked a while, then Matei returned. "How are your men? Are they ready? And what of the *Ifrits*?"

"My orta is ready to move upon your order. Two of the *Ifrits* are ready at your command. The other requires an axle repair, and there is some fume leakage around its naphtha tank. The crew says it will be ready to move within two days."

"Two days..."

Matei let that hang out there, as if they were words of warning. Then, "Can we leave it behind? Let it catch up?"

Usan nodded. "Of course, though I would feel better moving with all three. My orta has grown quite accustomed to following them into battle."

"And what have we learned of their so-called APCs? Did the *Chaldiran* give any details about them?"

"Yes," he said, "what little they know. Voivode Lupu's spies in the Diet are having trouble getting messages to the Moldavians. A major general from the Sunrise has been put in charge of capital security. He has locked down most veins of information to and from the capital. But what Mordechai Pesach tells me is that these APCs are wagons of reinforced metal plate. They are pulled behind an engine, much like our own tanks, just as wide, but taller. They resemble the old wooden war wagons of Hussite origin, but bigger, more durable. They will be formidable on the battlefield."

"But not impossible, I pray, to defeat."

"Nothing, my lord, can withstand a sustained line of fire from our *Ifrits*."

Matei stepped aside to deliberate once more. Usan waited, waited. Finally, the voivode of Wallachia said, "We will march at first light. And you inform the crew of that beleaguered *Ifrit* that they have today to make repairs. In the morning, they will move with us. This army moves together, Usan, or not at all."

Chapter 53

Library of the Collegium Academicum
Gyulafehérvár

Some of his closest advisors had recommended that he commandeer the Princely Palace as his headquarters, but Morris refused. "That's not a smart move, gentlemen," he said, pushing back. "Seize Rákóczi's home right after he dies? Nope. Let's come up with another option, shall we?"

So, it was decided that the best option, for now, was a tent overlooking the center of the battlefield, but it would not be fully operational until tomorrow. For tonight, then, the library of the Collegium Academicum would have to do.

Guards were placed outside each door. There were no guards inside, lest one of them be a spy and convey the details of the conversation to the opposition. The only people allowed in the room were those directly involved in the impending battle. That included all generals, regimental commanders, and one personal aide each, if needed. Morris had invited Ellie Anderson, for it would be necessary for her and Len to have full understanding of the plan as they helped facilitate communication between the key areas of the battlefield. Eddie Junker was also included since his Dvorak pilots would be in the air for most of the operation. Everyone in attendance was sworn to secrecy. Morris finished his introductory comments with a call to prayer.

"After the meeting, gentlemen, I'd like the Sunrise priests and rabbis to conduct—what you might call—an ecumenical, multi-denominational, prayer. I think everyone in this room could use a little spiritual support on the eve of battle, don't you think?"

No argument for that, including General Hatmanu, whose facial expressions through Morris' preamble suggested he'd rather be anywhere than in a room taking dictation from a Jewish general, or anyone else for that matter.

"And now, gentlemen," he said as Generals Renz and Higgins rolled out the battlefield map and secured its corners. "The plan."

He and Jeff Higgins laid it out, much in the same manner as they had earlier to Generals von Mercy and Renz, but with the inevitable interruption from pretty much everyone in the room.

"I'll allow Generals von Mercy and Renz to discuss troop deployment," Morris said, stepping back from the table and giving them the floor. "Gentlemen?"

Von Mercy paid deference to Renz, who stepped up to the map. The newly appointed field commander sighed deeply, scratched his thick, graying hair and beard, then began.

He pointed to the southern third of the map. "The Joshua Corps will deploy south to meet the Wallachian army as it moves against the capital. South and center, more accurately, for if they break through and begin to move to the center of the field to link arms with the Moldavians, which is possible, we'll need the flexibility to adjust. Colonels Shalit, Schiff, and Zelikovich—do you understand what I'm saying?"

The colonels looked at each other, nodded. Colonel Shalit answered for them all. "Yes, General. We understand."

Morris could see Shalit's dissatisfaction with the plan. He was the biggest proponent for the strategy of setting up rings of defense around the capital and then waiting for the enemy to attack. But that suggestion had been discussed ad infinitum and would not be considered any further.

"In addition," General Renz continued, "First Cavalry will serve with the Joshua Corps, providing flanker support as needed. Colonel Burkenfeld, I want you to meet cavalry with cavalry. Reports tell us that the Wallachians have a lot of Serbian horses on their side. You keep those bastards contained, you hear?"

Colonel Burkenfeld nodded. "Yes, sir. We will."

Morris could see Burkenfeld's jaw muscles working a mile

a minute. He was clearly upset that von Mercy had given field command to Renz. Morris just hoped that during battle, this mercenary colonel with a bruised ego wouldn't change his mind, tuck tail and run, or switch sides. Bonus ducats had been given to all commanders to help incentivize their duty to the Sunrise. Morris hoped it was enough.

"Captain Lazlo Guth," General Renz said, turning his attention to the center of the battlefield, "we would like your Hajdus to take the center and hold against any incursions therein. Both enemy forces are, by our estimation, of equal distance from the center. Their armies may move together, or one at a time. Either way, these stone walls here, here, and here, will provide your men adequate shooting positions in case either force reaches the center."

Captain Guth nodded. He leaned over the map and ran his hand across the area that Renz had designated. "I understand, General. Are we to be the only force protecting the center?"

General Renz shook his head. "No, sir. A regiment from the Zizka Brigade will follow you in." He turned to Colonel Makovec. "Colonel, you decide which regiment to deploy, and hold your other two in reserve with your APCs."

The Brethren commander nodded. "Yes, General."

"Now, our remaining mercenary infantry, comprised of Hungarians, Italians, Silesians, Scots, and Bohemian companies not affiliated with the Brethren, have decided to allow General von Mercy to be their overall commander."

"Yes," von Mercy said, wheeling his chair forward to get a better look at the map. He leaned up with a wince of pain and pointed to the northern segment of the map, where, at present, the Moldavians were moving to engage Brigadier Higgins' Silesian Guard. "Our original idea was to have these five free companies—designated as Delta, Echo, Foxtrot, Golf, and Hotel—shift as needed, from the center to the north. However, given the Moldavians' stronger and faster push across the Maros than anticipated, they will be deployed in full to the north."

"You are putting unwieldy mercenaries," General Hatmanu said, interrupting, "alongside my trabants, with no field commander in overall charge of their disposition. Why?" He pointed at Jeff Higgins. "You have already put a Silesian regiment into my lines. Aren't they enough?"

"My regiment will withdraw from your lines, General," Jeff said, "as soon as you return to your men. These free companies will be put in their place. They are of equivalent size and strength."

"Really?" General Hatmanu let his voice rise in pitch and a broad smile cross his face. "It was my understanding that your Silesians, Brigadier, were some of the finest soldiers in Europe. Surely a ragtag bunch of fight-for-hire ruffians cannot match your—"

"The Silesian Guard will be held in reserve," General Roth said, jumping to ensure that Higgins and Hatmanu's growing argument didn't come to blows. "Like Colonel Makovec's APC's, they will be moved to wherever, and whenever, they are needed."

General Renz laid out the plan in full for the Silesian Guard and the Brethren APCs. As he spoke, Morris measured the temperature of the room.

Some in attendance seemed to agree with the plan; others did not. He could almost hear what the detractors were thinking: Why hold such powerful forces in reserve? Why not move them into the field immediately? Good questions, he had to admit.

As far as the APCs went, they were new and not battle tested, not like this anyway. They had survived Impaler attempts at sabotage along the march, but even Colonel Makovec was hesitant to overcommit them to one place on the field. Hold them in reserve, he had recommended, and then move them to where they might have an *immediate* impact, as opposed to committing them to a defensive position that the enemy could simply avoid. The Wallachians and Moldavians surely understood the history of the deployment of Hussite war wagons just as much as anyone else. The current battle line was a wide front, several miles, so it was best not to deploy them, then have to redeploy them, then redeploy them again. Wait until the enemy had committed to a move, and then hit them hard with a powerful line of APCs.

For the Silesians, their best use was for pinpoint strikes, especially the Hangman Regiment. Use them as shock troopers in places where an overrun was imminent. Morris imagined that the most likely form of overrun was the Ottoman fire tanks. The thought of them made Morris' skin crawl.

"Now," General Renz said, "getting back to the northern segment. Second Cavalry will join General Hatmanu and the free companies. Colonel Callenberk, your responsibilities will be similar to First Cavalry: keep the infantry secure and well supported. It's also important that you help maintain the integrity of the airfield."

"It's my understanding," Eddie Junker said, raising his hand, "that some Saxon companies, fleeing the enemy's approach, will oversee its security?"

Morris nodded. "Yes, under Major General Lange's command. About six hundred men, give or take."

"It might be more prudent to put them into the field, General," Hatmanu said, "alongside my men. They would be tough fighters against an army that has destroyed their homes."

Morris nodded. "Agreed, but if the airfield is overrun, and the communication tower destroyed, we'll be in serious danger, General. That would give the Moldavians access to the capital. The airfield must be protected."

"It will be protected, General Roth," Major General Lange said, "by Princess Lorántffy's request that all Saxon forces and any Székely forces not under General Hatmanu's direct command be empowered to defend the streets of the capital, Gyulafehérvár will be secure by morning. I personally guarantee that, sir."

There were no guarantees in war, Morris knew, but he took Lange's assurances with a polite nod and then allowed General Renz to conclude.

"Finally, artillery deployments. Battery A will be assigned to General Hatmanu. Battery B to Captain Guth. Batteries C and D to the Joshua Corps. The Zizka Brigade and the Silesian Guard will be responsible for their own guns."

Batteries A, B, and C were normal field cannons. Battery D comprised six mortars. It was unclear exactly which part of the field might need them the most, but Colonel Shalit had specifically requested that they be assigned to his regiment.

"That is all, gentlemen," General Renz said. "That is the plan. Questions?"

There were, of course, many, and most of them confined to issues of supply and who had tactical control over battlefield decisions. In an army of mercenaries, it was often difficult for individual companies to be persuaded to follow an overall plan, but Generals von Mercy and Renz made it absolutely clear for the need to respect the chain of command. The battle that would likely commence in just a few days would be the first time that they had all fought together. With so many untried soldiers, so many raw recruits, so much could go wrong. Most of the Joshua Corps had never even been fired at. What would these young

Ashkenazi men do when facing down a charge of wild Tatars, or Serbians, or Janissaries? So much could go wrong so quickly.

They stood there, in silence, after the last question was raised and answered. Morris took a moment to look at them all. He then moved from man to man, quietly and firmly shaking their hands, giving some of them hugs, others firm pats on the shoulder. He met them, eye to eye, and smiled warmly to each. Even General Hatmanu, who, nearly incapable of showing the kind of warmth and empathy needed in a time like this, accepted his up-time handshake with a curt smile and nod.

"I'm proud of all of you," Morris said, feeling a little silly saying such a thing to men like this. "I know you will all do your duty. Some of you are here for pay. Some because you believe in what the Sunrise is doing. Some to protect your capital and country. Regardless of your reasons for being here, I want you all to know I'm honored to be your general, and I assure you that I will do my duty to see that you prevail."

He walked to the main doors to the library, opened them, and stepped aside to allow Jason Gotkin and the rest of the spiritual corps access. "Now, gentlemen, if you'll indulge me, let us pray."

Chapter 54

Field hospital
Grand Army of the Sunrise

Isaac gave young Tobias his orders, supplies, and sent him on his way. To the southern triage center, in fact, where he and other medics and nurses would wait for casualties. And there would be plenty. On that, Isaac had no doubt. More, perhaps, than he had experienced in Krakow. Much more than on that stone bridge years ago.

"Thank you, Oana," he said with a smile, handing her a basket of sanitized bandages and horsehair stitching. "Give that to Doctor Oberheuser, please. Ask him to review its contents, and if he is satisfied, he may hand it over to the field medics heading north."

"Yes, Doctor," she said with a sweet smile. She turned on her heels and walked away. Isaac watched her leave until a less attractive figure stepped into his view.

"Captain von Jori," he huffed, "surprised to see you here on the eve of battle."

"The eve? Maybe. Or two days, three. It all depends upon the enemy." Christian stepped aside and turned to watch Oana leave the tent. "Hmm. Pretty woman. You seem quite taken with her."

Isaac pointed a stern finger at Christian's good eye. "Watch yourself, Captain. Fräulein Dalca is a great caregiver. I cannot have you diverting her attention from the casualties that will be—"

Christian waved the comment away. "Peace, my friend. I did not come for that."

"Andreea Hatmanu is here somewhere," Isaac said, lifting himself up on his toes to look through the bustle of medical and supply staff.

"I didn't come to see her either. We've ... shared our words already." Christian straightened. "No, I'm here to see you. If you have a moment."

Isaac nodded, perhaps a little too enthusiastically. "Yes, of course. There's much to do before the battle, but now would be a good time."

They stepped through the flap and into the darkness. The light from so many torches and lanterns gave the evening an eerie glow, a kind of ghostly visage that swirled around them in the wisps of fog leaching through the camp. The activity outside the tent was almost as frenetic as inside. Somewhere in the distance was laughter and, as usual, Doctor Oberheuser's booming voice as he dictated simple tasks at the top of his lungs.

"So, Captain von Jori, to what do I owe the honor?"

"I wanted to drop by and see how you were. You know, ever since Kolozsvár, I've been worried about your—"

"My breakdown?"

"No, no, that's not what I going to say. I—"

Isaac waved him off. "Don't worry about it, my friend. I'm well versed in psychological trauma and stress. It isn't just soldiers that deal with such things. Let's call it what it was: a nervous breakdown. I'm fine now, Christian. Ever since I arrived in the capital, I've been well."

They paused. Isaac breathed deeply, catching the scent of meat roasting on a spit nearby. Some of the Saxon soldiers who had fled from the south were bivouacking nearby in support of the medical corps. They caroused in German. Isaac understood the words, but not the context. He was glad to see and hear them in such good spirits. Nervous laughter, perhaps, but any laughter in a moment like this was better than brooding silence.

Christian raised his chin toward the capital. "Right now, at the college, our fates are being decided by General Roth and his lieutenants." He chuckled. "Like the gods of Olympus high above us mere mortals."

Isaac raised his brows. "Ah ... you're a soldier and a scholar."

"No, I know very little about all that. But my uncle used to speak of such things when he would return from his mercenary work in Greece, Italy, France. It seemed like he'd been everywhere."

Isaac could see a spark in Christian's eye, a longing for, perhaps, those simpler days as a child, where stories of war were always less bloody than the real thing. Where heroes always vanquished the wicked. Where God's divine purpose always prevailed.

"You said you were going to tell me about your uncle and how he was the reason you became a soldier. We've got time now. Tell me about it."

Christian sighed, paused, then began. "Very well. My uncle, Klaus von Jori, was a mercenary. Most of his life, I suppose. He was my father's youngest brother. Captain Kinsky reminds me of him, a kind of brash, undisciplined fellow from a good family who struck out on his own in his youth and never regretted a moment of it. In winter, he'd come back to the homestead and stay with us for a few months, sometimes longer. Always with a fresh wound—a slash across his face, neck, chest. A broken bone, a limp, a bump on the head. He was a footman, which I always thought was surprising given his family's business. Another example, I suppose, of his rebellious nature.

"But I loved him. Not so much for who he was, but for what he did. He *did* things, Isaac. He stepped outside of Zurich, outside Switzerland, and did things. All my father ever wanted his family to do was to stay in Zurich and manage horses. Horses, horses, horses. I never passed a morning sunrise without hearing the whinny of a horse, a snort, a stamp or shuffle of hooves. It's surprising that I didn't grow to hate them.

"But unlike my uncle, I grew to love them. Depend on them. I can't imagine life without a horse, Isaac."

Isaac nodded. "I know what you mean. I can't imagine myself not being a doctor."

"Exactly. You understand. Anyway, my uncle would come home and tell us stories about his 'adventures,' as he called them, his time in Greece or Italy. France. He seemed to love France the most, though he never explained why. He'd tell stories about battles and all the fights he was in. If he ever got too graphic, too overzealous with his descriptions, my father would rein him in, sometimes kick him out of the house for the evening. But then I'd sneak out and find my uncle sleeping in the barn, and he'd quietly tell me more. Well, from there on, I knew what I wanted to do with my life.

"Then the Ring of Fire happened. News of it came slowly to Switzerland. It was months before we learned of the event. Of course, like many in Zurich, we thought it a falsehood, an evil lie. Fanciful Germans telling tall tales after drinking too much ale. But it was true, and the world began to change.

"Young men in Zurich left to head north, to see for themselves these up-timers who had come through some godless ring of fire to our time. Witches and warlocks, that's what they were called. But when things really began to change, when word of their successes on the battlefield arrived in Zurich, well, I had to see these people. I had to know for myself if they were real.

"I tried leaving in 1633, and I almost got away. But my father caught me hanging out the window. He didn't strike me, he didn't rage. He was calm and rational about it, and for that, I paid him the courtesy of staying for a while longer. But in the spring of 1635, I finally left. I stole a man's horse from our livery and headed north, into Germany. From there, I got work with one cavalry regiment after another, as a farrier, a blacksmith, a quartermaster's aide, until I got the chance to join a company."

Christian held up his hands. "And here I am: Captain Christian von Jori, commanding officer of my own company. I think my uncle would be proud."

"Your father?"

Isaac could see tears well up in his friend's eyes. Christian did not let those tears drop. Instead, he shook his head, rubbed his face. "I don't know. I left without saying goodbye. Left without kissing my mother, without telling my sister or younger brother where I was going. They probably think me dead."

Isaac felt a tear of his own begin to form. "Well, one day you will return home and regale them with stories about high adventure on the Transylvanian plateau."

That seemed to pique Christian's mood. He nodded. "Perhaps. If I live that long."

That last comment hurt. "Would you like to pray?" Isaac asked.

Christian shook his head. "No, thank you. I'm not very good with that. But, if you will, please say one for Lieutenant Enkefort and my men tonight. They deserve a good word."

Isaac nodded. "Yes, I will do so."

Isaac opened his arms. Christian did the same.

They hugged. A short, sweet squeeze and pat on the back.

"I must be off," Christian said, letting go and turning away. "Back to the company."

"Go with God, Captain." Isaac forced a smile, perhaps the last smile he would ever share with this man that he had grown to know and admire as a brother. "I'll see you soon."

General von Mercy's room

It was late, nearly one o'clock in the morning, but Morris could see a sliver of lamplight through the general's cracked door. He knocked lightly.

"Come in," von Mercy said.

Morris opened the door and stuck his head through, smiled. "Am I disturbing you?"

"Not at all. Please come, General."

Von Mercy was telling the truth. He was up in his wheelchair, sitting over a map of the battlefield that he had laid out over his bed. No one else was in the room. It was quiet, with the only light from the lamp focused on the bed and map.

"I hate to disturb you at this hour, General," Morris said, opening the door just enough to enter, then closing it behind him. "But I thought I'd go over the plan with you once more."

"Very well. Shall I call in Renz, or Higgins, or—"

Morris put up his hand. "That won't be necessary. We'll talk alone."

He wanted to go over the plan again, for sure, but that wasn't why he was here. But now that he stood before von Mercy, with the general sitting upright in his chair, waiting patiently for him to make the first move, Morris wasn't sure he could speak about what was really gnawing at his brain. He wondered if perhaps it was better to speak to Jeff on this matter. Up-timer to up-timer. Someone who, though younger and with less knowledge of Jewish up-time history, had at least enough knowledge of it to know what was coming. Or, at least, had a much, much better sense of what could happen if the Grand Army of the Sunrise failed in its cause.

Morris sat on the edge of the bed, disrupting some of the

pieces von Mercy had spread across his map. He sighed deeply. "I'm...concerned about the battle."

Von Mercy nodded. "Understandable. Is there something in the plan you'd like to discuss, go over again? We've time to make adjustments, if necessary."

Morris shook his head. "No, that's not what I mean. I'm satisfied with the plan. I'm worried about the men." Oh, hell, just say it! "I'm worried about the Joshua Corps."

Von Mercy said nothing, waiting, Morris supposed, to see if his commanding general would continue.

"They're green, General. Green as a gourd, as an up-timer might say. Yes, they've been given good training. They've drilled continuously before and during the march into Transylvania. In their minds, they know what to do. They've got enough muscle memory stored up. They're ready.

"But let's be honest: they're just boys. Most of them, anyway, and there's a big difference between shooting at a target and shooting—and killing—a real enemy soldier, a live human being. Someone who's bearing down on you with their own gun, their own sword. At the height of the battle, General, are their muscles going to remember what their minds forget?"

Von Mercy cleared his throat. "The Joshua Corps has good officers. Colonels Shalit and Schiff are both highly qualified commanders."

"What about Zelikovich?" Morris asked.

Von Mercy shrugged. "He's definitely less experienced. But the plan isn't to put his regiment into the front line anyway." Von Mercy fell silent, rubbed his beard, adjusted position in his chair. He cleared his throat again, said, "I'll radio Higgins to send one of his Silesian Guard regiments south in support."

Morris shook his head, stood, and walked over to the lamp. He let the light shine up onto his chin, creating an eerie glow on his face, the kind of glow he remembered as a child. On sleepovers late at night, he and his friends used to hold a flashlight under their faces to cast dark, twisted shadow masks while telling ghost stories. Those were the days. Good days. Simpler days. The flashlight was gone now, but the ghost stories remained.

"I can't just send in more troops," he said, "not right before the battle, anyway. What kind of message does that send?"

"Message, sir?"

"Yes, message. I'd be telling them right up front that I, Morris Roth—the guy they see as some Moses that's come to deliver them from their strife—thinks that they aren't capable of fighting, and winning, their own battle. What message does that send?"

There was a pause. Morris turned and stared at von Mercy, waiting for an answer, but knowing that a good one was unlikely to come. Morris didn't have a very good answer himself. His emotions were all in a tangle. Fear, dread, indecision. The kind of emotions best left on the cutting room floor on the eve of battle.

Von Mercy seemed confused as he tried working out an answer in his mind. Finally, he said, "Let me see if I understand you correctly, General. You're concerned about the battle preparedness of the Joshua Corps, and as such, you are worried that they will not hold against the Wallachians."

"Yes."

"As the commanding general, you have the authority to order additional troops to the southern battle line in order to shore up any weakness that the Joshua Corps may possess."

"Yes."

"And yet, you are unwilling, or reluctant, to make such a request because you are worried that doing so would make the Joshua Corps seem weak and incapable of fighting for themselves."

"Yes," Morris said. "You have it right."

Von Mercy huffed, shook his head. Morris saw a derisive smile curl the left side of the general's mouth. "With respect, sir, you are being foolish."

Morris put his hands on his hips, furrowed his brow. "Excuse me?"

"Sir, I've been in this war business for a long time. I can tell you this. A man is not a good or bad soldier because his skin is fair, or dark, or he's a Christian, a Muslim, or a Jew. He's a good soldier because he's been trained to be so, and he has something inside that makes him one. I've served with a lot of good soldiers in my life. I've served with a lot of bad ones. When bullets begin to fly, the good ones will rise, the bad ones will fall. Bullets don't give a damn for the color of your skin, or which God you worship."

"This is bigger than that, General," Morris said, stepping away from the lamp into greater shadow. "This is bigger than just defending the Transylvanian capital and honoring our commitment to the local people. I cannot allow the Joshua Corps to fail. But I also cannot allow them to believe that they cannot win."

"It's a good fighting force, General," Von Mercy said, wheeling himself away from the bed. "Yes, two of three regiments are green, inexperienced. I'm worried as well. But I've seen the best of them in action at Déj, and Colonel Shalit's regiment will be at the spear point of the attack. First Cavalry Regiment will be there as well. It's a strong position."

"You don't understand, General. You're not a Jew. At this moment, their psychology matters just as much as the bullets they pump into their barrels. It's my responsibility to support both. I cannot let them fall. I cannot let them lose faith."

He turned away and stepped to the window. It was a cold night. Not below freezing, but in the low forties. Light rain had fallen, though no one believed that a storm was brewing. Not one in the clouds, anyway.

"You've heard my position on the matter, General Roth," von Mercy said. "It's your decision. Send in one of the Silesian regiments right away, or wait and let the southern battle line evolve as it may."

Morris kept looking out the window. A company of Saxons had been put in charge of protecting the grounds of the college. Now they sat outside, around their campfires, huddled together, smoking, conserving as much warmth as possible. He could hear their muffled German mixed with the occasional Hungarian phrase.

"You know," Morris said, "if Uriel Abrabanel were here, he'd quote Shakespeare and recommend that I don a heavy cloak and walk about my men in disguise, to get the full measure of the common soldier." He chuckled. "It wouldn't work for me. They'd spot me in a New York minute."

"Then what shall it be, sir? If we send another regiment to aid the Joshua Corps, we must do it soon. Time grows short."

A Saxon soldier outside the window apparently told a joke in German. His campmates laughed. *I wish I were with you fellows,* Morris thought. *I sure could use a good laugh right now.*

"Do not send any Silesians yet," he said, closing his eyes and leaning forward to place his forehead on the cold window. "We'll stick to the plan...and see what happens."

Chapter 55

Southern battle line

From safety, Usan Hussein watched katyusha rockets fire along the Wallachian front. The six-pounders then fired, a swirling wall of whistling iron balls that struck the ground in front of the advancing Sunrise infantry and bounced into their forward ranks. The rockets struck in the center of the advancing men, hurling some of them up and forward in a mangle of twisted bodies, banners, and uniforms. The line seemed to waver; it paused to adjust to the men who had been struck down. Gaps were filled quickly, drums and commanding voices sounded, and the Sunrise advanced.

Somewhere behind the enemy ranks, mortars opened fire, answering the katyushas with their own arching wall of shot. The Wallachian soldiers below Usan's perch, three ranks deep, advanced slowly under this new veil of enemy counterfire, their muskets primed, cocked, and ready.

"Those are Jewish regiments advancing," Matei Basarab said, handing the spyglass back to Usan.

Usan adjusted the spyglass and had a look for himself. Yes, yes it was, and he had never seen anything like it, had never seen so many Jews carrying so many rifles. But there they were, rows upon rows of Ashkenazi, moving forward at the quick step and not to submit or surrender, but to fight. "Yes, it is. And it would appear as if they intend on attacking."

"Should we advance," Matei asked, "or should we halt and let them come to us?"

The field between the two belligerent forces was relatively open, save for a few modest farmhouses, a small stone wall, and a copse of thick brush. Not enough protection for a good defensive stance. "It is up to you, Voivode. It is your army."

Matei considered while both forces continued to endure cannon and rocket fire. Then he cupped his hand over his mouth, sucked in a deep breath, and shouted, "Forward!"

Northern battle line

The chaos below the *Chaldiran* had Vasile Lupu in good spirits. Tatar and Moldavian cavalry were attacking Transylvanian forces on a wide front. Forces that did not possess the kind of up-time weaponry that had ultimately thwarted General Radu's efforts at Déj. These so-called trabants, manned with Szekler commoners, still fought yesterday's war, with formations and tactics established well before the Ring of Fire. Facing an army that he understood, the voivode of Moldavia was joyous, rendered nearly speechless with tiny giggles and guffaws that spewed from his mouth in droplets of spit.

"Wonderful, just wonderful!" Vasile said, dangerously leaning over the starboard side of the gondola.

"Do not forget the cavalry behind them, my *lord*," Sergiu Botnari said. "They are a modern Sunrise force, and they carry the same pistol I have on my hip."

Vasile ignored the words of caution and continued to watch the unfolding battle below. Sergiu looked at the kafir Moshe, who stood quietly near the voivode on the starboard side, gazing through a spyglass. The rest of the crew—Mordechai, the janissary guard, and two other men with rifled muskets brought aboard for defense—said and did nothing, preoccupied with keeping the *Chaldiran* safe and in the air.

"My lord," Moshe said abruptly, "there are no aircraft on the enemy airfield."

"What?" Vasile said, grabbing the spyglass and looking for himself.

Sergiu stepped starboard. Quite a distance from their position, but at their height, he could tell, even without the spyglass, that the airfield was barren. A metal tower, a shack, and clearly, there were still personnel on the field, but that was all.

"They must have moved them back to Kolozsvár, my lord," Moshe said, "to keep them safe."

All the more reason to have allowed me to stay in the field with my Impalers. We could have destroyed those aircraft before they left. It was on the tip of his tongue, but Sergiu paused, collected himself, and said instead, "I'd now advise that you drop the firebombs upon the advancing cavalry. Dropping bombs on an empty airfield will do nothing but scorch the grass."

Vasile looked as if he were about to explode, but Moshe gave him a quick nod. "Very well," Vasile said. "Prepare the bombs, and take us lower."

"Lower, sir?" Moshe's eyes flashed concern. "We should not drop too low, my lord, lest we expose ourselves to excessive enemy musket fire."

"Dropping lower will allow us more accurate targeting," Vasile shouted. "Haven't you said that to me before?"

"Yes, my lord, but—"

"Then take us down. Now. I want to see who I am burning."

The Dixie Chick

Denise's assignment was to keep HQ apprised of any changes in the enemy's approach. What was the Moldavian army doing? Where was it moving its forces? How many units did it have? She had already radioed in a lot of information on that score. Now, she was shadowing the airship, watching it closely for any sudden changes in movement or action.

She saw that it was dropping while moving in a straight line, as if it planned on strafing the columns of cavalry moving to the front. Denise changed the channel on her radio and spoke loudly.

"Enkefort, Enkefort. Do you read?"

Chapter 56

Southern battle line

Jason Gotkin startled when he heard the first volley of whistling rocket fire. His chest clutched, and although he was far behind the advancing First and Second Regiments of the Joshua Corps, the fear of being struck by one of those whistling missiles made his head and heart ache. Surrounded by men from Third Regiment gave him comfort, but not enough to keep his faith from wavering.

I've made a mistake coming here.

But here he was, on the front, at his own behest. "I wish to volunteer," he had said to Isaac and Morris just last night in a sudden burst of cultural duty and pride. "I want to help your medics any way I can, medically and spiritually, where it matters." So here he was, standing in reserve with Third Regiment, on the right flank, listening to enemy rocket and cannon fire, distant howls of captains ordering their men forward, sporadic drums tapping out a cadence, rifles and muskets firing. Dying men screaming.

Young Tobias seemed concerned. "It'll be all right, friend," Jason said, laying a hand on the young man's shoulder. "Remember what the Talmud says about strength: Do not be afraid or terrified because of them, for the Lord your God goes with you; he will never leave you nor forsake you."

Tobias nodded and tried to smile. "Yes, Rabbi Gotkin. Thank you. Please forgive my weakness. I am glad you are with us."

Jason was glad he was with them as well. He just wished he

were in a more secure location, like the ridgeline behind them, where Batteries C and D continued to sound.

Colonel Frederick Burkenfeld of First Cavalry Regiment rode into camp on a tall, pitch-black horse, his staff riding alongside.

Colonel Getzel Zelikovich greeted him with a curt salute. "Colonel Burkenfeld, what is our situation?"

The cavalry officer removed his helmet, wiped his brow while trying to maintain control of his overexcited horse. "First and Second Regiments have engaged along the Wallachian line. Short-range fire, bayonet charges. So far, we're holding."

He pointed through the woods to the left flank, then the right. "Air reconnaissance indicates a large gathering of Ottoman sipahi and Serbian light horse, supposedly preparing to attack on both flanks."

"And are you going to greet them, Colonel?" Zelikovich asked. Jason could feel the man's anxiety. "Charge them in the field?"

Colonel Burkenfeld nodded, his brow wrinkling with annoyance at such a preposterous question. "Of course we are, Colonel. I know this business of war. I've already ordered my companies to defend both flanks. The *Smooth Operator* has radioed in saying that there is a large gathering of cavalry behind the enemy ridgeline. Thus, I'd advise you to get *your* men ready to set up a strong defense of these woods. Move forward to those small homes in front of your line and take that stone wall between them. Cavalry won't likely charge through the woods, but I've seen Serbian cavalry, with their blood up, dismounting like dragoons and bringing hell and bloody steel down upon a routing enemy. And let me tell you, Colonel: there's a lot of Serbian and Ottoman cavalry on that side of the battle line, just waiting."

Colonel Zelikovich considered the suggestion for a moment. Then he said, "My orders are to wait in reserve until such a time as Colonel Shalit orders me forward. I've heard no word from him yet."

"Indeed you haven't," Colonel Burkenfeld said, "and that's because he's got his hands full with Dorobanți infantry armed with rifled muskets firing Murad mini-balls. Our ZB-1636 rifles are just as powerful, but it's a slaughterhouse up there right now, Colonel. Don't worry about waiting for his orders. Again, I advise you to move immediately into a defensive position to protect and support the Joshua Corps. They may start falling back at any moment."

"Thank you, Colonel," Zelikovich said. "I'll consider your recommendation."

Colonel Burkenfeld shook his head, but saluted respectfully. "Suit yourself, sir." He slammed his helmet back into place, turned his horse, and trotted out of camp.

Jason kept his eyes trained on the Joshua Corps' new, untested colonel. For a moment, Zelikovich did not seem to know where he was, what was happening. Then a long, deep guttural howl echoed through the wood from the battle line, the kind of moan that would give even God a chill down his spine. The sharp strike of steel on steel followed the echoing howls.

"What do you think I should do, Rabbi?" the colonel asked, sweat beading on his face. "Should I order my men forward to the stone wall, or wait for Colonel Shalit's orders?"

What should you *do? I'm just a Rabbi.*

But it seemed as if everyone was looking at him, everyone, even the birds in the trees. *What should we do?*

Jason didn't have a clue.

Northern battle line

Cannon and musket fire aggravated Christian's thoughts and made his stomach tighten. It hadn't been long since he and his company had engaged the Moldavians, but it *felt* like an eternity. So much had transpired between the comparatively small battle at Déj and now. At Déj, he had had more control over the situation. Here, he felt like nothing but one tiny man adrift in a martial sea. The battle had already commenced up the road, and he (as yet) was not a part of it. That would likely change soon.

Lieutenant Enkefort concluded his conversation with Denise Beasley via radio. "Airship," he said, pointing upward. "Coming in hot."

Christian looked to where the lieutenant was pointing. The airship, nothing more than a speck on a bank of clouds, seemed far away, but it was, without doubt, drawing closer.

"Did she get a good look at the gondola?" he asked. "How many shooters?"

Enkefort shrugged. "She did not say. She's been ordered not to draw too close. Just keep an eye on it and report anything suspicious. She's reported: it's descending and coming our way."

"Halt!" Christian shouted to his men. It took another shout and Enkefort's effort as well to finally bring the company to a halt. "Can our ZBs hit it from here?" he asked.

Lieutenant Enkefort shrugged. "If it gets close enough, we could certainly give it a try, but I can't imagine that those manning it would be foolish enough to—"

"They're foolish enough," Christian said as he saw the vessel drop precipitously, and an object fall from the gondola. The object struck the cavalry column up the road and around a bend such that Christian could not see where it hit. Screaming men and horses made it clear, however, that it had struck soldiers. The erupting billow of smoke and fire made it clear what had been dropped.

"Move!" he shouted, reversing his previous order. "Move. They're dropping bombs!"

How foolish was he to have ordered a halt? The kind of attack he was imagining from the airship was nothing more than gunfire, random shots like those that it had taken on Prince Rákóczi and General von Mercy. Bad enough, indeed, but nothing like this. The bomb was a kind of area weapon that exploded on impact and spread fire in a broad, dangerous wave from its center.

Another bomb was released, this one striking the center of the road.

Men from Mitzlaff's and Truckmuller's companies farther up the column scrambled away from the spreading fire. Men burned and were tossed from their horses while the airship continued its rapid descent.

"Fire!" Christian and other company commanders began to howl. "Fire on that ship!"

Random shots rang out as men pointed their ZB-2s into the air and squeezed triggers. The dragoons of the regiment, those possessing the more accurate and longer-ranged ZB-1636 rifles, were already deployed and fighting alongside their Székely counterparts. Shorter-ranged pistols would have to do. Lucky for them, the pilot of the airship was a mad man.

A third bomb was released, but now, its gondola was so close to the ground that it almost felt as if Christian could reach out and touch it. The bomb struck a patch of the road in front of his company, exploding in a hot plume of fire and smoke, while men and horses scattered from the flames.

Another volley of pistol fire struck the gondola, including

Christian's shot, the left barrel and then the right, one after the other, as he tried to aim them at the few men in the gondola that he could see.

The airship flew over his company, but no further bombs were dropped. Finally, it lifted up, up until it was too far away for further pistol shots.

Christian collected himself, checked his body for wounds. None. Then he checked Alphonse. Nothing. He breathed a sigh of relief. He could not afford to lose another horse. Not now, anyway.

"How are you, Lieutenant?" Christian asked as Enkefort settled back into his saddle.

"I'm fine, sir," Enkefort said, checking his radio to ensure it hadn't been damaged. It was fine. That, indeed, was a blessing.

"Radio General Renz and let him know of this."

"Yes, Captain."

Christian reloaded his pistol and holstered it. He took a deep breath and checked his second pistol. Cocked and ready when needed. He raised up in his stirrups, making sure that he was seen by his men. "Move out. And keep good order!"

The Chaldiran

One of the musketmen that they had brought along on the *Chaldiran* now lay dead at Moshe's feet, his body battered with up-time bullet wounds. "My lord," Moshe said, trying to contain his anger. "We cannot drop that low again. The gondola will not be able to endure another round of that kind of sustained fire, the bottom of it, anyway. Our bombs can be dropped from a higher elevation with good accuracy and less risk. We must maintain a proper altitude, or the entire crew could be killed, including you."

He hoped that by personalizing the risk for Vasile, the man might finally understand the danger. It didn't seem to work.

"Did you see it?" Vasile beamed. "Did you see the flames? The explosions?"

Moshe nodded. "Yes, my lord, I did. But—"

"That was significant, kafir. We hurt them badly. Delayed them from reaching our battle line."

A few minutes at most. "Yes, my lord."

"We should go back and do it again."

Moshe looked at Mordechai, even at Sergiu, who surprisingly said nothing. The mercenary assassin seemed almost delighted at the dead man at their feet. "My lord, we have but a few bombs left. We should not waste them on trying to hit cavalry columns. The bombs were designed to strike fortifications, not—"

"My lord," Mordechai said. He was standing astern, looking through the spyglass. "Please, come and see. The center of the battlefield is nearly empty."

Vasile pushed Moshe aside, reached for the spyglass, and tore it from Mordechai's hands. He stared through it as Sergiu moved up beside him. Moshe stood back, feeling obligated to stay with the dead member of his crew. The man was not an official crew member, of course; he had just come aboard on Lupu's orders. Nevertheless, as far as Moshe was concerned, a man in the gondola was a crew member, plain and simple. He deserved someone to stay with him.

"It looks like less than a full regiment of infantry," Vasile said, "a few guns, some mercenary cavalry. You're right, kafir: not much at all."

"We should answer this with men of our own," Sergiu said. "We could sweep them quickly and take the capital. If we move now, Gyulafehérvár would be ours by nightfall."

Vasile considered. He rubbed his beard, grunted a few times, looked through the spyglass again. Finally, he said, "No, not yet. Our army is doing well. I won't take men off the front and divert them to the center, thus weakening our position against nothing but mewling trabants. We can defeat *them* within the hour, and be in the capital in a much stronger position." He paused to consider, then said, with a broad smile, "Let the Wallachians deal with it. After all, they have the Sultan's fire tanks and Janissaries."

Vasile constantly complained about not being given the orta and the tanks. Moshe looked at the Janissary standing guard beside him, thankful that he hadn't been hit by pistol fire in the barrage. The man stood like a stone, but seeing Moshe stare at him, rolled his eyes derisively.

Vasile handed the spyglass back to Moshe. "Fly to Matei Basarab's position, kafir. We'll order him to attack the center."

Moshe nodded. "Yes, my lord." He looked at the dead man at his feet. "What shall we do with him?"

Vasile shrugged. "Toss him over the side."

Chapter 57

Southern battle line

Usan could smell the faint scent of naphtha from the hull of the *Ifrit* to his right. Steam and smoke billowed out of its chimney and exhaust valves. It was primed and ready to go, as were his men, waiting patiently behind all three tanks. Waiting for his order to attack.

"The *Chaldiran*," one of Matei's aides said, pointing toward a split in the clouds.

From it emerged the airship. Like water bursting from a tube, it dipped lower, signal flags waving madly on the starboard side. Too madly, in fact, for Usan could not keep up with all of it. He tried waving to Mordechai to slow down, but the kafir could not or would not respond. Usan sighed and did his best to catch everything.

"What are they saying?" Matei asked, his voice high and anxious.

The voivode's sudden appearance startled Usan. He drew his own red flag and waved his acknowledgement to the *Chaldiran*. The airship confirmed his reply, sped up, and flew over the raging battle lines.

"What did they *say*?" Matei asked again.

"The battle is going well above the capital," he replied. "Victory is imminent."

"Is that all?"

Usan shook his head. He pointed to his right, up the Maros River Valley toward the center of the battlefield. "No. They also say that the enemy has a thin defense in the center, along the river in that direction." He paused, then: "They recommend that we move into the center and exploit this weakness."

"Is Lupu going to do so as well?"

Usan shrugged. "I cannot say, my lord. I could not catch all the message."

Matei spit and turned toward the ridgeline. Usan followed.

Artillery on both sides had all but ceased firing, as the lines were now too thoroughly entangled. Only the mortars on the enemy side fired from time to time, into the flanks. *Wasteful,* Usan thought. Such firing had done little or nothing to stem the steadied, patient Wallachian advance. Stragglers and wounded were falling back for protection on both sides.

Usan offered his spyglass to Matei. The voivode took it and focused on the left flank.

"It's time to really push them," Matei said. "Wouldn't you agree?"

Usan nodded. "Yes. The *Ifrits* and my orta are ready to go, my lord."

Matei handed the spyglass back. "I'm not talking about your men, Usan. I'm talking about the cavalry. Are Captain Dordevic's Serbians ready?"

"Yes," Usan said, "as are our Ottoman sipahi."

"Very well, then. Get word to our cavalry to attack in a—what do you call it—an envelope?"

"Double envelopment, my lord," Usan corrected politely. He suppressed a smile. Matei Basarab was no soldier, for sure. "A double envelopment led by cavalry, followed with infantry."

"Let us do that," Matei said. "Get word to Captain Dordevic, and to the sipahi, to attack on the flanks immediately."

"What of my orta?" Usan asked. "The *Ifrits*? If we attack the Jews now, my lord, we could rout them."

Matei shook his head. "As much as I hate to admit it, Lupu may be correct. If their center is weak, then it may be best to move your orta and the *Ifrits* there. If we break their lines there, Usan, then you and your men would have free rein in the streets of Gyulafehérvár.

"But let us be prudent. Let's wait to see what happens on the flanks here first, then we'll decide what to do with your men."

Usan was about to argue against such an action when he was halted by the low, rumbling sound of an engine.

He looked skyward, and there, one of the enemy's small planes, like the one he had seen fly over Meinbach a week before, sped across his vision, across the battle line, and straight toward the *Chaldiran.*

The Smooth Operator

Tuva flew as close as she was willing to get, then banked right. She heard a pop and saw a flash of fire and smoke from the gondola as someone in there took a shot at her. It missed by a mile, and Tuva forced herself not to laugh and make an obscene gesture in the gondola's general direction. It never hurt to rankle the enemy, but this was serious business. Men were dying on the ground below them, and her duties flying above it all were equally serious.

Tuva banked right. She'd take a quick look at what's going on in the center, and then swing back around and examine those columns of enemy cavalry.

Southern battle line

Colonel Friedrick Burkenfeld of First Cavalry was annoyed. Not because of General von Mercy's decision to promote Gerhardt Renz to be field general over himself...well, all right, that was annoying, and in Friedrick's mind, more than insulting. Right now, however, his biggest annoyance was the fact that Colonel Zelikovich seemed resigned to ignore his request to seize the stone wall.

What a fool!

But that was what happened, he knew, when you put an inexperienced, untested army into the field. True, the enemy probably had as many green troops as the Sunrise; the Wallachians had been an Ottoman vassal state for a long time, and their involvement with European wars had been minimal at best over the last few decades. But what did the Wallachians have that the Sunrise didn't?

Turks. Lots of them.

"What are your orders, Colonel?" Burkenfeld's aide-de-camp asked as they emerged from the tree line and into a small opening of rolling hills and farmland.

Burkenfeld reined his restless horse to a stop and surveyed the ground. Beautiful country, indeed, was this Transylvanian plateau. But rises and dips in the terrain made it difficult to know for sure where enemy cavalry were deploying and when it would strike. The only reliable sense in a time like this was one's hearing, and even that was hampered by the relentless gunfire just a mile away.

"What companies are deploying to the left flank?" he asked.

"Shaffenburg's, Vizthum's, Salm's, Raabe's, and Lapierre's, sir. Nearly five hundred horse, as ordered."

Burkenfeld nodded. "You make sure Vizthum's dragoons dismount and deploy. Tell him to find a good clump of trees or hillocks and hold those Ottoman bastards at bay, you hear?"

"Yes, sir."

"And send for Captain Gayling." Burkenfeld dismounted, handing the reins over to his personal aide. "Tell him to bring his dragoons and deploy here, right where we stand. If Colonel Zelikovich refuses to defend his position, then we will."

Chapter 58

Northern battle line

Elements of Mitzlaff's, Truckmuller's, and Christian's companies fired their pistols in caracole, then charged into the massive block of Moldavian infantry on the right flank. This was the first time Christian had charged into battle since early spring. The thought of it made his weak right eye ache.

This wasn't Déj, however, where he had fought against an inexperienced army with little knowledge of up-time weaponry. This infantry block had rifled muskets that fired Murad mini-balls.

The first line of cavalry fell almost instantly as the Moldavians fired into the charging cavalry. The second and third lines, however, reached the infantry flank and slammed into it, whipping their swords through the air, firing pistols. Horses, inflamed with fear and rage, bucked and bit equally enraged footmen on their flanks. Alphonse reared up on his hind legs as a pike was thrust toward his neck. Christian drew his second pistol and put the man down before the tip of the pike could puncture Alphonse's throat.

Christian holstered his spent pistol and pulled his sword from its scabbard. A footman on his right tried raising his musket and firing. Christian yelped and brought the blade of his sword down on the man's arm, cutting through his buff coat and hearing the crack of his arm as he screamed and fell. A rider from

Truckmuller's company galloped over the falling man and disappeared into a swirling morass of swords, pikes, and pistol shots.

Christian pushed farther into the mass as well, bringing his sword down left, then right, left and right. Another pike was thrust his way. This time, it struck meat, slashing his left leg and cutting Alphonse as well. The horse reeled backward, and Christian fought to maintain control.

"Whoa, Alphonse," he shouted, "whoa now!"

It was difficult to regain control in the midst of battle. For a moment, Christian considered dismounting, but Lieutenant Enkefort, on his own horse, appeared at his side. He grabbed Alphonse's reins and helped get the horse under control.

"Thank you," Christian said quickly and rejoined the fight.

The ground was becoming sloppy with mud, blood, dead and wounded men. The Moldavians, under reasonably good command, managed to fall back and reform their lines. Christian knew exactly what to do under these conditions.

He waved his sword in the air, and the company trumpeter sounded the retreat.

General headquarters
Grand Army of the Sunrise

Morris Roth paced back and forth as he wiped the unending flow of sweat from his brow. Ellie Anderson finished her radio communiqué with Tuva, put the phone down, and said with as much sincerity and grace as she was able. "Morris, please, calm the *fuck* down. You've got to pace yourself. The battle has just started. It's going to be a long day."

General von Mercy, who sat in his wheelchair studying maps and speaking with General Renz via radio, wasn't sweating. The messengers moving in and out of tent headquarters weren't sweating. Nobody in the tent was sweating except him, as a matter of fact, and why the hell not? Didn't they understand the magnitude of this engagement? Couldn't they see what was at stake here? If the Sunrise lost, then what did that mean for the Anaconda Project? And what did it mean for the thousands, the tens of thousands, of Jews who had put their trust in him? To see the Joshua Corps reel back in defeat? And right now, according to

Tuva's report, they weren't doing very well. *I should have sent the Silesians in. Should have sent them in.*

"Shut up, Ellie!" Morris snapped. "I'm busy here! I've got a battle to fight!"

"Hey, boss," Len said, "don't be so harsh. Ellie's just worried about you, is all. We're all worried."

Morris threw up his arms. "She can tell me to 'calm the fuck down,' but I say 'shut up,' and it's an issue? Both of you just do your duty, goddammit, and leave me alone."

All conversation in the tent halted as Morris stepped around the map table and to the flap. He did not step outside. He stood there, by the entrance, looking out toward the hospital and beyond it to the central battlefield. In the distance, he could see the Silesian banners waving in the wind, Brethren banners just beyond them. A massive number of men just waiting. *And such a foolish thing to do.*

No. He couldn't start second-guessing his decisions again. He had made his final decision with von Mercy. Ellie was right. The battle had just started. He had placed his trust in the plan and in his command staff. He needed to stand down, wait, and let them work.

Yes, Morris... calm the fuck *down.*

The Dixie Chick

Denise felt like she was in a tag team wrestling match. The airship was the opponent, and she and Tuva kept tagging in and out like twin sister lady wrestlers. The airship moved north, and Denise tagged in. South? Tuva. Unfortunately, their big, brooding hulk of an opponent didn't want to be dropped to the ring's canvas, and she couldn't get close enough to try a strong flip over the shoulder, even if she had the weight and wherewithal to do it.

But this time, she did fly closer, for her opponent had flown over the capital and was now circling the airfield. Fortunately, the Jupiter and the Dauntless had been moved to Koloszvár, and so, there was little or nothing to see down there. But given its propensity to drop firebombs, Denise was concerned. If it struck the radio tower with one of them, that could cause significant communication problems.

She flew under the craft and past it. She circled around, minding some wind shear, as men from the gondola tried taking shots at her. They all missed, as she expected, but the residual fire did distract them from attacking the radio tower.

The good news was that her harassment did force the craft to move along. The bad news was that, while she was trying to keep it from striking the tower, the Moldavian infantry that had been gathering in the hilly woods to attack the airfield were no longer there.

Where did they go? she wondered. They'd probably been called back to the main line. Why attack an empty airfield?

Chapter 59

Southern battle line

Captain Andrej Dordevic waited for his cavalry to slowly—too slowly, perhaps—assemble into nice, tidy rows and await orders. The voivode of Wallachia had already given that order, but Andrej had paused. Why?

Two reasons. First, Matei Basarab was no general, and he had little or no understanding of tactical preparedness. Dordevic's men simply weren't ready when the order was given. He had to wait until the Croats, arriving late to the battle, were in place and armed with proper weapons.

Second, that little aircraft that the enemy insisted on flying over their battle line had spooked their horses. Morale had teetered on a knife for a while as he and his staff had to convince the hopelessly gullible within his ranks that God wasn't raining death down upon them for what they were about to do. What they were about to do, Andrej had to convince them, was to drive this Jewish force out of Transylvania, and then reap the rewards accordingly. His men had already been given enough silver dinars to last many, many months. Imagine the treasure that full victory might give them.

The thought of those rewards had renewed Andrej's enthusiasm about this engagement. In his heart, he had no love for the Sultan or the Ottomans nor was he inclined to take up arms on their behalf, but if they could beat this Bohemian army and take Transylvania, well—

His pleasant thoughts were interrupted by a rider who came galloping over a hill. The young Serbian reined his horse to a stop, saluted, and said out of breath, "Captain Dordevic, enemy cavalry, just over the ridgeline, is attempting to deploy its dragoons along a small stone wall."

"How far are they along?" he asked.

"They've just arrived, sir. Starting to deploy now."

"Excellent!" he said, almost hissing. "Then we go, *now*, and strike them in mid-deployment."

Andrej rose in his stirrups, pulled his sword, held it high, and gave the order to charge.

Jason pushed the screaming man's bloody leg down until it was flat against the ground. Like many others of First and Second Regiments, he had staggered back behind the relative safety of Third Regiment's defensive line, had fallen to his knees, and had begged for help. Scores of Ashkenazi soldiers had done much the same.

Jason had helped the medical staff at the Battle of Déj, but nothing had prepared him for this.

Young Tobias moved quickly to place a tourniquet on the man's leg before he bled out. Jason was impressed with the young man's efficiency. Young, but apparently quite capable. In fact, now that he thought about it, he did recall Isaac saying how much he admired Tobias' quick mind and cool demeanor. Jason could see fear in the boy's eyes—who wasn't afraid at this moment?— but once casualties had begun arriving, his whole attitude had changed. Tobias moved from man to man, making quick triage decisions about their care: "superficial," "minor," "treatable," "priority," "expectant." Those with superficial or minor wounds were sent back into the fray; treatables were given care on the spot; priorities were placed in a wagon and sent to the main field hospital where Doctor Kohen resided; expectants were left to die. Jason lingered behind for those, giving them comfort in their last moments, praying with them, holding them even after death. The new Murad mini-ball was a devil of a bullet. So far, over a third who had managed to stagger back from the front lines had died from their horrible wounds.

"Heavy casualties," Tobias said as they moved to another group of fresh arrivals. Thankfully, most of their wounds were minor. It seemed as if not everyone fleeing from the Wallachian attack waited until the last minute.

"How much longer can we hold?" Jason asked under his breath, more to himself than to anyone around him.

"Have no fear, Rabbi," a soldier, one Tobias had classified as "priority" due to the severity of his leg wound, said as Jason helped other medics put men into wagons. "We're pushing them back!"

The man coughed uncontrollably, and Jason helped him find his resting spot in the wagon. *Pushing them back...* doubtful, Jason figured, although the corps' modern weapons were just as powerful as anything the Wallachians could wield. Perhaps even more so. He wondered what it might be like on the Wallachian side of the line, how their wounded were faring amid so much terrible gunfire.

He shook the thought from his mind. As much as he wanted to love and respect everyone, to think good thoughts about all people, even the enemy, he had to focus on the care of these men, *his* men, boys whom he had prayed and worshipped with during many Shabbos since the very moment they had joined the Sunrise. Right now, they alone deserved his respect and attention.

Tobias slapped the hindquarters of the horse at the front of the wagon. The driver responded with a snap of the reins, and the wagon was gone.

From his right and through the tree line, Jason heard a rising of voices, galloping horses, and shouting men. Everyone in camp could feel the tremor of charging hooves. A silence cascaded from one wounded group to another. Jason looked at Tobias. The young man's impressive focus on duty was suddenly washed away. In its place, abject fear.

A man charged out of the tree line. Winded, exhausted, he fell to his knees and shouted, "Serbians...the Serbians are attacking!"

Northern battle line

Another charge into the Moldavian infantry, and for a moment, it seemed as if they would break. But Delta and Echo, two of five free infantry companies that Generals Roth and von Mercy had assigned to the Székely defense of the northern battle line, paused to loot bodies, thus giving the enemy time to bring up Tatar and Akinji cavalry and slam into their flank. Delta and Echo held, wavered, then routed.

"This isn't like Déj," Captain Josef Kinsky said, as he was ordered to redeploy his dragoons to the right flank to reinforce Foxtrot, Golf, and Hotel, the remaining three free companies who were, themselves, close to breaking.

"Not at all," Christian said, barely able to raise his tired arms to shake Kinsky's hand. They met in the middle of Kinsky's men who were in saddles and rushing to the right flank. "Can't General Renz do anything? Can't we get that Silesian regiment back?"

Kinsky shook his head. "Apparently not. At least not right away. Lots of problems in the south. The Joshua Corps is getting hammered, I hear."

Christian shook his head in disgust. His neck, too, hurt, though he had not suffered many wounds on the charge, save for that leg slash and a cut across the left sleeve of his buff coat. Alphonse had suffered a few other minor cuts. "Too inexperienced an army. We got too many green men in the field."

Kinsky nodded. "Not to mention mercenaries more interested in personal wealth than fighting. Ahh, well, that's to be expected. At least Hatmanu's men aren't falling back like they did before. They're taking a beating, but thank God, holding."

Kinsky shouted orders to his men as they finished moving to their new defensive position. He turned and took a good look at Christian. "How are your men holding up, Captain?"

"Fine. Though, we're running low on ammunition."

"I spoke with Col—I mean, General—Renz. They're sending more, though he could not tell me when it would arrive."

Too late, probably, to do much good, Christian figured. In the midst of battle, wagonloads of supplies couldn't roll up into the middle of it. Wagonloads of wounded were coming out of those dangerous areas right now. The narrow roads leading into and out of the capital were already teeming with horses and men and wagons and walking wounded. A log jam would most certainly occur and, inevitably, at the worst time. It always worked out that way.

"Do you need assistance, Captain?" Christian asked. "I've re-formed my men—those I have left—to the rear. We can move on your order and give support to your redeployment, protect your flank."

Kinsky smiled. He leaned over and patted Christian on his dusty shoulder. "Thank you, my friend. That won't be necessary. Ulfsparre's company will take that role for now. But stick around. Things'll get dangerous, I'm sure."

General Hatmanu's aide-de-camp rode into view with a security detail, their Székely banners, bearing an armored hand clutching a sword on a red field, waving madly in the wind. He was courteous enough to wait until Kinsky's men had cleared the road, then he approached. "Sirs," he said, "General Hatmanu has asked that you attend him...immediately."

Christian rolled his eyes. Apparently, things were getting dangerous right quick.

Chapter 60

Field hospital
Gyulafehérvár

The wounds Isaac was seeing were not like those from Déj. The Murad mini-ball was a beast of a bullet.

It created a wound similar to the Sunrise's own ZBs, but this was the first time that he had seen those kinds of wounds in large numbers arrive at the hospital. At Déj, and even at Krakow, the wounds were of a more traditional sort, from match and flintlock muskets, wheellock pistols. The kinds of wound he was more familiar with. Here at the capital, the enemy had just as powerful weapons as the Sunrise, and they knew how to wield them.

Wagonloads of wounded began arriving shortly after the battle commenced, and it had not dissipated much since then.

Soldiers lay inside and outside the tent. Good people from the capital had volunteered to assist the Sunrise's beleaguered nursing corps perform many of the mundane—though important—tasks of nursing, such as cleaning, sanitizing, preparing medical equipment. Devorah, Oana, and Andreea worked tirelessly in helping Isaac and Doctor Oberheuser sift through the wounded to determine which ones would be cared for first. Simply put: those with serious, though treatable, arm and leg wounds were cared for immediately. Those with deep body wounds, if they survived an hour waiting, were then admitted for evaluation and surgery. It was a brutal decision that Oberheuser put in place as soon as he saw the numbers arriving. Isaac didn't like it, but didn't complain. The old man was in a right mood, and in truth, the decision was probably the correct one. Treat those who could be saved relatively easily, where the largest volume of patients could be sent on their way, either back to the front or into convalescence outside the tent.

Isaac now stood over a young Ashkenazi soldier who had taken a shot through the gut. A clean entry and exit wound. Rare, but treatable. If only the boy would calm down.

Oana and Andreea held his legs and arms down while Devorah administered a shot of morphine. "Keep still, young man," Isaac said.

"Will I die?" the boy asked.

Isaac shook his head. "No, son. Not if you keep still."

"There were hundreds, thousands of them," the boy spit, as Devorah pushed the syringe of painkiller into his arm. "We couldn't hold them. Nobody could hold them."

From the Ashkenazi arriving at the tent, Isaac had gotten dribs and drabs of information from the southern battle line. It was a mess down there: an inexperienced Joshua Corps trying to hold back an entire Wallachian army, and one with terrible killing weapons like the one that had punctured this young man's bowel.

Damn all wars!

Isaac waited until his patient was unconscious, then he stepped aside to allow Oana to clean the entry wound. "There's not much I can do for him," he whispered to Devorah. "We can clean the area, remove the shrapnel, sew up his bowel, and then pray he doesn't get an infection."

"I'll pray for him while you do the work," Devorah said.

Isaac nodded and smiled. *"Ja, meine Dame."*

It was always a joy working alongside Devorah.

Southern battle line

"Hold the line!"

Colonel Burkenfeld's order to Gayling's dragoons was received, but not acted upon in time, as Serbian cavalry charged down the ridgeline toward them in waves of flowing red robes and glinting steel. Wheel- and flintlock pistols fired sporadically along their charge. ZB-2 Santees responded in kind along the stone wall from those who had successfully deployed before the charge. Others scrambled to try to get off shots before the Serbians swept their position. They shot and fell back, shot and fell back, trying desperately to maintain good order.

Pechmann's and Lamotte's heavy cavalry slammed into the Serbian advance, and that helped divert a portion of the attack. But still they came on, screaming and howling like red devils. If it had been simply a scrap between evenly matched forces, Burkenfeld's companies would have held, its dragoons' more modern rifles forcing an easy retreat. But the sheer number and weight of the Serbian charge was too great.

His hastily formed defense collapsed.

Colonel Burkenfeld found himself in the middle of the fight, a heavy *Panzerstecher* in his hand, slashing and stabbing his way through a wave of Serbian red coats, his cuirass protecting him from most sword slashes threatening to drop him from the saddle. He howled and hacked and hammered, ignoring the fact that his vision was partially obscured by his now-broken helmet. He raised his sword in his right hand and drew his Santee with his left.

He cocked one hammer of the pistol while parrying an attack from his right. The Serbian's saber struck his hand, splitting the flesh between index finger and thumb. Burkenfeld shuddered in pain, dropped his sword, and turned his pistol to the right to address his assailant.

Shots were fired, but not from his pistol. Two Serbians to his front fired into his cuirass. One shot was deflected. The other punctured a seam in his chest plate and tore through his stomach.

He fired his pistol randomly into the chaos. Maybe he struck someone, maybe not. Nothing seemed to matter to him now as he dropped his pistol, felt the warm sensation of blood draining down his stomach and into his crotch. He leaned to the left and fell from his horse.

"Wheel," Colonel Zelikovich said, finally, with an air of authority and defiance, "and refuse the line!"

Jason could hear the tumult through the trees, a combination of shouting, screaming, muskets firing, and horses dying, the kind of sounds most often reserved for nightmares. But, it was midmorning. This was no dream, and the Serbians were coming.

"Shouldn't we pull back?" he said, grabbing young Tobias' shoulder and tugging him away.

Tobias was giving aid to a medic who had fallen back with fleeing men from Second Regiment. He had stepped on a stone and had twisted, and perhaps broken, his ankle.

"It'll be all right, Rabbi," Tobias said, seemingly resigned to the possibility that here, now, he might die. "Remember your words: be not afraid of them."

Them were now pushing hard against Third Regiment. A violent discharge of musket fire sounded through the trees. Jason could not see the discharge of smoke, but he could smell it. He could smell it everywhere. It made him want to throw up, to turn tail and skedaddle, as they say, to jump on the Jupiter and fly back to Prague and be with his wife, their children.

Be a proud Jew... Words he had shared with many over the past several months. Had they come back now to haunt him, to mock him in his fear?

He helped Tobias put the medic in the back of a wagon; the last wagon available to transport wounded to Doctor Kohen. More were on the way, but did it matter now? If Colonel Zelikovich's order to "refuse the line" failed, would anything really matter?

Another volley of musket fire, then a cold, heavy silence. A long, deep silence. Jason found that strange, for surely the battle had not ceased. Perhaps it was one of those so-called acoustical shadows that he had learned about in up-time school, where observers close to a battle could hear nothing, yet many miles away, the sounds were crisp and clear. He suddenly found himself yearning for those battle sounds again. The silence scared him more.

Then a volley of weak musket fire sounded. A pause, then terrified men from Third Regiment burst through the tree line. Another musket sounded, and one of them dropped. Another screamed, "Run! Run!"

Tobias' hand was on his shoulder. "Rabbi? You're right. It's time to go."

Usan had never seen Matei Basarab in such a pleasant mood. But, good report after good report from his runners confirmed what he and everyone had hoped: the Jews were on the run.

The double envelopment had worked. Partially, at least. The attack on the left flank, led by Captain Dordevic, had succeeded masterfully, pushing the Sunrise dragoons back into the wood line. And now, the two Jewish regiments that they had attacked frontally had fallen back to a defensive position along a narrow stone wall between a row of farmhouses. The entire enemy line was falling back upon itself. All it would take now to break completely was for the cavalry on the right flank to push a little harder. But the Turkish and Wallachian cavalry assigned to that attack had met with stiff resistance. So far, at least.

"The *Ifrits* and my orta would make short work of that flank, my lord," Usan said again, trying to goad the voivode of Wallachia into a decision. "Just give the word, and I will bring victory to you and to Sultan Murad, and we will be in the capital by nightfall."

From time to time, Usan had had to remind Matei who they really served. It was easy to forget, the Sultan being so far away and so preoccupied with other military matters. He had not heard word from the Sultan since arriving in Transylvania. But no one should ever doubt who was in charge of this endeavor, especially Matei Basarab.

Matei lowered his spyglass and shook his head. "No, that won't be necessary, Usan. These Jews will fall before the sun sets. It is certain now." He motioned to his right. "Fire up the tanks and move them and your orta to the center, as Vasile Lupu recommends."

Usan sighed. "My lord, it has been hours since the *Chaldiran* delivered that message. We do not know the nature of the enemy's position in the center. They may have reinforced it by now. If I'm to go, I would feel better if I could acquire some cavalry to defend my flanks. The *Ifrits* are powerful, indeed, but slow, and they can be easily outmaneuvered."

"Your Janissaries aren't enough to defend those tanks?"

Usan held his anger in check. "My lord, we are but a thousand men"—*and even less now after the attacks on Meinbach and Hermannstadt*—"and we can only do so much. Give me two companies of cavalry. One company."

Matei shook his head. "No, *corbaci*. I still need them for the flank attack. We cannot relent against the enemy still before us." He paused, stroked his beard, said, "But I will give you my Dorobanți reserves. A full regiment of a thousand men. More than you'll likely need, I'm sure. They're yours. Take them."

Usan bowed. "Thank you, my lord." He raised his musket in salute. "Victory for the Sultan!"

Chapter 61

Central battle line

Brigadier Higgins watched the airship slip through the clouds, heading north. If he had a good up-time sniper rifle, one like Julie Sims carried, he'd put it to good use and bring the mother down. Cause it a lot of trouble, at least.

The airship was using said clouds to screen its movements. Like using smoke to block line of sight on the battlefield. Jeff nodded, impressed. Whoever was piloting that thing knew what they were doing.

Colonel Makovec of the Brethren appeared at his side. "Brigadier, Tuva has just reported difficult times for the Joshua Corps. They are being pushed hard."

Jeff nodded. "Perhaps we should throw your APCs into that fight."

Colonel Makovec shook his head. "I do not believe that they would get there in time to make much difference, if what Fräulein Tuva says is true. Sending footmen would be more appropriate. Faster, too. Perhaps a regiment of your Silesians would suffice?"

Jeff stared at the Brethren colonel. Makovec was a closed book, nothing but a rigid, dirty chin sharp with gray stubble and scars. He couldn't tell whether the man was being prudent or cowardly. More likely the former, although Jeff wondered if the man wasn't a bit apprehensive in putting his untried APCs

444

into the fray for fear of failure. As per the plan, Makovec had already committed one of his regiments to Captain Guth's defense of the center, so it wasn't as if the man balked at a good fight. *But, your APCs will commit one way or the other, Colonel,* Jeff thought. *Why not now?*

"Any word from the north?" Jeff asked. "Where's General Renz?"

"As far as I know," Colonel Makovec said, "he is moving there to deal with the Moldavians. They, too, are pushing hard. The general is most concerned."

Jeff grunted into a half burp, tasting his breakfast. He cleared his throat. "Squeezed like a grape. And you know what that means, don't you?"

"No, sir."

"The center's going to pop."

In truth, he and Morris had hoped that, by keeping the center relatively weak, both the Wallachians and Moldavians would seize the opportunity and divert more forces there, thus alleviating the pressure in the north and south. Such hope had yet to materialize, and Jeff was beginning to think that perhaps it never would. Perhaps it was a mistake not to send his men and the Brethren right into the fight, especially his Silesians. The enemy's superior numbers at the focal points of the battle were beginning to have a serious effect. *Well,* he thought, *at least we're three armies to two.* He scratched his chin. *Hmm... like in* The Hobbit. *The Battle of Five Armies. I wonder if Hollywood ever made a movie of that book.*

Jeff cleared his throat again. "I want to get more information before I commit anywhere. I don't want to send my men south, then hear that the north has collapsed. Or vice versa. But I agree with you, Colonel Makovec. We should at least get the men up and ready to move... in one direction or another."

Northern battle line

Christian could not believe what he was hearing. "I'm sorry, sir," he said to General Hatmanu. "The Moldavians are withdrawing?"

Hatmanu nodded. "It would appear so." He adjusted the map laying open on a makeshift table constructed of empty wooden supply boxes. The wind was up, the tent they were in was flimsy, so his assistants held the corners down lest the map blow away. Hatmanu ran his finger across the sketched-in battle line. "Withdrawing along this line here."

Christian studied the map, muscling his way in between Colonel Callenberk and Kinsky who seemed, rightfully so, put out by this abrupt order to waste time with a tent discussion.

The battlefield that their men were fighting on was relatively flat, given the nature of the Transylvanian landscape. The flattest that Christian had so far experienced. The battle line that General Hatmanu was pointing at lay on the left flank. Székely forces were fighting hard along that line.

"That makes no sense to me, General," Colonel Callenberk said. "The Moldavians are in a good position, with strong interior lines. Why would they retreat?"

Hatmanu shrugged. "I cannot say. Nevertheless, they are. And we must exploit that foolish decision."

Callenberk nodded. "If they are indeed retreating, then I agree. We should attack immediately."

As they discussed a plan, Christian remained silent. He studied the map, the terrain that, if accurate, concerned him greatly. Finally, he broke his silence. "Sirs, if I may?"

The tent grew silent as all turned their attention to Christian. "You have something to add, Captain?" General Hatmanu asked.

"Yes, sir." He moved his finger from the Székely battle line and down a road leading north between two wooded hills. "This is where the Moldavian retreat will likely lead your men, General. Right between these two wooded hills. If they get riflemen into those hills, it'll be—oh, what do the up-timers call it?—a turkey shoot. I think this drawback is a ruse, sir, to get us to follow them here." He pointed at the map again. "I recommend that we *not* give chase, and instead, hold the line. After all, it is their charge to attack us. Not the other way around."

Hatmanu huffed. A slim, derisive smile crossed his mouth as he shot a glance at Colonel Callenberk. "It would appear, Colonel, that one of your officers has seen enough battle for the day. I never thought I'd hear a cavalry officer call for defensive battle over pursuit."

Kinsky jumped in. "Sirs, if I may?"

Hatmanu paused, sighed, then nodded.

"I'm the first one to always agree with attacking. But, in this particular case, I agree with Captain von Jori. We saw this in Déj. On a smaller scale, admittedly, but a similar tactic, when the Impalers set up an ambush on a wooded hillside and cut to pieces scouts from Neuneck's company. If Captain von Jori is correct, you'll be cut to pieces in a crossfire."

"*If* he is correct," Hatmanu said. He turned to his aide-de-camp. "Any indication from our scouts that the Moldavians have moved into those wooded hills?"

"No, sir," the aide said.

"Any word from our aerial reconnaissance to that effect?"

"No, sir."

"General," Christian said, trying to contain his impatience. "Those hills are heavy with trees. The *Dixie Chick* can see a lot from the sky, but not everything. Denise cannot see through the canopy."

"Then all we have is just yours and Captain Kinsky's speculation and—how do you say it—hunch?" Hatmanu shook his head. "No. This is an opportunity to beat these people once and for all. If we can force a full retreat and swing around behind their central and right lines, then we can destroy the Moldavian army. I made a promise to Princess Lorántffy to defend the capital, to avenge the death of Prince Rákóczi. I owe that to my country and to my countrymen."

Hatmanu turned to Colonel Callenberk. "Sir, will you assign at least three companies to my advance?"

"Marius," Christian said, discarding proper military protocol, "I implore you to reconsider. I'm telling you now, officer to officer: this is a *trap*. There is absolutely no good reason for them to withdraw their left line at this time. They are doing it to pull you into a dangerous salient and then pick you apart."

Hatmanu ignored Christian's final warning. "Colonel Callenberk? Will you assist in this attack?"

"Yes, I will," the regimental commander said, glaring at his two captains. "You will have Truckmuller, Horst, and Hanau. They will lead the attack."

Hatmanu nodded. "Very good. That is all, gentlemen. You may return to your—"

"Sir," Christian blurted, his anger a slow boil under the surface, "if you refuse to take my and Captain Kinsky's counsel on the matter, then why were we summoned?"

Hatmanu closed his eyes to slits. "Because I wanted to see if you would volunteer to lead the charge. I wanted to see if you were...man enough to do it. I was wrong. And so, since you are not the man I thought you might be, then my order to you, Captain, is to return to your command and maintain good order on the right flank. And see to it that they do not, as you say, turn around and enclose my advancing men into a slaughter pen." He moved around the makeshift table to stand in front of Christian. "Can you do that, Captain? Can you and Kinsky and all the other company commanders do that much? Or have you and your Sunrise come to Transylvania simply to loot and exploit its people?"

Christian fought the urge to draw his sword. He'd make short work of this little cretin, and who would blame him? He then thought of Andreea and his hand stilled. Sweet Andreea. She deserved a better husband, a better man, for sure, but not a dead one. At least not at the end of Christian's sword.

"Can you do your duty, Captain?"

Christian swallowed his anger and forced himself to nod. "Yes, sir. I will."

Chapter 62

General headquarters
Grand Army of the Sunrise

Len Tanner passed the word to Morris. "Tuva reports that their fire tanks are on the move."

"Where?" Morris asked.

"To the center, followed by the Janissaries."

"Is that all?"

Len shook his head. "Her radio was popping in and out, but what she tells us is that there's another large body of infantry moving in concert as well. She couldn't give exact numbers nor was she clear on who it was. Moldavians . . . Turks . . . she did not know."

Morris turned to General von Mercy. "What do you think?"

"I think they are now, finally, trying to do what we had hoped that they would do from the beginning," von Mercy said.

Morris shrugged. "Seems like a relatively weak move, though."

"It's too big a force to be seen as a diversion," von Mercy countered. "They're serious, and we in turn must address it, especially if they follow it up with more troops, or the Moldavians make a similar move."

Which was why they had placed both the Brethren APCs and Higgins' Silesian Guard in reserve.

"The forces we have there right now will hold them off for a little while," von Mercy said, "but not for long. With Janissaries, defensive battle lines rarely survive."

Morris nodded. "Very well, then." He turned to Ellie. "Please contact General Renz, and kindly ask him to send the Brethren and the Silesian Guard into the center."

The Dixie Chick

Denise's relief that the Moldavians were falling back from the northern battle line was quickly replaced by confusion. Why in hell were the Transylvanians following them?

She was no expert in the art of war, but her recent experience with it at Déj had given her some practical knowledge. That, plus the fact that she, unlike anyone else (except Tuva), could see the entire battlefield from above. She had already radioed in that the Moldavian infantry companies that had initially threatened the airfield were now missing. Further, she had reported that a large gathering of Tatar cavalry was forming in the distance. Those two events were not mutually exclusive, she knew. Did anyone in HQ have enough smarts to know that as well?

What's the matter with General Hatmanu? Does he have a death wish?

Chapter 63

Central battle line

Usan Hussein had grown to—if not love—then at least respect the mighty power of the three fire tanks that rolled slowly in front of his orta. In truth, he despised the Sultan's up-time-inspired weapons, manned primarily by Jews and Christians, and none of them adhering to the teachings of Islam. Especially these infernal *Ifrits* that trundled forward, leaving deep grooves in the ground with their large, wide, hard rubber tires, smelling of smoke, steam, and naphtha. But at this moment, there was no better way to greet the enemy than with long, deadly streams of fire, like the mighty Greeks of old.

Hungarian cavalry tried attacking first, a headlong charge right into the snapping tongues of flame. Both horses and their riders were cooked where they fell, while others managed to at least turn back and flee, their haunches burning, their riders screaming. What a foolish move, Usan thought, rash men too inexperienced with up-time weaponry to understand the nature of them. They did not try another frontal assault. Instead, the shocked cavalry regrouped and struck the flanks.

The Wallachian infantry regiment that had followed his orta toward the center took the brunt of the assault, shifting to the right as their ranks buckled under the weight of the charge. For a few deadly moments, it looked as if the Dorobanți would rout. Usan ordered the *Ifrits* to halt, turn their turrets, and fire.

451

The cavalry melted in front of three flaming tongues, reaching out like a frog snagging prey. Dorobanți fell under the fire as well, but far less than the charging cavalry. Janissaries, too, were doused, and as much as Usan hated seeing his own men burn, the fire, again, forced the cavalry to retreat. This time, for good.

The Dorobanți regiment collected itself and re-formed its lines. The way toward Gyulafehérvár was now clear, hopefully, of further cavalry attack.

Poor radio reception hindered Jeff's communication with Tuva, but he endured. "Say again, Tuva?"

"Cavalry attacked...burning...retreating before *Ifrits* and... Janissaries and other...infantry..."

The mention of the *Ifrits* scared him less than Janissaries. He'd heard about them even before the Ring of Fire. The elite fighting force of the Sultan, members of his household troops, culled from Christian areas. They were seized as children, circumcised, converted to Islam, and trained to fight and kill. The Janissaries were some of the best soldiers the world had ever seen. Even in this new timeline.

"How many Janissaries, Tuva?" he asked.

There was a pause, a long one, and Jeff wondered if the connection had dropped again. The radio then crackled, and Tuva's voice boomed, "A thousand, maybe?"

"That's one orta," Colonel Makovec said at his side. He raised a finger. "One regiment."

"Is that all, Tuva?"

Through a weak connection, she provided as much detail as she could before finally signing off. Jeff paused to listen to the sounds of distant battle. Just muffled roar of cannon, the occasional crack of musket fire, the very rare bellow of men and trumpet, staccato drumbeats. The fighting was close and yet not close enough for him to get an idea, purely by sound, of the state of the fight.

"Two infantry regiments and three tanks," Jeff said with a big sigh. "I think you better fire up your APCs, Colonel, and get them moving."

Colonel Makovec nodded. "Right away, sir. Will your Silesians join us?"

Jeff shook his head. "Still waiting on word from Colonel Shalit. We need to know what the hell's going on down south before—"

"Brigadier!" a radio controller shouted. He held up the phone. "It's General Renz, sir."

Jeff accepted the phone. "General, glad to hear from you. What's the good word?"

"No good words, Brigadier," Renz shouted over a better connection. Jeff could hear battle sounds in the background. *How damn close are you to the northern front, General?* "The Joshua Corps' position is wavering. Collapse is imminent, I fear. I've discussed the matter with Generals Roth and von Mercy. You need to get a regiment up and moving now to support the southern line."

"Just one?"

"Yes, sir. Hold the other two in reserve a while longer until we can get a better sense of the situation in the north and center."

"No problem, General." Jeff didn't want to delay, but he couldn't help but ask, "How *is* the fight in the north?"

A pause, then through more battle sounds, even closer, "Difficult. Renz out!"

The transmission clicked hard as the connection was severed. Jeff handed the phone back to his radio controller and considered the order.

Only one *regiment for the Joshua Corps? Would that be enough?*

He wondered. If the situation in the south was as bad as General Renz said, then why not two? Then again, commit both Second and Third Regiments, and what did he have left for the Janissaries but his own Hangmen? And what of the north? Renz had just told him that the northern fight was "difficult." What the hell did that mean, exactly? If it meant something bad, then Jeff needed to keep a regiment of Silesians in reserve to move in that direction if needed, which was probably why Renz had asked him to commit only one to the south. *And yet, the Joshua Corps...*

Jeff did not consider himself part of Morris Roth's Anaconda Project, though he had absolutely no objection to it. In fact, he supported it fully. Hell, here he was, perched on a hill in Transylvania, far from home, risking his own life and the lives of his men, to preserve this cause to secure a future where Jews could live in peace without fear of constant persecution and massacre. It was the right cause, a noble cause. To have the Joshua Corps, then, routed on its first real fight, what message would that send to the Ottomans? To the world? The USE and the Bohemians had enough wolves at their gates already.

He turned to his regimental commanders. "Sirs, get Second and Third Regiments moving, on the quick step, south to the Joshua Corps' position. We *cannot* let them break."

Southern battle line

Men of Third Regiment fell back into a fighting withdrawal as Jason followed Tobias and his medical staff toward the ridgeline where Batteries C and D were standing. The guns had begun firing again, lowering their trajectories to place shot into the advancing enemy forces. A large wall of Wallachian infantry had followed the Serbian cavalry into the heart of Third Regiment's position. If it wasn't a total rout, Jason didn't know what to call it.

Terrified men, boys mostly, ran past him, finding the courage occasionally to pause, load, turn, and fire back toward the advancing enemy line. An imperfect line, for sure, more like a mob of Wallachians, Serbians, and Ashkenazi, firing and stabbing at each other from mere feet away. Jason saw one Serbian drive his saber across the face of one of his own, realizing his mistake, and then falling dead from a ZB-1636 rifle shot into the back.

"Don't let me die here, Rabbi," said a Krakow boy who had just taken a musket shot in the chest. "Don't let me—"

But he did die, right there, in Jason's arms, looking skyward, his eyes glazed over in terror, confusion. Jason paused to give prayer and then closed the boy's eyes. Tobias pulled him away.

"Keep moving!" the medic shouted. "We have to get past the cannons!"

"Where are First and Second Regiments?" Jason asked.

Tobias shook his head. "I don't know. All dead, maybe."

That was unlikely, and yet, they hadn't received any radio report from them in a long while, ever since the Serbians had broken Third Regiment's line. When last they had heard, the rest of the Joshua Corps had fallen back to a line of farmhouses and stone walls and were desperately trying to stave off total defeat. Where were they now? Where was everyone?

It seemed to Jason as if all the world was retreating. There was nothing now but war and smoke and fire and blood, the whimpering cries of dying boys, the deep growls of angry men engaged in hand-to-hand, the *whoosh!* of smoke and fire from cannon barrels firing shot and shell into as many of their own men as the enemy. What was the old American Civil War saying? *This is a universe of battle?* He could not remember the quote exactly, nor did it matter. What mattered now was getting beyond the ridgeline and to, hopefully, safety.

Safety... The word lingered in his mind. *There is no safety anywhere in all the world for my people.*

Tobias fell at his side. Jason looked to his young friend and found a gaping wound in his back. "Tobias! Tobias!" But the medic lay there, saying nothing, a roll of bandages in his left hand, a satchel of medical supplies upended and strewn across the soft ground.

"Move!"

It was Colonel Zelikovich, far to the right, waving Jason forward. "Move, Rabbi! Move!"

Jason forced himself away from Tobias, letting his fingers linger in the young boy's dark hair a second longer before pulling away completely and continuing toward the cannon line.

By God's grace, he reached the line and passed beyond it, feeling through the ground the hard discharge of cannon fire as the rest of Third Regiment raced to safety.

Behind the cannons and mortars, men from Third Regiment huddled together, like terrified mice, not knowing where to go, what to do. *Should we keep running?* He could almost hear them ask the question. Would the enemy stop at the cannon line, or would they overrun that as well and keep driving and driving and driving until they reached the capital? Jason looked down at all the huddled, frightened men and knew the answer to those questions.

No... I cannot let this happen.

He reached down and scooped up a discarded ZB rifle and held it aloft. "*Rak Chazak Amats!*"

He shouted it again and again, until all the men below him quieted and looked up.

"*Rak Chazak Amats!*" he said to the beat of mortar fire. "These are our words, Joshua's words, given to him by God to lead the Israelites into Canaan, into the promised land, after Moses' passing. *Rak Chazak Amats!* Be strong and courageous."

He stumbled down the ridge. The men parted to let him walk between them. "I am an up-timer. My life as a Jew there was not perfect, but it was nothing like the life all of you have had to endure. But through the Ring of Fire, I found my purpose. I became a Rabbi so that I may know that you, my people, my brothers, never have to endure again the privations of the past, or the holocausts of your future. I say no more!

"Morris Roth has given us this chance, *this one chance*, to change our lives," he said, his voice cracking under tears, his throat dry, scratchy, "and we must take it." He pointed to the cannon. "The enemy that charges here are not Serbians or Wallachians or Turks. They are nothing more than Philistines in different clothing. They want to defeat you, suppress you, kill you, and I say to them no more. We are the Joshua Corps. We are Joshua's men, and if we are to die, then let us do it fighting for our lives, our wives, our children, our culture. Let us fight for the right to be *who we are*. We are Ashkenazi. We are Jews, and we are proud of who we are. Let us fight for Morris Roth, for Joshua, for God.

"*Rak Chazak Amats!*"

The chant grew and grew and grew until even the cannoneers began to shout it.

"Fix bayonets!" Colonel Zelikovich shouted. The men, who had previously huddled in fear, now gathered in loose ranks behind the cannons, and Jason filed in right beside them, the rifle still in hand, tears of joy and fear lining his face. Somewhere over that ridgeline, he knew, could be his death, and so be it. Young Tobias had given his life for this cause. *I can do no less.*

The cannons fell silent to allow the rallied men of Third Regiment to take their positions.

Colonel Zelikovich, giddy now with strength and courage, raised his saber, and shouted, "*Rak Chazak Amats!*"

Rabbi Jason Gotkin shouted the war cry until he could no longer speak. He raised his rifle, fixed his bayonet forward, and charged into the wavering line of Philistines.

Chapter 64

Southern battle line

Matei Basarab stood beside a hot cannon and watched as his once powerful advancing army now fell back across ground that they had already captured earlier in the day. "What's happening?" he asked Stroe Leurdeanu. "What's *happening*?"

"The Jews have rallied, my lord," Stroe said, his voice wavering. "All three regiments, including the one that Captain Dordevic and the Serbians had in full retreat. They shout *Rak Chazak Amats*, and our men fall back."

"What does that mean?" Matei asked.

Stroe shook his head. "I don't know, my lord. I can try to find out for you if—"

"Forget it! Where's Usan Hussein?"

Stroe pointed toward the center of the battlefield. "He has moved to the center, as you requested."

"What is his status?"

"I don't know, my lord. We've received no word. Though"—he took a step in that direction and pointed the spyglass toward rising smoke—"there are large pillars of smoke in that area one can see even from here. It is certain that he has engaged."

Matei closed his eyes and prayed. *Oh, merciful God, let those Janissaries see their way to victory.*

Central battle line

The hefty wheels of the fire tanks churned through the soft ground as musket and rifle fire from Hajdu and Bohemian gunmen, defending a stone wall, peppered their hulls. Usan was less afraid of taking a direct shot and more worried about ricochet, as lead whistled through the air like hornets, striking thick chassis, and dropping men in front of him, beside him. Enemy cannons behind the wall and set atop a hillock now fired. A cannonball struck the *Ifrit* farthest to the left; a burst of metal and naphtha flew out of the flamethrower barrel, and it seemed as if the tank would ignite and blow. It shook from the cannon strike, halted, righted itself, and continued, though Usan could see that its turret now seemed sluggish, harder for the crew to correct its trajectory.

He struck the hull of the tank in front of him with his rifle butt, a series of short, precise staccato taps that he hoped the crew inside could discern from the musket fire. They seemed to do so, as its turret swung to the left, paused, and let out a stream of fire that leapt through the deadly space between it and the stone wall. The fire doused very little, save for thick tufts of grass, a tree, a bush, and a few horse and human carcasses from the previous cavalry charges. The heat of the flame, however, forced the defenders of the wall to pause and step back a few paces lest their exposed skin be badly singed. Usan struck the tank's hull again, a different pattern this time, and the *Ifrit* reacted with a cough of steam and heightened speed.

Through smoke and the choking fumes of naphtha, he suddenly realized that the *Ifrit* in front of his men was the one that had had mechanical problems before the battle: an axle repair and fume leakage around its tank. All *Ifrits* had some amount of leakage, he knew. As good as the Sultan and his engineers were in adopting up-time military technology, many of their weapons were hampered by lack of refinement. Usan had grown to understand and accept that truth, but now he worried about it, as a cannonball struck the tank's hull and rocked it to the right. *Will its axle hold*, he wondered, *or will it break climbing that wall?* And what of the fumes? So far, it had proven unimportant, save for stinging his eyes, choking his throat. But as long as the flames fired forward, what concern could there be?

Right now, the biggest problem was the enemy at the stone wall, firing and shouting expletives, almost daring their assailants to charge. One Hajdu had the courage—and stupidity—to stand and expose himself and gyrate his hips as if he were fucking a goat. He was promptly shot dead, but Usan wondered, *Is it just boastful pride, or do they* want *us to come?* What foul devilment lay behind those cannons on the hill?

It did not matter now, he realized. The path to glory, the way to redeem himself in the eyes of Sultan Murad, of Allah, was forward. From his place in the line, Usan could already see the outline of Gyulafehérvár. So close. So, so close. There was no retreat now, regardless of what lay before or behind him.

He struck the tank again, raised his sword, and shouted, "Forward, men! Forward to the wall. Seize it, and don't leave anyone alive!"

The *Ifrit* belched fire and burned whole swaths of men in its stream. The Hajdu line buckled and fell back, and Usan ordered another push, into the wall and over it. The tank's tires scraped against the ground as its battering ram struck the wall and pushed, pushed, until its stones toppled over, leaving a breach. The cannons on the hillock fired again, striking the tank's hull in mid-lurch over the broken wall. For a moment, Usan feared a kill, but the *Ifrit* took the hit, settled, and pushed over the wall, slamming into the ground and broken stone on the other side.

His men shouted their joy and raced forward around the tank like water around a rock, drawing their yatagans and giving chase to the retreating enemy soldiers.

The other two tanks leading the Dorobanți regiment forward breached the wall as well, though the last tank could not bring its turret into the proper position to fire. Its naphtha stream had diminished to half the distance, a mere thirty yards. *It's done,* Usan thought, though its beleaguered crew did its best to keep it. The Dorobanți, however, were less enthusiastic with the breach. They seemed unwilling to exploit it.

In his capacity as *corbaci* and an envoy to Sultan Murad IV, Usan reached the wall, stepped onto it, raised his sword, and shouted, "Attack! Attack, you spineless—"

Then he saw why the Dorobanți had hesitated.

To their left and moving fast was a metal monstrosity, much like an *Ifrit* but long and twisting like a snake, with large rubber tires and thick armor, belching steam, and pulling equally armored wagons behind it.

And in front of where he stood, just beyond the hill where Bohemian cannons lay in defense, was another.

Chapter 65

Central battle line

Accepting the command of Usan Hussein, the Dorobanți colonel—half dead with bleeding wounds and a broken arm—ordered his men to re-form the lines, wheel, and advance against the armored APC to turn the damaged *Ifrit*'s flank. He was not successful.

The damaged *Ifrit*, the one on the far edge of the left flank, was overwhelmed by enemy soldiers coming up behind the parked armored wagons and swarming its hull. The crew inside, and those Dorobanți brave enough to respond, tried keeping the beleaguered tank from capture, but a swarm of musket fire from the wagons themselves sent many Dorobanți to the ground and the grave.

The second *Ifrit* and the one closest to Usan's position, had an even worse problem to treat with.

The steam locomotive from the APC whose occupants were giving the third *Ifrit* so much trouble detached itself from its lead wagon. Belching steam as it picked up speed, it bounded over a small hill like a sloop cresting a wave. The crew of the second *Ifrit* tried adjusting its turret to respond, but before it could get the proper firing arch, the V-shaped iron grate on the front of the locomotive slammed into the tank, rocking it backward and sending Dorobanți soldiers flying.

Usan could almost feel the impact of the strike as he tried keeping his focus on the evolving matter in front of him. But the struck *Ifrit*, its tires churning against the relentless push of the enemy locomotive, fell back through the breach in the wall. Usan tried rallying the Dorobanți around it, but their injured commander was now dead. The struck *Ifrit* managed to douse the locomotive with a tongue of naphtha, but it did little damage, burning more Dorobanți than enemy soldiers.

The struck *Ifrit* and the Dorobanți charged with its protection were now in full retreat.

Enemy cannoneers on the hillock in front of Usan's regiment fired again, several desperate shots that passed harmlessly overhead as his *Ifrit*, scorched, dented, but otherwise intact, moved to silence those guns forever.

Behind the protection of the back left tire, Usan raised his musket, aimed carefully, and put a round into the belly of a cannoneer trying to prime his gun. Someone tried taking his place, but he too was shot down. The remaining cannoneers fled. The *Ifrit* responded by moving forward, adjusting its turret, and sending an arching stream of fire into their wake, engulfing the last man in the retreat.

"Forward!" Usan shouted despite the fate of the Dorobanți and their two *Ifrits*, reloading his musket as his orta and the remaining fire tank pushed ahead.

How much naphtha did the *Ifrit* have left? Usan wondered. He tapped the tank with the butt of his rifle. The *mülazim awal* who had foolishly exposed himself to gunfire outside the Hermannstadt gate had done so on occasion to measure, by sound, the amount remaining. He couldn't tell, though he figured that there was far less than half. Was there enough to handle what was coming? That was the question.

And one he could not answer, nor did he have time to contemplate. The *Ifrit* pushed up the hillock where the cannons lay, and there, its battering ram struck the closest gun and crushed its limber and caisson. Like a crunch of bone, and for a moment, Usan was afraid that the cannon itself would ignite. Instead, it sank into the ground as its steel-banded wheels buckled. The fire tank rolled over it like a bump in the road.

The cannons were silent, now, forever. *Praise Allah!*

Up and over the hill. Now, Gyulafehérvár lay even closer. Usan imagined that he could smell the wood fires burning in its quiet homes. He imagined then his men running through those homes, burning them to cinder, burning and killing everything.

The APC he had seen in the distance had halted. It blocked a crossroads where his *Ifrit* had to travel to reach the capital in good order. Usan paused to see if there was any other way forward, any other path that they could take and thus avoid those armored wagons altogether.

There were certainly paths his men could take, but not the *Ifrit*. The ground was too hilly, too cluttered with rocks and bits of stone wall. The only way to glory was through those wagons.

Do we need the tank anymore? Its protection was really the only reason the orta had gotten so far. As strong as the Janissaries were, they would not have survived so long a march under such withering gunfire. No. It was the *Ifrit* that had provided the needed protection, had forced the enemy to retreat, men terrified of its demon breath, terrified of losing their souls to its tongues of fire. Usan would come to terms with his own fear and hatred for such a weapon later, would beg Allah forgiveness, when victory was secured. For now, there was no doubt: despite what had happened to the other two, the Janissary needed its *Ifrit*.

"To the wagons!" he shouted.

The Dixie Chick

Denise looked at her fuel gauge and winced. Near empty, and not enough to take another full pass over the battle line. *Damn! Damn! Damn!*

"We've got to return to the airfield," she said to her passenger, "or we'll end up a broken husk in those woods down there."

Her passenger wasn't listening. He was looking intently *at* those woods. Something was going on underneath the canopy. He took a shot.

"What did you see, buddy?" she asked.

"Can't say for sure," he replied. "A puff of smoke, a discharged rifle. Hard to know."

"Shall I drop lower?"

"No," he replied. "Don't do that. Let me try something else."

Despite his statement, she took the Dvorak down another one hundred feet to a comfortable cruising altitude of four hundred. Still out of range of anything the enemy might try to shoot her way, and it gave her passenger a better shot.

He fired again, and this time, even Denise saw it. "Return fire!" "Bingo!"

Where the man had heard the up-time expression, Denise did not know. But he was right. There were a bunch of musketmen under that colorful canopy; most likely those that had pulled back from the airfield.

The fuel gauge on her dashboard flickered. *Damn again!* She couldn't delay the return any longer, but she couldn't leave without first alerting them of the danger.

Before banking left and heading back to the airfield, Denise took up her radio and shouted, "Enkefort, Enkefort! Do you read?"

Northern battle line

Lieutenant Enkefort signed off and dropped the phone into the radio box. "Sir, Denise reports musket fire from a tree line about two miles or so up the road."

Christian frowned. "Right where Hatmanu's men are being led."

Enkefort nodded. "Yes, sir."

Fuck! If he had been the regimental commander in that tent, he'd have refused Hatmanu's request for cavalry support. The argument would have gotten heated and perhaps even dangerous, but three cavalry companies, plus a good portion of the Székely trabants, would not be heading to their deaths. *Fuck, fuck, fuck!*

"What do we do, Captain?" Enkefort asked.

"We have our orders, Lieutenant," Christian said with a big sigh. "We protect the right flank."

"Against useless Hansari light cavalry? They're nothing."

As was part of the Moldavian plan, Christian was certain. Provide just enough aggravation on the right flank to keep the Sunrise in place there, while pulling the Transylvanian forces into a no-win situation. And they picked the right general to fool: Marius Hatmanu. He wasn't leading the charge—he wasn't so bold—but he was following his men to their deaths. *Stupid man!*

"Radio Captain Kinsky," Christian said. "I have an idea."

"You're a fool, Christian," Kinsky said. "Hatmanu's a fool. Let him fall on his own sword."

They were a mere hundred yards from the front line. Kinsky's dragoons were holding a small cluster of farmhouses against a relatively modest frontal assault of light Moldavian infantry. Keller's and Ulfsparre's companies were in the saddle and aggravating attempts by the Hansari light cavalry to infiltrate the rear. Christian and Kinsky stood amidst a growing sea of wounded men who had fallen out of the line and were huddled near medical staff. Christian looked at the wounded and was thankful that Isaac was safely miles away, in the capital.

"Hatmanu's men are up there now," Christian said, pointing up the road. "They're going to get slaughtered."

"Yes," Kinsky said, "but I can't pull my dragoons out of the line now. The right would fall, and we'd have two catastrophes on our hands."

"Then give me Mitzlaff's men," Christian implored. "You're using them as dragoons, and they aren't dragoons. They're heavy horsemen. They need to be in the saddle and riding with me to save that son of a bitch." Christian paused, took a deep breath, then said, "You know what's up there, Josef. The whole goddamned Tatar cavalry corps, just waiting."

Kinsky pulled back. "Why are you even considering this, Christian? You despise Hatmanu."

"It's not about him." *It's about Andreea.* "It's about not allowing this Sunrise, that we serve, to fall. It's clear to me now that General Renz isn't going to send us Silesian reserves. Why, I don't know. So, it's just us. We've got to go and save our arrogant colonel, who is only interested in covering himself in glory, *and* General Hatmanu. If they fall, the whole battle line collapses. You know this."

Christian could see that his friend knew the truth of it, but was struggling with what to do. Kinsky removed his helmet, ran his hand through his sweat-matted hair.

"I'm sorry, Christian," Kinsky said, putting his helmet back on. "As much as I want to follow you in the charge, I can't pull my men from the line. That would be suicidal."

"Then give me *Mitzlaff's men*," he repeated with added urgency.

Kinsky shook his head. "I've no authority to do that."

"Fine!" Christian threw his hands into the air, his frustration on full display. "I'll ask him myself."

Chapter 66

Southern battle line

"Jason Gotkin," Colonel Samson Shalit said, keeping his helmeted head low at the stone wall. "I love you, Rabbi, but put a god-damned helmet on!"

Jason couldn't help but snicker. He'd never heard the man curse, especially in up-time parlance.

"I apologize, Colonel," Jason said, accepting a loaded rifle from a man nearby who had volunteered to load while others fired. "I can't find one that fits."

"Then find one that doesn't, for if I see you again without one, God forgive me, I'll drag you off the line myself and court-martial you in front of General Roth. You are too important to die!"

The Wallachians were trying to reseize the wall, and in a few places, they had managed to breach it. But *Rak Chazak Amats* was still being shouted along the line, and the gaps had been filled with zealous men chanting Joshua's words while firing rifles into the dwindling mass of enemy soldiers.

Jason picked up a helmet at his feet, bloodstained and messy with mud. He slipped it on. It covered his right eye. "Will this do, sir?"

Colonel Shalit slapped the helmet hard, driving it tighter onto Jason's head. He nodded and smiled. "That'll do. Now, raise your rifle and fire, Rabbi. *Rak Chazak Amats!*"

Jason raised up, pressed the butt of the rifle firmly into his shoulder as he had been shown, and fired. He tried to shout the words as well, but his voice was gone. Just a squeaky recitation of the chant escaped his dry lips. He was spent, exhausted, and yet, he fired. Not for himself really, though the fear of death was strong in his mind. He endured his weak body and fired for Tobias, for Colonel Zelikovich, Colonel Shalit, for every man along the stone wall. They were firing and dying still at his side, and he could think of no better place to be but here, at this moment, fighting with them.

"They better break soon, Colonel," the young man loading rifles said, "or we're going to be in trouble. We're running out of ammunition."

Jason could see Colonel Shalit working out that reality in his mind. *What must we do? Another bayonet charge? How many more of those do we have left in us?* Tough, tough decisions, for sure. Rise out from behind this wall and attack, and possibly get slaughtered. Stay in place, run out of ammunition, and be overwhelmed. *Perhaps I've done nothing but rally the men to delay the inevitable.*

He was about to state his opinion on the matter when a cadence of drum and flute burst through the morass of killing sounds. Faint at first, then rising, rising, like a tide that could not be overcome. Jason looked back to the tree line, toward the small farmhouses that now lay in burning ash.

A line of soldiers, in tight, steady lines, burst through the fog of smoke. Jason recognized who they were immediately, for there were Jews in their ranks as well.

"The Silesians!" he shouted, letting his tears, and helmet, fall. "The Silesians are here!"

Northern battle line

Captain Gregor Mitzlaff nodded. "Yes, Captain von Jori. I will ride with you."

A weight lifted from Christian's chest. "Thank you, Captain."

"But it will take some time to move my men off the front line and have one of the free companies move in as replacement."

"How long?" Christian asked.

Mitzlaff considered. "An hour. Maybe two."

Christian winced. *Too long!* By then, the entire Székely force could be destroyed. They had yet to hear word or sound of anything serious happening up that deadly road. That gave Christian comfort. Maybe they did have some time to muster.

"Do what you can to assemble your men within the hour, Captain Mitzlaff. We'll gather left of the center line."

"This is insubordination, Captain von Jori," Mitzlaff said. "It's in conflict with a direct order from Colonel Callenberk and the commanding Székely general."

"Yes," Christian admitted, "and I will take full responsibility if it fails."

Central battle line

Musket fire roared out of the tiny slats along the APC's side. *A clever design,* Usan thought, as he, like his men, kept close to the *Ifrit* to avoid being shot to pieces. The men inside the enemy wagons were fully protected by armored walls slanted slightly so as to force enemy fire to ricochet away harmlessly. *Clever, indeed.*

But burning naphtha would not ricochet, not in the manner that the occupants of the wagons might hope. Janissaries fired their muskets as practicable, but the *Ifrits* would win this engagement, Usan knew. If it was winnable at all.

A cannon strike to its front left wheel rim shook the tank and pushed it back a foot. One Janissary, too close to the right rear tire, screamed as he fell under the agonizing weight of the *Ifrit.* Usan forced himself not to run to the boy's aid. No stopping now, for any hesitation would bring a quick end to this endeavor.

With a powerful *whoosh!* the *Ifrit* opened fire, now only forty yards away from the APC. The crew turned its turret toward the locomotive and coated its wheels with fire. Thick, black smoke erupted from the flames and poured into the sky, giving both sides further protection from musket fire as visibility dropped. But Usan knew the wagons and its men weren't going anywhere. They had moved into a crossroads, and there, the APC would stand.

The *Ifrit* crew turned the turret down the length of the armored wagons, painting them with flames like an artist pushing pigment across a canvas. Musket fire from inside the wagons stopped as hot naphtha splattered through the slats and began burning the men inside. Usan could hear their screams. The crew of the *Ifrit* must have heard them as well, for it stopped its turret and kept pouring fire into the central wagon.

Soldiers inside the burning wagon tumbled out, through the top, the back, falling behind the wagon or in front of it. Those in front were cooked immediately. Those behind fled as other men rushed forward to try to retake the position. Cannon fire erupted once again, and this time, it struck well.

Flame shot straight into the sky as a cannonball struck the turret and bent the barrel upward. Burning naphtha cascaded down like a fountain, and Usan's heart sank. With all the fumes this tank was emitting, it might—

He beat out a hard staccato pattern with his rifle on the hull of the *Ifrit*, trying to warn the crew. He struck so hard the stock of his musket cracked and fell away in pieces. But the message was received: the naphtha stopped flowing through the damaged barrel and the battering ram was pushed out farther.

The *Ifrit* lurched forward and slammed into the burning hull of the central wagon.

The weight of the wagon and its attachment to its partner in the rear, and the locomotive in front, kept it from toppling over immediately. It was a strong position, and Usan wondered if he had ordered a mistake. The wheels of the *Ifrit* churned like a millstone on stubborn grain, as its battering ram struck the chassis of the wagon and cracked wood and iron. But the APC would not go down.

Then Usan saw a miracle. His men, his orta, moved around the sides of the tank, abandoning their protection in the rear. Under heavy gunfire, they slammed into the wagon and pushed and pushed and pushed, rocking it back and forth on its broken chassis. They howled to the glory of Allah and pushed.

The *Ifrit*'s tires finally found purchase in the muddy road, and its battering ram struck again. This time, the wagon collapsed backward.

Usan felt like crying. He had given the order to charge, but never in his life could he have imagined men under his command showing such drive, seizing the initiative with both heart and hands as they did now. A sea of red coats and white bork hats, faces smeared with blood, mud, and sweat, taking that extra commitment to ensure victory. He wanted to bow before them all, to present them to the Sultan personally, to shower them with imperial accolades. There was no denying his utter devotion to these men now, and he would die in the honor of their company.

"Attack!" he shouted, climbing over the toppled wagon and pushing forward with his beloved men.

He paused to look back at the *Ifrit*. It was not moving. Again, its tires turned, kicking up dirt and mud. It reversed, but it could not pull its battering ram out of the wagon's mangled chassis. It tried all steam ahead, but the crumpled APC, again, would not budge.

It's gone, Usan thought as he bid the *Ifrit* a fond farewell and watched as naphtha poured out of its broken turret.

His eyes widened. "Move! Move!" he shouted, raising his arms to his men to drive them forward. "Move!"

He turned and ran up the road, toward the capital and glory. Behind him, naphtha, running the length of the *Ifrit*'s hull, ignited, engulfing itself and the armored snake in flame.

Chapter 67

Northern battle line

Christian heard the horrific discharge of musket fire. The whole world heard it, he imagined. He and the world paused to listen, and his heart sank.

Wounded Székely soldiers fell back from the ambush. Christian could see the mass now, a red-coated shamble of terrified men who were still under heavy fire from the thick tree line on each side of the road. For a moment, he feared that he and Mitzlaff's cavalry would not be able to work through it, that their charge would be blunted by the chaotic retreat. *Should we withdraw?* he wondered. *Re-form and try another way?* Then he heard the faint rumble of horses' hooves beyond the retreating lines, and the recognizable howls of Tatar cavalrymen.

Christian leaned forward and put his head on Alphonse's mane. He stroked the horse's neck. *"Mut, mein Freund. Wir werden das gemeinsam durchstehen."*

Holding Alphonse's reins tightly, Christian drew one of his pistols and held it aloft. He looked left, right. His and Mitzlaff's men were in place, ready. Lieutenant Enkefort was at his side, fearful, Christian knew, but steady.

He cocked his pistol, both barrels. "Ready, men!" Christian shouted. "Ready...

"Charge!"

Central battle line

Jeff stepped back as the rider's mount slid to a halt in front of him, splashing dirt and pebbles forward. The boy in the saddle, his voice raspy and breathless, botched the salute. Jeff waved it off. "Give me the skinny, son."

The boy seemed perplexed by Jeff's words, but answered anyway. "Sir, the APC line has been breached."

"How?"

"One of their tanks struck, pushed it over, and then exploded in fire!"

Jeff's heart sank. "How the *hell* did that happen?"

The boy shook his head. "I don't know, sir. All I know is what they tell me. They say its battering ram struck the middle wagon and knocked it over. Then it got stuck in the wagon's carriage and—"

Jeff blew out a long, high-pitched whistle. "Damnation!"

The boy nodded. "Yes, sir. Apparently its naphtha tank was breached and then ignited, killing its own crew and many men in the APC, though some got away. But the Janissaries are coming, sir. They're coming!"

"What of the other APC?" Jeff asked. "There are two."

"The other is doing well, sir. Transylvanian soldiers following the APC swarmed one of the tanks and took it. The second tank was struck by the locomotive."

"What?"

The boy couldn't help but smirk. "They say its crazy pilot decoupled from his wagons and took off after it, struck it square and forced it to retreat."

Jeff grunted and shook his head. "That's a set of balls for you. May have to give that fool a medal when it's all over. Thank you, young man. You may go."

Jeff stepped away and walked to the edge of the camp, raised his spyglass, and looked out across the battlefield.

Large lines of smoke drifted into the sky. More smoke than he had, in truth, ever seen on a battlefield in this new timeline. No doubt created by those twice-accursed flame tanks. He shook his head. *To go down into the middle of all that...*

But two tanks were now out of commission, if the runner's report was correct, and the last one was locked in a fight with the other APC. So that left only the Janissaries to deal with. Easy-peasy.

Jeff couldn't help but laugh. *Easy-peasy, my ass.*

He tucked his spyglass away and turned to his aide-de-camp. "Sir, fetch me my horse. It's time to meet those Janissary sons of bitches."

The Hajdu made one more attempt at hitting the advancing Janissaries, but Usan's men, their blood up, pushed them aside as they had all other obstacles. The Hajdu were an impressive fighting force, he had to admit, a credit to their country. But nothing was going to stop him and his orta from reaching the streets of Gyulafehérvár. The path was wide open now.

Usan calmed his men and brought some order to their advance. He appreciated their energy and enthusiasm, but now was not the time for undisciplined movement. Re-form the lines and move together, one unified block of fire, shot, and sword. The *Ifrit*, which they had relied upon for so long, was nothing but a burning husk behind them. Going forward, they would have to rely on their own fighting prowess to bring victory.

He looked up and down the red-and-white columns of the orta, his lieutenants barking orders to maintain good form and pace. Nowhere near the number of Janissaries he had first met in that field in Timișoara. Their numbers now were well below full strength, some of them having fallen fresh in the fields behind him. But if any men could take a city... *let it be mine.*

Up and over a line of connected hillocks, through fields lying fallow for winter, past a farmhouse, and now, Usan could see the banners of the enemy waving in the wind, and the bright white canvas of its hospital. Oh, if he had just two, three cannons, what havoc could he force upon the enemy to drive them away! Why had he been so foolish not to demand cannon be brought with him to this field of battle? Matei needed them, of course, to push the Jews back in the south, and how was that battle progressing? He'd gotten no report of late from the voivode of Wallachia, nor any signals from the *Chaldiran*. The entire southern attack could have faltered; or, perhaps they had broken the Jewish line and were now driving into the capital themselves. Usan smiled at that possibility. *I will meet you at the Princely Palace, Matei Basarab, and there, we will drink a dead prince's wine in victory.*

Usan raised his yataghan, pointed to the white tent, and waved his men forward.

"To the banners!" he shouted until his voice broke. "To the banners!"

Jeff was off his horse and moving in a crouch along the line of men from his Hangman Regiment. Now, he could hear the orders of the Janissary officers as they closed on his hidden position. It wasn't the best place for an ambush: a half dug-out ditch alongside a dirt road, and if botched, the enemy could easily recreate "Bloody Lane" from the Battle of Antietam.

"Steady, men," he said, whispering his encouragement as he moved from soldier to soldier, giving them supporting pats on the shoulder, a nod, a smile. Most of them were elite, men who had engaged in many battles over the years. But some were new, and they needed all the encouragement he could give them. This time, they weren't facing Lithuanian magnates. This time, they were facing Janissaries, and there was a big, big difference.

"Are the volley guns ready?" he asked a member of one of the crews who had come down from the tree line above the ditch.

The man nodded. "Yes, sir. Ready to move into place when you give the order."

"Then I so order. Get the guns out from behind the trees and set them up as planned. Keep the barrels hidden until you"—he felt silly saying the next thing—"see the whites of their eyes."

Now was not the time to use old American Revolutionary War lines, but the man didn't know a thing about up-time wars, and thus, the phrase was new to him. And maybe it still meant something. If the volley guns could slow the Janissaries down and, perhaps, break their lines, then such a declaration would mean *everything.*

The first barrage of volley gunfire struck the orta. Usan instinctively ordered his men to drop. Some crouched, some lay flat on their bellies. In both cases, after that initial shot, most of the fire flew over their heads. The guns then paused, and Usan knew that they were adjusting their trajectories for another volley.

In front of him lay a dirt road that meandered both left and right into the horizon. But in the narrow space that they were heading toward, the road dipped out of sight for a good one hundred, one hundred fifty yards. That meant a ditch, and he knew now why those volley guns were firing from hidden positions along the tree line.

There are men in that ditch... waiting.

He did not shout the order. He did not rise to expose himself to gunfire. He simply ran forward in a crouch, yataghan in one hand, a khanjar dagger in the other. His men did not need to know what their *corbaci* wanted them to do.

Usan Hussein led by example.

The volley guns in the tree line fired again, but Jeff knew the Janissaries wouldn't—didn't—take the bait.

"Up, men!" he shouted. "Up, and fix bayonets!"

Officers of the Hangman Regiment repeated the order up and down the line, and the men rose from their positions in the ditch and clicked bayonets into place. Then they waited. Jeff wished he had a rifle of his own; he'd be clicking a bayonet into place with the rest of them. But this wasn't the olden days. He wasn't a captain or colonel anymore. He was a brigadier, and how many other officers had he admonished for being so foolish as to charge into battle and risk death? No. He would stay behind, find a safe place among the volley guns, and observe the fight with his staff. Besides, if he exposed himself to deadly enemy fire, Gretchen would kill him herself.

"Up!" he shouted again.

His men piled out of the ditch and stood on its lip, waiting.

"Set!"

Together, they shouted and set their bayonets forward.

"Ready... charge!"

Chapter 68

Southern battle line

"Silesians, my lord," Stroe Leurdeanu said, looking through a spyglass at the blocks of fresh soldiers pushing across the stone wall. "Our men are falling back and—"

"I know what they're doing, Stroe," Matei said, his left hand shaking at his side. "I don't need a spyglass to know that. I can see that with my own eyes."

We are beaten. The reality of it struck Matei's heart like a hammer. Or, perhaps more fittingly, a mace. There was no doubt now that the Sultan would bring his own mace down upon Matei's head for this defeat, and at the hands of Jews no less. It was just a matter of when and where.

For a time, it seemed as if the wolves in his dream had stopped howling. So much success in the early hours of morning. Now this defeat. Would the wolves ever stop howling?

Matei looked at his young assistant. A bright, intelligent man who would survive him and perhaps even go on to rule Wallachia in his own good time, assuming, of course, there was such a country in the future. Stroe's eyes were respectful, but accusatory. *We should have linked arms with the Moldavians and attacked together.*

"Any word from that *corbaci*?" Matei asked, incapable of saying the man's name.

"No, my lord," Stroe replied. "No word at all."

Matei didn't need word from him either to know what was happening. Scores of Dorobanți infantry had fallen back from their push in the center. Janissaries were tough, indeed. Perhaps the toughest men Sultan Murad possessed. But no one thousand men ever born could survive alone without full, dedicated support from its army, and Matei Basarab had no more support to give.

He sighed, deeply, closed his eyes, and nodded. "God's will. Order the men to fall back to the Maros. I want everyone still alive across that river by nightfall. And order our rockets and cannons to expend all remaining munitions. Let's give our men a fighting chance to escape."

"There are no more rockets, my lord," Stroe said.

"Cannons, then," he snapped, "and keep them firing until they too run dry."

Central battle line

Usan swiped his yataghan left, right, cleaving Silesian faces in two. He did not even care about the gunfire popping randomly around him, mini-balls buzzing past as the line between friend and foe collapsed. Nothing now but groups of men slamming into each other, bayonets buried into throats and bellies, swords slashing and stabbing, rifles barking, men screaming, falling. The bright red uniforms of his orta were enough to keep him from cutting down his own men, but the smoke and sheer numbers in the killing field made it difficult not to draw friendly fire. He had never been in such a fight in his life; both exciting and terrifying at the same time.

A Silesian in front of him tried raising his rifle. Usan shouted, knocked the rifle from the man's hands, and drove the khanjar dagger into his belly. He twisted the blade, watched as the life bled from the man's eyes, and then withdrew it and let him fall dead at his feet.

His ear was nicked by gunfire.

Usan fell to the ground beside the dead man, the sting of the shot hot and debilitating, sending shards of pain through his face. He dropped the khanjar and clutched his bleeding ear. A piece of it hung loose. He gritted his teeth and ripped the piece away, letting the blood flow freely down his cheek. His eye patch was still in place, thankfully, though he wished now that he had two functioning eyes. Then, perhaps, he might have seen the man, somewhere in the confusion, raising his rifle to fire.

Dozens of Janissaries raced past him, not realizing—or perhaps not caring now—that their *corbaci* was wounded and lying at their feet. Then hands grabbed the back of his coat and yanked him up.

"*Corbaci*," the boy who had pulled him up said with real concern on his face. "Are you wounded?"

Usan gained his balance by gripping the boy's shoulder. "I am fine. Thank you. Now...forward!"

The white tent and enemy banners were close now. So close. The only thing between them and the capital was the ditch. Cross the ditch and take Gyulafehérvár.

The Silesian line suddenly broke and fell back. Usan could not contain his joy any longer. He grinned like a hyena. He knew how those creatures smiled; he had seen one as a pet in a bazaar in Istanbul as a child. It grinned from ear to ear, yipping like a madman, and now Usan repeated the look, no longer a *corbaci*, an officer. He was a soldier now, a simple Janissary, one of many.

The Silesians who reached the ditch alive jumped into it. Usan imagined reaching the lip of that ditch and firing down, killing dozens, hundreds as they scampered madly up the back slope, trying to break free from the slaughter. But he had no rifle. He had smashed it against the hull of the *Ifrit* and had not bothered to find another. If necessary, he, like all his men, would jump into that ditch too and—

A line of hidden Silesian riflemen raised out of the ditch and fired a full, powerful volley into Usan's charging lines. Then the volley guns in the tree line roared again.

Usan took a shot into his belly and dropped. Lead buzzed over his head so thick it seemed as if he had wandered into a beehive. Oddly, he felt less pain from this gut shot than just a moment ago when his ear had been severed; less pain than when his eye had been destroyed. There was a warm, soothing quality to the wound, like the comfort he had felt in the arms of his mother, in the security of family. He was in the midst of family now, all the men around him taking shot after shot after shot as well, and he wondered in those last moments how they felt about him. *Do they blame me for leading them to their deaths?*

Do they blame me for not bringing guns, cavalry in support? What will Sultan Murad think of me, my decisions, when he learns of my death, my failure?

None of that really mattered now. All that mattered was getting right with Allah, and did he have time for that?

Usan slept. How long, he did not know. Then he awoke. He was nothing more than a pile of meat, bone, and blood, staring up into the overcast sky, staring into the silhouette of a soldier.

Not a Janissary. A Silesian. A boy. A nobody. Perhaps a farmer, a herder. He stood over Usan as if he were a king, ready to pass sentence, pointing a cocked pistol at his face.

Usan smiled and tilted his head up to get a better view of the boy. A handsome boy with just a small smear of blood on his chin, a spattering of mud on his uniform.

"*Görevini yap genç adam. Ben Allah ile barış içindeyim,*" Usan said as he stared deeply into the boy's eyes, waiting for the shot.

Instead, the boy turned his head suddenly to receive an order from a superior officer. The boy sighed but nodded, uncocked his pistol, knelt beside Usan, turned the pistol in his hand, and smacked Usan hard across the face.

Chapter 69

Northern battle line

His pistols spent and re-holstered, Christian drew his sword and slashed out at the closest Tatar face in his path. The man partially deflected the strike with his own sword. Christian's blade instead struck the man's shoulder, doing little damage but forcing him to reel back in his saddle. His steed, a dark-hided *mori*, raised up on its hind legs and took a pistol shot in the belly. It tumbled backward and knocked another Tatar from his mount. Christian split another face with his blade and spurred Alphonse forward.

He hacked left, right. The lines were confused, disorganized. Most of the dead or dying strewn across the ground were trabants, their bright red coats saturated with dark blood, even darker mud. Alphonse jumped over a crawling, screaming man as Christian drove his sword tip into the exposed side of a charging Tatar's chest. He felt the crack of rib reverberate up the sword blade, yanked the weapon back, and finished the job by putting his shoulder into the howling man's back. The Tatar dropped the reins of his horse and fell to the ground.

A *mori* slammed into Alphonse's left flank. Christian winced and tried to move, but the weight of the enemy horse pressed his leg hard into Alphonse's side. No cracked bone, Christian was thankful, but his ankle and foot screamed under the pressure of the hit.

Alphonse staggered to the right. Christian kept strong control of his reins, but the impetus of the blow was too much for the horse. Alphonse tumbled.

Christian uncoupled his boots from the stirrups and half leaped away from the fall. He struck the ground and slid several feet through mud and sharp pebbles, feeling the scrape of the rocks across his exposed neck. His buff coat and breast plate cushioned the blow. His weak eye pulsed. Strong hands grabbed him.

"Come on," Lieutenant Enkefort said, all but spitting the words into Christian's face. "Let's go!"

He allowed himself to be pulled forward. "Where are we going?"

Enkefort did not answer, but soon, Christian knew where he was being pulled.

Close to the center of the fight, a small cadre of men held defense behind a pile of Székely bodies and horses. It was General Hatmanu and his personal guard.

Let him fall on his own sword. Captain Kinsky's words rang through Christian's mind. It seemed like the right thing to do now. In the midst of all this chaos, all this death, who cared about such a one as the cretin that now lay in abject fear behind a pile of men who had died from his own hubris? *Let him fall on his own sword.*

Christian grabbed a discarded, half-cocked musket from the hands of a dead trabant, stepped over the body, and joined Hatmanu and his men in their defense.

They did not speak, nor did the defeated general recognize Christian's presence; he probably didn't even know that Christian and Enkefort had joined their little redoubt. Hatmanu lay supine under the weight of his own aide-de-camp, who was sitting on him to protect his general from gunfire. Christian cocked his musket in full, raised it up, and fired at a Tatar coming on in full gallop.

On and on it went, until there were no more muskets or pistols to fire, no more ammunition to load. Another loud exchange of musket fire erupted as the Moldavian infantry, hiding in the tree line, now emerged and moved in good order down into the road. They fired, and the man sitting on Hatmanu was shattered by Murad mini-balls.

Enkefort then went down to a shot in the shoulder. Christian dropped in response, letting the whistling lead pass over his head and *thunk!* into dead bodies providing cover.

He heard a death scream and peeked out from his position.

General Marius Hatmanu had, once again, made a foolish decision: he had exposed himself while pushing his dead aide-de-camp away. Mini-balls struck his chest, his shoulders, his stomach, and he fell dead.

The gunfire stopped. A large shadow crossed overhead. Christian dared to look up. It was the airship, flying low, dropping yet another firebomb onto the mass of men below it. Christian searched the ground for another pistol and found one. He cocked the hammer and fired, as did other desperate men, taking their shots at the airship, hoping beyond hope that they could do it some amount of damage, for no other reason than to try and salvage victory over this—Christian's—ill-advised charge.

Who was trying to cover himself in glory now? Christian wondered as another volley of gunfire sounded, and another firebomb fell from the airship.

"I love you, Isaac, my brother," he whispered. "I love you, Andreea. *Auf Wiedersehen.*"

Christian closed his eyes as more of his men fired at the airship, as more Moldavian gunfire slammed into the bodies around him, and as another firebomb struck the ground and engulfed his position.

The Chaldiran

Another round of gunfire struck the gondola, and this time, Moshe knew something was wrong.

The laughter stopped. There was a *thunk!* near the stern, and Mordechai shouted.

Moshe turned and saw his engineer leap toward Vasile Lupu but missed catching him by inches. The voivode of Moldavia collapsed, his limp body striking the gondola floor with a kind of sloppy snap that suggested broken bones as well as bullet wounds.

"He is down!" Mordechai said, dropping to his knees to cup Vasile's head with his hands.

"Take us up, Mordechai!" Moshe shouted as he fell to the gondola floor and crawled to his side. "Take us up! Now! I'll take care of him."

"You warned him not to go so low," Sergiu said, his face a mask of smug contentment. "He paid the price."

Blood pooled on the gondola floor near Vasile's midsection. Clearly a bowel shot, but not the only one. Blood seeped from the voivode's shoulder and face as well. There were likely other wounds too, though Moshe could not see them from the man's thick clothing. He pushed his fingers into Vasile's throat, leaned over and set his ear near the man's face.

"He is still alive. He's breathing, and his heart beats." He turned to Mordechai. "Turn us toward our base camp. We must return there immediately, so his physician can try to save him."

"Let him die!" Sergiu hissed like a viper. "We're on the verge of victory here, and you want to return to camp and have word spread about this? Cause panic? Pull up, yes, but do not take us off the front until this matter is resolved."

"He is not dead!" Moshe shouted. "And he is your voivode."

Sergiu spit, pulled his pistol. He cocked a hammer, but kept the barrel pointed toward the gondola floor. "He'll die soon enough with those wounds. Forget him." He raised the pistol and pointed it at Moshe's face. "I'm in charge now. We stay and finish what we have started. I've worked too hard, for too long, to let it all fall apart. I'll get what's mine, and—"

The Janissary guard shouted, pulled his sword, and rushed Sergiu. Moshe could see that the Janissary's initial move shocked Sergiu, but the mercenary assassin was too fast, too skilled a gunman to be deterred. He turned quickly and fired. The shot tore through the guard's chest. The man's momentum propelled him forward. Sergiu stepped aside and let the body strike the starboard wall of the gondola and slide to the floor.

God in heaven! Moshe mouthed silently while falling back from the sudden violence. He then saw Mordechai and the last rifleman rush Sergiu. He found the courage to rise and assist them.

Sergiu, distracted by the fallen Janissary, raised his spent pistol as a club. Mordechai caught his arm before it came down on the rifleman's head.

"Unhand me!" Sergiu shouted as Moshe's fingers found the man's throat and squeezed. "Unhand—"

He was strong, very strong, but three on one proved too much for the leader of the Impalers. Mordechai balled his fist and punched Sergiu in the face, again and again, while Moshe and the rifleman pushed him up and onto the larboard side wall of the gondola.

"Let me go! Let me...I'm going to kill you all! Damn you all to hell! Do you know who I am? I'm Sergiu Bot—"

Moshe grabbed Sergiu's kicking legs and with one strong shove, they pushed the killer out.

Mordechai and the rifleman fell back, but Moshe watched as Sergiu, screaming, tumbled through the air, struck the ground below, and promptly disappeared in the rolling gun battle.

His anxiety spiked, his heart raced. Moshe raised his hand and saw that it was shaking. He grabbed it with his other hand and took a moment to calm himself. He breathed in and out deeply and appealed to God for strength.

"What are we going to do, Moshe?" Mordechai asked, his eyes a glaze of shock.

Moshe shook his head. Everything had fallen apart so quickly, and how fast indeed had he joined his crewmen to kill. A terrible, worthless man, for sure, but nevertheless, he had grabbed Sergiu's legs and had helped toss the man to his death. He had never done anything like that before, and at this moment, he didn't know how to feel about it.

Moshe shook his head again to clear away the shock and knelt again at Vasile's side. He checked the poor man's pulse and pulled away a bloody hand. "He's still alive. Fly up...and get us back to base camp. Now!"

Mordechai took to the controls and the *Chaldiran* rose quickly and turned to cross over the Maros.

Chapter 70

Field hospital
Gyulafehérvár

Isaac received the good news like everyone else, from General Headquarters via Morris Roth. Despite dozens of wounded soldiers still needing attention, everyone, even the wounded, paused to clap, cheer, and give thanks to God for a bloody, but well-deserved, victory. A victory that Isaac almost thought would never come, given how terrible the news had been earlier in the day.

Just a few short hours ago, his brethren on the southern battle line had fallen back in disarray, close to collapse. Something, or someone, had rallied them and now, the Joshua Corps and Silesian Guard were forcing the Wallachians back across the Maros. Brigadier Higgins and the Brethren APCs and their crews had apparently stopped a regiment of Janissaries and their fire tanks from reaching the capital. And now, word from the northern battle line indicated that the Moldavians had paused their assault and were falling back as well. How had it all turned so quickly in the Sunrise's favor, Isaac couldn't say, nor did it matter. Despite the severely wounded men around him, Isaac could not contain his happiness. He smiled from ear to ear and his face reddened with joy.

Was Christian all right? That was the question now. Several wounded had come from the northern battle line, but there

485

had been no time to pause and ask for information. Too many wounded, too many responsibilities.

"Oana."

She turned to him. "Yes, Isaac?"

He handed her a roll of gauze. "Will you please see to this man's dressings? Wrap his ankle tightly and ask the orderlies to take him outside so that he may have some fresh air. I'll be stepping out for just a moment."

"Yes, Isaac."

He removed his gloves, scrubbed his hands, and sprinkled cool water on his face. He stepped outside the tent. Like Krakow, the air was sickly-sweet with the scent of gunpower, a residual effect of war that he did not like. But the hospital tent needed to be as close as possible to the action without actually being in the midst of battle, so the smell had to be endured.

"You there!" he shouted at a mere boy who was talking to another cavalryman at his side. "You on the horse. What regiment do you serve?"

They paused their conversion. The boy looked to Isaac, said, "Second Regiment."

"Are you well?"

The boy nodded. "Yes, I'm fine. I've been helping deliver wounded from the front."

"And how goes it on the front? How is Second Regiment?" Isaac asked.

The boy glanced at the other soldier, a wary look in his eyes as if he were afraid to answer. "It has been a while since I was there. But I hear it's bad, very bad. That Moldavian airship came by and dropped a lot of firebombs on the whole damn charge."

"What charge?"

The boy gestured as if the battle were close. "Mitzlaff's and von Jori's companies gave charge to Tatar cavalry hitting hard. Bombs were dropped. The whole damn area went up in flames."

Isaac's heart dropped. "And Captain von Jori. Is he all right?"

The boy shook his head. "I can't say, sir. The whole situation is confused now. I hear that their airship has retreated, and the Moldavians army is falling back, but—"

"Take me there."

The boy screwed up his face. "Doctor?"

"I said take me there. Right now!"

Isaac found himself reaching up the saddle and taking hold. He tried putting his shoe in the stirrups and pulling himself up. The boy tried helping but the awkwardness of the moment and the angle of his grasp made it difficult. "Doctor, I'm sorry, but I don't think it's a good idea to go there. Everything is all—forgive my language—fucked up and—"

"I'm a chief medical officer of the Sunrise, sir. I'm ordering you to take me to see my patients—"

"Doctor Kohen!"

Isaac turned and saw Oberheuser there, his apron lousy with blood and bile.

"What are you doing?" the old surgeon asked, a confused, angry look on his dour face.

"I'm going to the front! I'm going to help Captain von Jori and anyone else that needs my attention. I'm going there, and you're not going to—"

"Don't be a fool, Isaac!" Oberheuser said, moving closer, anger overriding his confusion. "You can't go there, young man. You have responsibilities here." The old, grumpy doctor pointed to the tent. "We've got men in there who need attention. There are medics at the front. They'll take care of the wounded."

"My friend needs me!"

"*We* need you, goddammit! Right now. Devorah, Oana. All of us. We can't do this without you. You cannot abandon your post! Get your head out of your ass and grow up!"

Isaac had never heard such an expression. Hearing it come out of that hoarse, gruffy mouth made him almost laugh. An up-time expression, for sure, and quite medically impossible to begin with. How exactly could one insert one's head into one's ass?

Isaac chuckled and his stress bled away. He breathed deeply, rubbed his forehead, tried not to tear up. "You're right, Doctor. My apologies. I don't know what I was thinking." He patted the boy's boot and stepped away. "It's okay. I won't be going. But will you do me a favor and go there in my stead and see to the situation? It's important that Doctor Oberheuser and I know what casualties to expect in the next few hours."

The boy nodded. "Yes, Doctor."

He stepped back and let the boy go.

Oberheuser turned brusquely and stomped back into the tent, cursing all the way. Isaac stood there listening, for the first

time in many, many hours, birds chirping in the nearby trees, a
light wind blowing across the space between him and the tent,
walking wounded loitering around the grounds. Distant sounds
of war were muted now, save for a few cannons barking to the
south. He turned his gaze north and saw several long streams
of smoke in the hazy distance. Again, he had to bite back tears.
What good would tears do now? As much as he hated to admit
it, Oberheuser was correct.

Time to get my head out of my ass and grow up.

Isaac stepped back into the tent and got to work.

Moldavian army headquarters
East of the Moros River

Moshe Mizrahi frantically worked the signal flags as the *Chaldiran* lowered to drop its tether lines. The last rifleman who had
helped them toss Sergiu Botnari to his rightful death dropped
each line as men on the ground scrambled to secure the airship
to posts in the field below. Then he unfurled the ladder. Moshe
dropped the flags and leaned over the larboard side, cupped his
hands over his mouth, and shouted, "Voivode Lupu is wounded!
He needs attention immediately!"

Men on the ground scrambled away to find a physician, and
Mordechai grabbed Moshe's shoulder and turned him around.
"We cannot stay here, Moshe. They'll kill us, two god-condemned
kafirs, just to have a scapegoat. We'll die for sure."

Moshe nodded, and whispered, "I know, but I'm not going
anywhere with him still in the gondola."

He pointed to Vasile Lupu, who, surprisingly, was still alive,
though the pool of blood soaking the gondola floor confirmed
he wouldn't be for long.

"We're coming up!"

Moshe leaned over the side again and saw two men grab the
rope ladder and ascend. The voivode's personal physician was one
of them. They reached the top of the ladder and Moshe helped
them in.

The physician moved quickly to attend to Vasile Lupu, ignoring the dead Janissary guard crumpled in the corner. The armed
man took up a position on the larboard side, eyeing Moshe and

Mordechai warily. Moshe felt his heart sink. *We've got to go now.*

The physician put his fingers against Vasile's neck, pressed his hand against his chest, checked for his breathing. He nodded. "He still lives. But we must take him down now."

He motioned for the other man to assist, but Vasile was too heavy in dead weight. "You there," the physician barked, "come and help."

The rifleman slung his rifle over his shoulder and helped the physician and his guard carry Vasile to the ladder. It was a delicate matter to lower him to the ground, all shot through, his clothing all bloody and mangled. In no time, all three men's hands were covered in the voivode's blood. The big man nearly slipped out of their hands twice, but Moshe helped keep the limp body stable while they took to the ladder and slowly, slowly, lowered Vasile to the ground.

"You men stay here," the physician's guard shouted up to Moshe. "I will speak with you soon about this matter."

Moshe nodded and watched them carry the voivode of Moldavia into a tent.

"Now!"

Mordechai moved quickly to untie each tether, the fore lines first and then the aft. The airship lifted when the last tether was dropped.

Moshe expected the camp to notice, to take up arms and fire at them as they raised up into the bank of clouds floating above. Two kafirs who had murdered their prince. But no. All their attention was on their wounded leader. Getting away was the easiest thing they had done all day.

"Where do we go?" Mordechai asked as he took the helm.

"To Wallachia," Moshe said.

"Not the capital?"

That had indeed been a thought at one point: defect to the victorious side, if things got desperate. Things were certainly desperate right now, no doubt about that, but at what cost? Defect to the Bohemians and perhaps live a quiet, comfortable life in peace, and thus condemn their families to death.

Moshe shook his head. "To Wallachia. We'll follow Matei Basarab's retreating army across the border and throw ourselves on his mercy. He's a fair man. He'll speak on our behalf to the Sultan."

Field hospital
Gyulafehérvár

The sun was setting, and the young cavalry soldier whom Isaac had sent to the northern battle line had returned twice already, with bad news each time. As he had stated earlier in the day, the area was chaotic, confused, nothing more than one big pulsing wound itself, as more dead men than alive were pulled out of the carnage. Thank God that the Moldavians were, indeed, retreating, but that didn't keep men from dying.

Isaac stopped counting the wagonloads of dead soldiers. He tried focusing on those patients that he could help. Burns, burns, burns! The number of burn victims were sobering, more than he had ever seen in war before. Second- and third-degree burns were the most prevalent and the only ones they bothered to treat. First-degree patients were triaged outside the tent and sent away. Pain medication was running low.

"Isaac," Devorah said behind him, her voice low, tired. Everyone had been going near nonstop since the first guns of the day had fired.

"Yes, what is it?" Isaac asked, finishing the stitching of a leg wound.

"Another wagonload of wounded from the north has just arrived."

He waved her off. "You know the drill, Devorah. Line them up for triage as usual. I'll be out directly."

"Doctor Oberheuser has asked that you personally see to the triage of these men."

Isaac groaned. *That man! Insufferable!* "Very well," he said, finishing his stitching and turning around to follow her out, "but if these are all minor issues, I'm going to—"

The man sitting upright at the front of the wagon was one he knew very, very well, despite his charcoal-black face and ruined buff coat. Isaac's heart leapt into his throat. He caught himself just short of running to the wagon with his arms open like a babe wanting his mother. Instead, he cleared his throat, straightened his collar, and walked calmly to the back of the wagon. He didn't hide his smile.

"Did you win the war, Captain?"

Christian coughed, winced, and tried straightening up. "The battle, maybe. The war?" He coughed again and spit. "Too soon to tell."

"I have a good mind to climb in and slap you across the face, my friend," Isaac said, helping one of the wounded step out. "You are one of the most reckless men I've ever known."

Christian tried to laugh but his pain was too great. He groaned, grabbed his side and leaned back.

Andreea stepped out of the tent. Unlike Isaac, she did not bother trying to hide her relief. She ripped her apron off and let it drop to the ground, ran to the front of the wagon, and threw her arms around Christian's neck, hugging him tightly and repeating the same Hungarian words over and over into his ear: "*Hála Istennek, élsz! Hála Istennek, élsz!*"

"Careful now, Andreea," Isaac said, helping Devorah clear a path to Christian. "You can hug him later. We've got to get him into the tent and check those burns."

There were many, but most were confined to his legs. Isaac checked them carefully. Second-degree, for sure. Then he saw Lieutenant Enkefort lying flat on the wagon floor, unconscious.

Isaac jumped in and checked Enkefort's vitals, his breathing, his arm. "Get the orderlies to take this man in the tent," he told Devorah, "and tell Oberheuser that he's a priority."

"Is he going to lose his arm, Isaac?" Christian asked, trying to lean closer.

Isaac shook his head. "I can't say, my friend. He's wounded badly. We'll see."

"Please do whatever you have to do to keep him alive."

Orderlies came and carried Lieutenant Enkefort away. Devorah climbed in and together, she and Isaac helped move Christian to the back of the wagon. Another orderly assisted and they lifted him up and out.

Isaac could see the dreadful pain on Christian's face as they moved carefully toward the tent. Andreea followed behind, whispering her Hungarian words and keeping her hand on Christian's head for support.

"We licked them, Isaac," Christian said, slurring his words as he wavered in and out of consciousness. "We licked them."

"Good, good," Isaac said as he helped the orderly lower

Christian onto a table for further scrutiny. "Have I told you how much I want to slap you right now?"

Christian nodded. "Yes, I think so. Here's my face." He turned his head so that Isaac had a clear shot at his right cheek. "Slap away."

Isaac chuckled. He leaned over and placed a light kiss on Christian's forehead. "I'll do it later, you reckless fool. Now, shut up and let me save you...again."

Part Eight

October 1637

As all dread strengths give way
—Sophocles, *Ajax*

Chapter 71

Forward Transylvania
Koloszvár

As soon as they entered the building, Ignaz Honterus and Elek Ferenc came to an abrupt halt.

"Holy—"

"Don't blaspheme," snapped Elek Ferenc.

Like most Szeklers, Ferenc was Roman Catholic and had a hair-trigger reaction to blasphemy and other sins. Ignaz suspected that was because a fair number of Szeklers had converted to Unitarianism and the Catholic Szeklers were exceptionally touchy on matters of religious doctrine because they viewed Unitarians as borderline freethinkers.

Ignaz, a Lutheran like almost all Saxons, was more secure in his faith. It was true that blasphemy was a sin, but he didn't really consider it equivalent to murder or worshipping golden idols. No sensible man he knew did. Lutherans, at least.

But he said nothing. In general, he and Elek got along quite well, and he saw no point in pursuing a quarrel over this issue.

Fortunately, the awkward moment was very brief. A young woman came up and said, "May I help you?"

"We'd like to speak with Gretchen Richter," said Ignaz.

"Is she expecting you?"

"Not exactly. We have no appointment to meet her. But we

495

spent quite a bit of time speaking to her in Szatmár and Zilah and told her we'd be coming to Koloszvár at some point in the future, and we'd like to speak with her again."

The woman looked uncertain for a moment, and then pointed to a bench nearby. "Wait here. I'll go see if she's free."

While they waited, Ignaz looked around the interior of the buildings, examining more closely the features that had brought on his near blasphemy. He'd been startled, having expected something far more modest in the way of a headquarters for a band of political organizers.

To begin with, the room that served as the equivalent of a storefront—except the windows had all been shuttered—was huge. Ignaz wondered what sort of goods had been sold there. But now, instead of racks and shelves holding items for sale, most of the floor space was turned over to desks and what he presumed were meeting tables.

All the desks were occupied by someone busily scribbling whatever they were scribbling about. Two of the meeting tables provided a workspace for several people at each table. Ignaz wondered what they were talking about.

The walls were covered with banners and political slogans, the largest being against the far wall and reading FORWARD TRANSYLVANIA. What he found most interesting was that none of the slogans seemed aimed at anyone in particular—neither the monarchy nor the aristocracy. Instead, they were devoted to broad social and political issues, such as SUPPORT FREEDOM OF SPEECH and SUBSCRIBE TO FORWARD TRANSYLVANIA.

In short, material that would certainly annoy the monarchy and aristocracy but did not pose a direct challenge or threat. There was a shrewd mind at work here and Ignaz could only assume it was Gretchen Richter's, even if it didn't seem to match her reputation as a flamboyant agitator.

The young woman returned. "Follow me, please."

Ignaz and Elek rose and trailed after her, as she led them into a corridor that ended in a flight of stairs. They took the stairs to the next floor and debouched into another corridor which led them in short order into Gretchen's office. The office was large, holding both a desk and a chair behind it along with two padded chairs and a divan in one corner of the room that were arranged for small meetings.

Gretchen rose and came around the desk, motioning them to take seats in the corner. They both sat on the divan and she took a seat near the window, whose curtain was still drawn. Ignaz wasn't sure, but he thought that might be a precaution against a would-be assassin.

"Welcome to Koloszvár," she said. "What can I do for you? Would you like something to drink?"

Both men shook their heads at the offer of refreshments. After a moment's pause, Elek said, "We were both surprised at the size and apparent breadth of your operation here. You've only been here, what? Two months?"

"Not quite that long," Gretchen said. "We started off much smaller, only renting a couple of rooms in the building. But then Prince Rákóczi was struck down by an assassin's bullet and never regained consciousness. As soon as that happened, we saw a rapid increase in people's interest in us. And when the prince died, leaving a muddied succession, our growth became not much short of explosive. The owner of the building wanted to sell it altogether and move to Hungary. Quite a few of the shopkeepers felt the same way, although not all of them. I bought the building to give us the room we needed."

Elek's brow furrowed. "Where did you get the funds?"

"From my own banks in the USE and the Netherlands. Well, mine and my husband's, but Jeff generally lets me handle our finances."

Both men stared at her. Gretchen's expression combined amusement and some exasperation.

"May I suggest you stop jumping to conclusions based on too little information? You came here for a reason. Why don't you just tell me what it is?"

She rose from her seat. "I'm going to get myself some tea. That will give you a bit of time to make up your jittery minds without me looking over your shoulders."

When she got back a few minutes later, her two visitors seemed to have reached a decision. As soon as Gretchen sat down, Ignaz Honterus said, "There's been a great deal of discussion north of here about the political situation. But none of us expected Prince Rákóczi to get himself killed. He wasn't the sort of reckless military commander who usually suffer such a fate."

"It's the new engines of war," said Gretchen. "You haven't had time to get adjusted to them. So, the prince got slain by a rifle shot from an airship."

Ignaz nodded. "Yes, that's undoubtedly what happened. His death, though, gave a great boost to a viewpoint that up to that time had been espoused by only a few people."

"What 'people' are we talking about?" asked Gretchen, bringing her cup to her lips and blowing on it to make it cool quicker.

"The majority are Saxons," said the Szekler, Ferenc. "Some are native to the area. More are recent arrivals fleeing from the Wallachian conquest of the big Saxon settlements in the south of Transylvania. They feel very misused. They had to bear the brunt of the fighting and suffered most of the casualties."

"While the Romanian and Hungarian nobility who comprise most of the big landowners and dominate the Diet stayed safely behind the walls of the capital, Gyulafehérvár," added Ignaz.

Gretchen took a sip of her tea. "How many Székelys are participating?"

"Quite a few," said Ignaz, "especially after Rákóczi died."

Gretchen set down her cup. "All right. So what's this new viewpoint? I'm pretty sure that's what you want to ask me about."

"Yes, but there's another question we need to ask first. Something that we're not clear about."

"Puzzled by, in fact," added Ferenc.

She took another sip of her tea. "So, ask."

"What is the nature of your relationship to Gustavus Adolphus?" asked Ignaz. "It doesn't seem to make a lot of sense. On the one hand, you are the preeminent revolutionary in Europe. On the other, Gustavus Adolphus holds three crowns. He's simultaneously the emperor of the United States of Europe, the king of Sweden, and the high king of the Union of Kalmar. He's now undoubtedly the most powerful monarch on the continent, leaving aside the sultan of the Ottoman Empire. You'd think he'd be moving heaven and earth to hang you from a gallows—just like you'd be expected to raise a revolution against him. Instead, you seem to get along quite well."

Gretchen laughed. "And I take it you find that suspicious."

"Well..." said Ignaz.

"Yes, we do," said Ferenc.

Gretchen set down her cup. "My relationship with Gustav Adolf is complex. To understand it, you need to understand the impact of the Ring of Fire and the ensuing American relationship to the man. They found themselves facing a stark choice. With their military prowess, they could have created a small—very small—republic, exactly to their liking. But faced with the combined hostility of every ruler in Europe, they would have had to turn themselves into a garrison state, which is not a good medium in which to have democracy and equality flourish. As Mike Stearns put it at the time—this was back in 1632, after the Croat raid on Grantville was driven off by the Americans in alliance with a force led by Gustav Adolf—'You can't build America in a fortress.'

"So, he negotiated with Gustavus Adolphus and reached a compromise. The Americans would provide the Swedish king with a formidable military capacity. In exchange, he agreed to respect the liberties they were accustomed to, as well as giving them a great deal of political control. The end result wasn't the sort of 'constitutional monarchy' that they'd had in their own universe, because Gustav Adolf exercised a great deal of power, especially over foreign affairs and the military. The American scholar Melissa Mailey once told me the arrangement was much closer to the 'constitutional monarchy' in the eighteenth century of their universe, than that of the twentieth."

She drained the rest of her cup and set it down on a small table next to her chair. "What was just as important to Stearns was that the arrangement gave the Americans and those down-timers who came to agree with them with far greater political elbow room than a so-called pure republic could have provided. What resulted over the next few years was a vast expansion of freedom and justice."

She shrugged. "It was far from perfect, but it was also far better than any possible alternative, given the realities of our time. In the early years, I myself was wary of the situation and had some major reservations about Mike Stearns. But, for me, those reservations were dispelled when Stearns brought his Third Division back into the USE from Bohemia, and smashed the reactionary forces that were seeking to crush the Dresden rebellion—of which I was one of the leaders. Since that time, I have come to share Stearns' view of our political prospects. As he once said to me, 'Don't let the perfect be the enemy of the good.'"

Ignaz and Elek looked at each other. "Well, as she said, it's complex," said Ferenc. "But I think our question is pretty well answered."

Ignaz nodded and turned back to Gretchen. "What we were wondering..." He hesitated. "I'm not sure how to put this because I'm now on unfamiliar ground."

"Here's the situation you face," said Gretchen. "Rákóczi did leave a clear heir, which is his oldest son, George II. But he's only sixteen years old so his mother would be the regent and she's what amounts to a Calvinist fanatic. Those factors make him unacceptable to too many nobles of Transylvania, most of whom are either Romanian Orthodox or Roman Catholic.

"As a result, some noblemen are plumping for one or the other of Prince George I Rákóczi's brothers, Pál or Zsigmond, but both of them have problems. Pál's health is not good and Zsigmond doesn't even live in Transylvania. He's a Hungarian nobleman, first and foremost."

She shook her head. "There are at least half a dozen other factions, all of them small and supporting unlikely candidates. Which means a long succession crisis for a principality that is now an enemy of Sultan Murad IV. The odds that any of them would be able to lead a successful war against the Ottomans are very low. Do you agree?"

Ignaz and Elek both nodded.

"In that case," said Gretchen, "the most intelligent course of action is for Transylvania to join the United States of Europe as a province. That would mean you could count on the very powerful USE for protection against the Turks."

Ferenc made a face. "But we'd be vassals again."

"That's nonsense. A province is not a vassal, it's a *province*. Especially if you joined with a republican structure, you'd have clearly defined legal rights from the very beginning. That would spare Gustav Adolf with having to deal with often fractious aristocrats claiming some sort of princely status. And the emperor has always been meticulously proper in his dealings with republican provinces. I know. I've been the ruler of two of them, Saxony and Lower Silesia. And the current prime minister of the USE is the former governor of the republican State of Thuringia-Franconia."

Ignaz and Elek looked at each other again. "That's a very clear and succinct presentation of the political viewpoint that has been gaining a lot of adherents in the northern counties," said Ignaz. He glanced at the door to her office. "And judging from the operation you're running here, it's a popular opinion in Koloszvár also."

"Which is the largest city in Transylvania," said Ferenc. He squinted a little at Gretchen. "But would Gustavus Adolphus agree?"

"Probably," said Gretchen. "But that's easy to find out. I'll reach him by radio and ask."

They were both back to staring at her again. She smiled and spread her hands. "As I said, my relationship with the emperor is complex."

Chapter 72

Field hospital
Gyulafehérvár

As the weather grew colder, there was much desire to try to find a warmer, more permanent place in which to house those soldiers still convalescing from their wounds. Both the Collegium Academicum and the Princely Palace had been crossed off the list by the Transylvanian court, much to Isaac's frustration. Both facilities had ample room for such patients, but the collegium was, after all, a college, and thus needed its space for students. And the palace was, well, the palace, and who in their right mind would consider soiling the opulent floors of the prince's home with the blood of mercenaries?

The search was ongoing.

In the meantime, two wood-burning stoves had been brought into the tent to try to keep those still recovering from freezing to death. Isaac wore as many layers as he could and still perform his duties.

He reviewed a patient's chart at the foot of bed number six. "Why are you still here, Captain? I need this bed for the wounded."

"Are you releasing me from your care?" Christian asked, happily sitting upright to await the answer.

"I am...if you'll allow me to check your burns one more time."

"Certainly."

Isaac pulled the blanket away to reveal a right nasty patch of burned skin on Christian's leg. Over the thigh and knee. As it turned out, the right leg had taken the brunt of the fire. The area was still tender, sore, and the rough scar tissue, which was beginning to form, would never disappear. It was healing nicely, however, and despite tightness and pain, the damage wasn't life threatening, nor would it keep Christian from walking.

"You're cursed, my friend," Isaac said, giving Christian's leg a gentle tap before replacing the blanket. "Your right side is cursed. Your right eye and now, your leg. Might I recommend that next time you foolishly charge into a regiment of Tatars, you show them your left side?"

Christian chuckled. "Assuming I ever charge into battle again."

Isaac raised a hopeful brow. "You've decided to resign your commission?"

Christian removed the blanket and turned to sit upright on the bed, a move he had been practicing for a good while for this inevitable moment. He sighed deeply and rubbed his face and did well to hide the pain Isaac knew the stubborn captain felt. "It's not quite that complicated with mercenary captains, Isaac. In truth, I could just walk away—or *ride* away, if you prefer—since we're not in the middle of a fight. But I haven't decided yet." He looked behind him, toward where Andreea and Devorah were taking care of patients. "I know what Andreea wants me to do."

"She's a good woman," Isaac said, handing Christian his cleaned and folded breeches before the man froze to death. "She'll make an honest man out of you."

Christian huffed, shaking the chill away. "I know it." He put his clothing on as quickly as possible, taking care not to stretch his thigh too quickly, thus aggravating his wounds and tearing the remaining blisters.

"I want you to promise me," Isaac said, "that you'll follow the therapy regimen I've written down for you. I want you to stretch that leg every day, in the manner I have described, to ensure that that scar doesn't tighten up. If you don't, I'll—"

"I know, I know," Christian said, waving him off. "You'll find me and kill me."

They both laughed at that, though Isaac could see that deep laughter brought serious pain to his friend. The kind of trauma Christian had suffered had affected his whole body, even if the most significant wounds were confined to his legs. In truth, Christian was breaking down, whether he wished to accept it or not. His youth would mask such trauma for a while, but not forever. He needed monthslong rest and therapy to fully recover from the trauma of both battles that he had fought on the Transylvanian plateau. Would he do it? *Please, please, my friend, resign, return to Déj with Andreea, and live out your days in peace.*

"Oh," Christian said, tying up his breeches with cold fingers, "congratulations are in order, are they not...chief medical officer of the Sunrise?"

Isaac rolled his eyes. "You heard, did you?"

"You can't keep something like that a secret." Christian winked. "Not when you have a nurse like Devorah Bayer in the tent."

Isaac made a mental note to scold the sweet lady later. "Yes, Oberheuser has resigned. He's returning to Kassa on the Jupiter later this afternoon with the rest of them. I've accepted the position, but...I don't know. I'm still young, Christian. I'm not sure I'm qualified yet to be the chief."

"Nonsense. I've said it before, I'll say it again: you're the doctor everyone wants to work with. They respond to you. They respect you. You have General Roth's confidence, for sure, or he wouldn't have appointed you." Christian turned carefully and placed his hand on Isaac's shoulder. "Just don't carry the weight of the world on your shoulders. Let me, Devorah, Oana, all of us, help you carry the load. All right?"

Isaac smiled, though his never-ending anxiety rose in his throat. He swallowed, nodded. "Thank you, Christian."

Isaac handed Christian a cane that Oana had given him, one that her father—whom Morris had recently gotten released from prison—had owned. He could tell that his friend didn't like using it, didn't like the symbolism of old age that it projected. If Isaac hadn't been standing right there, Christian might have tossed it away. Instead, he accepted the cane, turned and said, "Andreea? I'm ready when you are."

Andreea finished with a patient, a young Silesian guardsman sporting a terrible concussion who, in his delirium, kept claiming that he had *captured* the Janissary commander. She then joined them, giving Isaac a small bow. "Herr Doctor, with your permission, I will escort your Captain von Jori to his company."

Isaac nodded. "You may, and may you keep him well."

With the cane in his right hand, Christian placed his left in Andreea's hand. "Will you be joining us at the Jupiter this afternoon?" he asked.

Isaac shook his head. "No. I'm sending Devorah as my representative. Oana and I have important matters to attend to here."

"Very well. Then will we see you tomorrow night for dinner?"

"Yes," Isaac confirmed with a curt nod and a smile. "My treat."

As he watched them leave the tent, Oana waved him over politely. "Isaac? Can you give me assistance with this patient?"

Isaac raised his hand in acknowledgement. He smiled. "Of course, Oana. I'll be right with you."

Sunrise Airfield
Gyulafehérvár

The Jupiter was already fueled and running as Morris pushed Len up to it for loading. Len could walk, but Ellie insisted that her husband be loaded onto the plane to ensure he didn't start running away the moment his feet touched the tarmac. The badly wounded communications specialist didn't want to leave, but his shoulder was not improving at the pace that Doctor Kohen liked. The flesh was healing, but its mobility hadn't improved much at all. A quick flight to Kassa and then on to Magdeburg where they had superior medical facilities and procedures to deal with such problems. Maybe they could fix him, maybe not. Now that the battle was over, it was time to try.

Ellie was going with him, in addition to a few other patients whose wounds would benefit from better care than the Sunrise medical staff could provide. Retiring Doctor Oberheuser was going as well, and he had volunteered to oversee the care of the patients during the flight.

Lieutenant Karl Enkefort had, as predicted, lost his arm. At Ellie's behest, he had decided to leave the army and return to Prague. His radio knowledge and skills would help shore up her and Len's absence.

Enkefort's captain had come to see him off, as had Denise Beasley, who, Morris learned recently, had a strong connection with Second Cavalry Regiment. Also present was Andreea Hatmanu, clinging to Captain von Jori like a life preserver. Clearly, there were things going on behind the scenes that the Sunrise general did not know. *Time to talk to Isaac,* Morris thought as he brought Len to a halt, *and get all the scuttlebutt.*

Morris took Len's working hand and shook it vigorously. "I want to thank you both," he said, "for being here, for working with me. I know it was a difficult decision to make, leaving Prague, but as the old, stale cliché says, 'I couldn't have done it without you'?"

"What exactly have you done, Morris?" Ellie asked.

Good question, and for the moment, Morris wasn't sure of the answer. There was still much more to do to bring his Anaconda Project to full froth, thus wiping out any possibility that something like the Chmielnicki Pogrom could ever happen in this timeline. So, what *had* he done? A lot, in truth, but his ultimate goal was still to be achieved, and the ebbs and flows of life were never easy to predict. The past year had turned out in his, and the Sunrise's, favor. Who knew what the next year might bring?

Morris smiled, but ignored her question. "I also want to apologize for my harsh behavior during the battle. I—"

"Don't worry about it, boss," Len said. "Hell, Ellie sounds off all the time, as you well know."

Ellie giggled. "I do." She took Morris' hands into her own and squeezed them in strong affirmation. "You're forgiven, my friend, so don't worry about it any longer. Our friendship transcends time, and it always will."

Morris pulled Ellie close and hugged her tightly, not wanting to let go, but feeling Eddie Junker's eyes on him from the cockpit window, as if the pilot were pointing at his wrist and shouting, "Let's go. Time's money."

Ellie kissed Morris' cheek, then turned away as the Jupiter crew picked up Len in his wheelchair and handed him up to other crew waiting. "Hey, Len!" Morris shouted over the roar of the Jupiter engines.

"What?"

"Get the chess board ready. When I see you again in Prague, I'm gonna whip your ass!"

Len smiled, nodded. "You'll try, anyway!"

Despite the sadness of the moment, Denise was in good spirits. Yes, a friend of hers was getting on the Jupiter and leaving forever. But getting Enkefort off the battlefield was the right thing to do. His physical impediment would not have made his service as a cavalry lieutenant impossible, but certainly difficult.

"I hate seeing you go," Denise said as she stood with Christian and Andreea, his new lady love, bidding Enkefort goodbye under the shadow of the up-time plane. "In my opinion, you were the best radio operator in the field. The Sunrise is losing a star."

"Thank you, Denise," Enkefort said. Denise could see that he was still in quite a bit of pain, though the surgery to remove his arm had gone well. It would take a while for him to recover. She only hoped that he found good care in Prague once he arrived. "I wish I were staying."

"Doctor Kohen offered you a medical supply position," Christian said. "You turned it down."

Enkefort huffed. "I'm a mercenary soldier, Captain, and a radio operator. And I'm missing an arm. What good am I in that position?"

Christian nodded. "Fair enough. But, as Denise says, I too hate to see you go. The company is losing its best lieutenant, and I'm losing my right-hand man."

An awkward pause, and Denise saw that Christian realized his error. He started to correct himself. Denise jumped in.

"You'll have to forgive Captain von Jori's inarticulate comment, Karl. He's not thinking with his brains right now."

Christian got the crude joke. Andreea seemed confused. Christian chuckled, leaned into Andreea's ear, and whispered, "I'll tell you later."

"That's quite all right," Enkefort said. "And you're right, Captain: I'm no good to you in this condition. You'll find another to take my place. There are plenty to choose from."

Christian shook his head, his expression turning sour. "Not as many as there used to be."

"Indeed. But you'll manage, Captain. You always have. Goodbye, sir." Enkefort pulled away, then paused to salute.

Christian saluted. "Take Prague by storm, Lieutenant. That's an order."

They shared a smile, then Enkefort turned, and with help from the crew, climbed into the Jupiter.

Chapter 73

The Joshua Corps encampment

Jason Gotkin was late for Shabbos with the Joshua Corps, but it wasn't his fault. Morris had asked him to drop by headquarters first for a brief chat, but once he'd gotten there, he was told that the general had been called away on an important errand. Apparently, that important errand was lying to his rabbi.

For there General Roth stood, alongside Colonels Shalit, Schiff, and Zelikovich, all dressed in *tallis* prayer shawls. Brigadier Higgins and Gretchen Richter were there as well. Standing beside them were Isaac, Oana Dalca, and Devorah Bayer. Alongside them were other members of the medical staff and officers of the Sunrise that Jason recognized by their faces but not their names. Alongside them were the other priests and pastors from all the other faiths that had journeyed with the Sunrise into Transylvania.

"Attention!" Colonel Shalit shouted as soon as he saw Jason. The entire Joshua Corps, standing in tight blocks in the field nearby, snapped to attention.

"What's . . . what's all this?" Jason asked.

Morris stepped forward. "Rabbi Gotkin, for performing a valorous and life-risking deed in the service of the Joshua Corps, I wish to award you with our first service medal: the Sunrise Medal of Courage."

Morris held his hand forward and opened it. A small red ribbon, attached to a silver rising sun, lay in his palm.

"This is technically an up-time service metal that the Israeli Defense Force awarded its soldiers," Morris said, shooting a glance at Colonel Shalit. "But the medal itself has been modified to make it more appropriate to our time and situation. I hope you don't mind."

Jason dared to reach out and touch it. The silver was clean, smooth, and well-crafted. He worked to hold back his tears. "Thank you, General. I'm honored. But"—he looked at Jeff Higgins—"it was the Silesians who saved the Joshua Corps. Not me. If they hadn't arrived—"

"We did our part," Jeff said, stepping forward, "but it was you, Jason, *you* who turned it around. Without you, the corps would have collapsed before we got there."

"As long as I have lived," Colonel Shalit said, stepping forward, "I have never experienced the bravery that you showed on that day, Rabbi. You brought honor to yourself, to me, to the Joshua Corps, to every Jewish man, woman, and child alive today. You ensured that we did not break in the eyes of the enemy. You made sure that we found the courage in ourselves to stand, as Joshua did himself, against our enemies, and word of your courage will spread. And it will make a profound impact on who we are and what we are trying to do here in the Sunrise.

"You are a most righteous man, Rabbi Jason Gotkin. *Rak Chazak Amats!*"

The chant was repeated among the nearby ranks of Ashkenazi as Morris pinned the medal to Jason's prayer shawl.

It felt like a dream, like he had fallen asleep, and soon, he'd awake and it would all be gone. The praise and the award were much appreciated, but in truth, merely secondary. If they had just given him a quick "hurrah!" and a pat on the back, he would have been content. As far as he was concerned, he had done his duty for God.

What mattered the most to him was how his actions had affected the men. They seemed ecstatic, nearly giddy with excitement and pride. That was what mattered: that whatever he had done to save the corps would be turned into a drive and a strong, cultural sense of purpose for these young soldiers. That they would wear their yarmulkes in public places and not be afraid of doing so. That they would just simply be happy to be Jewish.

Soldiers came forward, hoisted him up, and paraded him

around to their continued chanting of *Rak Chazak Amats*. Jason felt uncomfortable on their rough shoulders, but if it meant that, in time, Morris Roth's dream would be realized, then so be it. Jason would be that vessel through which God's glory worked through the Grand Army of the Sunrise.

No Rabbi worth his salt could do any less.

Chapter 74

Forward Transylvania
Koloszvár

Gretchen tore open the envelope and extracted the sheet of paper within.

"Finally!" she grumbled. "It took them long enough."

Her husband was sitting on the divan in her office. "It's hardly surprising, my dear wife. This proposal is a lot more complicated than the deal Morris Roth made with Prince Rákóczi, in just about any way you look at it. The stakes are higher, the risk is greater—so are the rewards, of course, if it works—and it's quite a bit more expensive both financially and in terms of the troops required. You can bet the emperor consulted with everybody involved more than once before he made his final decision. So what does it say?"

Gretchen had already started reading the message. Although it had been transmitted by radio, it had much the same appearance as a telegram. Except, thankfully, without the constant irritation of plastering STOP throughout.

PROPOSAL IS APPROVED. MUCH STILL NEEDS TO BE
ARRANGED IN TERMS OF THE FINANCES INVOLVED, BUT
WE HAVE PLENTY OF TIME TO TAKE CARE OF THAT.
GIVEN THE EVENTS IN THE ADRIATIC, MURAD WILL
HAVE NEITHER THE TIME NOR THE READY RESOURCES
TO DEAL WITH A REBELLIOUS BALKAN PRINCIPALITY.

511

YOU WILL NEED AT LEAST ONE FULL DIVISION EITHER
OF REGULAR ARMY TROOPS OR TOP OF THE LINE
PROVINCIAL FORCES LIKE THE SILESIAN GUARD.
TORSTENSSON CAN SEND A BRIGADE FROM THE SIEGE
OF POZNAŃ WITHIN THREE MONTHS. WE CAN ALSO FILL
MOST OF YOUR AIRCRAFT REQUESTS FAIRLY SOON.

WILL BEGIN THE RAIL LINE SHORTLY, CONCENTRATING
FIRST ON THE STRETCH BETWEEN KASSA AND KOLOSZVÁR.
SHOULD BE FINISHED WITHIN A YEAR.

She looked up at Jeff. "Is that realistic?"

"If they put enough teams on it, sure. The straight line distance involved is about one hundred and seventy miles, but for a rail route you'd need to figure two hundred and fifty. About half of that stretch, from Kassa to Szatmár, is in the Great Hungarian Plain. They could easily lay a mile a day. From Szatmár down to Koloszvár, the terrain isn't as flat but it's still not particularly difficult. So figure half a mile a day. That comes to..."

His eyes got a bit unfocussed as he did the arithmetic in his head. "Figure about a year, like he says, but it could be less."

She looked back down at the message.

MORE TO FOLLOW.

What remained was only one line.

"Oh, damnation! I was afraid he was going to do that," she said.

"Do what?" asked Jeff.

She handed him the message. "Look at the last line."

A moment later, her husband was laughing.

"It's not funny!"

"Sure it is. Pure Gustavus Adolphus. CONGRATULATIONS ON YOUR NEW TITLE, LADY PROTECTOR OF TRANSYLVANIA."

Cast of Characters

Abrabanel, Rebecca   USE Secretary of State, wife of Mike Stearns

Ahmed, Semsi   Commander of the Gureba-i hava, the Ottoman Air Force

Alsted, Johann Heinrich   Calvinist minister

Anckermann, Heinz   Former platoon leader in the USE army, now a member of the CoC

Anderson, Ellie   Radio operator from Prague, wife of Len Tanner

Basarab, Matei   Voivode of Wallachia

Bayer, Devorah   Chief nurse, Grand Army of the Sunrise

Beasley, Denise   Teenage girl employed as an agent by Francisco Nasi; informally betrothed to Eddie Junker; daughter of Christin George; pilot in the Bohemian Air Force

Botnari, Sergiu   Advisor to Vasile Lupu; leader of The Impalers

Burkenfeld, Friedrick	Colonel, First Cavalry Regiment, Grand Army of the Sunrise
Callenberk	Captain, Second Cavalry Regiment, Grand Army of the Sunrise
Cerny, Lukas	Aircraft repairman, Bohemian Air Force
Corvinus, Janos	Szekler notable
Dalca, Oana	Teenage girl; volunteer nurse, Grand Army of the Sunrise
Donner, Agathe "Tata"	CoC organizer in Dresden, close associate of Gretchen Richter
Dordevic, Andrej	Serbian mercenary captain
Došek, Matej	Administrator of the Kisvárda district
Dreyzl, Tuva	Teenage girl; pilot in the Bohemian Air Force
Enkefort, Karl	Lieutenant, Grand Army of the Sunrise, aide-de-camp to Christian von Jori
Evhad, Hasan bin	Servant to Murad IV
Ferenc, Elek	Szekler notable
Fetzerin, Johanna	Staff member to Prime Minister Ed Piazza
Goss, Laura	Captain in the USE Air Force, pilot assigned to Rebecca Abrabanel
Gotkin, Jason	Rabbi, Grand Army of the Sunrise
Gustavus Adolphus	See "Vasa, Gustav II Adolf"
Hasslang, Jonas	Colonel, Third Cavalry Regiment, Grand Army of the Sunrise
Hatmanu, Andreea	Volunteer nurse, Grand Army of the Sunrise; wife of Marius

Hatmanu, Marius	General of Prince Rákóczi's red trabant Szekler infantry corps
Higgins, Jeffrey "Jeff"	Brigadier-General, Silesian Guard; husband of Gretchen Richter
Honterus, Ignaz	Saxon notable
Hugelmair, Minnie	Teenage girl employed as an agent by Francisco Nasi; friend of Denise Beasley; member of the Bohemian Air Force
Hussein, Usan	*Corbaci* (regimental commander) of the Janissaries
Ibragimov, Alim	Tatar captain
Jori, Christian von	Captain, Second Cavalry Regiment, Grand Army of the Sunrise
Junker, Egidius "Eddie"	Employed as an agent and pilot by Francisco Nasi; informally betrothed to Denise Beasley
Kinsky, Josef	Captain of the "Wild Elite," Second Cavalry Regiment, Grand Army of the Sunrise
Kohen, Isaac	Junior surgeon, Grand Army of the Sunrise
Krenz, Eric	Colonel in the Silesian Guard
Lange, Luthor	Major General and Provost Marshal, Grand Army of the Sunrise
Leurdeanu, Stroe	Close advisor to Voivode Matei Basarab
Lorántffy, Zsuzsanna	Wife of Prince George I Rákóczi
Lupu, Vasile	Voivode of Moldavia
Makovec, Reznik	Colonel of the Brethren and APC Commander, Grand Army of the Sunrise
Mercy, Franz von	Bohemian general, field commander, Grand Army of the Sunrise

Mizrahi, Moshe	Airship commander in the Gureba-i hava, the Ottoman Empire's air force
Murad IV	Sultan of the Ottoman Empire
Nasi, Francisco	Former head of intelligence for Mike Stearns; now operating a private intelligence agency in Prague
Oberheuser, Karl	Chief medical officer and surgeon, Grand Army of the Sunrise
Pasha, Halil	Chief Advisor to Sultan Murad IV
Pesach, Mordechai	Airship engineer in the Gureba-i hava, the Ottoman Empire's air force
Radu, Andrian	General of the Moldavian Army
Rákóczi, George I	Prince of Transylvania
Rákóczi, Pál	Brother of George I Rákóczi
Renz, Gerhardt	Colonel, Second Cavalry Regiment, Grand Army of the Sunrise
Richter, Maria Margaretha "Gretchen"	Leader of the Committee of Correspondence; Chancellor of Saxony; Lady Protector of Lower Silesia; wife of Jeff Higgins
Roth, Judith	Wife of Morris Roth
Roth, Morris	Commander of the Grand Army of the Sunrise; husband of Judith Roth
Ruppel, Werner	Leader of Gretchen Richter's guard detachment
Schiff, Velvel	Colonel, Second Regiment, Joshua Corps, Grand Army of the Sunrise
Schmidt, Otto	Major, Second Cavalry Regiment, Grand Army of the Sunrise; aide-de-camp to Gerhardt Renz

Shalit, Samson	Colonel, First Regiment, Joshua Corps, Grand Army of the Sunrise
Sommerus, Christian	Saxon notable
Stearns, Michael "Mike"	Former prime minster of the United States of Europe; now a major general in command of the Third Division, USE Army; husband of Rebecca Abrabanel
Suleyman	Commander of irregular cavalry and scouts (the *Akinji*) of the Ottoman Army
Tanner, Len	Communication Specialist; husband of Ellie Anderson
Tobias	Field medic, Grand Army of the Sunrise
Vasa, Gustav II Adolf	King of Sweden, emperor of the United States of Europe; high king of the Union of Kalmar, also known as Gustavus Adolphus
Veres, Gáspár Bojthi	Close advisor to Prince George I Rákóczi
"Young" Greta	Nurse, Grand Army of the Sunrise
Zelikovich, Getzel	Colonel, Third Regiment, Joshua Corps, Grand Army of the Sunrise